THE DAYS I LOVED YOU MOST

THE DAYS
I LOVED
YOU
MOST

AMY NEFF

PARK
ROW
BOOKS

PARK
ROW
BOOKS™

ISBN-13: 978-0-7783-1047-1

The Days I Loved You Most

Park Row Books
22 Adelaide St. West, 41st Floor
Toronto, Ontario M5H 4E3, Canada

Printed in U.S.A.

Recycling programs
for this product may
not exist in your area.

For Jonathan,

and the garden we have made.

"If I had a flower for every time I thought of you...
I could walk through my garden forever."

—Alfred, Lord Tennyson

One

Evelyn

June 2001

Joseph's words loom before us, waiting. I reach for his hand, calmed by the map of calluses, cuticles rimmed with dirt from planting bulbs this afternoon. My fingers shake in his grip. Sweat forms where our palms meet.

Our children sit across from us on the sagging couch. They are silent. The two lamps nearest us glow yellow beneath their shades. Joseph clicked them on as the room darkened, no one willing to interrupt the conversation to stand and flip on the lights overhead. Moonlight spills onto the dual pianos in the study, glinting off the ivory keys. The windows are open to the night that moved in as we spoke and the air is stale and thick, exceptionally hot for late spring in Connecticut. The only sound is the whirring ceiling fan above and the echo of waves from Bernard Beach around the bend.

When the kids were growing up and our home was still the Oyster Shell Inn, the coffee table hid beneath half-finished puzzles depicting New England lighthouses. Tonight, it's buried in appetizers, blocks of cheese that have begun to gloss and soften; stems of plucked grapes and a few lone crackers litter the platters. Joseph told me not to go to the trouble—but Thomas had come from Manhattan and we hadn't seen him since Christmas. This rare visit from our son gave me an excuse to walk to the new wine and cheese shop in town. The one across from Vic's Grinders that had been there since the grandkids were young, and Joseph pressed dollar bills into their palms before sending them to fetch wax paper–wrapped sandwiches for lunch on the beach. Joseph tried to talk me out of it but I can still find my way, though I move slower now. The mission kept me focused, my mind from drifting.

No one speaks, waiting for Joseph to continue his ominous preamble, the reason for this meeting. *We have something important to talk to you three about.*

Violet, the baby of the family, now a grown woman with a husband and four children of her own, sits between her brother and sister on the worn sofa. I reupholstered it myself, once the kids were out of the house and the inn was closed to guests, though it inevitably bore the faint stains left by our grandchildren, the filling softening in the center of each cushion once more.

Our kids were raised here in the Oyster Shell, as Joseph was. As I was, too, in a way. Me and my brother, Tommy, and Joseph, inseparable and constantly bursting through the screen door until Joseph's mother, waving her apron and laughing, shooed us out onto the front porch before we could disturb the guests. Years passed and before we knew it, our children marked reservations on a crowded calendar, and swept floors, and helped me roll and cut biscuits for breakfast. Our grandchildren pitched in, too, showed guests to their rooms, unclipped sun-bleached sheets from the line, rinsed sand from stacks of beach chairs with a coiled garden hose. The inn was always full but the faces came and went like static on the radio, background noise to the life we built. Even as we prepare to tell them, I can't fathom it, how we can leave it all behind. All I want is to begin again, together, at the start.

"There's no easy way to put this, to tell you. I don't know how to begin…" Joseph stammers, gripping my hand tight.

Jane, our oldest, fixes her attention on me, her expression difficult to read. She used to hide her emotions under her wild mane of hair. Now it is professionally relaxed and cut to her shoulders, a look more in line with the other news anchors. Her lanky limbs and long neck became an asset; she moves with a learned grace that escaped her as a gangly teen. I have to turn away from her gaze, afraid my face will betray what I haven't told her.

Thomas stares at Joseph, his mouth a hard line. How similar their frames are, shy of six feet, built like swimmers with wide shoulders and narrow torsos. But unlike Joseph, who had dark hair until his sixties, when it began to thin at his temples and turn white, Thomas started graying young. Silver threads glinted in the light beneath his cap when he graduated from NYU; how serious he was, smiling only for photos, even on a day of celebration. His face looks thinner now than at Christmas, and I don't know if he and Ann cook together at night or if he eats dinner alone at his desk. He wears a suit, here after a long day of meetings with other executives. He slid out of his jacket only because of the stifling heat. Even his sweat is contained, caught in his hairline, not daring to trickle past his brow.

"Your mother and I…" Joseph teeters on the edge, eyes filling. I'm not sure he will be able to bring himself to say the words. "You know how much we love each other, how we've always had each other in our lives. We love you all so much, too, please know that… It's just that we can't imagine life without the other at this point…" I nearly cut in, to carry the blame, to save him from being the one to break their hearts. Our children, our babies all grown up, who used to grab me behind the knees, all bursting love and need, clamoring into my lap, never close enough, and then they were walking to school, and driving away, and leading lives that had nothing to do with us, making friends and choices and mistakes and falling in and out of love, our blood and bone the fabric of their bodies but not their innermost lives, and all the while Joseph and I still here, an island of two, disoriented and mystified by the years that slipped us by.

He takes a deep breath, gathering strength. "We don't want to leave the last chapter of our life to chance, with some miserable, drawn-out end for everyone. I know this is going to come as a shock, it feels shocking to say it, it took us a while to come to terms with everything, but we feel it is the best decision…"

"And that is…" Thomas prompts, impatient when Joseph can't go on.

"We are planning to end our lives in one year. Next June." Joseph's voice breaks.

"I'm sorry—what did you say?" Violet's eyes widen.

"We don't want one of us to die before the other. We don't want to live without each other…we want a say in how our story ends." This explanation comes out more gentle, but his voice is pained, doing his best to ease our burden onto them, to conceal it in a love letter.

"*What?*" Thomas says.

"Yeah, what are you even talking about?" Jane sputters, setting her drink on the table as though she may need use of her hands.

"This will be our final year." It's surreal to hear Joseph speak the words aloud, although I had been the one to say them to him first. *This will be my final year.*

"You're joking." Jane stares back and forth at us, searching for the punchline.

"We're not joking," I say, desperately wishing we were.

"I don't understand," Violet pleads.

"Let us explain." I lean toward them, easing onto the edge of the couch.

"Please, because this is pretty sick." Thomas lurches back into the cushions, away from me.

"Your father and I, we are getting older..."

"You're not a hundred! *Jesus.* You're not even eighty," Jane argues. "What are you turning, seventy-six?"

This time next year I'll be almost seventy-seven and Joseph will be seventy-nine, paltry corrections I don't make. "We are *getting* older, I said. Please, let me finish." I rein in my nerves, all the justifications we've rehearsed now trapped behind my tongue, my throat thick with all the loss to come, everything we will miss, the grief we are inviting into our haven. Thomas shuffles in his seat, fuming. "We understand there will come a point of no return, when one of us may be unrecognizable to the other, when we may not be able to take care of the other, when we may not even remember each other. And there's no way to know when that day will be, no way to live forever as we are now. We have already lived longer than any of our parents, with the exception of my mother...and you all know how horrible that was for so many years. We don't want that burden for you, we don't want that burden for each other."

"There are nursing homes, for this reason exactly! There are rational solutions—" Jane interjects, but I barrel on.

"We don't want that life. We don't want a half-life. We don't want a life without each other," I say, feeling like I'm losing air.

"So what the hell are you proposing, seriously?" Thomas crosses his arms.

"We are proposing a final year," Joseph says. "A final year to live the fullest version of ourselves, to leave behind happy memories for you and the grandkids, to be able to go out on a high note instead of you all remembering some withered version of us."

"Oh, so you do remember you have grandchildren?" Jane scoffs.

"Of course we do." I barely get it out, tears threatening to fall. "We've put a lot of thought into this."

Thomas exhales through his nose, almost a laugh.

"What about us? What do you expect us to do without you?" When Violet's outburst isn't met with rallying cries from her brother and sister, it hovers in the humid night air between us.

Jane's eyes flicker between Joseph and me, then narrow on the cheese dish, as if it is hiding information. I can see her working through the facts, processing the things we've told her, comparing them to what she knows to be true, and coming up short on a *why* she can comprehend.

Joseph gives the saddest smile, scraping for any semblance of strength and certainty, and it tears me in two. "We love you all. We want this year to be a celebration, filled with time together as a family."

"Celebration?" Thomas asks, incredulous. "Sure. Okay. Never mind the million questions I have—is one of you dying or something?"

I offer a soft smile. "We're all dying, Thomas."

"Real nice, Ma."

"Seriously. Are you dying?" Jane is a hound, stock-still, ears cocked toward a rustle in the grass.

I had promised myself not to tell them. Not yet.

"Mom." The force of Jane's attention prickles my underarms, the lights too bright.

"Mom," Violet echoes, picking up the scent.

My diagnosis confirmed after endless tests, a name for my silent, secret battle. A reason. A thief of memory, of function, of being recognizable to myself, of recognizing the ones I love. The root of every fear bound in a single word. *Parkinson's.* Medications that should be helping, but don't. The disease advancing and aggressive in ways doctors didn't anticipate, can't explain. Part of the unluckiest third of patients, with hints of dementia to come, a nightmare I know all too well. The rot and bleach smell of my mother's nursing home, the way she yelled, slipped between decades, threw things, didn't know me. An end that would be more painful, even, than this.

"Why are you lying to us?" Jane wields the accusation, sharp against my throat.

"We aren't lying." I grasp at the loophole, clamping my trembling fingers beneath my knees.

"Well, you certainly aren't telling the whole truth."

"Evelyn," Joseph concedes, "maybe they'd understand..."

"Understand what?" Violet whips toward her father.

"Joseph—"

"They are going to find out..." His shoulders sag with the burden of what's untold, all his strength spent to lead us here.

"We discussed this." I resist an urge to hush him, to drag him into another room.

"Discussed what?" Violet's eyes ping-pong between us, a child begging to be clued in.

"I knew it," Jane says, throwing up her hands.

"I haven't said—"

"This is unbelievable." Thomas stands and stalks to the fireplace, leaning his elbow on the mantel.

"Tell. Us." Jane emphasizes each word, jamming keys into a locked door.

"Evelyn..."

"I didn't want—"

"You can't expect us to buy this," Thomas says.

"Mom, what's going on?" Violet's voice is tinged with fear.

"What could possibly be worse than you and Dad telling us you're offing yourselves in a year?" Jane asks, and despite myself, despite the absurdity of this conversation, or perhaps because of it, I stifle a laugh. It swells in my throat like a sob.

"You all treating me like fine china for a year. That would be worse." It comes out before I can stop it, a partial admission that is the first full truth.

"So you are dying," Jane says.

"In one year's time," I agree, desperate to get back to where we started. *One final year. Next June.*

"This is so fucked," Thomas says.

"Mom, come on." Jane's words are an outstretched hand, urging me to climb in the rescue boat. She, more than anyone, knows how it feels to tread water, braced for danger. "Did you really think we'd let this go?"

I exhale, my resignation an anchor. *Stage two.* Six months ago, stage one felt devastating. *It's progressing quickly...normally it could be months, years, between stages, there is no way to say, but with you...* Now, I'd give everything to clamber back down the rungs. Joseph is right, of course. The shelter I built around my condition is no more than sticks and twine. Even without my admission, they would dismantle it soon enough.

"I have Parkinson's. It's advancing quicker than the doctors predicted. I wanted to keep some semblance of normalcy as long as possible, but the way it's going..." I reveal my hand, my tremor a tell even the best poker player couldn't hide.

"Oh, Mom," Violet begins.

"Jesus," Thomas says.

"Mom, god. I'm so sorry. I wish you told us...but I thought, isn't Parkinson's—like Michael J. Fox? The fully functioning, not at all dying actor?" Jane asks.

"Different people respond differently. My doctor says it's an unusual case..."

"Okay, so let's see another doctor," Thomas says. "Have you gotten other opinions?"

"This is why I didn't want to tell you. I've spent the last few years getting poked and prodded, trying to find an answer that will lead to a different outcome, but there isn't one." My voice catches, the bare facts of it, the certain and inevitable course I bloodied my knuckles fighting, only to surrender now as though I had never stood my ground. "I don't want to waste what time

I have left in hospitals and clinics and waiting rooms with you three researching and spinning your wheels searching for some imaginary cure. This is my decision. My diagnosis is not up for debate."

"You should have told us... We could have helped," Thomas says. "This doesn't affect just you—"

"What can we do, there must be something—" Violet asks.

"Wait, okay," Jane interrupts. "So you have Parkinson's... I'm sorry, Mom, seriously, so sorry...it's terrible...but you said you both were... Wait. Dad, what do you have?"

"Oh my god—" new horror dawns across Violet's face "—what do *you* have?"

Joseph squints with confusion. "What do I have?"

"You said you both were ending your life," Jane says, her emotions in check, a doctor studying her chart. "What do you have?"

"I don't have—"

"Your father has made a unilateral decision that my death calls for his. If you three can dissuade him, I'd really appreciate it. I've been trying."

"Evelyn," Joseph warns.

"*What?*" Thomas says, rubbing his forehead. "Okay, you're both nuts."

"You're perfectly healthy?" Jane says, her voice dry.

"As far as I know."

"And you want to kill yourself because Mom is?"

"I would prefer we both live, but she has made it clear that's not an option," Joseph says, injured and gruff. Now there is nothing to hide behind, every card on the table, no trick to this disappearing act.

"Is this some twisted game of chicken between you two?" Thomas asks. "Because we can call your bluffs now."

"I'm not bluffing," I say, already wanting to turn back the clock, to end the night by hugging them close, by assuring them we would be there for them always, a lie I could make myself believe by sheer will. How badly I want it to be true.

"Unfortunately, neither am I," Joseph adds. Could he really go through with it? Could either of us? To confess it, to bear the weight of their pain and fury and grief from our words alone... but to *do* it?

"I don't even know where to start," Jane says.

"I thought you had more sense, Pop," Thomas challenges, glaring at Joseph.

"Thomas." My tone is firm, but not harsh. We expected Thomas to react this way. We prepared for it.

"Don't *Thomas* me," he sneers. "This is so selfish. How do you expect Violet and Jane to explain this to the kids?"

"We've thought about that." My tremor, out in the open now, distracts me from a lengthier explanation. Joseph grips my hand tight once more, steadying me, and I'm grateful.

"I don't think you have," Thomas shouts. "You're acting like lovesick teenagers—"

"Thomas, cool it. I can't think," Jane cuts him off, the authority of the eldest sister trumping the status he holds in the finance world. Our firstborn... It's hard to believe she, although never married, may soon be a grandmother herself; her daughter, Rain, confessed they have been trying. A baby I may never hold. A gnawing loss that leaves me raw, picturing Rain sitting in a hospital bed, her baby pink and new against her chest, a chair that should be meant for me pulled up to the bed as she hands her little one over, my great-grandchild, except I am not there. I will never see that life unfurl, will never feel those tiny fingers curl around mine, will never see my granddaughter inherit the secrets of motherhood, the way it binds us together. I held my babies as she holds hers, and I should be there to show her, to give her tired eyes a moment to close, to say, *give me that baby*, the one I've loved for as long as I've loved you, which is to say, before we ever met, for my entire lifetime and forevermore.

He turns his attention to his younger sister. "Violet, you can't be okay with this."

Smaller than her tall siblings, inheriting my petite figure while Jane and Thomas got Joseph's height, Violet reminds me of the porcelain dolls she loved as a girl, her wavy hair and full lips and eyes shiny with tears, her fragility beautiful and palpable.

"I can't imagine." Violet speaks but she is quiet, unsteady. "But I don't think they're selfish. It's devastating to think about, but also...kind of romantic."

Thomas tents his fingers over his nose, head bowed, eyes squeezed shut. "You're sick, you know that?" He lifts his gaze to his older sister. "Jane, be the voice of reason here?"

"I can't begin to process this." Jane twirls a grape stem between her fingertips. She picks at it, peeling back to reveal a raw green between the joints.

She doesn't cry and she isn't angry. She is trying to understand, but details will not help her. A decision like this is too foreign, unthinkable—loving someone this much terrifies her.

"You have both lost your minds." Thomas shakes his head, his expression clouded.

Joseph opens his mouth to explain, but I interrupt, trying to get this train back on track. "You're obviously upset, and we understand." Even as I speak, I know it's inadequate, but my mind fogs, can't find the words we had planned, the soothing explanation we hoped would give them peace despite their sadness.

"Upset? This is insane. You can't do this." Thomas's voice catches.

I continue, feeling myself fading as I speak. "It's a lot to take in, and you will all need time. But for now, we just needed you to know. There isn't anything left to discuss."

Joseph nods. I can sense him watching me. He has always been in tune with the slightest shift in my mood. His brows soften in the center when he reads what I am unable to hide. My stomach knots, what was hypothetical days ago is now set in motion, the timer set, the hourglass flipped. I don't have much more to give, the nerve I've worked up will fall away if they keep tugging, my certainty false and shattering as I look into our children's eyes. Tonight is no different, and Joseph knows what I need without me asking. "We hope one day you can understand and until then, that you trust us and our decision." He releases my hand and rises to his feet, signaling the end of the conversation.

"So that's it, huh, nothing left to discuss? Just trust you?" Thomas stews, furious. He glances at his sisters for backup, but at least for now, there is no fire left to storm the castle. Violet is deflated. Jane, solid ice.

"You're going to miss your train," Joseph says, his voice gentle.

Thomas opens and closes his mouth, and a moment passes where it seems like he might argue, or more will be said. There is a haze over the room, as if we are all sharing the same lucid dream. Thomas folds his jacket over his arm and stalks into the foyer. Joseph follows, and Jane and Violet rise, the spell broken. It suddenly feels very late. The waves roll endlessly, audible again in the space our children's protests had filled. I don't get to be hurt that Thomas didn't kiss my cheek or say goodbye. This is our doing. And yet, there is a pang when I watch him walk away. Jane begins to stack the dishes, and I motion to her not to bother; she ignores me and clears them to the kitchen.

Violet sinks beside me on the love seat, her knees folded beneath her like a child. "I'm so sorry, Mom. For what you've been going through, for how you've been feeling. It's awful. I wish I knew...but don't do this, please."

I can see panic creep in, leaching into her sadness, and the guilt I've been battening down swells. How to explain to them that death is the last thing I want. "I wish it were that simple."

Tears fall fast now down my cheeks. I hug her, burying my emotion in her curls.

I overhear Joseph, a final appeal to our son. "We're not asking for you to condone this. I know you don't. But don't disappear, Thomas, please."

Thomas meets his father's gaze with a glare, then walks out without another word. The screen door slams behind him.

"This conversation isn't finished," Jane says as she grabs her purse. She won't meet my eyes but she leans and gives me a hug before she follows her brother. She agreed to drop him at the station to catch the last train to New York before heading home, and I worry now if he will make it in time or be too upset to find the right platform. He should have stayed over, but he always travels back to the city before midnight.

Joseph escorts Violet out, and she threads her arm through his and lingers at the door as if memorizing the living room before it vanishes. She'll cut through the garden on her way to her house next door, the one I grew up in—my mother left the cedar-shingled cottage to Joseph and me when she died. I wonder when Violet will tell Connor about our decision. He's a good man who loves her but never learned to ask about the sadness written across her face.

Joseph returns alone and joins me on the couch. The living room emptied, echoes of all that was said float before us.

"That went well." His voice sounds strained from talking, like he needs to cough. "Should we not have told them anything?"

My heart is heavy; I think of the stem Jane couldn't stop twirling, of Violet's tears, of Thomas's anger. Joseph and I discussed whether to tell them at all, if it was more humane to give them time to prepare, if it meant a year of agony. But I know the cost of a secret, and this isn't one I could keep. "It was a lot to take in. They need more time."

"I hope you're right," he says, sounding unconvinced.

"You gave me up pretty quick." I swipe at my cheeks, don't admit to the sliver of relief within my anger, not to have to hide, to make excuses, to be discovered in a moment of humiliation.

"I know, I'm sorry…it seemed wrong, it didn't make sense, without them understanding everything."

"I wasn't ready." I sound petulant, but there is so little I have a say in anymore.

"I'm not ready for any of this." Joseph's attention lands on the empty sofa, his own pain an offering to their imprints left behind.

"That makes two of us."

We sit in silence, not the tense silence of moments before, but one taut with awareness of bearing either end of a heavy weight, complicit in each other's decision. Perhaps he's wagering I will change my mind, or that this conversation, my conviction, will escape with my fleeting memory.

"What now?" I ask.

"Now we spend this year together, you and me, and the family. Retrace the footsteps of our life…relive the memories we've shared. That's all I want."

"I knew you'd say that," I tease, his predictability both bitter to the taste, and a balm.

"Is it the worst thing to want?"

The lightness in my voice fades. "No, it's not. But you're healthy…you have more time."

"I've spent too many days without you."

I lean against him, ever so slightly. My years in Boston, his years overseas, memories so distant they belong to someone else. "So long ago. Certainly we've made up for it since then."

"I will never stop wishing for more time with you." His eyes fill once more, the reality settling between us, exactly how short one year can be.

"There will never be enough, will there?" My chin quivers, and he folds me into his arms.

"And you?" He whispers in my ear, "I know you've thought about it. I know you've dreamed of all the things we could do."

"Besides getting you to change your mind?" I pull away and look at him squarely, my eyes rimmed red. The finality of a single year reverberates through my body. When it was only me, it seemed less scary. Like I could float away, leaving only ripples to show I had been there. Now it is twice as heavy. Two stones, sinking to the depths, to the unknown.

"Please, Evelyn. Tonight was tough enough."

I back off, exhaustion shrouding reason. Conceding, if only for now. "You know the answer..." I shake my head. "But it's silly. It's not possible, I don't know how, or if I could..."

When I don't continue, he offers gently, "The symphony?"

I glance into the lamplit study at our dual pianos. The glossy black Steinway I rarely play. A showpiece my father bought in the twenties that I begged to use, but under my mother's critical eye, always felt like swing dancing in a museum, inappropriate, verging on reckless. I prefer the Baldwin, the one Joseph bought secondhand, with its warm honeyed wood, the yellowed keys, the bench that holds sheet music within its hinged seat, the cushion that sags in the middle. The piano I taught Jane to play on, where I attempted to teach Thomas and Violet, though it never stuck. Where I conducted beginners' lessons and entertained guests when the kids were young and every room of the Oyster Shell was full, impromptu concerts in our living room, bursting with music and swaying couples and laughter.

The biggest dream on my list: *play in the Boston Symphony Orchestra*. For a lifetime I've practiced, and that dream was the reason, the heartbeat humming beneath. An impractical, implausible yearning that bloomed within me when I held the hope of a different path, that I've never been able to quiet, despite reason and logic and the trajectory of my life. Even now, as I face its end. I don't acknowledge it, how much of a stretch this dream of mine has always been, how laughable it is now.

My idea seems small, selfish, in light of the anger on my children's faces. And yet, the need remains, pulsing and aware of the minutes ticking by.

Instead I say, "We'll have to find a way to say goodbye."

Two

Joseph

June 1940

I cut through the field to Tommy and Evelyn's house, the fresh
cedar shingles glimmering in the pink dewy morning. Their
yard was once dotted with trees that littered their leaves and shed
their needles, pinecones sticky with sap. But now the route is
exposed, the trees ripped from their roots by a hurricane. In the
winter, this meadow, like a bridge between us, becomes snow
covered and treacherous. Our boots leave slushy footprints or
slip-slide, cracking through its icy surface. In the fall it turns
gold, the grass dry and crunching beneath my feet. Spring is
muddy when the snow first melts, everything limp and dishev-
eled, a mess of crisscrossed tracks. Then, days like this, the slow
rise, the budding, the drying out and soaking up, the showers
ending in birdsong. The wildflowers grow inexplicably, steadfast, and the entire field bursts purple.

I am almost to their house when Evelyn flies out the front
door, slamming it behind her.

Tommy appears seconds later, calling after her, "Ev, stop! You can't scream at Ma and run off like that."

"What's she going to do, send me away?" Evelyn sneers, whirling back at her brother.

"What's going on?" I jog to catch up, and Tommy slows his pace to let me. Evelyn storms ahead of us toward Bernard Beach.

"Don't you think you're proving her point? She already thinks you're out of control."

"I'll show her out of control."

"And ungrateful."

"For what?" Evelyn laughs, incredulous. "Spending the next two years learning how to curtsy? I don't want her life. Alone in the house waiting for Dad to come home from work, the same thing every day?" She takes off at a run once more, hollering behind her, "I'd rather die!"

"What's she yelling about?" I ask.

"Ma's shipping Ev off to Boston, to live with Aunt Maelynn."

"Wait, what?" I halt midstride as Tommy barrels ahead.

"At the end of the summer. I know. We're as shocked as you." He waves me on, trying to get me up to speed on this strange turn of events.

"I'm so confused. *Maelynn?*"

"That's the one."

As far as I know, Mrs. Saunders and her sister haven't spoken in decades, and none of us has ever met her. Maelynn ran away when she was seventeen, but the details are murky and contested, a bit of small-town lore. She's known to be wild, a flight risk. It doesn't add up.

"Why would your mom want Evelyn to live with her?"

"She thinks Ev needs a bit of help in the acting-like-a-lady department, and apparently Maelynn is a teacher at some fancy boarding school for girls, Mrs. Mayweather's something or other. Apparently you have to know someone to get in."

We approach Evelyn at Bernard Beach like a caged animal,

no sudden movements, and sit beside her in the sand. She doesn't acknowledge us, simmering in anger.

Tommy tosses a thin rock, flicks his wrist as it sails over the water, skipping once, twice, three times. "Ev, you're looking at it all wrong. This is your chance to get away from Stonybrook, to live in a real city, to meet new people. An adventure. I'd give anything for that."

"Well, then, you take my spot," she mumbles, her hair hanging in her face. This is an Evelyn I haven't seen before, her cheeks lightly freckled by the sun are usually stretched in a grin, but now they're ashen, tense.

"A school full of girls? Sign me up!" Tommy elbows me, smirking.

Sitting beside them, I am struck by how alike they are. In a few weeks they'll turn fifteen and seventeen, their birthdays only two days apart, but that is not why they are often mistaken for twins. They share a confidence I never possessed, a sureness of who they are in their bones that I envied, a charisma that gets them, and me by association, equally into and out of trouble. How entwined in each other's lives they have always been, siblings and best friends, something I never knew growing up in my house alone. Alone, but never lonely, because they slid me in like a card missing from their deck.

Together we raced to the shore, down the dirt path that sometimes flooded on full-moon nights. Tommy leading the pack, our feet toughened by the end of each summer by the piercing rocks and blistering sand. We swam out to Captain's Rock, a submerged land mass jutting out of the water that warned sailors to steer clear, and felt for the bundles of mussels clinging to its slippery sides like bunches of grapes on a vine. We plucked enough to fill a pail and swam in, heaved ourselves soaking wet onto the wooden dock and lay exhausted, drying under the midday sun. We cracked the shells with our bare heels to reveal the mucous flesh within, white or bright orange, before clamping a

clothespin tied to string and sitting side by side, three lines dangling between our swinging legs, waiting for the slight tug of
a crab. I don't have a memory of our first meeting, and maybe
that's because there wasn't one, our families' houses side by side
for generations. There never was a *before* Tommy and Evelyn, not
really. I try to imagine the next two years without her, but I can
only see the imprint in the sand between us where she belongs.

"Those girls are going to be awful." She drags a stick in sloppy
circles between her knees.

"I'm sure they won't be," I say.

"And if they are awful, but *very* pretty, bring 'em home for
me, alright?" Tommy says.

She punches him in the shoulder, but she's smiling.

After a summer together, she is gone, not to be back until the
next one. Tommy and I spend the year as we always do, our time
divided between school, trading updates on the war and helping
my parents restore the inn, damaged in the Hurricane of '38.

The storm hit two years ago now, but the memory is crisp,
a branding leaving a scar. That September day started hot and
sticky, not unlike the rest that summer. I was fifteen. Tommy,
Evelyn and I swam in the swelling surf after school; my mother
unclipped linens from the line as it began to rain. Then it came,
an angry, living thing. We rode it out in our attic with petri-
fied guests, clinging to heavy trunks and each other, our shutters battened down against the gale-force winds and hammering
rain. The water rose, burst through doors and windows, fell-
ing hundred-year-old maples, snapping power lines and sending furniture floating through the streets.

We emerged wet and shaken, trudging through floodwaters
and mud, bracing for the fallout. The posts of the wooden dock
splintered like toothpicks, the beachfront summer cottages were
knocked inland off their stilts or reduced to piles of debris. Tommy
and Evelyn found me near an overturned porcelain tub and we

stood together in silence. My mother fell to her knees in the dark churned earth, gripped the exposed roots of a pine ripped from our yard, and sobbed. My father at her side, held tight to her heaving shoulders.

The Saunderses' place was back to its normal grandeur within months of the hurricane. Mr. Saunders paid some of his workers to cut out the moldy plaster walls, rip out the carpets and rebuild while he went to the office. The only sign of damage was the wide-open yard that had once been covered with mature trees.

At my house, the storm is still a recent enemy; my dad distracted at dinner as he stares at our bare rooms and rough-hewn walls. With Tommy's insistence, Mr. Saunders got my father a job working on the line at his factory, the Groton Ship and Engine Company. My mother took up shifts at the Red Cross, distributing supplies while Roosevelt's WPA cleared our streets. A temporary thing, my dad said, so we could save up money for the repairs needed to reopen the Oyster Shell. But two years later, he hastens to the garage as soon as his plate is clear, working past nightfall to construct furniture out of scrap wood. My mother paces and tidies the inn that is no longer an inn, peering with worried eyes through the window at my father, silhouetted by a bare bulb hanging low above him. Sometimes I discover them in an embrace, when she has determined it is late enough and steps into the dewy grass to fetch him for bed, wrapping her arms around his soft middle until he relents.

Although our activities haven't changed, Stonybrook has felt strange these months without Evelyn, and I walk around with a knot in my stomach like I'm forgetting something but can't remember what. I keep expecting her to turn up, pressing her nose against the windows, or biking behind us on the path from school. I knew Tommy would have a hard time without her, but it surprises me how much I've felt her absence.

"You remember when we were kids and Evelyn chased the Campbell twins with that giant spider crab?" I stop, my paintbrush suspended over new window trim. As I say it, something in me twinges, a notch out of place. I can't get her out of my mind. Evelyn, who wore overalls Tommy had outgrown, who tossed her head back, open-mouthed, when she laughed, who kneeled in brackish mud digging for razor clams with her bare hands.

Tommy chuckles. "Let's hope for everyone's sake there's a shortage of spider crabs up in Boston."

"You think they'll send her home early? Kick her out for bad behavior, or something?" I ask, trying to sound casual.

"Are you kidding? I'll be surprised if she ever comes back."

"What do you mean?"

"Stonybrook's boring. If I got sent to Boston, I'd never come home."

"What are you talking about? She loves Stonybrook."

Tommy wipes his arm against his forehead, leaving a white steak of paint behind. "She *loved* Stonybrook. She hadn't been anywhere. You really want to live here the rest of your life?"

The question has never occurred to me. I peer around at the Oyster Shell, built by my great-grandparents in the 1800s, the mold-spattered walls and rotted boards will eventually be restored enough to reopen. I'll take it over one day, raise my family here like my parents, and their parents. Four generations of Myerses along the Long Island Sound, my kids someday will make it five. Five generations running on the same sand, learning to swim in the same waves. There is no other place so deeply rooted in my soul, no other place I could so truly belong, the only place that calls me home.

"Stonybrook's enough for me."

I can't help but notice her as she steps off the train, a beacon among the gray smog of men in suit jackets and hats. It isn't until she is almost on us that I realize who she is. Even Tommy is caught off guard. He was craning to see, scanning New London's bustling Union Station for a familiar face seconds before she threw her arms around his neck. We were expecting Evelyn. But this girl—this woman—who floats toward us, carrying her leather suitcase and smiling at passengers as she navigates the crowd, she is a stranger.

Her dress hugs tight to the curves of her body, and it's the color of the wild violets that grow in the field between our houses. Her hair is parted to one side and pinned in a way that emphasizes her eyes. They are flecked with green, something I never noticed before. Her body looks so slender, so feminine, instead of just small. She even has a heel on her shined shoes, although in every memory I see her barefoot. A train sounds its horn in the distance, and the early summer heat becomes stifling. My chest tightens, my mouth dry.

Tommy holds her by her shoulders, at an arm's length. "Where is my sister?" He spins her and makes a show of peering behind her back. "What have they done with Evelyn?"

Tommy always strikes me as taller than he is, his animated gestures and hearty voice proclaim a room empty until he is in it, but now with her heels on, they are almost the same height. Evelyn giggles, and even that has a warming effect. She turns to me and hugs my waist. She smells like a flower I can't name.

"It's so good to see you, you have no idea." She beams, grabbing each of our arms. She raises her eyebrows, the way she always does before one of her stories. "You can't imagine the year I've had."

Tommy nods. "Well, Ev, whatever they did worked. Ma may actually faint."

Evelyn tips her head back in laughter. Warmth like sunshine spreads through my chest, her fingers hot against my skin. She glances at me, and then at her shoes, dropping her grip. "Don't be fooled. I thought about coming home all haggard but I don't actually want her to explode. Plus, Aunt Maelynn stuck her neck out for me quite a bit, and I don't need Mom to pile on. Let's say I wasn't a *total* hit with the headmistress."

"Why am I not surprised?" Tommy says.

"What is Maelynn like?" I ask. "She live up to the stories?"

"Yes, you have to meet her. She's incredible. She is the only one who actually teaches anything interesting. Gosh, we read Faulkner, Woolf, the Brontë sisters—" She registers our blank looks. "Okay, you have no clue what I'm talking about, but trust me. She's brilliant. The girls all adore her. It's hard to believe she's Mom's sister."

Tommy tilts his head, ready to gloss over things between Evelyn and their mother, as usual. "She's not so bad, Ev."

She shoots him a look. "Easy for you to say. You're her golden, angel child." As tough as their mom is on Evelyn, she becomes malleable and girlish when her son turns his attention her way, a chink in her otherwise steel facade.

"Well, that's because I'm a golden angel." He winks.

Evelyn shakes her head, threading her arms through both of ours, and with exaggerated politeness says, "Well, would you two *fine* gentlemen escort a lady home?"

Tommy tips an invisible cap then picks up her suitcase. I laugh, and it sounds higher pitched than normal, flooding me with embarrassment. My senses are heightened, taking in the softness of the insides of her forearms. Evelyn straightens her shoulders and sticks her chin out, making a show of smiling at everyone who passes by.

In the nights that follow I dream of her, always in the violet dress, or walking in a field of wildflowers, or naked, sticking blossoms through her hair. I can't remember a day when Evelyn and I were alone, but now that's all I want. I need to see how much she has changed. See if there is a place in her life where I still fit. It surprises me how little I know her now, even after all these years we've spent growing together along the same sea.

Although, truth be told, I am grateful for the time apart. I'm not sure how Tommy will take my new feelings; I flush thinking about the dreams. He is my best friend, the closest thing I've ever had to a brother. How can I expect him to accept this shift, this need to make his little sister laugh, this desire to hold her hand?

I can't casually ask Evelyn on a date, whistling at her on the street the way Tommy does the girls in town. Those girls laugh because they know he's a flirt, and still they fall for him. Tommy brings me along to keep the other girl company, the friend of the one he has his eye on. Sometimes those girls lean in, and we kiss, but my heart is still when their lips meet mine.

I'm not even sure what to think. It's *Evelyn*. Evelyn, who used to wrestle with us on the sandbar, challenge us to spitting contests, and ate fistfuls of wild blackberries without caring when the juice dribbled down her chin. Evelyn, who used to tackle me and demand piggyback rides, who laughed at Tommy's jokes until she got the hiccups. Evelyn, who now rolls her shoulders back, accentuating her curves under the fabric of her dress. Evelyn, whose sweet scent lures me like a spell, whose touch buckles me at the knees. Evelyn, who is home for the summer before she is back to school once again.

Today is Tommy's day off, and they both swing by the inn on their way to the beach, insisting I skip out for a few hours.

Tommy tosses a striped towel at me. "For old times' sake, before Evelyn goes and becomes more of a lady on us."

I grin. "We wouldn't want that." It makes Evelyn laugh and my smile widens, sheepish.

She wears a yellow cotton dress over her bathing costume and leads us down Sandstone Lane to Bernard Beach. I imagine the moment when she will undo the buttons, slip it over her shoulders. I'm grateful for the privacy of my thoughts, still surprising to me, although not unwelcome. Her sunglasses hide her eyes and I wonder about their changing color, needing to know the exact shade of blue or green.

The sand is cool under my feet this late morning, but won't be for long, the sun beating on my neck. Evelyn tosses her sunglasses onto a blanket and dashes toward the water, nearing high tide. She sheds her dress as she goes; it flies behind her before landing crumpled in the sand. She splashes her feet in the foam, yelps from the cold as she wades in and propels herself through a gentle wave. Tommy and I drop our towels and slip off our shirts before running in after her. I dive under, the rush of icy water against my skin, pounding on my ears, everything muted, and flowing over me. I break the surface; the air rushes back toward me, the sound clear and sharp. Evelyn floats on her back, her pink toes stick out of the water, her breasts rise, buoyant, face pale and shimmering like the inside of a clamshell. When the waves dip, I glimpse a white strip of her stomach, a sliver of the moon, before it submerges again. Tommy is off, tanned arms from working in the shipyard rise up and out of the waves as he swims away from us. I could stand, but I tread water to keep warm beside Evelyn, watch the water pool and drain off her stomach as she bobs in the subtle current.

"It's good to have you back." My voice is quiet, and her ears are partially underwater. She doesn't reply and I think she hasn't heard me. Then she sighs, not out of frustration or exhaustion but a happy sound, a breath so contented she couldn't hold it in her body any longer.

After a moment she says, "It's good to be back." She opens her eyes, watching the endless clouds drift above us. Her skin ripples from the cold, the water in June not warmed yet for the season, not yet refreshingly cool like July, certainly not the bathwater of August. A strip of filmy copper seaweed drifts by her thigh and is sent back the way it came.

Before I can stop myself, I say, "I've missed you." Right after I speak, I panic. It's too forward; we don't talk to each other this way. Maybe she hasn't changed after all. Maybe she has changed too much. Maybe I shouldn't say anything, leave her to float with the clouds, light and free.

She lifts herself to tread water beside me. "Well, now, Joseph…" She smiles and tilts her head to one side, a Tommy sort of expression that tightens my stomach with guilt. "Don't tell me that because I've come home looking like a lady, all of a sudden you're going to act like a gentleman."

"I mean…" I squint, glad for the brightness of the sun, another reason my face might flush. "Tommy and I, we've missed having you around."

"Mmm-hmm." She raises her eyebrows. "If I didn't know any better, I'd say you were falling in love with me."

She pauses, holding my gaze, her eyes bluer today, I see now, and I open my mouth, but no words come out. She laughs, breaking my guilty stare.

"I'm teasing! Loosen up!" she says, before plunging underwater. Tommy is approaching, coming in with strong, even strides.

He stands when he reaches us. "That'll wake you up, huh?" He shakes his head, hard, to flush water out of his ears. "Ready to go in?"

"Uh-uh, no way, it feels incredible. I'm never getting out." She kicks her feet like a mermaid, alternately flexing and pointing her toes. "If I were at school I'd be sitting inside learning about which fork belongs with which course, and how best to greet my husband after a long day of work."

"You? With a husband?" Tommy splashes her. "Please tell me they don't actually teach you that stuff."

"Oh, I promise you they do." Evelyn reaches up and twists her wet hair into a knot at the nape of her neck.

"Well, did you like any of it? Was any of it useful?" I ask, trying to sound casual. One ringlet falls loose from the bun and I resist the urge to reach for it.

"My weekends with Maelynn, those I'll miss this summer. We went everywhere, Fenway and the MFA, that's the art museum, and oh! Sometimes she'd pick a random number and we would ride the trolley that many stops and explore where we ended up. She's fearless."

"Sounds way better than here if you ask me," Tommy says.

"Hey, here isn't so bad," I say.

"Unfortunately, *most* of the time at school was pretty painful. Etiquette and sewing and proper dress and ugh, I'm boring myself even thinking about it. The only saving grace was I got to play piano a lot. Maelynn got me private lessons. That was really lovely."

I've only heard her play a few times, the music finding me while I sat on their stoop waiting for Tommy those nights it was too late for Evelyn to come out with us. I almost never entered; Mrs. Saunders rarely welcomed our chaos around their expensive mirrors and stiff furniture, but sometimes when the door was left ajar, I would glimpse Evelyn aglow in yellow lamplight. It was practically the only time her mother tolerated her in the house, fingers dancing on the keys, the jet-black piano humming beneath her. In those moments, she seemed like a stranger, combed hair damp from the shower, elegant and focused, her talent unmistakable. Even to someone like me, who only listened to records when my father put them on; a burly man who loved to dance close with my mother while our living room buzzed with swaying guests, and after, when they were all alone.

"*Lovely?* Oh, Ev, what have they done to you?" Tommy covers his face, shaking his head.

"Listen, yes. Most of it was dumb and I hated it. But…" She trails off, smiling. "People…they treat me differently when I act the way they taught me. When I dress and do my hair. I'm still me but, I don't know…never mind."

"You're saying you like the way the boys in town are looking at you now, huh? You really are a chip off the old block." Tommy splashes her again. My stomach drops, thinking of other guys in town seeing her, noticing her.

She splashes back, hard, spraying both of us. "No—well, maybe—but when you act a certain way people treat you a certain way. That's all. It's nice." She stands, cupping water and letting it rush between her fingers.

Tommy clucks his tongue. "Well, you're really growing up, Ev. So wise, and worldly. I'm proud, truly. I guess this means now you can't…oh I don't know…race us to Captain's Rock or anything. Wouldn't want to ruin your new image…" He lifts his eyebrows.

She raises hers in return, eyes wide. "Is that a challenge?"

"I wouldn't dream of challenging a lady—"

Tommy can't finish his sentence before Evelyn dives away, starting the race. I plunge in, her legs shining in and out of the water ahead of me. Tommy is last, caught laughing as he joins us sloppily. Tommy is a decent swimmer, but my limbs are longer, and I am faster. I propel forward, kicking my legs, pumping my arms, the splashes of Evelyn beside me. We are in sync now, swimming together and apart. The water is electrified between us, and we meet the slick, algae-covered stone at the same time, my hand reaches for it and finds hers instead. We surface, and she slips away from me, wipes the dripping hair out of her eyes, breath rushed, her lips tinged purple from the cold.

Tommy's words rush in, churning my stomach. *You're saying you like the way the boys in town are looking at you now, huh?* My thoughts follow without permission. *Evelyn, who is home for the summer before she is gone.*

Water covers our shoulders and undulates between us, the taste of salt on my lips. My heart thuds, skin blazing and numb at once. My eyes search hers; they are deep and open pools, earnest, waiting.

I reach for her hand, again, and this time, she doesn't pull away.

The next week, I bring Evelyn flowers, a fistful of wild violets from the meadow between our houses, purple petals lined in gold and white. I knock, self-conscious now that I am standing on her stoop, of the puny bouquet, of how she will receive it, but her smile as she opens the door steadies me. I hand it to her, an offering, an explanation, a hope. "That dress you wore, when you came home, you looked so beautiful…and it reminded me of these…and I thought you'd like to have them."

After that, I picked violets and hid them for her to discover later, our secret code, *these make me think of you*, something to make her smile, to think of me too. I liked to imagine her finding them everywhere she turned: in a jar on her front steps, in her pockets, pressed between pages of her favorite books.

The weeks passed with stolen gazes and discreet affection. Her arm brushing mine, my knee pressed against hers beneath a table, our fingers laced in the dark while my body pulsed in disbelief, *she wants this too*. Unsure of how Tommy would react, we were nervous to bring our secret to light, to name it, even to each other, to make it real, to let it be taken away.

Summer was just beginning, but it always kicks into full swing around Tommy's and Evelyn's birthdays, right after The Fourth of July. This year to celebrate sixteen and eighteen, Mrs. Saunders makes an exception and allows me over for dinner, a pork roast with potatoes soft enough to mash with a fork, and a buttery lemon cake.

As he lights the candles, Tommy clucks his tongue. "Even on my birthday you try to steal the limelight."

Evelyn gives him a playful shove. "Oh please, I'm the best birthday present you ever got." He grins at her, and they blow them out together.

Afterward, we head to Bernard Beach to watch the sun go down, leftover fireworks from yesterday's Fourth of July display popping past the jetty, illuminating the darkening sky with bursts of red and gold. The night cools and Evelyn wraps her arms around her chest, and I have to stop myself from pulling her close, wishing I had a coat to offer, but even that gesture would set off her brother's alarm bells.

Tommy stands, leaving a wrinkled imprint between Evelyn

and me on the blanket, and slips his father's silver flask from his back pocket.

"Let's liven this party up, huh?" He takes a long swig, shudders and passes it to Evelyn.

She puts it up to her nose and recoils. "It smells foul."

"Don't smell it. Drink it. Here, Joseph." He grabs the whiskey and hands it to me, and I take a short sip.

Tommy lights the cigarette hanging between his lips. "Come on, Ev, you're sweet sixteen! Don't tell me a lady can't drink."

She shuffles her feet, burying then freeing her ankles in the cool sand. "You really have to let this lady thing go. I'm the same."

"Oh, but you're not the same," he mocks, grabbing the flask from me, a roman candle illuminates his boyish features as they turn to stone. "Is she, Joe?"

Evelyn tenses beside me.

"She seems like Evelyn to me." I shrug but my voice wavers, my eyes cast down at my knees.

Tommy takes another long swig, then a drag on his cigarette, relishing the awkward silence. He shakes his head. "Listen, you two. I'm okay with it. I am. I just want you to admit it to me."

"Hey, maybe you should slow down." I motion at the flask, and Tommy backs away.

"I just started—listen, Joe, you're my best friend and if you want to be with my sister, fine. But I wish you had come to me like a man instead of sneaking around and kissing her in the dark." Tommy won't look at us then, he doesn't even sound angry. His voice is hollow, disappointed.

"We haven't been kissing!" Evelyn squeals, her voice like a bicycle tire losing air. It is the truth, but a technicality, not an explanation.

There is a pause filled with the crackle of emerald fireworks and the steady roll of waves. Evelyn is silhouetted in the moonlight, and I wish I knew what she was thinking, what she wanted me to say, to do. Tommy tosses his half-finished Lucky Strike onto the sand. The breeze raises the hairs on my arms, but my body is burning from the accusation, the truth in it. All those moments we were sure were subtle, hidden. Of course he knows. I'm a fool. A traitor and a fool.

I take a deep breath. "I wanted to tell you, I did, but I didn't know how you'd react. I didn't want you to hate me or go crazy. I didn't want you to forbid it. I was going to... I was waiting for the right time. I..." I trail off, my excuses falling away.

"You thought I'd forbid it?" Tommy laughs, and even in the shadows I can see his anger forming, a low rumble. "What am I, her father?" He lowers the whiskey, so it is hanging loosely by his fingertips.

I falter, my voice rough with uncertainty. "I don't know, I— You're my best friend. I wanted to respect you."

Tommy jabs his pointer into his chest. "Respect me by telling me. Don't sneak around. You know how weird I felt around the two of you?" He sweeps an arm out over the beach. "You think I didn't see what was going on?"

Evelyn jumps in, forcing a lightness to her voice. "Tommy you always had your eyes on some girl walking by." She tries a laugh. "Honestly I never thought you'd notice." She twists a curl of her hair, a nervous gesture that despite the tension makes my stomach flutter with longing. There is no going back, no out I want to take.

I open my palms to him, a surrender. "I am so sorry, Tommy. I really am."

Tommy pauses for another eternity before he exhales a loud dramatic sigh. "I know you are. You're a good man, Joe. If you're crazy enough to want to be with Ev, I'm crazy enough to let you. I just wanted to get it out in the open. Honestly, I am okay with it." He pauses, staring me in the eye, and warns, "As long as you marry her."

Evelyn freezes; my mouth falls open, stammering. "We haven't even talked about—"

"Oh geez, I'm kidding." Tommy howls, throwing his head back. "Sheesh you two are uptight. Here—have a drink, it will help."

We both laugh, a laugh like a release. Like coming out of our cove braced for a storm and finding the sun.

Tommy lifts his stolen whiskey in a toast. "To Joseph and Evelyn, may you live a long, happy life together, forever in love." He grins at us before putting the flask to his lips. We pass it around, all of us taking burning mouthfuls, making us giddy and stupid and finally free, blurring the night sky until we can't distinguish the stars.

Once Tommy knows, the rest of the summer is better than I dreamed. We aren't overly affectionate in front of him, but I can't help but hold Evelyn's hand, brush the hair out of her eyes. Tommy shakes his head and calls us lovebirds, and peers around for some girl to divert his attention. Tommy works at the shipyard most days, so Evelyn and I are often alone. She visits me at the inn while I chisel away at the list my father's left me, replacing warped flooring, rotted baseboards, missing shingles. I don't mind the work, my brain emptying of all else in the tinkering, fixing and sanding. There's an ease to working with my hands, and pride in a job well done, the giving back to a home that will be given to me someday. A way of imprinting myself into its history, the way I've seen my father, and his father, do for as long as I can remember. And I never mind her interruption. Evelyn sometimes reading on a blanket in the grass nearby, or steadying a ladder and handing up tools before we steal away and spend the afternoon together, swimming and sunning on the warm sand.

This afternoon, we lie on the dock, finding images in the clouds above us. Evelyn's hair is damp and windswept, my hand on her thigh. Touching her skin is both thrilling and comforting, as if we've always lain this way, as if our relationship was never anything less than this. I turn to face her and my gaze soaks up every inch, like a painter with a model, an artist and his muse.

"What are you doing?" She blushes as she asks.

"You want to know?" I ask, suddenly shy. I can't help it, the way she looks at me.

"Yes. I do."

"Memorizing you, at sixteen." It jolts me as I admit it, *sixteen*, the way it makes me want to see her at every age, to file this one away for later. To sort through my memories for this exact moment, for this part of our life together. The notebook tucked beneath her, containing lists of her most secret dreams. The places she wants to see, adventures to have, ideas swirling within her since she met Maelynn. Dreams she told me about but has yet to let me read, that she scribbled as she lay on her stomach on the dock, watching me swim. Sixteen, her skin tan and smooth, the thin scar across her elbow where she slipped and caught a splintered edge of the dock one summer, her body a raft I could float away on, drifting off into the bliss I feel.

She curls into me, presses her cheek against my bare shoulder, my lips by her forehead, her hair tickling my neck. "It's weird, how it's not weird. Isn't it?"

"You and me?" I ask.

"You and me."

"Feels like it was always supposed to be this way." As I say it, it feels true, like a secret part of me knew. Our destiny mapped, waiting for us to catch up. "Doesn't it?"

"I always hoped for it," Evelyn says. My stomach flips, imagining her imagining this.

I whisper, "One more year away and then you'll be home for good, you can do anything...what do you want to be, Evelyn?"

She smiles, tilts her chin to face me. "I don't know...I want to be like Maelynn, someone who has seen the world, who has stories to tell. Did you ever hear of these traveling concert pianists?" I shake my head. "Maelynn was telling me all about them. These people get paid to play piano in an orchestra, can you imagine? Maybe that. Or, I'll become a pilot and fly wherever I want."

I tease, "You can't be a pilot."

She raises her eyebrows. "Why? Because I'm a woman?"

I laugh, smitten by her, the way she believes in everything but her own limitations. "Because you're afraid of heights."

She clucks her tongue, no doubt considering all the times she chickened out of jumping off the highest point of Captain's Rock. "Oh, so now you know everything about me, Joseph Myers?"

Quietly I say, "I know some things."

"Well, if you're so smart, what do you want to be?"

"Yours." My heart thuds, like our bare feet on the dirt path, all our years together racing in my chest, as I pull her chin toward me, and for the first time, kiss her.

Three

Jane

June 2001

I sit across from my mother in the study, beside the bookshelf jammed with picture frames and waterlogged novels, at the Steinway. With its characteristic black sheen, it's the piano I tended to play growing up, for no other reason than to be different from my mom, who was always seated at the Baldwin. It's been decades since she gave me lessons, since I've spent any real time at it, but without a piano of my own, I'm drawn to this room whenever I'm over. Sitting on this bench helped remind me of who I was when years ago, I strayed so far I was sure I'd never speak to my parents again, never mind be enveloped in the safety and comfort of this room. I can't sit near these pianos and feel lost too long. I am in the thousands of strokes of my fingers on the keys, as my spine lengthened and my feet grew to reach the pedals, my mother beside me, music the one place we could always meet.

I don't allow myself to look at her, to calculate all the ways she has already changed that I somehow missed. The tiny fractures I chalked up to normal aging. I can't bring myself to face the real culprit, the one that can't be reasoned with, the diagnosis I should be focusing on, that would bring me to my knees if I weren't so bewildered by their response. Not when it's much easier to confront the flawed being that is my mother, to dip into the years we did battle and draw from them a shield to cover what I could be feeling, should be feeling. I can't be generous with her right now, offering condolences, without somehow agreeing there may be justification to her thought process. Not when they've made this decision without us, without allowing us to plead a different case. Not when *one year* is so arbitrary, when she might have many more. Not when digging for details, facts, timelines, all the ways I usually build a full picture, will point to *dying mother*. Instead, I play scales with my left hand, unable to fight the subconscious muscle memory. "So what did you want to talk about? Another bomb to drop on me?"

This is the first time I've seen her, seen either of them—although Dad is conveniently busy in the garden, leaving us alone in here—since they made that ridiculous announcement, presenting it to the three of us in a pleasant package, setting out appetizers and asking about our jobs before handing it over to detonate in our arms. Thomas was silent, cagey, when I dropped him off at the train station that night. We don't talk regularly; our schedules—me recording my segments in the studio early mornings, and my brother working until ungodly hours at night—mean we mostly catch up at holidays and on birthdays. So it was a shock when he called me the next afternoon, demanding we stop our parents before it's too late. Obviously, I agree. We can't let them go through with this. Mom, not now, not yet, at least. Dad, not ever. But they have always been this way, wrapped up in each other, codependent, and part of me is not surprised they would propose an end like this. A world where the end of one means the end of both. It seems like exactly the kind of thing they would come up with, and when I told Thomas that, he hung up on me.

"You've been avoiding us," my mom says, her tone cautious.

I normally come over every week or so, every couple of weeks at least, unless work gets chaotic. I hadn't been by since that night, although we've spoken on the phone a few times, briefly, calls I thought I was ready for. Until I heard their forced calm, voices dripping with concern when they asked in turn, *How are you?* as though they weren't the reason I may be a bit off. I have looked at it a hundred different ways, tried to put myself in their shoes. I imagined nearing eighty myself, being handed a debilitating diagnosis, and I have come up with the same answer every time. They haven't thought it through, not completely. And they won't do it.

"Like Dad's avoiding me now?" I peer through the windows at my father kneeling outside in the tiger lily beds, a pile of discarded weeds beside him. "He knows I'm here."

"I asked him to give us a few minutes."

"So you could guilt-trip me?"

"I expected Thomas to bury himself in work, to push us away for a while. But I'm surprised by you, actually."

My anger flares, the safest of my sparring emotions. "You don't really have the right to be surprised by anyone at this point, Mom."

"Fair enough. I just thought you'd have questions."

"I've been processing," I say, then on hearing my own bitterness, add, "I'm sorry. I can't imagine how hard this is on you. I'm not trying to downplay that, or be insensitive, because, *Jesus*, it's awful, Mom. But it's…a lot."

I've been punishing her, actually, and she wants me to admit it. Punishing her because it's easier than confessing I jolt from dreams where she no longer recognizes my face. Punishing her because I had to be the one to tell my daughter, Rain, to field questions I didn't have the answers to. To tell her first, that

Grandma is really sick, and second, that both her grandparents plan to end their lives because of it. I was even younger than Rain is now when I had her. She is my only baby, and we've never kept things from each other. As hard as it was to tell her, as irresponsible as it felt to continue spreading this idiocy, it would be impossible not to, it would be there every time we spoke, growling at me to bring her up to speed. I also wanted to tell Rain before she heard it from her cousins, didn't want that news to travel and arrive butchered via the game of telephone like every story shared with any member of the family. So I was forced to explain that I don't know if they mean it or not, but for now we had to take them at their word. I was the one who had to hold her when tears of confusion and preemptive grief fell, who stayed up past midnight analyzing a decision I couldn't justify or understand. I considered making my parents face their oldest grandchild, to look her in the eyes and say the words that would devastate her, sure it would be a slap of reality, maybe even a reason to reconsider. But the one it would hurt most would be Rain, to learn a harsh lesson about my parents I accepted a long time ago, that they would always love each other a little more than they loved you.

"Process away," Mom says, like she is being the reasonable one. She, who so graciously gave me time and space these past couple of weeks, waiting for me to come to her, when I should have been the one to be gracious, to offer to help her, to see how she felt, what she needed. Until she decided she had been patient enough and requested I come over, said there was something she needed to ask me in person. I, too, have a question. I want to know what it is about old age that has given my parents such a flair for the dramatic, because these big formal announcements are entirely too much for me to take.

"So, what was so important you couldn't ask over the phone?" I know I should be somber, but I can't play along. I feel out of my body. It is exhausting to be discussing this, to act like killing herself a year from now is a real and rational option, her only option, and it isn't. Can't be.

"Does Marcus still have connections to the *Boston Globe*?" Mom asks.

I resist the urge to ask if she is high. Given our history, a comment like that would not amuse her. But surely, she is going to open with a retraction of their twisted plan to reenact some elderly version of *Romeo and Juliet.* Or she could at least offer more explanation, some context, information I can look into, names of her doctors, test results, treatment options. She did not ask me here to make some ridiculous request of Marcus. Marcus, who they've only met a handful of times, and never really with my permission. They've run into him at the news station when they came to visit me for lunch, and my mom is always incredibly obvious, elbowing me and asking probing questions and inviting him out with us. He is always gracious when he politely declines, because he's a news anchor who is paid to be smooth and affable. He knows I make the call if, and when, he joins. And I'm not ready.

I may never be ready. I have the worst taste in men, it's not worth trying, anytime I get close, I swear, I jinx it. Marcus is good right now. He's nearly perfect. No ex-wife, no kids, his biggest traumas belonging to other people, horrors he witnessed as a war reporter for years. No baggage in our relationship except for mine, and I have enough for the both of us. There is only down from here. And what's the point? Look at my parents. Aunt Maelynn too. If that's what real love requires, if that's what it can do, they can keep it. He wants more, he's patient but clear about that, but I assure him it's easier this way. No one needs to get in too deep, nothing needs to get weird at work and no one needs to spend extended time with anyone's parents. And my mother certainly doesn't get to start asking for personal favors.

I suck in my breath, willing myself patience. "Why do you ask?"

"I have something of a final request."

I grimace, my fingers still. "Come on. You and Dad aren't going through with this."

"That's the plan, at least for me. Your father is impossible, but you could try to work on him."

"There's no way—"

She cuts me off, "Do you think Marcus knows anyone at the Boston Symphony Orchestra from the years he worked at the *Globe*?"

I shake my head, unable to believe her ability to be so single-minded. "You really think we're going to let you do this?"

"I need something from you, Jane."

"And I need you and Dad to stop talking crazy." I dismiss her with a shrug, a nonstarter. She had been prepared to lie by omission, to hide the real reason, and that knowledge is a barb tearing into me anytime I soften against her. If she truly thought it was possible to conceal her symptoms, then either, one, she thinks we're idiots, or two, she's giving up way too soon. She may have many years of quality life left. I don't blame her for not wanting to live past a certain point. I don't want to see her in pain, or totally lost to herself. I wouldn't want to go that way either; I don't think anyone does. But I'm baffled as to why she would pick a random date and call it quits without seeing how things go. And that doesn't even get into how dumbfounded I am at my father's response. It's wildly distracting, won't allow me to react to my mom's very real diagnosis like a normal human. With concern, sadness, fear for her future, for what it means for all of us—which quite honestly, pisses me off. Somehow it paints us three as the bad guys, insensitive to her plight, selfish, even, to be thinking of ourselves at a time like this.

That said, Dad leaking a hint about her condition was a surprise. Normally, my parents are impenetrable, a united front to a fault. I doubted the level of their devotion once, doubted everything I once knew. We are in such a better place now, we've been in a good place for years. They have everything they worked for their entire lives—each other, their family and freedom from running the Oyster Shell—it doesn't make sense to cut that short, by even a day. But I do know they would do anything for one another. Even if that means blowing up the island they've always inhabited, leaving us with the fallout.

If the situation weren't so grim it would be funny. Me, the rational one in the family? Mom and Dad are delusional, Thomas is sulking like a child, and don't even get me started on Violet, the only human in existence that can romanticize everything but her own marriage. It's maddening. She still reveres our parents like she's a kid and they're the grown-ups, and she's incapable of looking at any of their actions critically. I told her their plan is incredibly flawed, and they are going to back out when it gets too real. She disagreed, convinced they've always known they couldn't live without each other, that they had probably agreed to something like this ages ago. She said she can't imagine one without the other, that maybe it's better this way, so they don't have to be lonely or heartbroken. This is when I consider I am not the only one in the family who has done a lot of drugs.

"It's important," Mom insists. It takes me a second to register she is still referring to the symphony, that somehow *that* is what she deems important at this juncture.

I whip around, a cornered bull. "So is this."

If she wants to do this, we can do this.

She pauses, in that exaggerated way she does when she wants to be clear that she hears us. It feels condescending, especially now. "I want to play. With the BSO. I've always wanted to. And I'm running out of time."

"You're *choosing* to run out of time. I understand you say you're getting worse, and fast, and I'm sorry for that, really, but to pick a date, to not even *try* to hold out as long as you can—" I screech. "This conversation is absurd!"

"I want you to play with me."

"You can't be serious."

"At the symphony. I need you up there with me."

Her insistence makes me laugh, cruelly. "First of all, I have no idea if Marcus even has those strings to pull. Second, I haven't played a concerto in years." I'm lying, of course. Marcus has deep ties to the Boston area, he grew up in Roxbury and became a bit of a local celebrity. He was the first African American to win the Worth Bingham Prize for Investigative Reporting. He spent years at the *Boston Globe*, frequently interviewed politicians and diplomats on television before a heart attack at thirty-six prompted him to question his fast-paced career, to leave Boston entirely and settle into a quieter life along the Connecticut shore. One call would probably be all it took, and the city would jump to its feet. The concerto is another story. I am not lying that it's been years since I've played at such a high level, but her question has me wondering if I still could.

"You never forget."

"Why do you need me there?"

"I'm afraid I won't be able to do it alone."

I let my gaze fall to her hands, trembling against the keys, and a brick loosens in the wall I built. "Why didn't you tell me?"

Thomas's question that night, *Is one of you dying or something?* It can't be true.

"Self-protection, I guess." She sighs. "But now you know why I need to take control of the rest of my life, follow this dream before it's too late. You have to understand."

She plays this card, the trait we share. The driving force that carried me through late nights while I studied journalism, and worked full-time as a bank teller, and raised Rain as a single mom. It's not my fault she didn't get to follow her dreams, but I get why she wants to. My mother and I, as my grandma always chided, never satisfied. A criticism I wear like a badge of honor. Intense, some people call me. Relentless. They can call me what they want, it's gotten me far. My mom, less so, but she prioritized things I didn't. Her marriage, for one.

She smiles. "Don't you want to know what we would play?"

"I haven't even said yes yet, and you've already picked out the music. You're unbelievable." The nerve on this woman. But against my best judgment, my curiosity is piqued.

"So you plan on saying yes?"

"Depends." I look up at her for the first time, this entire conversation so absurd I lean in, following the White Rabbit to Wonderland. "What did you pick?"

"Mozart's Piano Concerto number ten, designed for two pianos." She pulls the sheet music from the hinged seat, and sets it in front of me.

"I'm not done talking about this." But I begin to toy with the notes, finding my footing, my shoulders softening as the music unfolds before me. A memory rises to the surface, unbidden, a Christmas when I was a teen, right before I moved out, my mom and I constantly at odds. Dad came up with the idea for us to surprise her by playing "Have Yourself a Merry Little Christmas" and singing together, a corny kind of gift only he could get away with. He enlisted Violet, immediately on board, to recruit us. I begged for something more interesting to play, an actual challenge. Thomas, of course, took a lot of coercing.

We rehearsed for weeks—far more than necessary—when Mom was out giving lessons. On Christmas morning, Thomas and Violet and Dad sang along with the music, standing around me in their pajamas, with the tree and the crumpled wrapping paper littering the floor, their voices off-key and kind of terrible, but trying. Mom could barely speak after, thanking us through tears. I haven't thought about that in years, completely forgot about it until now. I'm not sure what reminds me but my throat catches as I contemplate Mozart's score.

I don't know what this year will bring, or what my parents will decide. But it could be a way to stall. A worthy distraction to look forward to, to work toward, playing together with the Boston Symphony Orchestra. Something to give my mother, a dream she never fulfilled, for all she has forgiven of me. Something to give myself, a part of me I've let wither, a reminder of our earliest harmony. A memory to hold on to if what they say is true, if, despite what I believe and despite our protests, at the end of this year, they really are gone.

Four

Evelyn

June 1942

The train lurches out of South Station, headed back to Stonybrook after my second year away, my last year at Mrs. Mayweather's School for Girls. I lean my forehead against the cool glass window, settling in. The man across from me reads a crinkled newspaper, a picture of the war savings bond girls plastered across the front page. I watch as the grays and browns of Boston are replaced by streaks of green and blue, countryside and sky.

My body aches with restless energy; the closer I get, the harder it is to be anywhere but home. The cabin is stuffy with cigarette smoke and I yearn for the sea breeze, the chorus of cicadas in the marsh at night, my bare soles sinking into wet sand. But there is something new, a layer of grief beneath my excitement. Leaving Maelynn, my piano lessons, an outline of a new life I had begun to color in. The instructor at the Boston Conservatory, Sergey, a Russian who notoriously rationed his compliments, once said I had *real promise*. The possibility of a spot there next year, the call he offered to make. The late nights Maelynn's liv-

ing room glittered with writers and artisans and musicians, as I
perched on her couch drinking in their stories, dizzy with their
nectar. The lists she encouraged me to indulge in, dreams I felt
too silly to show anyone but her and Joseph. *Dip my toes in the
Pacific Ocean. Visit the World's Fair. Ride an elephant.* The Boston
list we made together that she stuck to the bathroom mirror. The
thrill as we checked things off, *sail on The Charles, visit Egyptian
mummies at the Museum of Fine Arts, eat salty peanuts at Fenway
Park.* The streets of Boston humming with smartly dressed people with somewhere to be. The freedom to board the trolley in
Brookline and travel anywhere I chose, to meander for hours,
pulsing with possibility.

But staying would mean casting off the life I left behind. Saying goodbye to Joseph at the end of last summer was one of the
hardest things I've ever had to do. We kissed, the world spinning
and muted around us, until I was sure I'd miss my train. I've
loved him as long as I can remember. Probably because he was
nothing like me, nothing like Tommy—all noise and bravado
and jokes. Joseph was a stone rubbed smooth by the crashing of
our waves, a calming pebble you pocket and carry.

I knew about the dates he went on and the girls he had kissed.
I never let on about my feelings; I was scraped knees and tangled hair, he didn't think of me that way. He had always given
me his attention, the brotherly kind, and a friendship formed
because we were two moons orbiting the same planet, but until
last summer, he had never really *looked* at me. Never like that—
like I was a dream from which he didn't want to wake, his eyes
following me with a gaze like physical touch; I could feel it
even when I turned away. When he first kissed me, my heart
jumped, a staccato drum.

The year passed with the constant crossing of letters and
quick stolen visits at holidays. Always a goodbye on the heels
of a hello, and the constant ache within me, for the next letter,
the next visit, the next kiss. Wherever I was, I was halved. In

Stonybrook, I missed the buzz of Boston; in Boston, I missed Joseph's arms, the feeling of belonging, of home.

The train shudders into Union station and my heart surges. I grab my suitcase and heave it over the seat, rushing past passengers easing out into the aisle. I pat my hair, adjusting a pin, cursing where it flattened in the back since I boarded. I lean out of the car and spot Joseph, a head above the merging crowds, and Tommy beside him, both dressed in short-sleeved buttondowns tucked into their trousers. This time I run to Joseph first, drop my suitcase and jump into his arms; he lifts me off my feet, our kisses like gasps for air, filling me and making me whole.

"Alright, you two." Tommy laughs, shielding his eyes, a cigarette bouncing between his lips. I unwind from Joseph's embrace and give Tommy a tight squeeze. "How was your second year? Are you even more ladylike than when you left us last?"

"Oh yes, of course. I've got grace and poise coming out of my ears," I say, with my widest smile and an exaggerated curtsy.

"Well, you look beautiful." Joseph grabs me by my waist, kisses me again before reaching for my abandoned suitcase. "Welcome home."

Home. The word feels strange, fluid.

Back at the Oyster Shell, Joseph pulls his dad's Ford into the driveway, and together we walk to the front stoop. I can't help but gush about our reunion, one I had imagined again and again, buoying me through every patch of loneliness this past year. "It's such a relief to know we've said our last goodbye. We can finally all be together again. For good," I say, beaming at Joseph, then Tommy, expecting a nod, a smile. Their faces are gray, Tommy stares ahead. Joseph drops his gaze to his feet.

"What?" I stop short. "What? Tommy, are you going to Mrs. Mayweather's now?" I laugh. Their expressions don't crack and I stop short, a boulder caught in their stream. "What's going on?"

"You want to tell her?" Tommy juts his chin toward Joseph.

His face alarms me with its flatness, like a mask of my brother, a grave doppelganger.

"Tell me what?" My grip tightens. Joseph's muscle pulses under my fingers, and I shift my attention to him, a compromised fortress. "*Joseph*, tell me what?"

He looks down at me, his eyes rueful when they meet mine. "We enlisted."

I drop their arms as though they are live wires, my mind fills with fog, cloaking the bliss that had guided me home. "You can't…"

Tommy fumbles in his pocket for a distraction, anything to avoid my face. "We did. We had to."

"You didn't have to do anything. They're not even drafting nineteen-year-olds!" My legs weaken.

Joseph reaches for my hand, holding it in his against his chest. "It's only a matter of time."

"You don't know that." My eyes well up, and I blink furiously.

Tommy lights a Lucky Strike. "Ev, we wanted to make something of ourselves. You more than anyone have to understand. We didn't want to wait until they forced us." He exhales a thin cloud of smoke. "Come on, you get it. You've been sent away these last two years."

I shake my head. "No. Not the same. There isn't much chance of me dying at school."

Tommy lifts his eyebrows, his mouth a lopsided smile. "Not even of boredom?"

"That's not funny."

He waves me off. "We're not going to die."

Die. The word sends my legs wobbly. I want to argue, to yell the questions careening through my mind, but nothing comes out. I stand there, my limbs dangling uselessly by my sides.

"Well, I'll leave you two alone. I'm sure you have lots to talk about." Tommy squeezes my elbow and cuts through the overgrown verdant field, leaving us on the slanted front steps of the Oyster Shell.

We stand, not speaking or touching. The sky is a cloudless blue, the warm breeze and sunshine unsettling. I yearn for the cover of night, for the somber patter of rain, to curl into myself in a gray room alone. The seashell wind chime jingles. Joseph fumbles with a loose button on his shirt.

"How could you?" My eyes begin to fill. I focus on my shoes, heeled Mary Janes, and scuff their bottoms on the wooden slats of the porch.

Joseph rubs his knuckles against each other, with force that looks like it may hurt. "I don't know what to say... You know how Tommy is, he wouldn't drop it. I told him we should wait and see, but he kept talking about going in as men, and he said he'd sign up with or without me. I couldn't let him go alone... and you wouldn't have wanted me to."

I sink onto the front steps, tearing at my hair. "How do I say goodbye to you again? To both of you? What if something happens?"

Joseph sits beside me, his fingers loosely clasped between his knees. His leg is inches from mine, but he doesn't lean it against me, and I can feel the space between us like I would feel his touch. "I don't know. I'm taking this very seriously. I know what it could mean. But you have to understand...he's like a brother to me too. I can't stand the thought of leaving you, but I would never forgive myself if something happened to him while I was safely at home."

Hot tears begin to fall and I take a deep breath as he kisses my cheek, his strong arms encasing me gently. "Please don't cry."

I search his eyes for the first time and am met with the fuzzy outline of my reflection in their russet depths. "When do you leave?"

"Two weeks."

"Two weeks?"

"We don't have a choice."

"But I came home to be with you," I plead.

"What do you mean?" Joseph asks. "School's over...you came home because it's over."

"There was this spot, maybe, I don't know if I would've gotten in, at the Boston Conservatory, but I said no because it would be four more years—"

"What are you talking about?" He pulls away, brows knit in confusion.

"I could've stayed. Why am I here if you won't be?"

"Because this is where we live..." Joseph says. "And I'll be back before you know it, and we'll start our life together again, right where we left off."

I cry without apology now, my voice thick with emotion, with everything I've lost and everything still left to lose. "How do we say goodbye again?"

He rubs his thumbs over my cheeks, brushes away the smeared rivulets as my chin trembles in his palm. "We don't. You don't ever get to say goodbye to me. Not for good."

He holds me close, and I lean into his shoulder until I am calm, his shirt wet and streaked from my tears.

The morning Joseph and Tommy depart is foggy and drizzling, Long Island hidden in the haze across the sound, Bernard Beach muted by the spitting rain. Tommy dresses in his Class A's. Dad salutes a farewell at the stoop, Mom kisses him on the cheek, her face glowing with pride. The handkerchief in her grip an ornament, bone-dry. Their hometown hero, off to be a real one.

We pick Joseph up from the Oyster Shell and find his mother weeping into his shoulders on the porch. He bends low to embrace her, and she grips the fabric of his uniform so tight it wrinkles when he stands tall. His father, a match for his height but hefty like a grizzly, wraps him in a hug. "Don't just be brave, you hear me? Come home. And bring Tommy with you." His eyes bloodshot like he rubbed them dry, or hadn't slept, or both.

Joseph's parents are older than mine, skin lined and hair streaked gray. They struggled for years to have a child, so when Joseph came into their world, they clung to him. His mother was always squeezing him, his father lifting him on his broad shoulders when we were kids, launching him with a splash into the water. They were affectionate with him, and each other, even as he grew. Watching them say goodbye exposes the ache in me I tried to bury these last two weeks together. A blur of joyful moments etched with worry, days like a shortness of breath, a last supper.

At the station, it is only the three of us. Tommy and Joseph stand opposite me in their olive drab side caps, jackets and ties. Surrounded by a dismal tableau of girlfriends, wives and mothers in their best hats and dresses, damp and clutching on to final hugs, kisses and words of reassurance that are flimsy and fleeting. Another day in June, like so many summer days we have spent. Except nothing about it is like those days—sunny and blue skied and free. I feel the shift like a hairline fracture to a bone, a dull pain that deepens with time.

Tommy leans against a column, blowing smoke rings as he watches the other men board. "We'll be back before you even miss us. Between my charm and Joe's good looks, those Germans may surrender." He gives me his biggest grin, wiggling his eyebrows.

I try to return his confidence, but my jaw feels tight. "Be safe, both of you." My voice is steady. Tears had found me the night before but left that morning, exhausted. "Tommy, please don't do anything stupid."

He laughs his last smoky exhale and extinguishes the ember with his toe. "I wouldn't dream of it."

I force a smile. It strains my cheeks. "I'll see you when you get back. Love you, big brother."

"Love you, too, Ev." He folds me in a tight hug, his wool jacket rough beneath my chin. I feel my tears return and swallow hard. It is right before our birthdays. How could I celebrate without them?

"Joe, I'll grab us some seats. See you in there." He snatches their bags and Joseph watches him board, nodding, before turning to me.

"Please take care of him, take care of each other..." I am stammering now that Tommy is on the train, now that they are really leaving.

"I will. Evelyn..." He lifts my chin so I can't turn away. Those lips that spent so much time parting mine, the softness of his tongue pressing and warm. The jawline that I ran my fingertips over on lazy afternoons, trying to capture it all, to memorize everything. Those deep brown eyes staring so intently at me now that I can see my hazy outline reflected in them, disarming me like a mirror within a mirror, an endless glimpse into the deepest part of me. "I'll do everything I can so we come home to you."

"Promise me." My voice wavers, giving me away.

Joseph winces, his eyes closing as if in pain. "I can't promise that... I will do everything I can—"

"Promise me, Joseph. If you promise me, you can't break it... maybe it'll keep you safe...let me try to keep you safe." I begin to cry then. I am not making sense, but I can't stop blubbering about promises, my legs trembling, and he holds me close and I feel myself steady in his solid arms.

"I promise," he whispers, his lips brushing my ear. He pulls back so our noses nearly touch. "I love you, Evelyn."

Any lingering strength I have vanishes with those words, said for the first time, and the train whistles through the smoky, soggy air as the remaining passengers on the platform rush around us to get on board. I am struck silent, my heart shouting but trapped, unable to find a path to my tongue. I want to tell him. I want to say, *I love you, too,* but it is the extra beat of hesitation before leaping off the cliff that stops me cold. I can't say goodbye and I love you in the same breath. If I don't say it back, he has to come home to hear it. He has to. I tear myself away from the cove of his arms, conscious of the wet tracks of tears down my cheeks, the wool irritating where it rubbed my exposed skin, pink splotches rising around my collarbone.

I love you, Joseph. But I can't say it.

Instead, "Come home, okay? Both of you." His eyes search mine, begging a question I won't answer, those mirror eyes... but the train whistles again and I kiss him, stroking the hair below his cap, and press him toward the steps, with what feels like a whimper. "Come home to me."

And then he is gone. I stand there, empty. I reach into my pocket for a handkerchief and find violets, like velvet on my fingertips. I stand thumbing the petals in my pocket until I can't see the blurred outline of the train, and then after.

What stands out about the days since Joseph and Tommy left? Sore wrists. Sore wrists and an ache in my chest. I count the days that drag like seaweed through the tide, my body a placeholder for the three of us, for the life we'll have here again, once the war is over. I pass my time playing piano, writing letters and sewing parachutes. There is a whole room of us at The Arnold Factory, a brick building in town that was once a schoolhouse, women awaiting lovers and brothers and sons behind whirring sewing machines, sharing worries and updates from the front lines. Some girls I went to school with before Mrs. Mayweather's look much older than eighteen; foreheads creased by dread, we acknowledge each other but not our collective bated breath, the odds against us that all our soldiers will return. Every loss a devastation, my sympathy mixed with guilt, private gratitude that their telegram wasn't sent to my door, selfishly praying to be spared their pain. Sewing parachutes feels like I am doing something tangible. I am saying, *Here, hold on to this, let me help you fly.* In my dreams, the parachutes I sew billow out like clouds, like jellyfish, but when they hit the ground, they are always empty.

Joseph signs his letters, *Love.* I sign mine, *Yours.* I am his. I do love him. I always have. Enough not to tell him in a letter, not to send that hope across the ocean. I reserve those feelings, confess them on pages I never send, scrawled longing I can't bring myself to mail. I write to Tommy, too, tease him with updates from Stonybrook, things like, *All the prettiest girls in town work in the hospitals.* He jokes back, *I might get injured on purpose, if that's the case.*

I keep Joseph's letters in a nightstand by my bed, along with flower petals that have long since dried. Sometimes I hold them and, although they are fragile, pass them back and forth between my cupped hands. I like the way they feel against my skin, like to imagine Joseph holding them when they were soft, his palm the last thing they touched before he slipped them into my pocket. I like to read the first letter Joseph wrote. It reached me weeks after they left, weeks I spent mostly by myself. I sit on the dock where we first kissed, listening to the crash of the ocean, and read it again and again. How much louder the waves sound when I am alone.

Dear Evelyn,

I can't stop thinking of how we said goodbye. I don't know what to make of it…the words you didn't say, how you pushed me away. I know you're strong; maybe you were afraid to tell me how you feel. Afraid it would somehow make you weak. But please know I want my love to keep you strong too. You don't have to be strong on your own.

I meant what I said, and always will. I love you, and I shouldn't have waited until the last minute to tell you. I wanted to tell you countless times…on the dock, in the ocean, together on the sand. But I never did because I didn't want it to seem like I was saying goodbye. But when it was time to leave, I couldn't walk away without letting you know. I didn't get caught up in the moment, if that's what you think.

You don't have to tell me how you feel. Maybe this isn't the time, or the way. But I have faith that when I return everything will be as it was. I trust we will keep growing in our love, and that it will outlast every test we put it through. Even this time apart. Even war.

In my letters I won't write about my time here, please don't ask me. There is no need for you to worry about things you can't change. I don't want to waste these pages recounting violence, instead I will fill them with love. Please fill yours with the same and send them back to me. That's all I need to bring me home.
Love,
Joseph

I do as he asks. I fill my pages with love but without using the word.

I tell him about the piano, the escape it provides. My fingers dance their swift choreography, creating something apart from me, but a part of me, because the notes hum deep in my core even when I step away. I tell him of the parachutes, the bolts of endless silk. My thoughts wander at every stitch, back to when we were kids, snapshots projected in my mind. Tommy scooping a translucent moon jellyfish, devoid of stingers, and placing it jiggling in my palm. Joseph perched on the jetty with my foot in his lap, brow furrowed as he extracted a jagged shell embedded in my toe. The three of us leaping off Captain's Rock, plunging into the icy depths. Tommy and Joseph climbing higher to jump off its craggy top while I whooped and hollered from the surf below.

I tell him how I sew the initials *T.S.* and *J.M.* at the corner of each parachute before it is packed away. Small stitches that go unnoticed by anyone but me. But I do it every time because they are the reason I sew, and I hope it brings the men who use them luck.

I don't tell him about the petals, or the way I think about them touching his skin. I don't tell him of my daydreams of Boston, the rumble of the trolley underfoot, the maze of brownstones that made me feel so big and so small. The winding cobblestone streets that let me be lost and found, imagining an alternate future all my own. Of deadlines and chances missed, another life swept away in the war, an answer I'll never know, the girl I left behind.

That is what I will remember from this time apart. The longing, the music, the petals, the parachute silk, the letters sent away as if caught by the wind, hoping for a safe landing.

Five

~

Joseph

July 2001

The tide is high, spilling over the dock when we claim our usual spot, awaiting our children and grandchildren to trickle in throughout the morning. The Fourth of July fell a few days ago on Wednesday, timing that extends and dilutes the celebration, the sky booming and popping every night for a week. Cardboard hulls of spent fireworks litter the dunes.

Our oldest grandkid is twenty-seven years old, Jane's only daughter, Rain. She was our first grandchild to get married, last summer she said I do to Tony Sanducci, a stocky Italian boy who works for his father and grandfather at Sanducci's Auto Body off Boston Post Road. They rent a garage apartment in town, so they are quick to join us, striped beach chairs slung over their shoulders. Jane, finished with her morning segment of the local news, is a few steps behind. When they reach us, Rain drops her chair and seizes me in a long, tight hug.

She knows.

There it is again, the pang, the simmering remorse, the low

tremble of guilt for the grief we've invited into our haven. Even today, Evelyn's seventy-sixth birthday celebration, is steeped in sorrow.

Violet and Connor wait for their two oldest to arrive by train for the holiday weekend; Molly, twenty-two and settled in Providence after graduating from Roger Williams, Shannon, twenty, lives in Brighton for the summer while interning at the Museum of Science, padding her résumé before her senior year at Boston University. They show up before lunch toting coolers of sodas and grinders, Violet and Connor, and all four kids: Molly and Shannon, along with Ryan, his last summer home before college, and Patrick trailing behind, ten years younger than their oldest, a happy accident at twelve years old, consumed by his Game Boy. He tucks it away when he sees me, sheepish. More long hugs, faces that look like towels wrung too tight. I expect questions that don't come, their pained stares follow me even when I close my eyes. Our decision lurks like a lengthening shadow, a dragnet catching moments thick with melancholy. Violet blinks away tears when Connor leans over to ask Evelyn how she's feeling. Jane stares across the water, lost in thought. Thomas's absence is glaring, a staked flag brandishing his disapproval.

Rain drags her chair beside me. "Grandpa, tell those stories from when my mom was a kid. About how she was always getting into trouble?"

Jane lets out a low laugh. "How much time do you have?"

"You know all those stories," I say.

"I want to hear them again," she says, leaning her head on my shoulder.

Since today is Evelyn's birthday, we all try our best to forget, or pretend. We eat cellophane-wrapped sandwiches with salt and vinegar chips and bagged cherries, spitting the pits into the sand. The blue sky endless above us, streaked with thin clouds like leftover jet streams. A plane roars past towing a banner advertising fresh lobster for $6.99 per pound at Hal's Seafood Shack. The sun warms us after each swim, drying our bathing suits as we lay on towels stiff from the clothesline, chasing away the sadness we all feel heavy like a stone.

As the tide goes out, a game of touch football ensues on the sandbar, the grandchildren muddy when it inevitably turns to tackle. I press myself to standing, wanting to join them, all my grandkids, playing here together once more.

Is this the last time?

Evelyn reclines beside me, her hair is pulled back and dry; she's opted to stay out of the water when she woke this morning feeling so unsteady on land.

"Feel up to a walk?" I ask.

"You go ahead." She shades her eyes with her hand. "I'm getting a kick out of watching."

I follow the familiar footprints, avoiding colonies of snails and hermit crabs. Cheers as I approach, my grandkids smiling, their torsos and thighs and shoulders streaked with mud.

"Hey, no taking out the old guy." I lift my hands in mock surrender. "But we can toss it around a little." Ryan grins and rinses the football in the water seeping toward us, the sandbar already shrinking, before throwing it to me. His last summer before college, nearly an adult, all that's behind me is his now to unfold. We form a wide circle and pass the ball, alternating between catch and keep-away, reciting memories that exist as family folklore from all the times they've been retold, until the water passes our ankles, sending us back to shore.

Behind our chairs, Evelyn stashed a box of empty wine bottles and a couple of well-rinsed jam jars, along with notepads and pens wrangled from the junk drawer. *Send a message in a bottle.* A line from an ancient dream list brought back to light, one of many we hoped to cross off this final year. Dreams, and little pleasures she wants to hold one last time, like the strawberries we ate off the vine, small as my thumb, ruby red and warm from the sun. Chocolate malts and salted fries. The first bite of a ripe nectarine. Sleeping with the windows open to the summer air.

Most of all, days like this.

Evelyn assigns bottles to each of us, passes out the pens and paper, and the kids kneel nearby, taking turns writing against the wooden armrests or each other's backs.

I fake a peek at Evelyn's page and she whacks me with her pen, laughing. "No copying, mister."

So I write the only thing I can think of, *J&E*, like carving our initials into the trunk of a tree, testimony, proof, *we were here*. We roll the papers like scrolls, stuff and seal them, and wade together past the sandbar, water to our knees, chasing the setting sun. Evelyn counts down from three and we toss the messages as far as we can, watching them splash, then bob to the surface, drift with the current and disappear.

"You know these are probably going to end up back on our beach, right?" Jane says.

"You have to ruin it." Violet sighs.

"Most things end up back where they came from, honey," Evelyn teases, bumping her hip against Jane's. "But it's still worth letting it find its way."

Everyone heads back to the house to clean up before supper, the grandchildren shouting dibs on the outdoor shower. Evelyn and I stay behind, unwilling to miss our favorite hour of the day. The time when the other families have packed up, when the sun sinks and the slightest breeze chases the warmth lingering in our tanned skin. Tomorrow, the shoreline will be peppered with candy-colored umbrellas once more, but for now we are alone.

I ache for endless days like this, low tide rippling away from the sandbar that stretches the length of the shore like an open arm. Breathe the musky brine into my lungs. The time for sweaters buttoned and towels draped over knees, when the beach is still and the sea the only sound. Countless evenings spent here with Evelyn, watching the sun set over mirrored sky.

Waves seep in and recede, tugging at my memories. Pigtailed Jane, dripping mud between her fingers to form a craggy castle. Violet somersaulting in the surf, demanding attention. Thomas, aloof, skipping stones off the dock. Evelyn racing behind the children, scooping them up with a giggle toward the sky. Collecting green crabs too small to eat in plastic buckets before easing them back into the surf. Showing how they should be held with a thumb and forefinger between the back legs so they couldn't pinch, to flip them over to check the sex by the shapes of their underside markings. The grandchildren bobbing out to Captain's Rock, four redheads led by the North star of their oldest cousin, Rain. The oversize raft that they tied to a mooring and played king of the mountain on, wrestling each other into the water. Their squeals reaching us in our sand chairs, alternately reading, chatting or succumbing to the luxury of a nap in the shade of a tilted umbrella.

Evelyn sighs, content. "What a beautiful day it was."

I nod. "Just about perfect."

I consider her lined face, the age spots on her cheeks. Our entire life like a series of shorter marriages to each other, linked in their similarities, but distinct. Familiar, but changed. Even in marriage she has never been mine, even now as we face our end together. She has never belonged to anyone but herself, and I have never belonged to anyone but her.

"Are you scared?" I ask. We fumble through our murky beliefs, loosely tied to hope rather than religion, to a connection to our world we feel in our bones but never name. The Christianity we were raised in was a narrow tunnel that collapsed, a boulder blocking the entrance with each loss.

She pauses. "I'm scared for the kids, how they'll feel. I'm scared of not being ready. I'm scared of wanting to change my mind."

When the day comes, I don't know if we will be able to go through with it. To hug the ones we love and walk away, knowing it's the last time. But that's the choice we've made because of the question that brought us here, that haunts me still. Will this final year be too long for Evelyn to hold on to herself as she is now, or could we have many more years like this?

Her hand is a frail bird in mine, and I give it the lightest squeeze. "We can always change our minds, Evelyn. Nothing says we can't."

"*You* can. You should."

"We both can."

"Please don't say that like I have a real choice."

I don't argue. What constitutes our own choices is a raw point of contention. Instead I search for comfort, for the reasons I hold like a talisman when doubt finds me in quiet moments. "We don't get forever, but at least it's on our terms. At least we don't have to keep saying goodbye." I kiss her knuckles, swollen at the joints and shaky in my touch. I murmur, "We are the lucky ones."

She smiles, wrinkles deepening around her lips, her voice almost a whisper. "I think we always were."

Pink clouds stretch across the horizon. The Long Island Sound is calm, the surface rose-tinted and so still it could be an extension of the blossoming sky. We sit until the sun is too low to give off any warmth, until the day closes, with the promise of more warmth in the tomorrows that will predictably, and undeniably, end too soon.

Later, at the house, the door opens and the echo of two sets of footsteps in the foyer carries into the kitchen—one the tap of dress shoes against tile and the other the distinct click of high heels. Thomas and Ann are here. Jane raises her eyebrows at me, and then at the clock in the corner as she places the rolls on the table without a word. I hear her loud and clear. It's Saturday, they had all day to get here and, still, they cut it close.

Evelyn wipes her hands on her apron and abandons her spoon in a pot of gravy as she rushes over to kiss them hello, her relief bubbling up into affection. We haven't seen or heard from Thomas since we told him last month; the four messages we left went unanswered, one that included the details for tonight.

I hug Thomas, a fleeting embrace he slips out of, and say, "Glad you both made it."

He plucks a piece of lint from his sleeve. "Yeah, sorry. Some work things came up that couldn't wait."

I lean on my chair at the head of the table. "It's Saturday, Thomas."

Thomas takes off his sports coat, hangs it on the back of his seat at the far end across from me. "New York doesn't stop on Saturdays, Pop."

"I swear I never see him either, if it makes you feel better." Ann gives me a side hug and passes me a bottle. Her arms are sculpted twigs, her sleek dress hangs off her slight frame, her blond hair glossy and straight. She is nearly as tall as Thomas and equally as successful, a director of an advertising agency in Manhattan, their offices a few blocks apart. She always brings something for us from the city to add to the meal, gourmet cheeses, imported liqueurs, intricate pastries. They treated us to dinner at Windows on the World when we took Rain to see a Broadway show for her sixteenth birthday. Evelyn got a little woozy at the height, and Rain couldn't stop leaving our linen clad table to press her palms against the glass, in awe of the doll city below, miniature and infinite.

I accept the red wine, thanking her. "I know your schedules are busy, but it's an important day. And the beach was beautiful. I wish you could have been here."

"Well, we're here now, aren't we?" Thomas is noticeably short with me. "How's dinner coming, Ma?"

"We are setting it out now. You're just in time," she clucks happily, adjusting silverware that was already in place.

"How are you feeling, I think, is what he meant to ask," Ann corrects, then turns to Evelyn with tenderness. "How are you feeling?"

"I'm better now you're both here." She squeezes Ann's arms. "But enough about me, food's getting cold."

The rest of the family takes their seats and we dig into our steaming plates, ravenous after a day in the sun. Violet and Connor sit apart, their children between them. When they first met, they nearly shared a chair at dinner. I don't think they've shared more than a few words today. Violet to comment that Patrick needed sunscreen; Connor to ask if she wanted a ham or turkey sandwich from the cooler. Their relationship hung together by kids, by logistics of a shared home. We can't leave them this way, dangling above the depths, without knowing if they will find a foothold, without providing a rope for them to grasp. I have always liked Connor. With the first handshake, he struck me as genuine, steadfast through their whirlwind romance and swift engagement. Still, I like Connor. Still, I root for him.

As everyone has their fill, and conversations turn to talk of work and school and summer plans, I stand to make a toast. Wineglass in hand, I gaze over the heavy pine table, the mismatched chairs scoured from all over the house, everyone squished elbow to elbow around its perimeter. The dishes brim with roast pork and gravy, corn on the cob, potatoes au gratin, sautéed green beans. A chipped butter dish is passed along with salt and pepper shakers adorned with sailboats. The closet door behind the table is ajar, exposing the teetering pile of board games and puzzles. Expectant faces turn my way, forks and knives paused, the slightest breeze blowing in the open windows, our house a solitary lit bulb in the dark.

"Evelyn, it's hard to believe another year has passed. You're seventy-six today, and you're still as beautiful as you were at sixteen, getting off that train. I don't think we could have imagined what all our years together have brought us." I pause, nodding toward the rest of the family. "All the joy you *all* have brought us." I turn back to Evelyn. "Thank you for spending your life with me. It has meant everything. I love you. Happy birthday."

Glasses clink, happy birthdays echo around me. Evelyn, her eyes shiny with emotion, says, "Thank you."

A tear trickles down Jane's cheek, our independent and stoic first child. I think of California, of her wildness, all limbs and hair and fury. I can't remember the last time I saw her cry. She shakes her head, defiant. "You're not doing this." The table grows silent.

Violet, always quick to show her cards, sniffles loudly. Once, as a child, she found a robin's egg in the grass, far from any nest. She wrapped it in a towel and kept it in a box by her bed. I could hear her sing to it at night, but it never hatched. Her tears as she buried it made my heart heavy. Their tears now almost make me reconsider everything. Take away the pain, hatch the egg, set the bird free to fly.

"It's irrational." Thomas glowers.

Ann swats his arm. "Save it, okay? This isn't the time."

"Well, according to them, we don't have much time left."

"It's our life. It's our decision," Evelyn says lightly—perhaps too lightly. "Do you really want to have this conversation in front of the kids?"

"It's not just your life. It affects all of us. Including them." Thomas gestures to the grandkids with his fork as they look down at their plates.

Evelyn concedes. "Well, that's true. Violet, Connor, are you okay with this?"

Violet nods. "They're adults now, and anything you say will make it to Patrick whether we like it or not. It's important they hear it from you."

Thomas cuts in, his voice sandpaper, "How are you going to do it?"

"Why do you have to go there?" Connor speaks for the first time, his Boston accent coming through, his reddish brows narrowed at Thomas.

Thomas leans forward. "Because if they have thought this *all* through I'd like to know. How?"

"Don't be sick, Thomas." Violet's face is white. The grandchildren are silent. There is not even the scrape of forks against plates. Patrick has always been dragged into conversations he is too young for, growing up with much older siblings, but now I turn to him, afraid this is too intense for any twelve-year-old, even him. His cheeks are pink, eyes downcast. I worry about the memory he will carry of tonight. How this discussion will inform his own thoughts on life and death, how our decision will mark him, change him, and his older siblings, and Rain too.

"It's a fair question," Jane says.

"It's not magically going to happen. You have to do something. And someone has to find you when you do. Any volunteers?" Thomas glares at his sisters. "That's what I thought." He turns to us. "We need more information if we're supposed to be on board."

"Pills, Thomas, alright? There are pills that will do it. An ambulance can take us away. It doesn't have to be traumatic." Evelyn's tone is flat, controlled. "There isn't a pretty way to put this. We know what it means. We know it sounds crazy to you—"

"You think?" Thomas takes a swig of his wine.

"—but you are all going to have to live without us someday, and at least this way we can prepare, and really make the most of the time together."

"But why set a date? If you *really* don't want to live without each other—which is a separate issue we'll get to—why not wait until one of you goes, and then off yourself?"

"Jesus, babe, the kids," Ann chides.

"That *is* what we're talking about here! What, I'm not supposed to say it?"

"Grief almost killed me once." Evelyn's voice is firm. She pauses, faltering. "I don't agree with your father's decision, but I can understand it. I can't imagine life without him either."

"We've had so much loss… I know exactly what I'm in for," I say, reaching for her hand. *Stage two.* "And I wouldn't survive losing you."

"But that's life," Jane says. "People die, people find a way to move on."

"Maybe so, Jane. But I don't *want* to live without your mother. She doesn't want to live without me. Heck, there's no guarantee I don't go first, out of nowhere, leaving her alone as she continues to progress. If we don't do this…if we let fate decide, we could be widowed for years, decades, even, if either of us lives as long as Grandma did." *Widowed for decades* ripples through me, roots me again in certainty. Gives me strength to assure them without stumbling. "This has nothing to do with how much we love you all, please know we love you so much. But you have your own lives, separate from ours, and those lives will go on. Our lives—" I gesture at Evelyn "—have *always* contained each other. I've only known this world with your mother in it. A world without her, frankly, isn't one I want to wake up in. Please, Thomas, try to understand."

He is stone-faced, our thoughts and fears heavy on the table.

"I think it's beautiful actually," Violet pipes up, wiping her eyes on a paper napkin. "To love each other that much."

Connor, silent at the other end of the table, fumbles with his place mat.

"Not again with this…" Thomas throws up his hands.

Jane interrupts, "That's a nice idea, but it's bullshit—"

"Mom…" Rain warns, cringing.

Jane plows on, "I'm sorry, but no, I don't think your life ends when one of you is gone. Hell, I'm alone, and I'm perfectly fine. What about continuing to live for yourself? Mom, what about all you wanted to do?"

Evelyn nods. "That's what this year is for. That's why the symphony is so important, and why I need your help. I can't do it without you."

"But you could have many more years," Jane sputters. "And if one of you went before the other, you'd still have so much to live for."

"Thank you!" Thomas slams his palm on the table, startling Ann, visibly tense by his side.

"What about that Death with Dignity thing they passed out in Oregon? A few years ago?" Jane asks. "Mom, if you wait until you're really sick, we would all support that. None of us want to see you suffer, obviously."

"I considered all the options before making my decision. I'm not going to Oregon, or Switzerland, or anywhere so far from home. I *am* going to die. And I want it to be here."

"And of course," I add, "I wouldn't qualify, even if Evelyn went through all the red tape. So this way ensures we can go together."

"Of course you don't qualify! You're not dying." Thomas nearly laughs.

"Dying isn't the only thing that kills us, son," I say, and the table falls silent.

"I won't know you kids. That's a certainty. I won't know myself. I don't want to deteriorate into someone you don't recognize. What it did to my mother...how she was at the end, she had no idea who I was most of the time. I don't want you to be so exhausted by the burden of my care that my death is a relief. I won't put you kids through that."

"But you seem really good, Mom," Violet pleads. "What if in a year you're the same, couldn't you just wait and see?"

"Making the decision now, when I'm of sound mind, that's the only way I can be sure I have the strength to go through with it. If I keep pushing it off, I'll never do it. There will always be another day, just *one more day*, worth living for." Her voice catches.

I'm relieved they know about Evelyn's diagnosis, even though she resisted telling them. She didn't want to be treated differently, she said. But that wasn't it. When she told them, it became real. It's not something a year from now, her choice, in her control. It's facing the thief while he is still in the house, knowing you're helpless to stop him.

"I can't protect you, although I wish I could…" Evelyn falters. "This isn't going away, and it's not going to get better. I know it's hard to imagine, but you'll be okay, all of you."

"You don't know that," Violet whimpers.

"Yes, I do," Evelyn assures her, then turns her attention to Jane. "I've always wanted to live life on my own terms. And my death? It isn't any different." Evelyn lifts her chin toward Thomas, her eyes softening. "And, honey, I'm not asking you—I'm not going to change my mind."

The family grows quiet again.

Evelyn peers at all the faces turned down, studying their plates. She smiles, mischief in her eyes. "Enough with all the long faces. It's my birthday. And we are going to celebrate." She stands, pressing her weight into the table. "You know what? I didn't go for a swim yet."

Thomas looks up, jolted. "What?"

"You heard me. Let's go." She turns and walks out the front door without another word, the screen door clattering behind her. Everyone gapes over the remnants of dinner, unsure what to do.

I shrug, and push back my chair to join her.

Outside, a warm breeze blows through my hair and I limp to catch up, my leg acting up this late at night. I hear the screen door creak behind us, once, twice, three times, amid the distant pop of fireworks. She grins at me, her eyes shine in the moonlight. "Are you sure?" I ask. The sharp pains she has been complaining about worry me, the slowness, the shaking. How quickly could she continue to progress? Maybe playing it safe will keep her longer.

"I don't have much to lose, do I?"

Maybe she has every right to be reckless.

We make our way down the narrow driveway in the dark, paved with the crushed shells that gave the Oyster Shell Inn its name. I offer Evelyn my steady arm, but she slips out of it to walk on her own, a subtle refusal I expect even before reaching for her. We don't need light to guide us. The familiar crunch underfoot, the path that empties into Sandstone Lane lined with fragrant swamp rose in full bloom, the road that curves east toward the sea, passing towering oaks and switchgrass–covered dunes until we turn the bend marking Bernard Beach, the ocean opening before us, resetting something in me each time. I know my way like I know Evelyn, vividly and completely.

Together we reach the sea, her entourage trailing confused in her wake.

"Don't let your grandma beat you all in there."

"Mom, no. This isn't…you shouldn't—" Violet starts.

"And you wonder why I didn't want to tell you kids?" she teases, her voice twinkling with an inside joke all her own, amused anyone could tell her what she shouldn't do.

She holds on to my shoulder and slips out of her shoes, sinks her toes in the cool sand. Then she walks alone to the water, and I let her go. She doesn't need me now, in this moment, she is her own guiding light. I watch her until she is nearly enveloped in the dark, stars shimmering above her, the moon reflecting off the water in bright flowing rings.

On a night like this, I can't help but think of my own parents; I wasn't ready, there was so much I wanted to share with them, so much I wished they got to see. I would never have been ready for goodbye, although I always knew, at least in theory, that it would come. Children are supposed to bury their parents, that is the natural order of things. I can't prevent their grief any more than I can prevent my death, the best we could do is delay it.

But losing Evelyn, outliving the person who is the source of my heartbeat, or watching her wither into a rag doll version of herself, a pianist who could no longer use her hands to create the music she loves, or to wait until she doesn't recognize me, until she ceases to be Evelyn at all, to walk through the halls of our home alone…that would be impossible to endure.

How many more years could we share, if we left it to the stars? I remind myself we've had more years together than most, and somehow, that will have to be enough.

Our grandchildren run past whooping and cheering, fully clothed, and dive off the dock. Jane follows, tugging me along by my elbow before chasing after the kids. Rain and Tony run after her and leap off the dock in synchronized flops. Evelyn has made her way up to her knees when I reach her, past the gentle break, and I am grateful for the calm of Long Island Sound, the lakelike ease of entry not found in the harsh crashes of open ocean. The hem of her skirt moves with the subtle current, the water icy and ocean floor uneven beneath my feet. Violet rushes after her children and Connor follows suit, cannonballing into the blue-black surface. Only Thomas and Ann remain on shore.

Evelyn's face glows. "Let's join them, huh?"

"I'll follow you anywhere."

She grabs my extended arm, and we slide farther in, floating in the familiar depths in the moonlight.

Jane calls out to her brother, "Thomas and Ann, come on!"

Thomas's voice booms, "You all are crazy. Jesus, Ma, you're going to get pneumonia."

"It's July! Come join your crazy mother!" Evelyn screeches back.

The grandkids cheer.

"I can't believe we're doing this." Thomas and Ann walk toward us, carefully slipping off their shoes. Thomas rolls his pant legs, and they ease into the water up to their calves. "Happy?"

Jane and Violet share a grin, dart toward Thomas and tackle him at the knees. They grab for Ann, and she flees, splashing through the water, but they are faster and soon she is under too.

They come up, sputtering and chuckling, soaked and finally surrendering to the game.

The three-quarter moon shines bright on the water around us, illuminated with flashes of red and green and gold, the air rich with laughter, splashes, and the boom and crackle of distant fireworks, Evelyn in the center of it all. My stomach tightens, knowing what this swim will cost her, of what the next day will bring, but she is not thinking of tomorrow. The ocean a black and sweeping lullaby, our children and grandchildren swirling beacons around her, like fireflies, like silver minnows glittering beneath the surface, flecks of dust dancing in a stream of sunlight, like the clearest night dotted with stars.

Six

Joseph

May 1944

My wool uniform is sticky with sweat against my back, plastered to the undersides of my legs. The drab olive green Plymouth's windows are open to the warm salt air but there is ice in my chest, heavy and scraping as we rumble through town. The Long Island Sound opens before me; it is low tide, calm and glassy, but it does nothing to soothe me.

Time became an eerie echo when I was overseas; memories tossed around in my mind for two years returned to me distorted, in a voice I didn't recognize. Those hazy, languorous days on Bernard Beach belonged to someone else entirely. A boy who knew nothing of war. A dream. The damp plaits of Evelyn's hair across my chest as we lay in the sand became the wet, gummy blood of someone's arm against my back in the dirt. The smell of musk and brine, the lapping of waves warped into the stench of gunpowder and flesh, the cries of men.

As we drive, everything is as I remember. The sandbars stretch the length of the shore. The reconstructed wooden dock where

I first kissed Evelyn is exposed to its support beams when the water recedes. Captain's Rock shimmers in the afternoon sun. The dirt path that I scrubbed from my feet before bed kicks up dust behind me when I drive, rounding the bend of Sandstone Lane toward home. Everything is the same.

Except nothing is the same.

Too soon we are here, passing the signpost that used to announce The Oyster Shell Inn but is now a bare stake at the end of our drive, the sign whipped from its chain during the hurricane. It was never found, although for years I expected it to turn up in the sand covered with dried seaweed, or nestled in the rock jetty. My father said he would make a new one, but the inn has been closed to guests ever since. What use was a sign, a landmark to a place that had washed out to sea? They planned to reopen, someday, but that was six years ago, long before Pearl Harbor, before Tommy and I enlisted.

The car jostles on the driveway, and the crunch of the tires signaling I am home churns my stomach. I try to thank Sergeant Allen, someone the army provided, but all I can manage is a nod before I step out of the back seat. My throat is a clenched fist, and sweat beads beneath my cap, so I slip it off and tuck it under my arm. My right leg throbs, my wounds dressed but raw beneath the bandages. I favor my left, giving it more of my weight. It is not the walk of a hero. *Hero.* The word tastes like lead in my mouth. Limping, slow, hoping to somehow never reach the porch. Not sure if news has reached them, if a telegram beat me home.

The screen door creaks open and Evelyn runs out, throws her arms around me, the door clattering behind her. She hugs and kisses me, her hands on my face and my neck, my body is numb, unsteady in her embrace. She looks around, realizes it is only me. Me, all alone. There is no second car winding up the path, no one climbing out after me. She steps back, registering my expression for the first time.

"Evelyn…" I reach for her arms, and make contact with her wrist. She rips it away. The Plymouth that delivered me vanished, the only sign it was there is the faint crunch of tires, the engine fading in the distance.

"He was injured too. He's coming in another car." Her voice is firm, controlled, her gaze fixed on mine.

I can't speak. My mouth opens but the ice tightens around my heart; sharp edges sinking into tissue. It is a pain I have never experienced—watching her eyes cloud over, watching her realize what I cannot tell her, have no words to explain.

"The telegram said he was injured. You both were injured. Tell me. *Joseph*…tell me he's coming soon, he's on his way." Her voice becomes a screech as she pounds on my chest, her hair falling loose from its pins. "Tell me! Goddamn it, say something!" I catch her wrists again and pull her into me. My vision blurs with tears. I bury my face in her neck and all I can say is, "I'm sorry… I am so sorry."

She lets me hold her for a moment, and then her body stiffens in my grip. She straightens, shoulders heaving, and steps away from me. Her eyes are dark clouds reflecting nothing—no love, barely even recognition. They flicker toward my face, bluer today than I have ever seen.

Her voice barely a whisper, "You promised me."

The ice twists, shards cutting deeper.

"Evelyn…" My voice doesn't sound like mine.

She backs up, her eyes never leaving me. Flicking left to right across my face, as if reading something written there. Something written in a language she can't understand, something foul. She turns and I reach for her arm but she yanks out of my grip and runs away from me. The sun glares; my vision swims, purple and green distort before me, fuzzy and surreal, as she sprints through the field blooming with violets, toward their house.

Her house.

Hers.

Night swims are my salvation. I sneak out to Bernard Beach when I can't sleep, when my heart is a bolt screwed too tight. It is the only place I can breathe, plunging into the frigid depths. The sky so black above it's almost a new color, the universe glowing and infinite. In Italy, there weren't stars like this. The air was filled with smoke and gunpowder, gray soot, ashes of crumbled buildings. When I think of it, my throat constricts, oxygen becomes thin. A woman slumped in her doorway, her neck lolled back. The way her son screamed, caked in dust. Was that real? Is this?

I wake before the sun, restless, my pillow damp and smelling of the sea. I limp out to the field between our houses. Evelyn still works in town sewing parachutes, but then hides in her room, no signs of her except the curtains drawn until morning. I want to ask if she still sews our initials into the silk; if she can bear to write one without the other, whether stitching or omitting both etches a deeper scar. Before bed, she flips on her lamp, a tiny square of yellowed light I know is her, moving around in her room. The window where I used to sling crumpled messages and secret places to meet, a lifetime ago. Does she stare across to the weathered gray Shaker inn, wondering about me?

She hasn't spoken to me since that first day. Not even at the funeral, the weight of the casket on my shoulder, the jolts in my leg as I marched, the uniformed body tucked inside that wasn't Tommy, couldn't be. Mrs. Saunders clutched a crumpled tissue at the front of the church, her face pained, reciting the prayers. Mr. Saunders stoic, shaking each hand. Evelyn mute, draped in a loose black dress, echoed my emptiness as they lowered him, a sorrow carved so deep it changed her features. Two wax figures, two strangers, unrecognizable. One laid to rest beneath the darkest earth, one hollowed from the inside as she stood at the edge of the grave.

The army honorably discharged me because of the shrapnel that tore through my leg, the limp that causes people to stare, to lower their eyes in pity, or worse—thank me. I don't have the slightest desire to get involved now that I'm home. Not at the navy yard or collecting scrap metal; I already gave everything I have. All I want is to stay in Stonybrook forever, to swim, let the cool water rush over my skin, the way it did before I left and the way it always will. Doctors told me to go easy, I was lucky to walk at all, I would limp for the rest of my life. I can't accept that, a constant reminder of that day. So I swim, kick through the waves, relishing the pain until the cold and stinging needles turn me numb.

But my days and nights blur with thoughts of her.

Evelyn, sucking the salt out of a wet curl of her hair. Evelyn, holding my wrist and aiming my finger at shapes in the clouds. Evelyn, tucking a blossom behind her tiny ear curved like a shell. The first time I reached for her hand, at Captain's Rock. The first time she showed me her lists, cross-legged in the scratchy meadow, the pages she filled with ink and dreams. The first time I kissed her, lying together on the dock. The first time I told her I loved her. The tears in her eyes as the train pulled away. How she looked at me, face clouded over, when I came back alone.

She leaves for work each morning, and each morning I pick violets and bring them to her. A reminder, an offering, a plea. I stand where her cobbled walkway meets Sandstone Lane, a fistful of flowers against my chest, heart thrashing like a fish trapped in a net. When she reaches me, I offer them. She stares, vacant, unyielding.

I say, "I'll be here every day until you speak to me."

She is expunged of her familiar mannerisms, a floating bubble popped, ceasing to exist. Unreadable, she refuses to meet my eyes before she pivots toward the street and walks away. She does, however, match my stride, slow and labored as it may be. We walk, the air between us thick with uncertainty and silence.

When we reach The Arnold Factory, she disappears through the iron gate without acknowledging I had been there at all.

This morning, like each one before, I pluck the tiny stems once more, discard the elephant-ear-shaped leaves, and gather a bouquet of velvet petals. But this time, I hang back to see if my absence registers, or if I am merely a phantom beside her.

Her door swings open and she is there, in her tan unadorned uniform, her hair in a tight bun at the nape of her neck. She crosses the front steps, gazing at her feet, same as every day. She glances up only when she reaches the walkway, and I see the shadow of disappointment, the slightest turn of her head before she takes off down the street.

She hesitated. She expected me.

I hurry, my leg throbs as I strain to reach her. My calf burns and the flames spread all the way to my chest, the ache like lightning striking metal, but I push through the pain.

"Evelyn!" I call out to her, a few paces ahead.

She turns, startled to a stop, allowing me to catch up. Close enough to hold her, if she let me.

"I'm not going anywhere. You don't have to talk, just listen. Please don't walk away." I hold the violets out to her, my breath labored. Her eyes flicker to my hand. She pauses, she is going to refuse. But then she wraps her slender fingers around the stems, grazing my skin in the exchange like the tickle of a yellow buttercup she once brushed against my throat. In a whispering lisp, missing a baby tooth, she had told me: *Close your eyes. If you move, you're made of butter.* A kid's game, a memory, jarring in its exactness.

I didn't expect her to stop, and now the speech I practiced each day on our silent walks comes jumbled and rushed. "I never should have made that promise to you. I was trying to protect you, to make things right before I left. But I couldn't keep it, and it rips me apart." My voice wavers, my hands empty and useless at my sides, wanting desperately to reach for her, to know

she is real. "I wasn't there when it happened. If I was, maybe…
I don't know, maybe something would have been different…"

My eyes swim. Before this moment everything was numb.
I see the colonel coming to tell me the news. See the bandages
around my leg. See his lips moving and the sound muffled as
though I am underwater, I'm drowning, I'm dead. I feel everything then nothing. Seeing Evelyn resets something inside me,
and it's all I can do to get the words out before I'm submerged
once more. "I wish I could change it. I wish it had been me. I
miss him too. Please tell me you understand. Tell me…"

The flowers fall to the dirt like spent matchsticks and she
reaches for me. I bury my face in her neck and the release of
her touch takes away all my strength and I sob, shaking because
I can't change it and because it feels good to finally let go, because all I have wanted since I left was to be back in her arms.

She whispers firmly in my ear, my shoulders heaving, "Don't
you ever say that! I wanted you both to come home."

I hold her tighter, her touch paining and healing me. "Why
wouldn't you see me? I need you, Evelyn."

She tilts back, our noses inches apart. She stares at me, seeing
me for the first time since I came home. There is little warmth
in the gaze. "How could I? How could I look at you and not
be reminded of him?"

"But I can't lose you too."

My stomach drops thinking of my mother. The tumor found
while I was away, growing rapidly as she weakens. The nights
my father paces, staring out the window at nothing. The inn
that is only an inn by name, the paint unfinished and guestroom
windows boarded up. They hadn't planned to tell me about the
growth on her side, their fear of what it means, but I walked in
on my parents at the kitchen table. My father weeping into my
mother's outstretched palms. And Evelyn doesn't even know.
An impossibility, this thread we don't share.

Evelyn's voice brings me back, almost a whisper. "I can't…
Joseph, it's too much."

The breeze carries the smell of dewy grass, of dirt. It ruffles
the hem of her skirt and she folds her arms against the chill. I
resist the urge to reach for her. If we can't navigate through our
words, will our hearts recognize each other in this new darkness? Can we find our way by touch? I search her face, defined
angles replacing her full pink cheeks. I say, "I love you."

She lifts her gaze to mine, her blue-gray eyes rimmed with
tears. "I'm leaving."

It's as if a gale-force wind comes in for those words, carries
them to sea. "What did you say?"

She shakes her head. "I'm leaving Stonybrook. For good.
Maybe when the war is over, maybe sooner. I can't stay here
anymore, there's no point, everything reminds me of him."

"Say his name." Desperation seeps into my voice like rising
water.

"What?" Her body jerks, startled.

"Say his name. You haven't said his name since I told you, I
haven't heard it once."

She hisses, "Why should I say it? It feels like I'm screaming it.
I spent two years waiting for you both to come home. *Two years.*
What good does saying it do? What does it change?"

"How can you leave if you can't even say it?"

She leans back, a raised scorpion's tail. "Why are you doing
this?"

"Because you can't run away. You can't ignore what you feel,
ignore me and pretend none of this happened." I am panting
now, panting with the effort of holding back all this love and
anger and grief. I run to the street before he was shot, run with
his body, his living, breathing body. Run through the bullets
soaring through the air and dodge each one, run across the
ocean now, waves like stepstools propel me forward, to Bernard

Beach, to Stonybrook, to this life here we shared. This life I must somehow now carry on my own.

"I can do whatever I want." Her face is stone; the arms that hugged me are folded across her chest.

I take a deep breath, cautious. "Yes, you can. You can leave, you can run, if that's what you truly want. But I'm asking you not to, I'm asking you to stay with me." I pause, my throat raw. Mrs. Mayweather's School, a mother's order to leave town. A tumor growing, forcing its way through. The draft, looming and threatening. A bullet, shrapnel, tearing through flesh. My life, spinning out of my control, into hers.

"I have to go. I can't stay here." Her voice is cold, even and unfamiliar.

"Then I'll go with you." The water rises, I am losing air. I rub my knuckles, a nervous friction.

"I don't want you to. Can't you see that?"

"I need you. I know you need me too." The scene slides away, everything is getting smaller, black and fuzzy around the edges.

"It's *you* I can't stand to be around. Not here, not in this place." Her eyes fall to the violets, splayed across the walkway. "I thought being together would be enough. But the life I waited around for, it's gone… I can't stay, trapped here, wishing we could go back to the way it used to be." She takes a deep breath. "We should say goodbye."

I reach for her, her cheek hot against my palm. Her eyes are sunken, features sharpened. "I told you that you never get to say goodbye to me, not forever." She turns her chin slightly, averting her eyes. A single tear falls from her lashes and slides down my thumb. "I know you love me too."

"I have to go." She steps back, the contact broken like a life vest swept up in a wave. The surf rising, sloshing around me.

I can feel where her tear grazed my skin. Gravel in my throat, I ask, "You do love me, don't you?"

Her eyes well up as she stares at me, pleading. "Don't wait for me anymore...in the mornings. Please."

"Evelyn..."

One last look, her haunted beauty like a blade, slicing me open. She turns, and at a pace she knows is quicker than I can match, slips away.

A month later, Evelyn's darkened window gives me my answer. There is no lamplight to announce her getting into bed, and after three nights it is clear she has moved, left Stonybrook, left me. It is only a few days before their birthdays. Tommy would have been twenty-one. The boom of July fireworks becomes shellfire when I hide alone in my room, the flashing reflections in my window warnings to retreat. I smoke an entire carton of cigarettes waiting for the explosions to stop and then puke until I am empty.

On the fourth day I venture to her front porch, my thoughts a minefield. *What if I never see her again? What if she hates me? What if she meets someone new?*

Mrs. Saunders pries open their heavy front door a crack, her eyes sunken and skin taut against her cheeks.

"Mrs. Saunders, hi. Is Evelyn here?" She stares at me with distrust, as though I am in on some wicked prank. "Do you know where she went?"

"She didn't tell me. I thought you would know."

"Did she move back to Boston maybe? Do you know how to reach her?"

"I don't know, she didn't say. All I know is she's gone too. Now go on, please. There's no one here for you anymore." She backs up and closes the door.

I'd never felt particularly welcome inside the Saunderses' house, but this was something new. This wasn't a desire to keep the house pristine, to avoid our roughhousing around their fragile decor. My presence is a cruel twist of luck; the soldier who returned, when hers didn't. How many times had I waited here, right here on the second step by the railing with its hairline crack from a rogue baseball, but now the two people I wait for on this porch no longer live in this house. They no longer run barefoot down Sandstone Lane, dive into waves at Bernard Beach. They won't cut through the field to the inn, or jump off Captain's Rock, or exist here at all except in dreams and memories.

I am unmoored.

I drift through the next few months that drag like years. I battle inwardly, a fight I won't win. *She doesn't want me.* We need each other. *She said seeing me is painful.* We belong together. *She asked for space.* We'll never heal if we stay apart.

At night I wrestle with a soldier in my dreams who is built like me with Tommy's face and my father's pained eyes—I can't beat him. He strangles me until I wake.

The morning after Evelyn told me not to wait for her anymore, I left one last note, tucked in a bouquet of violets in a glass jar I set on her steps. *Leaving won't stop me from loving you.* She never responded. I'm not sure she saw it at all, and if she did it didn't make any difference. Weeks later, she was gone.

Something inside me breaks off like an overused hinge, fragments sent adrift. Weeks, months pass without my notice. I float aimlessly through the places that reek of her, of Tommy. I smoke more cigarettes. I contemplate swimming out to Captain's Rock at low tide and securing myself to a jagged outcropping until the water rises above me.

I have to go. There is no life for me here, without her.

I would follow her anywhere.

I board the train to Boston, suitcase in hand, following the address on a faded letter Evelyn had sent me years earlier. *Mrs. Mayweather's School for Girls, 239 Walnut Street, Brookline, Massachusetts.* Evelyn isn't in the telephone directory, so I start with the best lead I have, and pray I still know her enough to trace her path.

On first look I mistake the school for a museum, an ornate brick building with white Grecian columns and an oversize doorway. A scowling secretary greets me when I ask for Maelynn, then instructs me to wait outside the headmistress's office, a musty room of old books and plush leather couches. When Maelynn arrives, she is smaller than I imagined—in Evelyn's stories she is a strong and fiery goddess, a woman who fills a room, but in reality she is very close in size and stature to Evelyn. She wears a navy pantsuit and a knowing expression as she beckons me toward her, her head nodding a command with the confidence of a woman who is rarely refused.

"So, you're the Joseph I've heard about?" She raises her eyebrows and the resemblance to Evelyn sets me off-kilter.

I stumble my reply. "Yes, ma'am. I'm here to marry her, if she'll have me. I came to this city with a plan to find her. Please, I don't know where to start." I wish for a stronger opening, to match her self-assurance, to be a gallant suitor, not a hometown boy offering a weak plea.

"Well, that doesn't sound like much of a plan to me." Her eyebrows lift, knocking me off course once more. "Listen, I don't think it would be right to let you barge into our home without her permission." She pauses. "It certainly would not be right to let you know she works as a secretary on Boylston Street, or that she buys her lunch at twelve thirty at the little market across from the Copley Square Hotel. It would not be right at all for you to have that information, though I really do wish I could help." She winks and says, "It was a pleasure to meet you," turns and walks away, the office door swinging shut behind her.

I am stunned by the ease of it. I left Stonybrook only hours before; I imagined myself searching tirelessly, thrown off course, led astray. Three months have passed since I have seen Evelyn. Months lost to my grief, caring for my bedridden mother, devising ways back into Evelyn's heart only to bully myself out of each idea, and now I am too close, with a plan and a landmark on a map that leads to her. I am stricken with fear that she will run, that Boston will suddenly not be far enough, that I will force her to retreat. I had convinced myself in our time apart that she missed me too. But what if I was wrong, deceiving myself because I desperately wanted it to be true?

Having come this far, I rush to the Brookline Village trolley stop, still carrying my suitcase and chastising myself for not getting settled first, at least for the night, for showing up with luggage like my decision to stay hinged on her answer. But I am determined to make it to Copley Square while I still have my nerve. The only thing worse than finding her, would be not finding her, so I pray Maelynn is right.

The streetcar arrives and I pop my head in. "Excuse me, will this take me to Boylston Street?"

The conductor grunts, "Inbound train," and urges me on board with the others, trading coins for tickets. We heave forward on tracks through the city, jostled at every stop as the car empties and fills, fills and empties, the space around me constricting. I grip a fabric handle to stay on my feet, coats and hats and elbows and shoulders press against me as I fumble through what to say when I see her. *I don't know how to live in Stonybrook without you. I don't know how to live without you.* Nothing feels right. Nothing says quite what I need her to understand; I'm not acting out of weakness or desperation. There are no violets to offer, only the golden leaves of October. I don't want to bring something that symbolizes change. I want her to know I am constant like the sea, tides rising and falling, waves rolling into eternity. So, it will have to just be me. Me and the words I can't find.

The market across from the Copley Square Hotel is plastered with posters declaring Food Is a Weapon, Don't Waste It, and Buy Wisely, Cook Carefully, Eat It All, and Help Win the War on the Kitchen Front. I plant myself by the entrance, lean against the rough brick, my focus aimed across the street, unsure from which side she will come. The autumn wind whips through the flags atop the hotel, and despite my wool coat and hat, I have to blow on my hands to warm them. The scent of fresh bread and cured meats tantalize me each time the door opens beside me. My stomach rumbles; I had been too sick with nerves to have breakfast. The minutes crawl until I am certain I've missed her, or that I am in the wrong place, or that Maelynn misled me on purpose.

Then, like a mirage, a trick of the eye, Evelyn appears.

She wears a sleeved green dress, cut below her knees. Her curls are long and pinned away from her face, a contrast to her tight bun all summer. She smiles at the Copley Square Hotel's doorman as she passes, a polite gesture, not a joyful one. Then she looks both ways and crosses the street toward me. My palms sweat so I shove them in my pockets, my body electrified. She approaches the market but hasn't noticed me. I open the door for her, and she turns to thank me, a stranger in a wool cap, then stops, her mouth open in surprise when she sees my face.

"Joseph!"

"Hi, Evelyn."

An agitated man in a brown overcoat stands inside the threshold, and we step apart to let him pass.

"What are you doing here?"

"It's good to see you." Her face is fuller than when I saw it last; there is something fiercely adult about it, now that she is nineteen. Her dress casts her eyes a shade of emerald, an ominous forest I am desperate to explore.

Seeing her again, here, is like stumbling upon her in another life entirely, as if we could be born again and meet for the first time outside this market, and yet, even then we would know each other. My soul would recognize hers as a stranger in the next life exactly the way I understand her now, in an ancient, absolute way. All I want is to hold her, but I refrain, unsure of how much is still wounded, if she would bruise like an overripe peach in my grip.

"How did you find me?"

"Maelynn." Her soft lips, those lips I could recognize against mine in the dark, are still parted in disbelief, so I continue, "I told you leaving wouldn't stop me from loving you, and it hasn't. I miss you so much. I need to be near you, with you. I'll move here, if that's what you want, I'll do whatever it takes…"

She shakes her head. "You'll move here…to be with me? Oh, Joseph…"

"I don't want to scare you off. I know it's a lot, showing up like this, but I didn't know how to reach you, or what else to do—"

"I don't know what to say…"

"Have you missed me, or…is this life here…this is what you want?" I ask, desperate for the answer that won't tear me in two.

"It's not that simple."

"It can be."

"I wish that were true."

"I'll go, I swear. I'll leave you alone forever, if that's what you really want. But I need you to know if there's any chance you love me, I'll be here."

She takes a deep breath. Then she meets my eyes, a mystical siren's gaze I would gladly follow to my destruction. "Okay."

"Okay?"

"Yes, okay." A hint of a smile. "It's okay that you're here."

"Is it okay if I have lunch with you?"

She laughs, surprising us both, and nods. "Yes, that would be okay."

We share a ham sandwich on crusty bread from the market that is a cacophony of brined olives and cured meats and musky cheeses, a sanctuary of delicacies I thought had disappeared with the war. I am used to cubes of tough beef in stew, cookies made with corn syrup, canned beans grown in victory gardens. But here, ration stamps buy foods that taste like peacetime, like salt-water swims and flowers in Evelyn's hair.

We buy what we are allotted and savor lunch, that day and

each day after. A tacit arrangement we keep even after I start selling suits at Filene's, my first job ever that isn't at the inn. I was hired thanks to Mrs. Moretti, a widow with kind eyes on the trolley who noticed my limp and asked if I had served in the war. She offered me her spare bedroom; she had kept it for her son, another soldier who never returned. And she wrote the name *Filene's* on a slip of paper with an address and told me to ask for Sal, the manager there. When we met, he questioned my limp, asking in a thick Italian accent, "You seem like a good kid…but you'll be on your feet dealing with customers, can you handle that?" I placed my weight on my injured leg, letting it throb, and swore I could. He nodded, his leathered skin crinkled in a smile, and told me he needed a suit salesman, and I could start right away.

Once I begin to work, I hop on the Main Line Elevated at Downtown Crossing and take the subway three stops to Back Bay, and then run from there to Copley Square where Evelyn waits with half a sandwich for me, and half for her. We only have minutes together but it is worth it to catch her smile when she sees me from across the street, cracks in the shell she had formed to keep me out.

We sit huddled on a bench, clutching our sandwiches with frozen fingers, and Evelyn says, "You know I can type twice as fast as the other girls? All those years at the piano."

"Maybe they'll start paying you twice as much."

She exhales a laugh. "Yeah, right. Maybe then I could afford more lessons. I miss it."

"Can you convince Maelynn to get you a piano? Then you could practice on your own."

"And where would we keep it? There's barely room for the two of us, and she's been generous as it is, letting me stay with her."

I think, but don't say, *You already have a piano, waiting for you back home.*

"Can I ask you something?"

She chews, her eyes level with mine, careful not to agree to something she won't answer.

"What changed your mind? That day I showed up...I wasn't sure you'd be willing to see me."

"Honestly?" She crumples the wax paper, slides her hands into gloves. "Every day since I left...every time I walked out of work, a part of me hoped, somehow, you would be here too."

I don't say, *You always knew where to find me.*

I regard her honesty with care, a conversation to pocket for when we are on steadier ground. Our days spent like this, oscillating between what we are willing to say and what we cannot, what we share and what we keep tucked away.

I confess I don't particularly enjoy selling suits, but the money is fair and the hours steady. I consider answering ads for handymen, or inquiring at one of the hotels, but my job at Filene's seems easier than chasing shadows of a life we left behind. Rebuilding the Oyster Shell never felt like work because it was mine, but my sweat would be lost on someone else's building, would be as empty as pedaling pocket squares. Evelyn worries about the time I spend walking through the city, and standing around the store, because of my leg, the limp designating even these happy times as *after*. I shrug it off, saying I have to push it if I want to get stronger. Other than my leg, we don't talk about the war, or Tommy, or Stonybrook, or our parents; here in this new life we don't have to. There are no unexpected triggers to our painful memories, a familiar scent or sound to transport us home. Boston smells like exhaust, like strangers on the subway, rain in the streets. There is no hint of salt air, or fresh earth, the musk of low tide.

Here, we can start again.

Evelyn's cheeks are rosy, mittens wrapped around a brown paper bag, one end of a crusty loaf of bread exposed to the night air. Our boots make sloppy footprints on the slushy cobbled walk. I readjust the rations in my arms, fumbling, distracted by her. Her knit hat has shifted so I can see the curve of her earlobe, pink from the cold. Snow falls as we amble back to Mae-lynn's house, a rented colonial off Walnut Street, through the garland-draped Brookline Village at dusk. The streets are empty and hushed; everyone hunkered indoors beside crackling fire-places. Her hair is dotted white; I have an urge to steal a snow-flake and feel it melt against my fingertip.

The Evelyn I used to know would instigate a snowball fight, or sprawl on the powder, arms sweeping angel wings. This Ev-elyn does neither, but walks with her head raised, her chin lifted. This alone is a triumph because beneath her straightened shoul-ders she is balled up under the heaviest quilt, missing Tommy. I am not disappointed; it is merely an adjustment, a change in her I must accept. And I do. I'm learning who we once were is not always who we become.

A wisp of memory drifts in like smoke, Tommy's last morn-ing in Stonybrook. He was quiet as he shoved his suitcase in the rack overhead and slid into the train seat beside me. His hands swept his pant legs to smooth invisible creases in his pressed uni-form. He looked back at Evelyn's retreating figure as our train chugged away, the air thick with steam and burning coal, and with an unsteady voice said, *If anything happens, you'll take care of her.* I nodded, and we rode together in silence as we watched the girl we both loved shrink, and disappear. That moment haunted me after he died, how he looked, for the first time that I had ever seen, afraid.

It wasn't easy to move away from Stonybrook, and as I walk with Evelyn, even on a night like this when everything feels right, when the air is cold but not bitter, when I can smell wood-burning stoves and see smoke rise from chimneys, ev-eryone tucked inside and warm, there is an echo of guilt in my footsteps. Abandoning my mother, and my father, who brought her dinner on a tray each night, as she shrank and the tumor grew. He sat beside her on the edge of their bed, forgetting to eat. I fetched him glasses of cold water, urged him to drink, but I found them full each morning, a wet ring on his wooden nightstand. And yet, my parents knew I meant it when I said I needed to go, and for the second time they hugged me good-bye. I choked down a sob when I felt my mother's ribs where there had always been a soft place for me, a cushioned embrace that smelled of flour, sun-bleached linen and home.

Today in the snow, two months after our reunion, I am in awe of Evelyn's beauty once more. Flakes fall silently, resting on her hair and shoulders. She hoists the bag on her hip as though it were a child. The snow hasn't stopped for days, and Evelyn began to worry they would run out of food if they didn't stock up. I was visiting for dinner, Maelynn served dried-out macaroni casserole, cooking not one of her talents, so I offered to run to the market and Evelyn insisted on coming with me.

She catches me staring and smiles back, shyly, as though we just met. I try to freeze time, to never forget the way she looks right now, this very second, the pink blush of her cheeks, her self-conscious smile, the breeze playing with her curls. I'm lost in the moment when she stops, shifts the bag to hold it with one arm.

"Joseph…" A snowflake lands on her eyelashes, and she says, "I'm so happy you're here."

I brush a stray ringlet behind her ear, forgetting myself and the unspoken distance we've respected until this moment, desperate to feel her skin against mine, and the emotion overtakes me. "God, you're so beautiful. I haven't told you because I didn't want to scare you away, but I can't help it. You are so beautiful, and I'm so in love with you."

She reaches up, her wool mitten damp against my cheek, and she kisses me. She kisses me and it feels like it did before the war, before my limp, before Tommy, before everything was so heavy. She pulls away, her dreamy expression a gift I want to wrap so I can open it once more, and I kiss her again. We let our groceries slide to the ground, not caring that the bags will get wet and tear, not caring that we still have blocks to walk. She kisses me back and I have been waiting for this and all I want is to kiss her again and again, endlessly.

She tilts back, her smile etched with sadness. "Thank you for not letting me go."

I press my forehead to hers. "I couldn't even if I wanted to."

"I love you, Joseph. I'm sorry it took me so long to tell you, but I do. I've always loved you."

I wrap my arms around her and lift her off the ground. I nuzzle my face into her neck, overcome with the three words I have been waiting for, the feeling that I always believed in but never once heard from her lips. Her hair tickles my cheeks and I whisper, "Marry me."

She is silent, and I untangle myself from her embrace, afraid I went too far, that she will flee. Her lips are parted in surprise, the same expression that greeted me outside the market. This time, her eyes brim with tears.

"Do you mean it?"

I nod, dizzy in her gaze. "I've never meant anything more in my life. Marry me, Evelyn."

She leaps and throws her arms around me so quickly it sends me off-balance into the snow, spilling one of the bags of groceries as we topple backward. She falls on top of me, and kisses me right there on the snowdrift, the streets empty and lights twinkling in the night settling around us. I am so happy—we could be anywhere; we could be nowhere at all. There is only Evelyn, her weight against me, her lips, and the snowflakes in her hair.

"Yes." She kisses me, warmth spreading through my chest, her vow a hearth that becomes our home.

Seven

Evelyn

August 2001

The screen door creaks open and Rain's and Tony's voices fill the room, popping over unannounced, as they often do, our foyer always a revolving door of our children and grandchildren, shouting out hellos before raiding the refrigerator or grabbing sand chairs on their way to the beach. All except for Thomas, who keeps himself at an arm's length, a visitor when he enters, more distant than ever now.

Tonight, Rain peels and slices cucumbers to go with dinner while Tony disappears to help his grandfather-in-law tend a leaky sink. They are both fixtures here. Tony assists with repairs or offers a pair of strong arms, Rain works beside Joseph in the garden; he taught her to identify weeds, to deadhead the spent blooms, how to support climbing wisteria by lashing it to stakes with twine, at peace in the house where she was raised until Jane found her footing. The Oyster Shell is her home; it has always been her home, as it always has been mine.

We sit down to eat, but before we can fill our plates Rain blurts out, "I can't wait anymore! We have news."

Joseph puts the salad bowl down, and I place the tongs back on the platter of chicken, giving them our full attention.

"I'm pregnant!" Rain says with a girlish giggle. Tony grins, and we jump up to hug and congratulate them both. It seems impossible she could be twenty-seven with a child growing in her womb. She was just a baby herself, babbling between my ankles as she dumped sand from a plastic bucket.

"How far along are you?" I ask, breathless with excitement.

"We just found out," she says, beaming, "we haven't even gone to the doctor yet, but I took, like, five tests. I know most people keep it secret for a while, but...given everything..."

I nod, shame rising in my cheeks. The whole family is feeling the weight of time.

"When are you due?" Joseph's voice is tinged with joy as he pulls out Rain's chair, gesturing for her to sit.

"May," she says, and her smile falters.

May. The month before we say goodbye. A great-grandchild we may barely meet, entering this world as we leave it. A newborn we may hold for a moment, only to miss the first word, the first steps, the child the baby will become, the mother Rain will grow to be. Her swelling belly a reminder of all we'll give up. Of all I'm taking from Joseph because I'm afraid. An immeasurable loss. A new crater forms in me, deep and throbbing.

"I thought if you knew, maybe—" she looks down, not meeting my eyes "—it would give you a reason to stay."

My throat constricts, my sad smile a meager offering. "I wish it were that easy."

"Let's not talk about it anymore tonight, huh?" Tony says. "My only job so far in this thing is to keep my pregnant wife happy. Tonight, we celebrate."

"Agreed," Joseph says, almost too eagerly.

"Can you do something for me?" Rain rests a palm against

her still-flat belly. "Can you make the baby a blanket? Like the one you made for me."

Rain was over a year old when Jane brought her home from California, more toddler than infant, but she dragged it everywhere she went until the pink edges were frayed, for years after.

"Of course. Of course I can." I say with false confidence, hoping it's true. And I hug her, hug them both; the mother and the baby, while I can, maybe the only way I ever will. Rain's child not yet formed into pudgy legs or tiny toes, still merely cells, an absence of a period. The crater within me widens. Nine months to grow, ten months to say goodbye.

Days later, the needle trembles in my grasp and misses the pastel yellow cotton, once, twice, three times, and I glance up, grateful Joseph hasn't noticed. I don't want him to ask if I'm okay. Okay compared to what? I try to focus on the task at hand, use my thimble to force the needle through and the string tangles. I'm having trouble seeing clearly, my vision sometimes like living inside of a soap bubble, the light refracts and ripples into distorted rainbows, shifting and sliding before me. I blink, try tracking backward, but the passage is too narrow, my aim unsteady, so I will have to cut it, tear it out.

The living room is flooded in harsh morning light, another hot August day guaranteed to chase us into the ocean by lunchtime, a reprieve I look forward to. Floating on my back, weightless, eyes open beneath a powder blue sky, before the sunset sail out of Mystic Seaport Joseph planned for tonight. *Ride off into the sunset*, a Hollywood dream, two glasses of wine, breeze in our hair, someone else at the helm as the colors fade to twilight. I fight the urge to sleep until then. Joseph fills an armchair, reading glasses perched low on his nose, his head covered in thinning white hair. Built like his father, solid as the trunk of an oak, he has begun to wither; crepe-paper skin loose around his muscles, his stomach a soft pouch. If he still mirrors Mr. Myers at this age, it's impossible to say. He is twenty years older now than his father ever was.

The phone rings, and I am grateful for the interruption. My heart leaps as I answer. "Hello?"

"Morning, Mom." It's Violet. "I'm headed over soon. Is Dad waiting for me?"

"He's reading the paper, no rush." This Sunday morning her youngest, Patrick, has baseball practice and Ryan, following his older sister Shannon's footsteps, is away at freshman orientation at Boston University. That would leave Violet and Connor home alone, but instead she'll come here, preferring weeding to time with her husband. I nudge her, recognizing a worrisome pattern. She's forty-five and still underfoot, eager to help, to play her part. She left teaching when Molly was born, and chooses to spend her days with us, stirring a steaming pot for me in the kitchen, or crouched in the soil beside Joseph. "But if Connor's home, don't feel like you have to come by. Or bring him."

"No, he has stuff to do around here. I'll see you soon."

I rest the phone back on the receiver with a soft click. I don't realize I am glaring at it until Joseph peers over the top of his newspaper. "Not Thomas, I presume?"

I shake my head and resist the urge to dial his number. He's never been one to reach out first, but he always followed up between meetings or when he had a moment at his desk, our conversations rushed yet consistent. Since we told him our plan, he has yet to return a single call.

"He'll come around," Joseph says, his calm tone grating against my frustration.

"How many times has he been home since we told them? Twice?" My brain shuffles through the past two months, my mind a sticky deck of new playing cards. Moments from years past slide around in my mind—three-card monte, and I can always find the queen. But recent memories are stiff, glossy, and the bridge I bend riffles clumsily, cards spilling away.

Joseph's brow furrows; he thinks I should know this. "He's been home only once since we told them, for your birthday. We all went swimming, remember?"

Of course. That night, everyone diving into the water, the moon shining above, life was a palatable thing. The memory sharp as it dings into place. The froth of the blue-black tide turning over on cold mottled sand. Thomas, sputtering in the surf after his sisters dragged him under, an oyster pried open, a tiny pearl of boyhood, of playfulness and wonder, glimmering inside.

"Once..." I stare out the window at the sunlight filtering through Joseph's garden, a symphony of bursting color, the soothing notes of lavender, bright and brassy tiger lilies, steady chords of deep blue hydrangeas. "I knew he wouldn't understand, but this?"

Joseph flips a page in his newspaper. "You know how he is. It's how he protects himself."

"I don't know how Ann does it." My gaze lands on a pewter-framed photo of their wedding, Ann clutching a bouquet of calla lilies as they retreated down the aisle, her demure expression, his restrained pride. On their wedding day, the ballroom was packed with their coworkers and business associates. Between greeting tables, Ann released her hold on Thomas's elbow and intertwined her fingers with his. He turned toward her, his face aglow, and kissed her. Her joy, his tenderness, was so intimate I looked away, back to the half-eaten cake littering the tables. I always knew he cared for Ann, I knew she cared for him, their relationship made sense, but that was the first time I glimpsed the depth of their private affection for one another.

Joseph folds his newspaper in his lap, and I hope he doesn't come over to join me; his comforting touch would loosen a valve I am desperately wrenching shut. But he stays in his chair, tapping his fingers together. "I think he feels like if he calls, he is supporting our decision. He needs to work it out on his own."

"I want to shake him sometimes, you know?" I laugh, a forced gust of air. "I'm worried, there's only so much time… I don't know, I worry about them all, there's still things they don't have figured out, important things…" My gaze traces the dozens of framed photographs. The grandchildren kneeling in a pyramid on the sandbar; Rain and Tony dancing at their wedding; Jane, Violet and Thomas, faded figures in their footed pajamas beside a Christmas tree.

Joseph pauses, his expression one I've seen before, an ax splitting me in two with the force of its love. "You know if there was anything I could do for you, I would, right?"

"I know." My eyes soften; my guilt bubbles up once more, for being selfish, for not being stronger, willing to face whatever comes. "And what can I do for you?"

"Stay strong for me." His voice has a husk to it, emotion creeping in. "Stay as strong as you can until June."

Violet arrives in jean shorts and her faded Tufts University T-shirt, her hair a messy knot at her neck. I follow her out back with my sewing and settle on the wooden bench Joseph built for our anniversary one year so I could keep him company. He is already digging up and dividing overgrown hostas with a metal shovel, replanting them in smaller bunches so they flourish. Sunflowers tower beside him like nosy neighbors supervising his work, thriving in the late summer heat. I've learned there is much more to gardening than planting seeds and watering, it is a constant battle of weeding and fertilizing and pruning that I find exhausting. But not Joseph; he is steady in his care, patient with the elements outside of his control. Joseph seeks no recognition for his labor, his joy is in watching them blossom on their own.

The garden sprawls an acre from our back door to Violet's house where I grew up, where my mother lived until she was found roaming the neighborhood, disoriented, forcing us to send her to a nursing home. My father had died much earlier, a heart attack, and she deteriorated into her dementia, and her death, mostly alone. I imagine the air around me smells of dirt and pollen and the richest potpourri, but scents, too, have become a memory, a locked gate. Never did I imagine my suggestion to spruce up the yard would turn out like this.

When we closed the Oyster Shell, Joseph didn't know what to do with himself, his steps hollow without the jingle of keys in his pockets, without the constant tinkering required of a house in overuse. He hovered while I practiced, picked at what I cooked, sampling diced tomatoes or sticking a finger in cake batter. I pleaded with him to find something, anything, that was his own. I had so often wished for more time together while we toiled separately during peak seasons, imagining days on Bernard Beach like those we shared as teens. But without the Oyster Shell to occupy his time he became buzzing and tiresome, a knot between my shoulders.

The meadow had long sat untouched, home only to clover and the occasional game of croquet. Sometimes I imagined it a sprawling garden, and as my frustration grew the idea took shape. Something I could ask, a gift for me, that was secretly something for him. He agreed to my suggestion one night as we lay together in bed, although I felt his embarrassment like a festering wound as he struggled to admit he didn't know how to spend all this time he suddenly found himself with.

In order to turn the meadow into a garden, Joseph first had to tame the wild violets. They grew without abandon in the first few weeks of May until the entire field burst purple. The fragile flowers hid the strength of the roots beneath; they spread with the fervor of weeds, stifled anything in its path. They were beautiful, and yet, without malice or intention, they could strangle to survive. He boxed them in to save them, a protected bed where they could blossom. All I could think about while I watched him was how he showed up each morning at my doorstep clutching violets in his fist. I wondered if he thought of that, too, as he fumbled with the fertilizer and overwatered the plants. I feared this wasn't what I meant at all, he was chasing some ghost, Tommy, or his parents, or the life we used to have.

But soon it became so much more than a favor to me. He researched which flowers grew best in New England, which varieties preferred shade to sun, how to organize seedlings so something was constantly in bloom. He came home with stacks of books and read them long after I had fallen asleep. He carved out beds to represent each of our children. Daisies, their hope and innocence for Violet. Lavender's virtue, to represent Thomas. Gladiolas' strength of character, for Jane. As the years went on, he cleared space for a larger garden, planted a dream bulb by bulb. He took each of our grandchildren to the nursery and let them choose their own, snapdragons, zinnia, marigolds, lilac, primrose, peonies, daylilies, irises, to create a rolling tapestry of color. It started with violets, it all started with violets. Now there is an Eden, a dewy secret garden of our love and our family.

Joseph and Violet kneel side by side in the earth. I wonder even now as he works if he already misses it, like as a newly-wed I missed Joseph even while I lay in the crook of his arms.

Who will tend to it after we are gone?

Violet yanks a stubborn root, then stops to brush the hair out of her face with the back of her wrist, her exhaustion palpable. "Dad, can you stop for a second? I need to talk to you both." Her expression is pained. Always our popular one, our vibrant one, our beaming light. I'm not sure where she has gone, can't find her in this woman with tired eyes. She straightens and sits beside me on the bench, takes a long gulp from a sweating glass of iced tea.

Joseph senses the weight in her words. I can tell by the careful way he gets up to join us, deliberate, as if any sudden movement could cause the eruption of tears.

"We know this is hard," I begin, preempting her fears.

Violet shakes her head, and blurts, "I think I want a divorce."

My eyes widen, and I peek at Joseph. If he's surprised, he

hides it better than me. Violet has always leaned on us, confiding in her parents because she lost many of the friends she used to have, kids and husbands overtaking girl-talk and sleepovers. I knew they'd been struggling; her marriage eroded in the usual way, the same way pebbles become sand—imperceptibly, without permission. But I had no idea it had come to this.

She continues, "I…I don't know. I thought it would be different. Marriage. I thought if we loved each other, it would be enough. When we got engaged, we were so happy and so young, and it happened so fast, and that was so many years ago, and I don't know…it's never been what I imagined."

I try to counter, but she plows through, her voice hurried and breathless.

"And I thought I had to accept my life as it was…but when you told us your plan, I—" She begins to cry, tears racing down her cheeks. "I felt so many things. I was terrified to lose you both, and still am, and I was in disbelief, but mostly I felt envy—" Her words are getting hard to discern, muffled by sobs. "Envy because I don't think Connor loves me like that, and I don't think I could do it for him either, and all I've ever wanted is what you have, and I thought Connor was it, and I thought I could wait until the kids were out of the house to figure everything out, but I can't. I want the happily-ever-after, and I don't want to waste any more time." She stops abruptly, breathing heavy, and wipes her nose with the hem of her T-shirt.

My underarms prickle with perspiration. We fractured an already delicate vase. Violet, our strongest advocate for love. I didn't think *divorce* was in her vocabulary.

Joseph speaks up first. "I know you and Connor have drifted apart—"

"But that doesn't mean you throw it all away," I interrupt, finding my words, drudging up old questions in me, battles fought years ago. "Marriage isn't always easy, Violet, because life isn't. Not every love is worth fighting for, but think of the family you've built, the partnership you have. Yours *is*."

"I see the way you and Dad are. You've never had to work at loving each other."

"There were difficult years for us, trust me. You don't know everything about our marriage...there were times life didn't make it easy at all." I yearn for her to understand, to decipher my cryptic message. A secret from my past bubbles up, nagging. A day I almost left it all behind.

"Have you talked to him?" Joseph asks, although we both can guess the answer.

"He should be able to see I'm not happy."

"I'm sure he can, but he may not know why, or what to do," Joseph says.

"But I don't even know how to explain it, I don't know how we got here...there isn't that spark I used to feel about him, or about life, it's all so—" she's worked herself up again so she fumbles through her words, caught on her emotion "—so ordinary and so boring."

I can see her ambivalence and disappointment form, and Connor at the center of it. Connor, who had never done anything wrong except become a steady and ordinary husband. Settling for ordinary, to Violet, was its own betrayal.

"Sometimes it's easy to focus on what's missing, instead of all of the things that are right." I'm hyperaware of the echo in my words, the things I wish I could go back to, tell myself. "But the way you loved each other? No one could deny it, seeing you together. It was a cosmic force. To take that and build a life together, to start a family, that's what *real* love stories are made of. It may not feel the same as it did then. You were twenty-one, honey. Of course it doesn't." My shame reverberates, history repeating. A mistake I nearly made.

Joseph rubs at a streak of dirt on his forearm, agreeing. "Things were tough between your mother and I after the war, but if we had given up because it was hard, we would never have experienced the best parts of marriage, the closeness that comes from being tested and coming out the other side." Violet sniffles. "Do you still love him?" Joseph asks gently.

Violet wipes tears from her cheeks. "He's a good man, and a great dad, but we've grown so far apart..."

"Talk to him." I put my arm around her shoulder, the way I should have let myself be held back then, to release what I had bound so tightly inside. "Tell him how you feel, what you need. It may take time, and work, but what you have is worth it." I need her to see, although I am afraid it may take losing us for her to understand how rare the love is that she and Connor have found. It is not something to rip out like weeds. Real commitment requires cultivation. It's not about the tingle in your belly and a rush of adrenaline. It's not magic, or fairy dust, that sustains a spark. Steadiness over time is what makes it beautiful.

Violet begins to cry again. "But, how can I? If you're gone? Who will I talk to? I'm afraid he won't get it. You are the only ones who understand..." She hides her face, shoulders heaving, and now I know this isn't really about Connor at all.

"I know, sweetie. It'll be okay. You'll be okay." I make hushing sounds like she is a child, my resolve breaking. The oppressive sun beats down, the panels for Rain's baby's blanket in a crumpled pile on the wooden bench, Violet shaking in my arms, the weight of a deadline, of all we will miss. The weight of those we leave behind.

Eight

Evelyn

May 1945

We plan a simple ceremony at the Arlington Street Church in May. I choose a knee-length white dress, and Joseph buys a black suit with his employee discount. I clutch a bouquet of violets, and Joseph's eyes crinkle as I glide toward him, the organ playing "Ave Maria." His parents in the front pew, beaming, beside Aunt Maelynn, and our friends. My parents declined, blaming the travel, as though Boston was not merely a morning's drive, but a world away. (*To them*, Joseph reasoned, *it's a big city. Maybe it is.*) Their excuse stung, but theirs wasn't the face I ached to see, the teasing grin, the pair of suits at the top of the aisle that met me in my dreams, *he should be here.* Joseph kisses me when the priest pronounces us husband and wife, and my tears are of joy as well as sadness. Joy that he will always be mine, and sadness that there will always be a sliver of emptiness in every happiness we share.

When he lays me on our bed in our apartment, it is the first time for us both. Although I tried to entice him many times over the years, Joseph would not be taken by my touches or whispers, not even after midnight with my legs wrapped around him on Bernard Beach. Tonight he doesn't hesitate. He slips the straps from my shoulders, strokes my collarbone with his fingertips and then his lips. My dress falls to my ankles and I work the knot of his tie until it comes undone, his jacket in a heap on the floor. I undo the buttons of his shirt, exposing the sprout of dark hair on his chest. His hands roam until I am naked, unhooking my bra and sliding my stockings and panties over my knees and my feet to the floor. He guides his trousers and underwear to his ankles, his eyes never leaving my body, then he presses himself against me. He kisses me, and all I can think about is his skin against my skin and how soft it all feels, like petals. Then there is a sharpness like pain but it falls into something else, something new, and it somehow makes me want to cry, and laugh, but then it is over, and all his weight is on me, my chin on his shoulder, and his face in my hair, and all we are is breath. He kisses my cheeks and asks me if I am alright, and I giggle, a spontaneous sound, because for the first time in a long time, I am.

Months later, his father calls us, his voice shaking, "Come home, son…she's gone."

Walking through Stonybrook unearths a hurt I thought I buried. Joseph had returned once a month since he left, his mother disintegrating with each visit, but I couldn't bear it. The streets were full of ghosts.

Joseph's father is a shell when we see him, dressed in his nicest suit but empty and thin, like the mannequins at Joseph's store. We see my parents briefly at the funeral when they came to pay their respects. After Tommy died, I expected my mother to turn to me, for our grief to be the language we finally shared, but instead our pain wielded itself like a dagger, each day spent in silence dug a deeper wound. My father buried himself in work, my mother slept all day and smoked alone on the porch all night. When she saw me packing, she hid in her bedroom. She never asked where I was going or how she could reach me. My anger surfaces as we approach them in the dispersing crowd outside the church, daring her to speak first, to break our impasse.

My father steps forward, his bushy mustache muffling his congratulations on our wedding, clearly uncomfortable.

"Joseph's parents made it, even though she was sick," I say, an accusation, not an update.

My mother nods. "I heard. We're sorry for your loss, Joseph." Neither offer a place to stay for the night, rightly assuming we are staying with Mr. Myers, a preference I'm sure they clock. The family I coveted, now mine.

Leaving Joseph's father again feels like pushing off from a deserted island, knowing he is stranded ashore. On the train back to Boston, Joseph presses his head against the window, fogged with the cold. I say, "I don't want to go back again…it's too much."

Joseph doesn't argue; the guilt he carries from enlisting with Tommy and coming home alone an anchor he drags everywhere, no matter how I try to assuage him. Now this. A last year Joseph will never share with his mother, a goodbye he never said. His father left alone with no family or inn to keep. To be with me. A sacrifice, raw to the touch.

I think of the letters he wrote while overseas. A stack signed *Love*; envelopes bursting with longing, with hope of the future. I think of the jar on my porch brimming with violets, flowers meant for the girl I used to be. The note tucked inside, *Leaving won't stop me from loving you*. No question, no demand. A statement, asking nothing from me. It was almost worse that way, my silence a cruel response when all I wanted was to slip into a new life where grief couldn't find me. His devotion a gift when I had nothing, a steadiness I wish I knew how to offer him now, he who has given up everything for me.

Back in our apartment, we lay foot to head, resting on our elbows, and I run my fingers over the scar, exploring the jagged lines with the tips of my fingers for the first time.

"What happened?" I had never asked him. Our unspoken agreement, we never talk about the war.

"A bomb went off during a raid, we were in Rome...the day before Tommy was shot." His eyes clench in pain and he gets quiet. We learned of the details of Tommy's death later, the supplies his squad carried, the trap they walked into, the bullet in his stomach, the doctors who said he'd recover, the infection like snake venom that took him later.

"How did it feel?"

"I don't remember anything. I woke up in bandages."

"Nothing?"

"Nothing." Maybe he is trying to protect me. Or maybe he really has no memory of the moment, not pain, not the smell of burnt flesh, not even the sound of the explosion, only a white expanse in his mind like an uncharted map he refuses to explore.

"I killed her, you know," he says, voice quavering.

"Don't say that."

"My enlisting killed her, she worried so much it built up inside, and it killed her." I start to cry, his pain intimately mine. "And I left her again, when I knew she was dying, I left her... and now I left my dad..."

"Come here." I turn to face him and press him close, his wet cheeks against my chest. I hold him as he falls into sobs, all he says is a repeated apology, one not meant for me, that I feel I am overhearing, whispered into the ether. "I'm sorry... I'm so sorry."

I left Stonybrook to chase a bigger life, but when Joseph followed me, it shrank around us. Our whole world exists between these walls, and within this bed, a thin mattress in our tiny apartment on Tremont Street, a lodging house full of immigrants and crying babies. I wake to the sweet sound of trumpets and saxophones and guitars. Jazz music wafts through the open window like the scent of a freshly baked cake, and I drift in and out of sleep, unsure which part is a dream. At night we cling to each other, afraid if we don't one of us will get taken away by morning with the moon. Joseph has become my only solace, and I, his. This seems to comfort him, but it frightens me to love him this much. It's one more thing to lose. I don't know how to describe it, except in moments, notes on a page, that build to create something beautiful and uniquely ours. His arm wrapped around my abdomen in sleep. Threadbare sheets woven between our legs. The rough scratch of his chin against my bare shoulders as he kisses me awake. The movement of my body against his in the morning, his against mine, making love out of our joy and our anger and our hurt. We ease into the space where nothing else exists, collapsing into breath and holding on to each other, so as not to disappear. We lie together and I gaze at Joseph's clothes hanging in the closet, comforted by his things interspersed with mine, his jackets next to my dresses, his ties by my blouses. Sometimes if he works late at the store, I run my fingers over the fabric of his shirts, smell the soap and musk on his collars, as if to remind myself he lives there. That he will come home to me.

Joseph surprises me with tickets to the Boston Symphony Orchestra for our first anniversary. He confesses he's been stashing coins into the heels of his boots in our closet for months, saving so he could splurge on the thirty-cent admission. I leap into his arms and he spins me around the apartment and for the first time in a long time we laugh like we aren't shattered inside.

The night of the performance, Joseph wears his suit once more and I wear a shimmery gown I borrowed from Marjorie at work, and we take the train to Symphony station. It's impossible not to feel like we are entering something sacred as we step into the hall. Even Joseph, who has never played a note in his life, is hushed by the sanctity of it. He squeezes my hand, echoing my excitement as we navigate the crowd to find our seats. Gilded balconies adorned with wine-colored velvet provide a bird's-eye view of the orchestra, marble statues displayed in decorative alcoves. There are plush red-carpet aisles and burgundy exit doors, but otherwise the entire room is a sharp white. We are awed by the massive organ pipes, towering golden trunks that reach the ceiling, looming so high as to extend to heaven itself. Glimmering carvings outline the stage, an elaborate shield with the name Beethoven inscribed at the center.

I point it out to Joseph, and wave over one of the ushers. "Excuse me, I'm curious, why is Beethoven the only name carved into the border?"

The silver-haired gentleman peers over his glasses to meet my eyes. "That's a great story, miss. You see, the original designers of the venue wanted to pay homage to the very best musicians, ones that would never fall out of favor. But the only name everyone could agree on was Beethoven, so the rest of the plaques they made to honor other artists were left blank."

He grins at me, our shared appreciation of the symphony like a code between us, a club I could belong to. "Thank you." I beam. "It's our first time here."

"You're in luck, tonight they're performing Mozart's Concerto number ten. The dual arrangement is a sight to behold." He straightens up and helps another woman to her seat.

Classical music was the backdrop of my youth; my mother floated through our foyer greeting my father's work associates as I perched on the stairs, eyes closed, straining for the faint notes beneath the hum of chatter and clinking china. But this is the first time I hear the music as it is intended, and I am overcome. It's like splashing in a puddle for years before discovering the sea. Tears stream down my face as the piano concerto soars around us, and something inside of me cracks open, light streaming through the slightest tectonic shift of my sadness.

After the show, I hold Joseph's arm as we stroll through the city, night falling around us. I am taken back to years ago, walking to the trolley at dusk with Maelynn, after my first piano lesson at the Boston Conservatory. Arm linked in mine, she said, *Evelyn, you know you could be a concert pianist, right? You're so*

talented, and it would be a wonderful way to travel the country, to see
California, the world even, to begin to check things off your list.

The idea glitters inside me once more. To be a part of the
Boston Symphony is to exist inside music itself, to stand in the
center of the universe, a Milky Way melody, a chorus of plan-
ets swaying and spinning around my cadenza sun.

As Joseph and I undress for bed I can't shake the thrill of it,
like something amusing remembered in an inappropriate moment, twitching beneath the surface. As he falls asleep I whisper, "I'm going to play with them someday." And I lie awake,
the concert ringing in my ears, dreaming of the power of the
music up close, the steady hum inside of me mirrored and soaring through the pulsing air; an explosion of color and light, pure
emotion etched in song.

Last week we received word that death had come for his father.
Mrs. Myers was fifty-five when she died, and he lasted only
eleven months without her, passing at fifty-six. He had no symptoms, and no health problems to speak of. Death by heartbreak.

Guilt rushes into the crevices of my cluttered mind that
aren't already occupied by loss. My parents are both alive, but
we never speak. All this heaviness and yet I am only twenty-
one, and Joseph twenty-three. Is it possible that five years ago
we shared our first kiss, our eyes on the clouds floating by?

My thoughts drift as I study him in the glow of the city lights
seeping through our window. I allow myself to picture Joseph
before the war, before his limp. Joseph at eighteen, shoulders
broad, tanned skin, his thick hair ruffled by the wind, one hand
on my thigh as we lay in the sand on Bernard Beach.

He has been quiet since he heard the news and it scares me to
think how this loss will affect him. The first two brought him
closer to me, he hid his sorrow deep in the curves of my body,
but this feels different. The loss of his father, a man who lived
for nothing more than to run the Oyster Shell Inn, to love his

wife and his son, leaves Joseph adrift, a sailor without a compass or the light of the moon. I undress shyly tonight, wondering if he would like to be alone with his thoughts, in the way I needed to be alone in my grief.

When I slide under the covers, he pulls me toward him in one motion so I am against him, my toes touching his shins when we are face-to-face. He wraps his arms around my back, lifts me onto him. Then he does not move, does not kiss me. He holds me, gripping me tightly, and I cling to his cliff edge, terrified to let go, feeling all the sorrow, all the hurt pressed between our bodies, and away, into the night air.

Joseph lies awake, sheets kicked away in the suffocating and stale city heat. He has been irritable all evening, his leg bothering him. I sense him stewing and roll onto my side. "What's wrong?"

His eyes are on the ceiling, visible in the yellow glow of the streetlights. "I hate this apartment."

"Please don't start…"

"I want a house. I want to go home."

I shake my head, preparing my usual argument. After Joseph inherited the Oyster Shell he became haunted by its emptiness. "Our life is here. Our jobs, our friends, Aunt Maelynn… everything."

A flimsy defense, at best. Coworkers I began to think of as friends quit to start families, moved out of the city to Newton or Quincy. Younger girls replaced them at their typewriters, bubbly and incessant. Maelynn returns from a new city with a new boyfriend seemingly each time we call, barely contained by her teaching job at Mrs. Mayweather's. Maelynn, a star-shaped peg that won't fall in place, a fact tolerated by the school because she's an acclaimed writer, a trophy they flaunt. Her tether to Boston growing thin, an alluring breeze all it would take to carry her away.

When she's in town she invites us over, and sometimes I go, desperate for that feeling I had when I lived with her, knees tucked beneath me on her couch as she entertained painters and poets, inhaling their smoke and their stories. The promise I held in their eyes at seventeen. Maelynn at my side, smelling like peppermint and something I couldn't name; her dresser covered with amber bottles of ancient oils, vouching for me, her priceless jewel, a pianist who was going places, talented enough for private lessons at the conservatory.

But we haven't been to see her in months. Blaming our time apart on Brookline being too far, especially after a long day of work. Blaming it on the green line, always delayed, unpredictable. I don't tell her how it feels to be around her friends now, the awareness of them turning away while they stand before me, a twentysomething stenographer, riffraff who had wandered in from the South End, ears cocked for a more interesting conversation.

"Our life is in Stonybrook," Joseph says, nearly pleading.

"Not anymore."

"But it could be."

I roll away, facing the wall. "Don't do this, okay? It's late."

He touches my hip. "I know you're scared."

"I like our life the way it is," I say, not even convincing myself.

The future I had imagined for myself, of music, of exploring and adventure, has settled into the steady drone of typing, elbows pressing on the trolley, steep rent payments and crowded markets. Out of time and money and energy to desire more than my feet up at the end of each day. Maelynn made it all sound so glamorous, easy, to see the world at my age, the men who would sweep her off to London and Greece. She'd leave them behind, returning with cashmere scarves and hand-painted bowls and tales of her escapades. She never explained how she had money to travel or how she made a living during that time, and I didn't ask in the way I wouldn't ask a magician to lift his sleeves. She was young and beautiful, and the world was hers. It *could* be that simple, couldn't it?

For Maelynn, maybe. But where have I gone, really? The only city I was banished to, and stayed, building a half-life with Joseph that has caged us both. Stonybrook is pink sunrises and indigo twilights, wildflowers and waves lapping against the sandbar. Boston is brick and brownstone, muddled masses in the streets, a feeling of impermanence that leaves me uneasy. And yet, at any minute I could take the train to the end of the line, hop off and start anew.

Going back to Stonybrook means going back to Stonybrook forever. It means opening the Oyster Shell Inn, raising the fifth generation of Myers on the same shore, the life expected for Joseph, the life he gave up when he followed me here. The life erased by Pearl Harbor, by the thick stench of the departing steam train, and wives and daughters and mothers huddled around radios, and Tommy's stomach infection spread and he wasn't coming home and I forgot how to breathe on my own, and there was no Oyster Shell Inn, just a big empty house, and Mrs. Myers was dying and Mr. Myers became a skeleton and was it all a dream? I was lost and falling and ran to the only other place that ever felt safe, but then like a mirage Joseph was there, and he scooped me up and laid me in what became our bed, and together we soaked in the sadness until like fawns we found our feet, but those feet lost their path home, we pushed Stonybrook from our minds until it ceased to exist. How can there be an Oyster Shell Inn without any of them? How will we ever fill its sun-soaked rooms when all I want to do is draw the shades?

He jolts up, gesturing around in the dark. "You like this? We can barely afford this shit apartment and there's a massive house waiting for us back home."

Joseph never curses.

"Let's sell it. If we aren't going home, why keep it?" he asks, his voice raw.

"We can't sell it."

"What do you want from me, Evelyn?"

"I don't know." I pull my knees to my chest.

"I get what it means, moving back, and you don't want a baby, but..." He pauses. "If we started a family, we could run the inn together...and if we were back in a place you loved, I know it would make you so happy."

My face tightens. "You think I don't want a baby?"

"You never want to talk about it."

"Because I'm terrified." I bite the inside of my cheek, play with a fiber fraying on the sheets, anything to keep my tears at bay. To keep us in this limbo, this alternate life, this place where memories can't find me.

"Oh, sweetheart, come here." He reaches his arms to me and I scoot over, closing the gap between us, the thick heat compressed like an accordion.

I wipe my dripping nose with the back of my wrist. "But what if we have one, and something happens? I can't lose anyone else... I can't."

"We can't hide out here forever." He brushes a stray curl out of my eyes. "But if you're just afraid... I am, too, and we can be scared together." He pauses. "What do you want?"

I take a deep breath, shift to meet his gaze, and say the words that have rattled around my head for months, ones I have been afraid to admit even to myself. "I want a baby."

"You do?"

Every time I pass a mother pushing a stroller, I feel a surge of envy I batten down like shutters in a storm, picture a baby that looks like Joseph, running along the shore that still sings me to sleep, the place we both belong. "I want to go home." I wrap my arms around his neck and he lifts me onto him, burying his face in my hair.

"I know this will make us so happy. Thank you, Evelyn, I love you so much." But as he kisses me, all I can feel is the rush of fear in my chest, like a riptide overtaking me.

Nine

Thomas

September 2001

My rental, a silver Audi, smells like stale cigarettes and something lemony and artificial emanating from a pine tree hanging on the rearview. The sky is almost absurdly blue, and I open the windows to the fresh air as I turn off the highway. I hate rental cars, having to acclimate to new dials and switches, fumbling for levers to adjust the seat, but it doesn't make sense to own a car in the Upper East Side. I told Ann we could more than swing it, hell, Goldman would probably get me a car if I asked. But it's easier to rent one the rare weekends we disappear upstate, or for those times we drive to see specialists, like today.

I tell Ann, we're in New York City. People travel *here* for the best doctors. But she found some neurologist outside Green-wich, specializing in migraines, and I finally conceded and moved some meetings around. I've been putting her off for years. Climbing the ladder so quickly, the youngest executive director in the history of the company, grinding eighty-hour weeks, I'd be more concerned if I *didn't* get headaches. Who has the time to take a day off to drive to Connecticut for a bunch of tests, only to find out that they can't tell me what's wrong? Or that there's something wrong, but they can't fix it? Like my heart murmur. Or Ann's eggs. So many waiting rooms, months after months of needles, the bolts of her exposed spine turned away from me, leaning on the pedestal sink in our bathroom, braced for impact. Hating myself each time I drove the tip into her exposed flesh, knowing the jabs could be futile, the hormones relentless, for putting her through all this, only to be devastated when the embryo didn't take. For what? Year after year of trying. Ann's face tightening when well-meaning colleagues asked her when we were going to have kids. The nights I held my sobbing wife in our bed while we grappled with the reality that it wasn't going to happen for us.

I hoped for kids, too, but more than that, I wanted Ann to be able to be a mother, to give her everything she wanted. We knew couples who adopted, who jumped through hoops for years, who had false starts, birth mothers who changed their minds. In the end it was Ann who called it all off, she couldn't take any more, we had been through enough. We kept our struggle private, let people assume what they wanted, our heartbreak a secret we shouldered. We committed instead to our work, to each other, to making the most of the life we built, to the freedoms a child-free existence could bring. Late nights at the office without coordinating sitters, after-work drinks with clients, jetting off to the Hamptons. We commented on how our colleagues' careers stalled after their priorities shifted, our friends frazzled and exhausted and unrecognizable. We celebrated our promotions with expensive bottles of wine and fresh sushi rolls, things she couldn't enjoy if she were pregnant, consolation prizes we offered each other, reasons it wasn't meant to be.

But sometimes I imagine what it could've been like. Ann hand in hand with her little blonde miniature, pointing at seals at the

Central Park Zoo. Chasing after their cousins on Bernard Beach.
She would be a bit like my own mom, the clear matriarch, me
relegated to the background, like my dad. I wouldn't mind; Ann
was built to run a company, a family, the world. She left the Mid-
west as soon as she could, her acceptance to NYU her ticket to a
new life. She moved into the dorm across the street from mine,
we met swapping clothes at the laundromat around the corner
that reeked of wet socks and Chinese takeout. We bonded over
our embarrassing lack of local knowledge and kept each other
company during marathon study sessions in the library.

New York City felt like mine, like me. The organization of a
planned city grid, subway lines, people walking with purpose,
how easy it was to get around, find your way, and I was taken
with Ann, how forcefully she navigated her own path. There was
nothing keeping me in Stonybrook. I had no interest in inheriting the Oyster Shell, and in fairness, my parents never pushed it
on any of us. They hoped I'd fall for some girl in town, always
urging me to go out on Saturday nights. But all I knew about
love is that it was a reason people stayed put, that it was mea-
sured by what you gave up. It never seemed worth it. Until Ann.

We were together for nearly five years before I proposed.
I never had any doubt she was the one, never needed to date
around to be sure. But Ann's parents are divorced; she and
her sisters grew up bouncing between houses on weekends and
holidays, so she wasn't sure she believed in the institution. So I
waited, let her lead. A piece of paper binding us legally wasn't
important to me, we were as committed as anyone could be.
Then her younger sister got married, a big wedding in Boise. I
never thought of Ann as the type of girl who needed permission for anything, never mind something as big as marriage, but
that's what that wedding was to Ann, with its buffet overflowing with mediocre Midwestern fare, poufy bridesmaids and an
overzealous band. Permission to make our own mistakes, to
try. She drank a ton of champagne and confessed she wanted

to get married, too, that she felt like she could, that we should. The next morning, sober and emboldened, she confirmed it was still true. She basically proposed to me. I bought a ring the next weekend.

We went into our marriage with eyes wide-open. At some point, as hard as it is, you have to be realistic; dreams don't come true because you want them to, and nothing lasts forever. This plan my parents concocted is so twisted, the same way love is glamorized by books and movies, something to die for, love proven through sacrifice. It's cowardice, disguised as devotion. Love is giving the injections, it's the spots knotted black and blue from the needles, it's knowing I could live without Ann because she would want me to go on, rather than to martyr myself in her name. How much stronger they would be to stay, to eke out every last second of their life together.

I tune the radio, try to redirect my thoughts as I near the doctor's office. The only thing I miss about driving is listening to the news, calming in a different way than reading a folded paper while crammed on the subway. My BlackBerry starts pinging, probably an analyst needing to check something. Or another voicemail from Mom.

Ann says I have to stop avoiding them, that it won't fix anything, or make them change their minds. But I'm furious that they've put us in this position to be their conspirators. Nothing about this is okay. I am not shocked, knowing how they are. Jane said pretty much the same, though I didn't want to hear her let them off so easy. I wanted her to be pissed like I am, riled up and ready to fight, like the old Jane. But she's not wrong, it *is* something they would do.

Their relationship embarrassed me growing up. The way Mom would perch on Dad's lap after dinner, or sit between his knees on a shared towel on the beach, instead of keeping their distance like normal parents. Jane is convinced Mom is the one we need to sway, and Dad will go along with whatever she decides, and she's probably right. Dad has always been putty when it comes to Mom. I gave him a hard time about it one night when I was young, something about him being on a short leash, a phrase I heard a guy say at school that I didn't fully understand, but repeated for effect. He stopped what he was fixing, and looked at me, more serious than I had ever seen. *Your mom gave things up for me, son. To move back, to raise you kids here, to reopen the inn. I have never forgotten that. You shouldn't either.*

I didn't understand them then, putting each other over their own individual happiness. And now, dying for each other. I'd do anything for Ann, anything but this. I can't condone it, and at this point even the knowledge of their plan feels reckless, complicit.

Which is what I tried to tell Violet, but she's even worse than our parents. She reaches for justification, trying to convince me to make the most of our time left, like I'm the one who set the ticking clock. I thought I had Jane on my side. She can be a lot, but at least she's logical. Or so I thought, until she emails me an invite to some show four months from now, in January, at the Boston Symphony Orchestra. She wrote that her coworker Marcus pitched the idea for a community outreach event, "a performance to highlight local pianists," and she and Mom would be one of many to perform. Marcus arranged the whole thing, got us all tickets. She's mentioned his name—even to me, and we barely talk—more often than is normal for any colleague. So obviously, they're sleeping together. She's weird about relationships, and it's none of my business. I don't really care what she does as long as it doesn't create issues for the family again. But this move took me aback. She's usually unyielding, especially when it comes to Mom.

I don't want my mom to suffer, of course I don't. I hate everything about this. Her prognosis. The pain she kept from us. That a mother's illness could possibly be divisive. My anger that won't allow me to be there for her, for them both, because they've forced us to choose sides. The idea of losing her in little ways then all at once…but doctors aren't psychics, they can't predict the future and sometimes bodies respond in ways we don't expect. New treatments could become available, clinical trials, experimental drugs. Ann and I tried to the brink of breaking, contorted our hope and followed its faintest shadow until we had nothing left. It was the only way we could live with ourselves. There is no way to know what the future holds, not really, if you cut it off at its knees. I can't believe Jane is indulging her in this way, fulfilling a dying wish based on an arbitrary death date Mom chose. I don't know, in my mind the only leverage we had over them was holding out together, a united front that condemned this decision, and now I feel as powerless as I am.

Another series of buzzes. We pushed that meeting, what possibly can't wait a few hours until I get back? I try to peek at the screen and miss my turn, throw the phone into the console, ignoring it as it rings, circling back around, so I don't catch everything the broadcaster says.

"…plane…crashed into the World Trade Center…"

I brake without meaning to, turning up the dial. *The hell?*

"…something devastating has happened. There are unconfirmed reports of a plane crashing into the towers. We are trying to get more information. There is smoke billowing out of one of the towers, a very disturbing scene on the ground, we are trying to figure out what happened, all we know so far is a plane flying lower-than-normal altitude, appears to have crashed into the middle of one of the towers…"

I pull over. Call Ann and get an error message: *Your call cannot be completed, please try again later.* Call again. *Your call cannot be completed, please try again later, your call cannot be completed, please try again later.* Call the office. *Your call cannot be completed, please try again later, your call cannot be completed, please try again later.* Call Ann again. Nothing.

My meeting this morning. In that very tower. Postponed.

Holy shit. Holy fucking shit.

Panic rises. *Was the pilot drunk?* My hands shake on the wheel. I know some of those people, their poor families… I try to take deep breaths, the coverage on the radio drowned by the thud in my chest. Ann is uptown. I'm okay. I'm sitting here, somehow, in this car.

The near miss of it. *Oh my god.* A freak thing.

Then the second plane hit.

I nearly break down the front door wrenching it open. My mom and dad leap up from the couch, news blaring. I rush in white-faced and unsteady and lean down to grip Mom in the tightest hug. Between sobs I stammer, "I'm sorry, Ma. I'm so sorry." She almost falters under my weight, the shock of it all.

I turn toward Dad and clutch him, desperate. "Dad, I've been awful to you. Please, I'm sorry, I'm so sorry."

"It's okay, son. It's okay." He is at a loss, and speaks in a low voice, patting my back. "You're safe, thank god…we've been losing our minds, trying to reach you. Where's Ann?"

I pull away and stumble, trying to explain, rubbing my forehead raw. "I don't know. I can't reach her. Phones are down. I don't know." My legs are about to give out; I sink onto the coffee table, my head in my hands.

"I don't understand. How are you here?"

I shake my head. "Ann…she has been begging me to go see this specialist not far from here. I've been having really bad headaches, but I never have the time. But she kept bothering me about it. She made an appointment for me this morning… I was supposed to be at the North Tower today. I rescheduled my meeting for tomorrow. *Because Ann didn't want to lose me.*"

"Oh, Thomas." Mom crumples beside me.

"And when I heard it on the radio, I tried to get back to the city, to Ann, but they're saying everything is shut down. Trains, the bridges, there's no way in. Phones are all out of service. I'm freaking out." My breath is raggedy, unstable. "I don't know where she is, if she's safe… I couldn't be alone, I didn't know what to do. So, I drove here… I think I sped the entire way. I don't know if I stopped at one red light. I can't remember."

Dad's voice breaks, and he puts his arm around me. "We're so glad you're here."

The tragedy plays out on loop on TV, surreal footage I can't wrap my head around. Smoke billowing out of offices I was supposed to be inside, the Twin Towers engulfed. Mom grips my hand. When was the last time I held Mom's hand? I don't know what is happening, but I'm terrified. I'm terrified and feel my throat closing, I can't breathe. *Ann.*

We watch the banners screaming across the bottom of the television screen, "Planes Crash into World Trade Center." We watch, frozen where we sit. We watch, waiting for answers. None of this makes sense. Nothing makes sense as the news team pieces together scattered information, but there are no answers and their anchor masks fall away. They weep as the cameras roll, the rules we once played by shattered. All I can think about is my wife, racking my brain for any hint of where her meetings were, what she may have told me, anything that will cut through my panic. All I can see is the crumbled towers, the debris and ash filling the streets. The black smoke billowing. The endless blue sky, stained.

We watch as the South Tower collapses into ash and smoke.

I feel my scream, but nothing comes out. Mom's hand flies to her open mouth. Dad doesn't move, rapt by the horror on the screen. On the table there is a vase of sunflowers from the garden, the sky through the window still cloudless and impossibly blue.

I call Ann's cell and her office, over and over, even though it won't go through, furious with myself for being so far away, for how futile it is pushing these buttons when I should be running to her, but I am stuck here, powerless, desperate to hear her voice, replaying our rushed goodbye this morning. Did I even kiss her before she left? What was the last thing I said as she slipped out the door?

"Let's try Violet and Jane again. Tell them you're safe, at least." Mom says they tried calling me as soon as they saw the news but kept getting my voicemail, probably directed there while I dialed Ann on repeat. When they spoke to Violet she was home, staying by her phone. She hadn't been able to reach her kids and she didn't want them to get the answering machine. Connor has gone to pick up Patrick from school. They leave another message for Jane, likely summoned to the news station.

We watch the ash-filled sky overtake our screen.

We watch the collapse of the North Tower.

Dad puts his arms around Mom. I'm frantic, pacing.

We keep dialing. *Your call cannot be completed, please try again later.*

All these people…all their families.

Ann. *Where are you?*

My phone rings and we all jump. I rip it off the table, nearly dropping it. "Ann?" My shoulders collapse in relief. "Oh my god. Thank god." My nose runs, and I wipe it on my sleeve. "I love you. I love you so much." I can barely hear her through the crackle and noise, something about a pay phone, people waiting, she walked to Brooklyn, across the bridge, she's okay.

She's okay. The call drops, and I hang my head, my relief nearly unbearable. "She's safe." My breath ragged, voice choked, I tell them, "She's safe. Oh god, oh god, she's okay. I thought I lost her… I thought…" I sob, hiding my crumpled face in my arms.

Ten

Evelyn

August 1951

I wake throughout the night, not because Jane's crying, but because she's not crying. I need to make sure she can cry, she can breathe, so I jolt from frenzied nightmares with a desperate need to check on her. Tonight is no different. Sleep evades my body, still sore from giving birth, my mind races. I slip away from Joseph and pad down the hall, my resentment mounting with each nighttime feed. Up once more, haunting the house, while he remains sound asleep on his stomach, the unbothered slumber of fatherhood, unscarred from pregnancy, untethered to this tiny being, all consumption and need. After four years in our tiny apartment, I had nearly forgotten how sprawling this place was, our innkeeper's quarters separate from the guests', three whole bedrooms for us, a place meant to grow a family. Our future laid out, a blueprint for a good life.

The Oyster Shell Inn fascinated me when I was a girl. There was a comfort in its messiness, its mismatched floral furniture, everything soft and plush. The dust on the bookshelves in the study, granules of sand in the foyer, everything smelling faintly as though it had once been wet. The way the light fell hazily through the windows, inviting you to cuddle up in an armchair. The odd little doors that led to storage nooks, no taller than a child, but if you knew to push aside the boxes and brush away spiderwebs, they connected in narrow passageways. Joseph and Tommy and I played hide-and-seek during the slow season, contorting in the dingy crawlspaces, straining to hear footsteps. I'd wrap my arms around my knees, eyes closed tight, and wish for the Oyster Shell to be my home.

I steal into Jane's room, across from another bedroom, empty except for an ironing board and drying racks. Once intended for Joseph's siblings, hoped-for-babies who never came, his mother used it instead to press the linens. Joseph said it was better to leave the third bedroom as is for now, that we could fill and decorate it when we had more children.

More children. He always tacks it on at the end of a sentence, like it is something to add to my grocery list. More butter, more milk, more children. Romanticizing a big family before we even had our first, before I knew the white-hot pain of labor, the terror of hearing the umbilical cord was wrapped around her neck. Before swollen breasts, nights blurring into days, before distrusting the murky landscape of my own mind. The rocking and holding and bouncing, her intoxicating newborn smell and the overwhelming depth of my affection, the feeling of always being on the brink of tears. How much I could love her, this tiny person I made, that I just met. How little desire I had to put myself through it again, to tear myself in two in childbirth, only to split myself further in motherhood, slicing and slicing until I am a wisp of a woman, unrecognizable.

I slip into the nursery, a faint light from the lamp on her dresser illuminates her. It's funny to me that someone so little can have her own dresser yet here it is, one Joseph made as she grew inside me. He loved all the projects, painting the room, build-

ing the crib. I don't think I have ever seen him so happy. Ever
since we got home from the hospital Joseph has shouldered the
operations of the inn, open for a few months now, after weeks
of cleaning and restoration, a brand-new carved sign declaring
The Oyster Shell Inn and *Now Open* since May, the guestrooms
filling as the temperature rose. Which leaves me alone with
Jane, and the days and nights spent feeding and washing dia-
pers and hanging towels to dry stretching endlessly before me.
Stirrings of longing for my old life, when hours were lost playing piano, when I had lists of dreams, things I was sure I would
have done by now, places I would have seen. How improbable
it all seems now, how long ago it feels. No way out of this new
reality, this all-consuming motherhood. Demanding more of
me than I could have imagined, the saddest happiness I've ever
felt, because she's already bigger today than yesterday, already
a little less mine. I'm already missing the baby she is, desperate
to remember moments I'm certain to forget.

When I was pregnant, Joseph ran his fingers over my stretched
skin, put his ear to my stomach and whispered to the baby at
night, but his affection couldn't calm my nerves. As we packed
boxes he approached timidly, asked, "How are you feeling?" and
wrapped his arms around me and my growing belly, holding us
both. I couldn't answer. He squeezed me close, then left me to
my thoughts, swirling storm clouds in my mind. I could never
have handled the truth of all to come, the certainty I have now,
that those nine months were the easiest part.

There is silence in the hall as I approach Jane's room. Before
she was born, we considered different names, but when I held
her, I knew she was Jane. Jane, like Jane Eyre, from the novel
Aunt Maelynn bought me from that bookstore in Boston when
I was homesick. Jane Eyre, an independent and fiery girl who
believed in and sought out love. There could be no other name
for the beauty I saw in my arms, the sudden fullness in my heart
as she clutched me, burrowed into my neck like I was the safest

home. Before Jane I couldn't understand why everyone talked about a baby's fingers and toes, but now I know. I could sit with her in my lap all day and touch the soft pads of her feet, watch her toes curl, and her impossibly tiny fingers ball into fists. Even at one week old she can have her own dresser, and her own room, and she can hold my whole world in her tiny hands.

Joseph was right. I am happy we had her, I'm happy we're home. My childhood wish, whispered into the darkness, granted by kismet or grand design, or sheer force of will. The boy seeking me, all the times I've been found. But I am also scared. Scared because so many babies stop breathing, and eat the wrong things, and get sick and hurt, and people we love get taken away for reasons I'll never understand.

Jane sleeps on her stomach, pudgy little arms by her ears. I stride close, put the back of my wrist near the tiny O of her mouth, wait for the tingle of her breath on my skin. I wait for five breaths before I exhale, lean my chin against the top of the crib, watching her, pleading to a god I'm not sure I believe in, bargaining everything I have to keep her safe.

Joseph

November 1953

Mrs. Saunders gives her bun a pat to be sure her hair is in place, and chides, "Support his neck, dear." Evelyn does not reply, but her lips tighten. Thomas cries in her arms. She stands, bouncing him as she circles the sofa. Only two guestrooms are occupied tonight, a newlywed couple who has barely left their room and an older man visiting his daughter, so we have the place mostly to ourselves. If it were a warmer day, she would walk him along Sandstone Lane, but winter has come full force now, night falling early and bringing a cutting wind. Jane sits by the fireplace and throws blocks across the room.

"Hush, Thomas…it's okay, baby. It's okay." Evelyn coos at him but her face is stone. A block hits her in the ankle and she turns with a scowl. "Jane, enough. Stop throwing."

"Evelyn, have you fed him? That's the sound of a hungry baby." Mrs. Saunders's voice is shrill, though she sits calmly on our couch, her hands folded in her lap. Her mother doesn't seem to remember this is not Evelyn's first baby, or how she managed with Jane without help.

When we moved back to Stonybrook a few years ago, she dreaded returning even to the periphery of her parents' world. Evelyn hadn't spoken to them since my father's funeral, and even then, their conversations were strained. But when we stepped back into the foyer of the inn, even with dust-coated furniture and the rotted wood on the front porch, I could imagine our children running through the field behind the house, could see a piano tucked into the study and Evelyn and I directing guests toward the beach. I looked at Evelyn, desperate to know if she saw what I did, and she laced her fingers with mine. The Oyster Shell Inn. Our home.

We dropped by that first afternoon, Evelyn begrudgingly, and knocked on their door to let them know we were back, and here to stay. The porch was littered with leaves, the yard overgrown, the brass knocker tarnished. The front door creaked as Mrs. Saunders appeared behind it, squinting her eyes against the daylight. She had always been thin, but there was something eerie about her structure, like she, too, had been neglected inside the house.

If she was surprised to see us, she didn't show it. "I was wondering about the inn, sitting there vacant all these years. Your father is working, but I'll relay the message." Her eyes flickered down to Evelyn's curved belly, but her face gave nothing— not anger or joy, just a sunken expression as she said, "I never thought I'd see you pregnant. I thought…"

Evelyn cut her off as she turned away, "Yeah, well, you didn't seem that interested in our marriage, so I don't expect you to spend time with our baby, don't worry."

We didn't see much of her after that. She never came to Bernard Beach, and there was only the occasional lamplight and glow of her cigarettes on the front porch after dinner. We were busy with the inn, with Jane, with navigating our new life that was a strange, inverse reflection of our old one. Then Mr. Saunders died, a heart attack at sixty-one, and Evelyn's mother didn't have any friends or other family to turn to. Her husband had rarely been home, never showed her affection, but I assumed his lingering cigar smoke as he came and went filled the house with the pretense of his company. After he passed away, she must have felt alone enough to swallow her pride, and when another grandchild came along, a boy, she found herself at our door. Evelyn, delirious with exhaustion and desperate for an extra set of hands, accepted their ceasefire.

"Yes, I've fed him. Of course I have. He cries all the time, fed or not." Jane throws her blocks again. Evelyn's eyes harden.

"He should be changed," Mrs. Saunders insists. "I thought he smelled when I held him."

"He is fed and changed, I told you, he just cries. Please stop."

A knock on the swinging door from the sitting room stops the conversation short, a white-haired gentleman, our frequent guest, pokes his head in to ask for extra towels. Evelyn hands me Thomas and follows him out, and I am grateful for the diversion. Thomas calms from screams to a low moan. My heart slows, and I hadn't realized it was racing until that moment, Evelyn's stress acutely mine.

That night as we get ready for bed, Evelyn is quiet, lost in her thoughts.

She gets under the covers and turns toward me. "We did the right thing, right? Letting my mother back in our lives?"

"I know she can be tough sometimes—"

"All of the time."

"Okay, all of the time. But she doesn't have anyone else, and besides Maelynn, she is the only family we have. I'd give anything for my parents to know our kids."

"So would I—you know I loved your parents. But my parents, they're different." She pauses, winding a strand of hair around her finger. "Do you know I haven't cried about my father? Not even when I've been alone. He was so busy working, I never really knew him, and he never tried to know me. And I am still so angry at them for acting like Tommy was the only one worth anything. When he died it was like—" She stops herself, and sighs. "And then she comes here telling me how to raise my kids? Like she knows anything about it? She sent me away. What kind of mother does that?" She pauses, then quieter, "What kind of daughter doesn't cry when her father dies?"

I open my mouth to reassure her just as Thomas screams, awake again in his crib. She sighs, then yanks back the covers to tend to him.

"Want me to?" I ask, but she waves me off, agitated. He is a much more trying baby than Jane was, and I see the gray circles under Evelyn's eyes in the mornings after a long night of feeding and rocking him.

I feel guilty sometimes, for pushing for children, but four years was a long time to stay alone in the island of our bedroom, holed up in sadness under our covers. Those four years became a new lifetime; Tommy's death split our life into halves—a before, an after. The memories of before a hazy daydream, the three of us suntanned and bobbing in the gentlest waves; the after marked by my limp, by loss, by the feeling of being scraped out from the inside and somehow standing upright, as though I wasn't made of rapidly escaping air. Running all those years didn't change anything, our grief lay dormant here, awaiting our return.

After we settled in, I bought a secondhand piano, a wooden Baldwin, and surprised Evelyn, a scarf over her eyes as I led her to the study where I had polished it until it looked new. She played concerts in the evenings, Jane in her lap, as the guests sat clutching glasses of scotch or wine, the windows open to the salt air, seeming at peace once more. But when Evelyn told me she was pregnant for a second time, her face was white. She withdrew, brushed me off when I reached for her belly. She didn't want to talk names, even many months in, "Just in case." But on the day she gave birth to our son she was overjoyed again, smiling in a way I hadn't seen in months. She held him and stroked his cheek, Jane cuddled up on the hospital bed next to them.

I sat beside them, kissed her forehead. "How about Thomas?"

She had tears in her eyes, whispering, "Thomas," and she reached for me, and I reached for them all. Our family, now four.

Now that Thomas is a few weeks old, I feel Evelyn drifting further into herself again. I watch her in the hallway, swaying the baby in her arms as he wails, her body hunched with exhaustion. She is twenty-eight but this second pregnancy aged her, her cinched robe hides the soft pooch of a maternal stomach, the faintest stretch marks on her swollen breasts. She moves with the cadence of a sentry on duty as she rocks him. This time, she is not drifting with me, into our secret, sad oasis. She is drifting to a place that is becoming hard to wrench her out of. A tense, distant place.

"Let me take him." I approach her in the hall, cautious.

"Oh, now you want to help?" She scowls, turning him away from me.

I follow her into Thomas's room. "What's that supposed to mean?"

"Convenient." She makes a loud shushing sound in his ear. "You sleep right through it in the middle of the night."

"We talked about this." My voice is even, treading on hot coals. "I have to work during the day."

"And what do I do?" she snaps, razor sharp over Thomas's screams.

"I know your days are hard too. I'm not saying that," I say, my hands up in retreat.

"Just forget it. Go, get your precious rest." She shoos me away as she sits in the rocker, eyes closed, Thomas pressed against her chest, too furious to look at me.

I thought moving back was the answer, if I could only get her to the sea, we could recover some of that ease we craved, but now I am not sure. There are rare moments when I glimpse the old Evelyn. Glimpses that gave me hope she would again find her way back to us. One summer night as we cooked together, Jane in her high chair, dark clouds rolling in. Suddenly it started to rain, then pour, and she ran to grab the sheets from the line. I turned off the stove so dinner wouldn't burn, rushing to help. She stood unclipping pins and balling towels in her arms, racing the storm. Then she stopped, drenched. She tilted her chin up at the sky and laughed. I wanted to join her, to grab her and kiss her, to share what she was feeling, but I stopped in the doorway. It seemed sacred, the way she smiled at the rain. It was fleeting, if I had looked down I would have missed it.

She stopped laughing when she caught my eye, but called out, "Isn't it beautiful, Joseph?"

I couldn't look away from her, the droplets falling down her cheeks. She ran in to meet me, her dress soaked through. And she kissed me. But those moments were outweighed by the heaviness she carried, like rain-soaked laundry straining the clothesline, dragging it toward the earth.

After a day jammed with late checkouts and a difficult-to-trace roof leak, my leg throbs from overuse. I reach for my pain pills on the nightstand, and knock Evelyn's book, a tattered copy of *Jane Eyre* she is rereading for the hundredth time, onto the floor. When I lean down to pick it up a folded page falls out, *Dreams* written in bold letters and circled in a cloud.

"It's been a while since I've seen one of these," I say, lifting the crinkled sheet and turning it over in my palm. "I didn't know you still had them."

"It's stupid, Joseph. I was using it as a bookmark." She grabs it from my hands, stuffing it back inside the book without finding her page.

"Evelyn Myers, I have never known you to think a dream is a stupid thing," I tease. "I think you should keep it up. Why not make a new list?"

She used to smile every time I called her by her married name. A name I heard her repeating once, as she applied her lipstick in the mirror, when she didn't think I was listening. She smiles now, but it holds a trace of sadness. "Well, maybe Evelyn Saunders didn't, but Evelyn Myers has no time to spend on a young girl's dreams."

"It'll get easier, with the kids. You'll see." I kiss the backs of her knuckles, and wish her good-night.

After a moment she asks, "What if we make one together? A dream list, for us."

"Marrying you, running this inn together, that's my list." I trace her arm with my fingers. "Making you happy, starting a family...to be honest those are the only dreams I've ever had."

Her face sours. "I hate when you do this."

"Do what?"

"Act like everything is perfect."

I suck in, gut punched. "You're twisting my words."

"I barely have a second to shower. You're killing yourself running this place on your own. *This* is really what you always wanted?"

"Damn it, Evelyn." I pull away from her. "Yes. This *is* what I want. It doesn't mean it's perfect. But most people would be happy here." My stomach tightens with her contradictions, this homecoming she asked for, that she said she wanted, that she treated like a death march. "But not you, no, no it's never enough."

"You try watching the kids all day and see how you feel."

"You wanted this. You said you wanted kids."

She tips her head back at the ceiling, infuriated at my incompetence, apparently, my insistence on reality, the terms we created somehow my fault. "It doesn't mean it's all I wanted."

"Okay, so you unclog toilets and scrub showers and fix the roof and I'll go play on the beach with the kids if it's that horrible for you."

She lowers her eyes at me, her voice cold. "You say things like that and it makes me hate you."

I should backpedal, I know how hard it's been on her, I know her days are long and draining and tedious, I know life with a toddler and newborn is far from easy, but I'm too mad, I'm too tired, and I'm sick of feeling like the bad guy, the one who always has to say the right thing, do the right thing, be patient and understanding and gentle, never upset her, never overstep, never ask for anything because I've already asked for this one big thing, to be with her, to go home. "Am I wrong? Or do you have the better end of the deal here?"

"*You* made the deal. That's the point."

"We both agreed to this. I didn't force you into anything."

Her arms cross, defiant. "Well, maybe I've changed my mind."

I reel back. "What's that supposed to mean?"

"I don't know."

"Well, that's a pretty big statement."

"Well, I feel pretty trapped."

"Trapped?" I ask, incredulous. "Okay, then, go. Go, if that's how you feel. If this life is so terrible, and you hate me, and you hate being with the kids and all you want is to go play piano and live in some made-up fantasyland where you have no responsibilities."

"Don't talk to me like that."

"I'm saying go! You're trapped? Then go."

"Like that's a real choice," she says, pure venom.

"I'm not forcing you to be here!" I yell. "I don't want you here if you don't want to be."

"Just forget it, okay? You don't understand."

"Great, sure." I throw my hands up. "You hate our whole life and I'm supposed to forget about it."

"Now who's twisting words." She storms off to brush her teeth, tossing her book onto the bed as she goes. It hits me in the knee, the paper poking out, taunting me. I wait to hear the water rush in the bathroom, unfold her list and steal a peek, fuming, before sliding it back in its hiding place. The words float in my mind, a line added to the bottom of the list, in different ink, fresh.

Perform with the Boston Symphony Orchestra.

A banished dream, a relic from another time, brought back to life. I lie awake long after she stomps back in, pulls the covers over her shoulders, her back to me as she clicks off her lamp. Afraid for her again, afraid, for the first real time, for us. Afraid she may go, that she may be happier leaving us all behind, and that this time I won't be able to find her and bring her home.

Eleven

Joseph

October 2001

We are driving down the coast, adventuring to cross another
line off a list from long ago. *Touch the sky.* A biplane ride, open
to the air as we climb, gliding over the tree line, autumn co-
lours at peak, above the shoreline we have only known from
the ground. It astonishes me, after all this time, that something
imprinted so deeply can still be seen anew. Evelyn sits beside me
in the car, her chin juts forward, opened-mouthed, as she dozes.
Even her posture betrays how she is fighting and losing. It tears
at me, each time she fumbles with the buttons on her cardigan
or finds her keys in the freezer or drifts through the house at
night like a phantom, unable to sleep. It is a new kind of heartache, watching her. But we don't dwell, instead we look ahead
by tracing a route she mapped years ago, *dance a waltz, search for
buried treasure, learn to speak French*, line by line, like leaping from
rock to rock, a way from here to there.

For me, there is no scrambling for greatness, no unanswered
ambitions that surface, there is an unexpected relief in know-

ing what is done is done. The seeds planted, soil turned, and all I can do is enjoy what blooms. As I face it, my death is abstract, an idea, and as we get closer it shape-shifts and slips away from me. It is something I've always known is coming and yet I've never prepared for it. How do you prepare to cease to exist? And yet, here we are. October, with the crunch of golden leaves underfoot signaling our last fall, which will bring our last winter and final spring. Eight months to memorize the wrinkles around Evelyn's knuckles like counting rings of an oak tree, to watch Rain's swelling belly and await the kicks from my great-grandchild beneath her stretched skin, to smell the brine-soaked wind coming off the ocean as I cover the youngest plants with burlap to protect them from frost; eight months to immerse myself in this life, the only way I know how to prepare to die.

Evelyn wakes, eyes on the trees as we pass. I tap her thigh to get her attention, and say, "When we get back, you should see if Jane wants to come by and practice."

She doesn't turn toward me. "Practice? What for?"

My stomach plummets. "You don't remember?"

"I remember." She whips around, insulted. "But look at me, Joseph. Look around. It feels so silly."

"It's not silly."

"I'm an old woman."

I laugh at the claim, an identity she would not own except to win an argument. "And I'm an old man. So what?"

"No, I mean…" She fumbles for her words, frustrated. "Everything is so much bigger. I've lived a great life."

"You're not making sense."

"It's selfish. Everything… I'm selfish." The news cycle a steady source of shame—loved ones desperate for closure, pleading for answers in the rubble, searching for meaning in the devastation, while Evelyn and I walk willingly into death.

"Giving up on your dream, what would that solve?"

She shakes her head. "I don't know."

I pause, prodding gently. "Do you still want to go through with it…with everything?"

She is quiet. "I don't know."

I offer, "We can wait and see how you feel."

Her voice sharpens. "It would be too late by then."

"We don't have to decide now."

She is silent. I press one final time, leaning dangerously over a precipice. "Either way, giving up the symphony doesn't honor those families."

"But choosing it. Deciding to do it. Isn't it worse?" she asks, sounding strained.

I pause. "We can change our minds. We don't have to do this."

"*You* don't."

"Neither do you." A lame retort, our scales visibly uneven, both playing a losing game.

"All those people…they had no warning, no final year to live out their dreams. No time to call their families, to say goodbye. And here we are, dying at will. It's not fair."

"Nothing about this is fair," I say, emotion creeping into my throat.

We pass two massive oaks marking the entrance, their leaves blazing reddish orange, and pull into a parking spot. Her fingers tremble on her thigh, although I can't tell if it's from her nerves or Parkinson's; her fear of heights has stopped me from planning anything too daring before.

She has been on a plane before, big commercial aircrafts, but nothing like this. After retirement we booked a few trips for us, even a family vacation to Disney when the grandkids were young. Evelyn had always wanted to see California, the sunshine and waves of the Pacific calling her since Maelynn moved away, so we went one year, crossed the Golden Gate Bridge by bicycle, dipped our toes in the Pacific Ocean, swirled wine in glistening glasses in Sonoma, buttery and heady, or tasting of citrus, flowers, earth. California held a different memory for me, but for Evelyn, who had dreamed of seeing it, I went back. Before then, her feet had never left the ground and touched down somewhere completely new, she never watched the earth get smaller and smaller as she rose, weightless. She gripped my hand during takeoff, but once we were in the air, she pressed her palms against the glass, awed to be above the clouds.

The pilot guides us onto the tarmac, and hands out two leather aviator hats and goggles. Evelyn ties her long silver hair back and slips it on, flaps over her ears. I follow suit, and we both help guide her onto the stepstool, over the wing and into the seat behind the cockpit.

I scoot in close to her and grab her knee. "My love, if the hat is any indication, you'd have made an excellent pilot."

She laughs. "Missed my calling," and pulls the goggles over her eyes as the pilot starts the engine, the rumbling cutting off any further conversation, vibrating through my body. We give thumbs-up to indicate our readiness, and he begins to drive along the runway. Evelyn's excitement and fear thrum in my own chest, her hand in mine, the tightest grip as we ease off the ground. We are bundled in heavy coats, grateful for the layers as we begin to climb, the air whipping past us a deafening static, like a radio between stations turned all the way up. Evelyn raises her arms above her, stretching to the sky, her mouth open in a laugh, the sound carried off in the wind.

We leave behind stretches of copper trees, follow an arc of gulls, the pilot pointing out inlets and secret coves, The Thimble Islands a craggy constellation in the distance. The clouds a sheet of cotton above, the sea a cerulean expanse below, and us, hand in hand, suspended between. When we land, our legs jelly and shaking, I feel like I could whoop, beat my chest, fly us back up only to dive out of that very plane, guide a parachute back safely to land, the thrill of it, of being alive. I see it in her too. The wild-eyed girl I knew from the beach, treading below, daring me to jump.

The girl who always wanted to fly away to Boston, to California. I've always been afraid to lose her, of what she would find, who she would become. Evelyn wants to fly away again one last time. And I'll let her, because I know this time I can go with her, and together we can soar into the light.

A few nights later, we plan to have the family over for Thomas's birthday. The morning of, we almost call off the celebration. Evelyn is irritable, her body aches, her tremor roaring. After lunch she gets some sleep, and she seems enough like herself when the children arrive that the evening feels as though it could be a normal night, in a normal year. We enjoy a delicious and simple dinner, a beef roast with mashed potatoes and green beans. Thomas didn't want anything extravagant for his final birthday with us, as I don't want anything extravagant in our final year. Just time with our family.

Violet digs out boxes of old photos, ones I hadn't seen in ages, and we all crowd around the kitchen table, carrying bowls of warm apple crumble heaped with scoops of vanilla ice cream, already melting around the edges. We went to an apple orchard yesterday, picked a bushel of Macouns that we shined on our shirts and sampled as we strolled, so sweet and tart and perfectly crisp. Decades of taking our children and grandchildren there, climbing trees and racing down the rows, their grins at the crunch, sinking their teeth into the first satisfying bite, wiping their mouths on their sleeves.

"Jane, your hair!" Violet giggles as she slips a picture from the stack. "I forgot how big it used to be."

"My hair?" Jane laughs. "What about your outfit?"

Patrick, the only one of Violet's kids around to poke fun since the others are back at school, grabs the picture from Jane. "Mom. This is seriously embarrassing."

Violet shrugs. "It was the sixties, sweetie. That was in, believe it or not."

Evelyn meets my eyes and laughs. "I'm lucky we didn't take many photos when we were young. Though Grandpa could tell you all kinds of stories. I was more the ugly duckling than the beautiful swan when I was little."

"You were never the ugly duckling. But the swan was hiding a bit behind all the dirt and overalls." I chuckle at the stack of black and whites. "Look at this. How young we all were." I slide it over to Evelyn. It is one of the first photos we ever took together. Tommy, always the star, stood between us, his arms around us both. I was about thirteen, and already a head taller than Tommy, and although the image has faded, I could tell we were suntanned, our grins wide and genuine, not merely posed for the photograph.

I can't help wonder what it would be like if he were still here, reminiscing and cracking jokes beside Evelyn. Losing him was realizing that a day went by when I didn't think of him, and being racked with shame. *How could I forget?* Gradually, that day became two, and then three, and soon I could string together a week that wasn't marked by the dull ache I carried. Missing him became the dust covering every surface, that floated in the air, unnoticeable unless I caught it in the right light, then it burst and refracted, glittering into view. A simple moment, like the first time Jane learned how to dive off the dock, shallow to the surface with her toes pointed, a shared glance between Evelyn and me—*Tommy would've loved to see that.* The infinite things he missed.

What a life we have built since; we never could have imagined it then. So much has changed; new stores and neighborhoods have popped up where I remember only fields and dirt roads. Like Hayes Farm, where we'd steal fistfuls of wild blackberries and cut through the pasture on our bikes to get to school, where now a coffee shop and pizza place stand. It shouldn't surprise me, the land was sold many years ago, but every so often when I turn the corner I expect it to be there, somehow. That version

of Stonybrook is so vivid, yet I can't remember the color of the
paint on the barn or if the blackberries were tart or sweet. I can
almost hear Tommy's whooping call from below at Captain's
Rock, and feel the hardened soles of my summertime feet, and
somehow in this moment, Stonybrook is the same, as if it is only
the two of us who have changed.

Jane riffles through the stack, then stops, her eyes softening.
"Wow…look at this. Rain, Tony, here's your future."

Tony places a kiss on Rain's shoulder, beaming, and peers at
the photo. "I've never seen a picture of Rain as a baby before.
Jane, you look so young."

"I was so young. Nearly a baby myself."

"Let me see." Evelyn gestures for him to hand it over. A chubby
two-year-old Rain, a dark mop of curls, wrapped in the skinni-
est arms. Jane back from California, her wild mane of hair filled
half the frame, her eyes fixed on her daughter, whose little fists
were blurred in motion.

"Well, I'm calling dibs on any old clothes. You guys had
style." Rain giggles, flipping through a stack until Jane swats
her away from the photos.

"Who is this?" Connor asks, sliding a photo across the table
to me, a young man in his twenties behind the front desk, an
easy grin on his face, as he lounged in my chair. Sam. An unexpected tug of bitterness in my gut. The first and last time we
hired a stranger to work with us, a face I had almost forgotten.

"Just an old employee." I avoid Jane's eyes, find another in
the pile, a distraction. "I love this one." I pass it around to Ann.
"Thomas and his planes."

Ann leans into Thomas and teases, "Seems like you took
them very seriously."

He squints closely at the photo. "That's the Bell X-5 fighter
jet. I loved building that thing. I wonder where it is now."

Evelyn shrugs. "Probably in the attic along with the rest of the stuff from you kids. You'll have to go through it all together, see what you want to keep."

"Don't say stuff like that, Mom," Jane says, her eyes on the photos.

Thomas clears his throat. "I understand now, you know." His face is solemn, gaze landing on Evelyn and me. "I didn't before— I'm still not condoning it—but—" he grips Ann's hand "—when I thought I lost you…god, I can't imagine…" He looks at her, his eyes welling. "For a moment, I knew what it felt like…to lose the person you love more than life itself."

My throat tightens, and all I can manage is, "Thank you, Thomas."

A hush falls over the room, a seriousness I was hoping would not find us that evening. We don't fight it, though. It is a part of our choice.

"I love this one," Violet whispers, her eyes brimming with tears. Across from her, Connor visibly stiffens at her emotion and makes himself busy with another pile. It is a photo from our wedding; I run my fingers over the glossy finish. I can see the deep purple of the violets in Evelyn's bouquet even though the image is black-and-white.

The night goes on that way, passing photographs and trading stories, the need to be together tangible. An entire history spoken in a glance between siblings, a laugh, as though recognizing ourselves in each other makes it all real, preserves the parts we fear losing. A pregnant Evelyn, no date inscribed on the back, the group trying to determine which child she carried. Photos of Mrs. Saunders, her signature tight-lipped smile and taut bun, first a grandmother and then a great-grandmother. There is one grainy picture of my parents, standing on the inn's front stoop, my mother in her apron and my father looming above her, his arm over her shoulder. Violet and Connor's wedding, Thomas and Ann's… Violet pregnant in many of the pictures, with one child or another. All five grandchildren making a pyramid on the beach. Evelyn and I dancing at Rain and Tony's wedding, our first grandchild and the only one we will see marry. Evelyn and I caught with our mouths open as we entered a restaurant, a surprise fiftieth wedding anniversary party the children threw. Fifty-six anniversaries in all, but most were never frozen for us in a photo. They were days spent marking the day in little moments between us, a touch, a kiss, a *can you believe it*, and *how did we get so lucky*, and wondering how another year passed without our permission.

Twelve

Evelyn

May 1955

I select my swing dress with the checkered skirt, and run my hands over my blouses as if browsing a department store, as if it matters, as if this is the decision that will change things. My suitcase open at my feet, I drop the dress, the fabric spilling over the side, as though it merely slipped from my grasp. I nudge the luggage deeper inside the threshold with my toe, hiding it from view. Then I shed two shirts from their hangers with urgency, barely registering as I toss in cardigans, capri pants, a thin black belt, the stockings with a run in the ankle from chasing Jane through a bramble bush, kitten heels with the worn soles.

A rustle in the hallway. I freeze. A beat passes in silence. I glance in the mirror, the empty hallway projected behind me. The woman staring back through the glass holds my gaze like an accusation. Flyaways wrestled into a low ponytail, wrinkles etched into her forehead, face angular and expressionless, eyes gray and lined with exhaustion, in a plaid housedress hiding widened hips that will soon be covered with an apron. I feel sorry for her; I don't know her.

Downstairs, there is a crash followed by the sound of something shattering. Loud voices, muffled but angry. I flip the lid shut and squat to buckle the clasps, shove it to the back of the closet, hidden behind a pair of heavy winter boots I've yet to tuck away now that spring has arrived. I sprint into Jane's and Thomas's rooms, where I had left them playing with a set of Lincoln Logs and a promise to be right back, and find both empty. *Shit.* I careen down the narrow back stairway into the kitchen, also empty. *Shit, shit, shit.* Push through the swinging door into the dining room to find Joseph with his back to me, seizing Jane by the wrist, Thomas clutched in his other arm, frantically apologizing to a guest. When I get closer, I see it's Mr. and Mrs. Whitaker, first-time visitors, and their table is covered in spilled orange juice and the smatterings of eggs. Jane's hair hangs in wet streaks and her clothes are soaked, a red splotch of strawberry jam on her chin. Joseph hears me enter and whirls around in a mix of anger and relief.

"Take. Them." He fumes, presses a sticky Thomas into my arms, and releases Jane with a push toward me. I scoop her wriggling body, nearly too big at four to be carried, with one arm, and Thomas with the other, desperate to get them out of sight. The full dining room is silent, my face burns with embarrassment. "So sorry, everyone…" Joseph stammers an apology as we exit.

Inside the kitchen, out of view, Jane stares at her bare feet, twists her toes into the grout of the tile, a chunk of egg falling onto her cheek. I reach for the wooden spoon to spank her and grab her by the wrist, but Thomas's face crinkles, and he begins to wail. My eyes dart toward the door, the guests on the other side trying to enjoy what's left of their breakfast.

"Upstairs, now," I growl, throwing the spoon onto the counter. Jane races ahead and Thomas follows, whimpering when he reaches the stairs even though at two years old, he can manage them. I snatch him to my chest, my dress already moist from where I carried him, my neck streaked with jam from his cheeks. Upstairs Jane has stripped off all her clothes and left them in a heap on the carpet.

"Jane. In the bath, *now!*" I kneel and undress Thomas, overtaken with the stench of fresh poop, his cloth diaper heavy and leaking onto his legs. Jane sucks on a jam-covered strand of her hair. My eyes fill with tears.

I test the bathwater with my wrist and clean up Thomas as it fills. I scrub them and rub shampoo in their hair, work my fingers through the snarls and sticky jam, as they yelp and contort away from me. My knees ache on the tile floor. It could be any morning, it could be any night. The water rises higher now, high enough, and I reach to turn it off. I place my fingers under the faucet and hesitate, feel the rush over my skin, close my eyes, imagine it rise higher and higher, filling the room, flooding the entire house until we are all suspended in its muted embrace, in sweet silence.

The bathroom door jerks open, and I'm jolted by the appearance of my mother. I am faintly aware the bathroom reeks of orange juice and human waste, the stained clothes and full diaper beside me. The water is still running in the tub, Jane and Thomas splash each other, soaking the floor around the rim.

"What in the…" My mother's mouth is parted in disbelief. Her hair is tied back neat as always, lips painted, her skirt pressed and shoes polished.

I register my appearance in her eyes, my unwashed hair, wrinkled dress spotted with food, naked lips and pale cheeks. I shut off the tap. "Hey, enough—stop splashing."

She shakes her head. "I have no words, Evelyn. You ask me to take the children so you can go to your appointment and this is what I walk into? Joseph's downstairs sweeping up a mess of broken china, and look at you. What did you do? Or better yet—" she points a thin finger at Jane "—what did this little hellion do?"

I shrug, too exhausted to protest or explain. Jane ducks her head underwater, and Thomas giggles.

"Unbelievable," she scoffs. "You're lucky you have me. I didn't have any help when you were young. You two, out of the tub now, come on." She clucks her tongue and delivers their folded towels with the tips of her fingers, as though they too are filthy, and follows the kids, dripping, out the door. She sticks her head back in to add, "This is why you can't give children too much freedom. It makes them wild. I made that mistake and look at you—" she pauses "—you've never been happy with what you have."

I swallow hard. "I'm going to take a bath."

"Well, I hope so," she snarls, and closes the door behind her.

I flip the hot water tap back on, filling the tub until it scalds. Run the taps, plug the tub, drain the tub. Wash the clothes, hang to dry, iron, fold. Cook, serve, clear, clean. Make the beds, strip the beds. Scrub the tubs, wipe the sinks. Run the taps, plug the tub, drain the tub.

Into eternity.

The Oyster Shell Inn felt more like mine when I lived next door. Now that I sleep in the master bedroom and make biscuits for guests and fold the sheets with crisp corners, this place doesn't belong to me anymore. Sometimes I catch a familiar whiff, blackberries or a musty towel, and am transported, but those echoes are fleeting. Still, Joseph needs the security of a worn-in house, banisters smoothed by our own hands, by his parents and grandparents. To sit at the same table each morning to drink his coffee. I don't think he has ever wondered about the music the Pacific Ocean would make, and if he had, he would favor a more familiar song.

I peel off my stained dress. Sink into the tub, let the water run. Minutes pass. The distinct creak of the stairway, my mother leaving with the kids. Water rises to my chin, and I plunge lower so my mouth is submerged, play with the water flowing between my toes. Finally alone at last, I yearn to be even more alone, alone from myself, from everyone and everything pushing in on me, closing in.

The faucet runs cold now. I hold my breath, my eyes just above the surface. Count to ten, watch the water flirt with the rim. I lean forward to switch it off, but hesitate, staring at the place where the rushing water interrupts the calm surface. I listen and hear nothing in the hallway. My heart pounds as the water climbs, now barely contained by the porcelain. Crane my neck toward the door. Silence. I stand, rivulets drip down my skin, watch the waterline recede to fill the space where my body had been. I wrap a towel around me, stiff from drying on the line.

Run the taps, plug the tub, drain the—*What if I don't?*

I hear cascading water slosh onto the tile floor, the perfect distraction, as I close the bathroom door tight behind me.

In my bedroom, I slip into the navy shirtwaist dress. I paint my lips a deep red and towel-dry my hair. The empty-eyed girl stares back at me again. There is the faint *whoosh* in the background, and I wonder if, when it comes, if it will be enough to drown in, or if it will spill out in the streets, bursting through the windows like the hurricane surge, carrying me to the sea.

The door swings open, and Joseph enters. "What happened out there?" he asks, furious. "I thought you had the kids?"

I watch him through the mirror, his voice sounds so far away. "My mother has them now. I have a doctor's appointment, remember?" I press my pinkie to my lips, erasing a smeared edge.

"What appointment?" Joseph stops himself, cocks his head toward the door. "Is the water running in there?"

I ignore the question and grab my purse. "I'm already late. I'll be back later."

He tugs my elbow. "You really got to be on them—"

I don't meet his eyes. "You know... I hear it now too."

"What?" He turns his head back and in the quiet we both hear the distinct sound of rushing water. "Oh no."

He runs toward the bathroom as it seeps from under the door, spilling out into the plush hallway carpet.

"I have to go!" I call out, but Joseph is already behind the door.

"Can you grab towels?" he yells, and I pretend not to hear.

I steal the suitcase from its hiding spot and race down the back stairwell, each step betraying me with a creak. The keys hang on a rack by the door, so I snatch them with shaking hands and walk with forced calm to the car, nodding as I pass a family on the way to the beach, hoping to conceal my luggage behind my full skirt. Don't want to invite questions, conversation, reasons to stall, to turn back, not now, when I am so close.

Then a phantom voice, my mother's—the one I have tried to keep out, that I have tried to bury deep inside, pushes back—*I made that mistake with you, and look at you…you've never been happy with what you have*—floods my mind as I yank open the station wagon door, toss my suitcase in and wedge myself inside.

Then there is Joseph. His words fill me, too, as they swirl with my mother's, pull me beneath the waves, the sound muted and pressure pounding in my ears. *I want a baby. I want to go home. I think it will make you happy, make us both happy.*

And suddenly I am almost thirty years old with two children, and a husband, and a mother that lives next door, and my life is nothing like I dreamed it would be, nothing like I wanted. I imagine myself, sixteen, before children and marriage and war. Sixteen, when my hair hung loose and wet against my back after a swim, when my skin felt tight from hours in the sun, when I ran through the field and jumped off the dock and splashed in the waves, when I recorded all of my wildest desires with certainty I'd see them through. That Evelyn would have taken one look at this life and swam to the end of the ocean, never turning back.

I jam the key into the ignition and my hands tremble. I grip the wheel to steady myself before backing down the driveway, a jarring acceleration that knocks the suitcase from the back seat to the floor, tires crunching as I approach Sandstone Lane and the new sign that reads The Oyster Shell Inn, to replace the one yanked from its chain by the hurricane so many years ago, the hurricane that lingers now that we are back in this life. This inn stands and yet Joseph is stolen from me, swept away in the shadows of the storm, because I don't see my husband anymore. He wakes before the sun to restore echoes of damage, the roof shingles that split and leak or the shed lined with mold, and tends to guests, driven by guilt that his parents never saw the inn reopen. He stays up late balancing the books long after the kids have gone to sleep and I have crawled into bed, my bones aching from a day's labor.

He is not the Joseph who taught me to skip rocks or who twisted his finger in my curls as we lay on the dock, imagining figures in the clouds. He is a shadow that creaks through the house and the jingle of keys and the fragments of clothes I glimpse as he slips in and out of doors, and I am the one holding the children and vacuuming the carpets and folding the linens and making sandwiches. I am the one who has her dress tugged, and her hair yanked, and gets spit-up on her blouse. I am the one who lives in a house that doesn't feel like mine, trapped in this town that I desperately wanted to escape.

Swim to the end of the ocean, never turn back.

I navigate without thinking and find the highway, drive to put space between me and my conscience, trailing me and gaining speed. In my pocket the letter from the BSO, *Dear Mrs. Myers, Thank you for your interest in the Boston Symphony Orchestra. We are in immediate need of a traveling concert pianist and are holding auditions on May 10…* The morning ticks away along the lines of the road, grass and trees for miles, other cars whip around me, smears of color as they pass.

I flick on the radio to drown out the silence. Nat King Cole croons at the piano, and I shut it off. Joseph bought me a piano after Jane was born. He said he knew what would make me happy. A house, a piano, children. When she was small, I played with Jane in my lap, nestled against one arm, Bach and Mozart and Chopin, music that made me feel part of a world I had left behind. But then I was pregnant again, and my back ached and my ankles swelled and I couldn't perch close enough to the keys to comfortably play, and Jane wouldn't sit still and the house was full of clatter and conversation, a racket that was sound but not music, that pounded between my ears so loud I had to open the windows to let it out.

When Jane and Thomas discovered the piano on their own, it added to the noise, slapping of palms against the ivory, the cacophony of all the wrong notes. The pounding gave me headaches and disturbed the guests so I covered the keys, kept them covered so the children would forget that beneath the piano's wooden door there was a stampede they could create with every smash of their little hands. I kept it covered so long I forgot there was music, soothing, and beautiful music I could create with mine.

I drive past signs I barely read, merges I never register, all the way to Boston, to the symphony, to a life I lived before, a life I almost started on my own.

I amble by the Boston Conservatory and feel that pleasure-tug in my gut, the thrill of the memory of my first private lessons. A building I would know intimately if only I had applied, gotten accepted, stayed. The people I would have met, the futures that would have diverged from walking through those doors. The second chance, now, of a whole new start, a renaissance of possibility at my feet. I pass the Berklee College of Music, students lugging instruments in cases, Boston apparently brimming with musicians, my desires admirable, commonplace even, here. My body implausibly light and unencumbered, no one grabbing at me, reaching for me, needing me, my limbs swinging free in the warm May sun. Sheltered by brownstones on both sides, strangers stride past without a glance, my suitcase tucked in my trunk, the implication of it parked on a side street in Back Bay.

Where to begin? Hours before the audition, and only a short walk to Symphony Hall, the morning open before me like an outstretched hand, eons I am unaccounted for, responsible for no one, walking in whatever direction I choose. Tea, *sitting* and drinking tea, at a café, alone—the urge strikes me and makes me giddy, how time could be spent this way, so frivolously. I order a tea latte, a luxury I've never had, the order so elegant, European, and waste away the morning on a cobblestone patio. Grateful for the warm mug nestled in my hands as the breeze picks up, the fluffy steamed milk hiding the scalding liquid beneath, burning my tongue. I study the women my age, and younger, and older, alone, and pushing strollers, and in groups of other women, and their arms linked with men, as they brush past or navigate passing cars to cross the street, and consider who they may be, where they may be going. Delighted to be mistaken for someone who lives here, sipping my usual order in my usual café, on my way to somewhere too.

How long ago it was I first arrived. Fifteen years. Maelynn picked me up from South Station, her navy trousers buttoned high above the waist, standing out in the horde of ladies in floral dresses. Her painted fuchsia lips, the tortoiseshell sunglasses she lifted onto her head when she saw me. *Well, what do you know. You're an easy one to pick from a crowd.*

I wore denim shortalls my mother hated. Maelynn looked me once over, put her arm through mine, and said, *I think we'll get along just fine.*

If only I could go to her now, find refuge once more in her second bedroom that she used as a writing space, the room that became mine, bathed in daylight and filled with books and exotic plants, spidery limbs hanging over their clay pots, a twin bed against the window that she bought just for me. To be that fifteen-year-old girl, none of her choices made for her yet, a girl who lost afternoons lazing on that Turkish rug, talking with Maelynn and toying with the feathery tassels and following the paths of red threads until the design became muddled, the way a word repeated too many times no longer sounds like anything at all.

Maelynn would be upset if she knew I was so close, and not calling. But I don't have anything to tell her, nothing I can explain. The suitcase, locked in my car. Preparing for not just today, but for the possibility of days that bleed into weeks and months, mornings spent like this after nights performing with the BSO, strolling and sipping and people watching, until my conscience muddles in the same way. Questions I haven't asked myself, answers I don't explore, traced and repeated until they too mean nothing, hurt no one.

I grow cool in the shade of a striped awning, a French name, Patisserie Lola, scrawled across the front, my tea drained except for the bitter dregs, my adrenaline waning, my urge to drive now displaced by my need to walk until my legs burn, to see how far I can get on my own two feet. I pay my tab and loop around Newbury Street, up and down side streets, explore Boylston until I reach Copley Square. The memories of meeting Joseph here for lunch, sharing sandwiches, rises unbidden. That first time he waited for me, his own suitcase in hand. Now even Boston is no longer mine, it is a hideaway we share. I push past, desperate for a place in this city that still belongs to me. Pass the Arlington Church, where we said our vows. Promises that trail me as I turn my shoulder against the cutting breeze, blocking my view.

I reach the Public Garden, circle the pond, geese drifting lazily on its surface, surrounded by beds of tulips. Across the footbridge, clogged with lovers and tourists, I follow the green grass of the Boston Common down to Charles Street. One of my favorite spots, tucked in Beacon Hill, the brick sidewalk lined with shops and restaurants that weaves its way to the Charles

River, sailboats drifting in the wind, the nearest thing I could come to the sea. Maelynn took me here that first Christmas, when I was so homesick for what was familiar. For my mother's gingerbread puffs, for snowball fights with Tommy and Joseph on the way to school, for the cigar smoke swirling around my father after dinner. Maelynn noticed me sulking, so we took the trolley to Park Street and sipped on syrupy cocoa, strolled by storefronts lit with twinkling lights and lampposts wrapped in garlands. She bought me a copy of *Jane Eyre* in a bookstore filled with dusty fringed lamps and oversize armchairs and we walked, kicking little chunks of ice and peering at window displays until our toes went numb and I stopped missing home.

That store is gone now, replaced by a clothing boutique. The street is quiet, most people working on a weekday, and I take my time, admiring mannequins and contemplating menus until I reach the Charles. I can see the boathouse, and the amphitheater across the water, a stage for free concerts in the summer. An experience I missed, returning to Stonybrook at the end of each school year, that Joseph and I never took advantage of for reasons I can't fathom now, can't recall how we spent our time, the recollections gauzy with grief. Our entire time here is a sliver of what it should have been, embedded in me now as another loss. Joseph, physically here with me, but wedded to the inn, his destiny like a getaway car idling outside our window.

I, too, felt the neglected house calling me back, even as I clung to the lie of leaving it all behind. Standing on the docks now, I am transported to the Oyster Shell Inn of my memory. The kitchen was clanging pans and the scent of yeast and flour that followed us through the swinging wooden door as we darted by, stealing a fingertip of fresh jam or a wedge of cheese. Mrs. Myers's laugh was honeyed, switching our behinds with a twisted towel to chase us away, she was a welcomed hug in her doughy arms. Mr. Myers was the jingle of keys on his belt as he repaired leaky sinks and swept the floors, he was foil-covered chocolates slipped into my palm when no one was looking. My parents' home was marble sculptures and mahogany furniture, cold to the touch; the Oyster Shell was the warmth thrown from a crackling fire. There were guests in summer dresses who laughed and drank tea on the front porch, and there was a hum to it all, a brightness and belonging I have chased ever since.

Thoughts of Joseph creep in, and I imagine him putting the children to bed tonight. Waiting. Worrying. The panic that would take over. The pain once he found out the truth. Shame burns through my skin. The suitcase I packed, an escape hatch to a life I agreed to. I hear Thomas whimper, see his crinkled face illuminated in the hallway light. I see Jane walk out of her room, her shirt inside out, saddle shoes untied, spinning to show me how she got dressed on her own. I feel Joseph's lips on my shoulders, his knees pressed behind mine as we lay like spoons. My head feels dizzy, disjointed, floating above me. Thomas reaching for me, Jane smiling, dancing in the morning light. Joseph's body pressing into mine. The sails in the distance blur, and it is only then I realize I'm crying. A nearby church bell strikes five times.

The audition. My heart quickens, a steel drum.

My tears fall faster, my vision swims, I am a fool, letting the day slip away from me. Protecting my one chance the way a mother sends a baby in a basket downstream, a hope set adrift without a real plan, with little chance of a future. My time slot passed with the strike of the clock, the audition that would tell me if I had what it takes, if I was good enough. The audition I'm not sure I ever intended to see through. It was never them I wanted to leave. It was Joseph's dream displacing mine, an anchor he inherited in birth. But without him, without our children, even the most captivating music is meaningless. Boston is an empty song.

I need to go, to get away from the river, the imposter sea, the elusive fantasy of some alternate life. The sun is blinding as it sinks, and I stagger down the path to the grass, and lean against a towering oak, close my eyes against rough bark to catch my breath.

Then I see them. I see them all and my knees buckle until I am in them, violets stretched along the riverbank, an endless purple pillow I melt into. I am crying harder now, flowers in full bloom by my ears and tickling the undersides of my arms. Crying for my father, for Tommy, for Joseph's parents and for Joseph, who loves a girl we have both lost.

The drive back to Stonybrook is a blur of exit signs and head-lights as the day fades into night, my chest tight with the guilt of leaving him, leaving them all behind, and knowing it could never be taken back. Before I reach Sandstone Lane I stop, hide the suitcase in the trunk, rake my fingers through my hair and lick my pinky to rub away the dregs of smudged mascara.

The tires crunch on the driveway, announcing my arrival. The bedroom windows are lit behind drawn blinds; the guests must have retreated for the night. Joseph appears at the front door, a silhouette in the yellow glow of the porch lights. I walk with what I hope appears to be a casual gait, but when I reach the steps I can't help but throw my arms around him.

I whisper in his ear, "I'm sorry." My eyes well up and I am thankful they are buried in his shoulder.

"Where have you been?" His voice simmering in anger. "I thought something happened to you." A question I will have to deflect, its answer would beg more questions, would eat away at him because he would never understand a mother's urge to flee.

"I needed...I needed a day."

"Christ, Evelyn. You needed a day?" He pulls back from my grip, his face cool, distant, shut off to me.

"I'm sorry." I tug his sleeve, but he won't meet my gaze.

"Where did you go?" he repeats.

"I needed to drive, to get some space, is all. I should've told you."

"It's dark."

"You never feel that way?"

"Of course I do!" he shouts. "But I don't act on it! Because you can't just leave when things get hard. We're not eighteen anymore."

A silhouette of a couple on the driveway approaches the porch, passing through from a moonlit walk. He leads me out of earshot, inside, into the kitchen, his hand pressing the small of my back, the only thing propelling me, keeping me steady, and something releases in me, something I had been holding on to for all this time. The lengths our love has gone, the depth of my need for him, surges within me like a life lived once before, like the sudden dinging into place of a forgotten memory, like the inexplicable feeling of having been exactly here, in this moment, like tracing footprints swept away by the sea. Once hidden behind the swinging door I clutch on to him with yearning, a language we had lost. My mouth falls open, press my tongue against his, caught by surprise but meeting me there, in this natural, primal place we once retreated inside a lifetime ago and made our own.

He slides his hands down my lower back and over my thighs, lifts me as I wind my legs around him, my lips on his neck as he carries me upstairs to our bed. He unties my dress and slips it from my shoulders. I unbutton his shirt and pants and he covers my bare stomach in hungered kisses. I trace my fingers across his shoulder blades, and his weight is my anchor. He moans and I press against him until I am falling into our movement, falling so far into him nothing else exists. I call his name and I am free, swimming to the end of the ocean with him beside me, our bodies rock in the waves, come to rest on the shore. I wrap my arms around him as our breath and heartbeats slow. He nuzzles his face into my neck, and I know he is thinking, like I am, of the girl we both thought we had lost, the girl that came rushing back with the cool air blowing through the open window. Joseph, you have found her again. I am home.

Thirteen

Violet

November 2001

I return from a morning run, annoyed to see Connor's car still parked in the driveway. I peel off my gloves and stow my hat and windbreaker in our overstuffed mudroom, an explosion of puffer coats and mittens and muddy boots. With Patrick already off on the school bus, I was looking forward to the respite of our empty house. My lungs jagged from the cold, only a few more weeks of my usual loop to Bernard Beach and through town before winter sends me back to the Y. Not like it makes much difference. Ever since my parents told us their plan, things that usually bring me peace, like the cadence of my feet against the pavement, the calm of low tide at dawn, do nothing for me.

Especially since I can't escape them. There they were, the pink streams leftover from sunrise, Captain's Rock glowing in the morning light past the shrinking sandbars and my parents, huddled together on that massive quilt we use for beach picnics, unaware of me as I huffed past. When was the last time Connor and I set out on purpose like that, packing a blanket and a thermos to watch the day begin? I rack my brain but come up empty, mornings dictated by routine, by children, by tackling the chores that consume us, but rarely sunrises.

I bring a glass to the sink, run the tap and see my father once more, visible out my kitchen window, raking mulch beds. The porch door opens behind him, and my mother appears, bringing him a cup of coffee, leaning on the railing to hand it off. They linger in conversation and my cup overfills as I watch them, trying to decipher their body language, desperate for a hint of disquiet between them, but as always, there is only ease.

I can feel the rank smell of cold air and sweat on me, and cock my ear to the stairwell, hear the distant rush of water, Connor running late and only now in the shower. I'm grateful he isn't poking around in the kitchen, grateful I don't have to pretend to be fine. Meanwhile, my parents still manage to fit romance into their morning, despite everything. A more romantic morning than I can remember having in years, no less. How sad, how sick, to be jealous of my mother in her condition, to make this about me—it makes me hate myself—but I can't help but compare our marriages as they play out side by side.

What would Connor do, if I stripped under the cover of steam, opened the glass door and slipped in behind him? It's laughable. I usually undress with my back to him in the dim lamplight, aware that my nudity is only a necessity between changes of clothes, rather than something that excites him. If I joined him now, he would say, *I'll get out of your way*, or, *I gotta run*, or worse, *thanks, next time, ok?* Gratitude laced with pity, recognizing my attempt but not wanting it, or me, at all. He would step out, still dripping, my naked figure no longer something that could make him late to work, but rather like the bathroom decor, something picked out ages ago that barely registers.

I fight through piles of faded sheets shoved in the hall closet to find a towel. Then step into the kids' shower, now just Patrick's, not wanting to wait until Connor is finished, and partly hoping he leaves before I reemerge. I can't bear to be near him since my parents told us. I'm self-conscious of taking up too much space, of breathing our shared air, of existing beside him, my thoughts of divorce a concealed weapon I am sure he will uncover.

Not that I'm in any rush to get ready. My calendar is open until Patrick's orthodontist appointment at two. I am careful not to touch the shower walls with any exposed skin, the grout discolored, shower curtain liner streaked with mildew, and now I know how I'll be spending my morning. Patrick is supposed to keep it clean, but he has soccer practice and trombone and more homework than I ever remember having in middle school. A lesson I learned with the other three, with Connor, too—if I want it done, I'm going to have to do it myself.

I linger under the hot stream, stalling, circling my neck as the water loosens my shoulder muscles. Connor is supposed to be at work by now, but if he doesn't leave first thing he waits until after rush hour, so he doesn't get caught in traffic on the way to Groton. There are some perks, this flexibility especially, to reviving the family business, this house not the only thing we inherited from my grandparents. The Groton Ship and Engine Company was left to my mother after my grandpa Saunders died, long before I was born. It maintained a shaky existence, trading hands and managers until Connor came on as chief engineer. A source of insecurity for Connor, our life constructed on the shoulders of my parents, their parents and a constant taunt from my siblings, *of course Violet gets the house, Violet, the favorite.* But the truth is neither of them wanted Grandma's house. Neither of them wanted the company either.

I never loved her house, myself. I always thought it was a bit of a monstrosity, the marble foyer and ornate doors, dark and overfurnished, not to my taste. But it had more than enough room to raise our four children, it was a reasonable commute for Connor and my parents certainly didn't need it. It didn't make sense to sell it and buy something farther away from the beach, only to invite some strange family into our enclave, invading the lot we share. I prefer the house I grew up in, and I've tried to replicate its homey comforts while making it our own. I replaced heavy window treatments to let in more light, found wicker furniture, linen fabrics. But it was too much house for us even when the kids all lived home. We could never keep it clean, the cavernous rooms packed with toys, sports uniforms peeled off and tossed in the corners, fossilized apple cores found beneath couch cushions. Grandma would have been horrified. But their chaos, their noise and their mess, three little redheads, and later, their littlest baby brother, was what finally made it our home. The clichés all turned out to be true, the one about the good old days, the way a heart can expand, how happy a life together could be.

I am dreading winter more than ever this year, when everyone cocoons inside and our emptying nest is even more apparent, three of our four already off on their own. Patrick more prone to hiding out in his room now that he's nearly a teen, no older siblings to draw him out with overheard debauchery, drama unfolding in the living room or the thrill of watching someone who is not you getting in trouble. Winter, which will lead to spring, to June, a countdown I can't silence in my own head. My parents' final year. I can't fathom it, and now, only seven months to go. I scrub the soles of my feet, hard, working at the dead skin around my ankles, elbows, trying to banish the thought. But it bucks back, no matter how red my skin gets. The sudden panic, the feeling of falling that startles me from sleep. The loss that wells up swift and loud, as though grief is a sound, a passing train between my ears. Soon, my constant guides, the two people I count on most, my paradigm for a life well lived, for true love, will be gone.

Jane doesn't believe them, or that has been her party line, a way for her to not deal with her emotions, as usual. Jane, the prodigal daughter, who somehow gets the honor of Mom's grand finale, their performance at the symphony. Even though I'm the one who has been here, who they can depend on, who helps them call the cable company, and booked that bus tour of the Grand Canyon for the entire family, and spends Sundays weeding their flower beds.

I was the one who worked on Thomas when he was barely speaking to anyone. I told him—even though I hate the very thought of it, and I can't imagine their house without them in it, their voices never again on the other end of the phone—I also can't imagine one of them without the other. I told him he would regret it if he squandered the little time we have left to make a point. Punishing them won't keep Mom healthy, won't stave off grief or change Dad's mind. My siblings don't get it; they think I'm crazy, but they don't live next door. They don't see what I see every day. The flowers Dad clips from the garden, the hours Mom spends keeping him company while he works. The walks they take together, the lit windows that follow their path at night, moving together through the house. The impossible bar they have set, the one thing I'll never forgive them for.

I've brought up couples counseling, but Connor doesn't believe in therapy. He's from Southie, a place where people mind their business, don't invite strangers into their problems. He thinks we are dealing with normal life, our relationship giving way to the demands of running a business and raising four kids. He's not wrong, not solely to blame. I, too, had settled into what we had made. I slept better on my side, away from him; the couch was more comfortable when I could recline alone. I stopped recounting my days, not wanting to bore him with stories about volunteering at the kids' school, the library, charity 5Ks, gardening, all the ways I filled my time that never elicited follow-up questions. I packed lunch boxes and set out dinner plates as he came and went, and at some point he stopped kissing me hello and goodbye, or I stopped kissing him, and I'm not sure either of us noticed until it became a pattern, too late to protest. The exhaustion building with each child never subsided, never let us carve a path back to each other.

But he doesn't know that sometimes, in those rare nights we fumble in the sheets, an autopilot routine that gets the job done, I think about my high school boyfriends. About the ways we explored each other, the ache of desire, of being desired. I would never share this with him, even in therapy. I'm embarrassed by it, forty-five and fantasizing about boys I once knew, younger than my oldest son now, but frozen in time as nearly men, virile and wanting me.

I had never said the word aloud. *Divorce*. Not until months ago, when I told my parents what I was considering. I had never entertained it. The kids came first, creating a stable, happy home for them. Connor is the kind of dad that knows how to butterfly a bandage, helps with long division and makes egg-in-a-hole toast. He is not the kind of man you divorce. I know women in town, whose husbands had strayed, and they are still married. How could I justify it? Even the logistics—where would he live, where would I live, what would holidays look like, how would I support myself, would I have to return to teaching, a career I barely began, didn't feel confident I could jump back into after a twenty-two-year hiatus—and my biggest fear, would the kids hate me, stopped me in my tracks.

Until June, until my parents sat us down, setting our unspoken agreement, a marriage that was good enough, to flame.

Because there's no hiding from the truth now. I have a husband I care about, who I don't wish bad things on, who I want to be happy. But I don't have a husband I would die for, who would die for me. Jane and Thomas may think it's twisted, but don't I deserve to find a love like that? Doesn't Connor? Don't we all?

A vague shout in the hallway, and I turn off the shower. I towel off, wrap and tuck the fabric in place to walk to our bedroom. Peek out the window, the driveway empty.

I don't even have a husband who makes sure I heard him say goodbye.

I turn on *Good Morning America* to keep me company as I dress. An image of the wreckage, firefighters still working through rubble. Since the towers fell, everything feels more tenuous. Thomas appears to have found some clarity through the tragedy, but all I can think about is all of those people, the way it should feel to lose someone, the absolute devastation. But if I lost Connor, I could go on. I would be shattered for the kids, for the loss of their father, but I could exist in a world that he left behind. Maybe wanting it, believing in love, waiting until we find our way, isn't enough. You shouldn't have to work tirelessly, to talk the other into staying.

Love is walking hand in hand, following each other into the light.

Later that morning, I tip a wrinkled bag of flour into a measuring cup, level it with my finger and pour it into a mixing bowl. I'm making muffins from a bunch of brown bananas Mom forgot about, while she keeps me company at her kitchen table, a knit blanket tossed over her knees. The sun peeks from behind a cloud, fills the kitchen with a false sense of warmth. Illuminates the dog-eared cookbooks, the copper kettle, the floral aprons on a hook beside the pantry, jammed with repurposed coffee tins and canned tomatoes and hefty bags of sugar. I pour the batter into muffin tins and lick a bit off the edge of my thumb. I pop them in the oven and sink beside her at the table, spread the woven blanket over us both.

"How are you feeling?" A question I know she hates, but I can't help but ask, hoping for a new answer, one that means we can reverse course, talk about this years later with disbelief, the near miss dodged because we held out hope.

"Alright." She tries to smile, to reassure me, but it comes out like a grimace.

I snuggle close, can't help but revert back to her daughter when we are tucked in side by side. Try to keep the tremble from my voice when I ask, "Are you scared?"

"Sometimes." Her face smooths and turns to stone, the masked expression I've noticed before, one of the symptoms I've learned to measure, to clock, the real answers to my questions. "But, honey, I'm more scared of staying, of being alone at the end in my own head."

I trace a scratch across the antique oak table, etched with fork tines and stamped with murky outlines of sweating glasses left too long on its surface. "I know. I really do understand…more than anyone else ever will. I'm terrified of being alone."

"You won't be. You have Connor."

If it were true, she wouldn't have to say it. No one has to re-assure her about Dad. They are the wisteria vine, he is the struc-ture around which my mom has flowered, my mom giving life to what would otherwise be an empty frame. Connor and I have grown away from each other in the most mundane way, as the kids left to build their lives. No one to lash us together except our baby, who is no longer one, who will soon be on his own. And what then? It haunts me, how little I have to say to my husband across an empty table. I can't remember the last time we hugged.

I pause for a beat, my voice shaky and uncertain. "I still think about leaving." I lift my gaze, scanning for her reaction, needing her to tell me to do it, to not do it, to assure me I'm not hor-rible for feeling this way. "I wonder what he would do? If he'd fight for us? Maybe it's what we need."

Mom exhales slowly, giving nothing away. "I left once."

My eyes widen. A trick of her mind, maybe? I've read about confusion like this, the ways her thoughts may begin to distort, her memory jumbled. "What are you talking about?"

"I left your father. Or I tried to. When Jane and Thomas were little, before you were born."

I am stunned for only a moment, before I shake my head, sure one of us misunderstood. "No, you didn't, you couldn't have. You and Dad love each other so much."

She nods. "Yes, we do. I loved him even as I packed my things. But…I felt like my life wasn't mine anymore." Her eyes clear, locked on mine, here with me completely, her lucidity terrifying because it makes it all true. "I was overwhelmed with motherhood, and the inn, and I didn't recognize the person I was becoming."

My mouth falls open, unable to hide my shock. "But you love each other…"

She gives a sad smile. "It wasn't about your father. It was about feeling like my life wasn't what I expected. Like I was drowning and everything I wanted was out of reach. I was terrified if I didn't do something I'd be lost forever."

A tear escapes, I'm relieved, and stunned and devastated, to hear her echo my darkest thoughts back to me as her own. "I've felt that way."

"I know. That's why I'm telling you this. Because I *did* leave, and I am so thankful I didn't get far. I wouldn't have gotten to experience the best parts of my life. And I never would have had you." She grabs my hand, gives it a squeeze.

It can't be true…not my parents. Not my mom… I have so many questions, don't know where to begin, try to piece together this new image against the one I hold of their marriage, the one I've pocketed and carried, a photograph worn thin from all the times it's been studied. "So what happened?"

"I got in the car and drove to Boston. I don't even think I had a plan outside of a vague dream of playing for the symphony, of putting space between me and a life that was trying to swallow me whole…but I couldn't do it. I had planned to audition but missed my time slot, by accident…or maybe even a little on purpose… I don't know, I just broke down. All I could think about was your father and what this would do to him. I tried to picture a life without him and I couldn't go through with it.

Losing him and hurting him was more terrifying than anything we could face together."

The reality of actually having the conversation with Connor twists my stomach. Sitting him down, saying the words. *I want a divorce.* To think it is one thing, and to share with the locked vault of my parents, another. But to him? I had played out the *after* in a surface level montage—the small cottage I make my own, recipes I'd learn to cook for one, driving solo to visit the kids in college—but I never allowed myself to imagine the moment the words left my lips, to watch the shock and pain etch across his face. A man who doesn't deserve it, who would never see it coming, who has been head down in this life for two decades, raising kids and paying bills, sure we would come out the other side. The trust we've built, the friendship that exists beneath, irreparable. The certainty within me that he would never devastate me this way, never ask for the unthinkable while I sat before him, blindsided, made the fool.

"I'm so sorry. I never wanted you kids to know. I never even told your father. I was so ashamed and felt so guilty for so many years." Her voice cracks and tears begin to fall.

I reach for her and hold her tight. "I understand, Mom, I do."

"Then you need to understand this—" Mom pulls away, looks into my eyes once again. "The choice to leave is not one you can take back. You need to be sure there isn't a more important reason to stay."

I nod and lean into her, her decision mingling with mine, my shoulders shaking as my tears fall. Mom puts her arm around me, and she cries too. I cry for my parents, for my kids, for Connor, for everything I can't face, everything I stand to lose. I cry for the little girl who dreamed of love, and for the grown woman who is beginning to understand what it means.

Fourteen

Joseph

April 1960

There is a loud crunch of tires as someone roars up the driveway, and I peek out the window to see Maelynn's teal Chrysler.
Evelyn, in the middle of cleaning up from the guests' breakfast,
wipes her hands on her apron and goes to the doorway. Thomas
peeks from behind her hip.

"What are you doing here? What a surprise! My mother isn't
here, you could play with the kids for a while."

After too many arguments with her sister when their visits
coincided, snide comments about Maelynn's travels, about how
she shouldn't be left with the children since she never had her
own, Maelynn prefers to visit only when we can be alone. Evelyn's mother still comes by, especially when the inn is booked
solid and we need to turn morning checkouts over by early afternoon, but not as often as she used to. She has less patience
with the children now that she and they are getting older. She
tolerates Thomas, an obsessively neat child for six, who is never
far from either of us, ducking behind our legs. But she lets out

audible sighs when she spots Jane in the meadow, barefoot with her braids undone as she digs in the dirt.

"Evelyn, I'd love to, but I really must hit the road." Her smile is wide, her voice tinged with excitement, gesturing at her back seat full to bursting with suitcases.

"Where are you going? Why are you all packed up?"

"Los Angeles—LA. I'm moving, *finally*." She emphasizes *finally*, like the waiting has been particularly dreadful, although it's the first we've heard of the idea. She is vague about her frequent visits to California, there has been talk of someone special living there, but she's shared no details, only hints at his existence. Evelyn and I figure she has been seeing him for years, but she refuses to admit it.

"LA? What will you do there?"

"What does it matter? I'm fifty years old. I want to move, so I am!" This part is unsurprising; after we moved away Maelynn's only tie left to Boston was the school. Evelyn had told me her poetry was selling well, and she couldn't stand the newest headmistress, so she was probably not long for that place. Maelynn reaches for Thomas. "Goodbye, Thomas, be good for your mommy now. Where are Violet and Jane? I must hug them." She pokes her head in to where I sit in the front room balancing the books. "And, Joseph, you, too, come on now."

Evelyn fumbles as if she is short-circuiting. "You're leaving, right now? This second?"

"Yes, dear. Didn't you ask why the car was packed? I wouldn't be packed if I wasn't leaving! I'm driving all the way." Her voice is so light, each word lifted by a laugh. "Why wait?"

"I can't believe you didn't tell us until now." Evelyn calls into the house, "Jane! Violet! Aunt Maelynn is here!"

I walk to the door with the sensation of standing up too quickly, caught off guard by this sudden arrival and departure.

Maelynn grips Evelyn in a tight hug. "Well, don't be too

upset. I just decided. Life is a crazy thing, isn't it? Do tell me you'll visit."

Evelyn's voice is muted, nearly a whisper. "I've never been to California."

Jane, eight years old, rushes through the doorway to hug her great-aunt, knocking Thomas aside, and Violet, four, dawdles after her.

Maelynn shrugs, as though Los Angeles is the next town over. "Well, all the more reason for you to come by! Girls, I am off."

Jane cocks her head at me, then at Maelynn. "Off where? You just got here."

Maelynn, known to steal Jane away and bring her home with a scrape or two, brimming with secrets, tugs on one of her curls until she giggles. "Yes, well I did, and now I'm off! I'm moving to California. Your mother will take you all to visit me, won't you, Evelyn?"

"Cool." Jane hugs her great-aunt again, her eyes wide with the promise, another adventure for them to share.

Violet begins to cry. "Aunt Mae, you leaving?"

"Yes, dear. But don't be upset! It is a beautiful thing! Now give me a kiss." She lifts Violet, and Violet wraps her arms around her neck, giving her a wet smooch on the cheek. Maelynn hugs us both, urges us once more to visit. Then, as quickly as she arrived, she leaves, her headscarf fluttering behind her as she walks away. Her car sputters and is gone.

For weeks after, Evelyn talks of nothing but California, of traveling and exploring distant lands. She is so impressed that Maelynn started a new life, in a new city, at fifty, because she wanted to. To me, it isn't glamorous or brave. It is sad, lonely, to have built so little around you that you can pick up and leave at a moment's notice. But Evelyn won't let it go.

One night, I see her scribbling on a list, a habit she picked back up after she got pregnant with Violet, when I felt the shift in her I never quite understood, a happiness that bloomed like a flower growing through a rock wall, resilient and inexplicable. She uncovered the piano so it could be played again, rather than used as a shelf for picture frames, and taught Jane the basic notes and chords. It was the only time Jane sat still, and even then, she itched to play faster, louder, to learn every song. Even Thomas liked to press his pudgy toddler fingers against the keys while he sat in her lap. Newborn Violet often fell asleep burrowed into Evelyn's neck while she cradled her in one arm and played with the other. Years passed like this, a new golden age of ease and contentment I wasn't sure we would ever find again.

Evelyn, brightening the inn with her music; in the evenings, our living room full of neighbors and guests and wine and laughter and she is the shining center of it all. In the summer, we hustle through our work to soak up rare afternoons together on Bernard Beach. She kneels beside Thomas, pushes an armful of sand to create a foundation for his castle, Jane flips through slow rolling waves, Violet giggles as I swing her toward the surf. It is something we both need, to be near the ocean; it relaxes us, reminds us we are a part of something bigger. Being landlocked reminds me of war, of dust and heat and anger. I need the cool calm of the water lapping against the shore and the smell of the sea to feel at home.

When Evelyn goes to brush her teeth, I peek between the pages. On a fresh sheet she wrote: *California.* It was crossed out, and beneath was: *Fly to California.* That, too, was crossed out, and at the very bottom simply: *Fly.*

Three more years race by before we know it. It's Thomas's tenth birthday, and we're struggling to come up with money to celebrate. Over the summer, the Vietnam War tightened the purse strings of our regular guests, and the usually overbooked inn had multiple vacancies. Evelyn teaches piano lessons in town a few times a week, which helps, but it barely covers groceries. By October, the children had outgrown their clothes, the car needed new tires and the Oyster Shell continues to show its age, demanding a new roof, paint, carpets, seemingly all at once, and now we've come up short on funds for a celebration. Evelyn and I stay up late reviewing bills, balancing and rebalancing the ledgers, but we are at a loss.

"I wish we never did that historical house registry thing, the repairs just cost more now." She says this with blame, like I created the standards around which we must now operate.

I try to reason with her, our records covering the kitchen table. "You know the inn slows down after the season. It'll pick up by Christmas, it always does."

She rolls her eyes. "I'm not talking about Christmas. I'm worried your son will be disappointed on his birthday—ten's a big deal."

"Why do you have to say it like that? *Your son.* Like if he's disappointed it's my fault."

"Well, *you* were the one who wanted to reopen the inn."

I sit up straight. "Are you serious?"

"You think running the Oyster Shell was a big dream of mine?"

"You've got to be kidding me." I rub my forehead, incensed. "What about what I want, huh? Just because I don't have these wild dreams like you, what I want doesn't matter?" Evelyn says nothing. "Let's not forget, we did the Boston thing. We tried. It didn't work."

"No, it didn't," she scoffs, a jeer disguised as agreement.

"Damn it, Evelyn! This isn't about you. For once. There isn't any more money. I can't make more money appear because you want me to. What would you like me to do?" I yell. I never yell at her.

Something snaps, and she growls. "Maybe you should stop making promises you can't keep." She stands from the table, slamming the chair in behind her.

"Evelyn! Stop."

She whirls around, fuming. "What?"

"You can't use that to win a fight. I don't care how upset you are." She freezes, caught picking an old wound, a promise I had made so many years ago, that I had broken, to keep Tommy safe, for us both to come home. I lower my voice. "You can't."

Shame dislodges her anger like a popped cork. "You're right. I'm sorry." She sighs, deflated and chagrined. "God, Joseph, for once, would you fight dirty back?"

"You didn't mean it."

She shakes her head. "I should've never brought him up."

"It's okay. We're both frustrated."

"No, it's not. It's not okay that I attack you because of my issues."

"Come here."

She sinks toward me and I wrap her in my arms, burying her burning face in my chest. I hold her tight for a moment, recollections of fighter jets jostling into an idea, a solution forming clearly, and I whisper, "Maybe we can do something special that doesn't cost anything at all."

The sky is a cloudless blue and the air is crisp, like life renewed, the trees burst orange and red as we near Hartford. Evelyn and I wanted some alone time with our son, who often gets lost in the fold, so we leave Jane and Violet with their grandmother, much to Jane's preteen dismay. Thomas is quiet in the back seat as we pass golden hills, no more of a presence alone than he is among his sisters. A wicker basket sits to his left, ham and cheese sandwiches, apple cider and pumpkin cupcakes inside, his eyes flicker over the fiery landscape as we pass. There is something different about his silence now, neither cold nor distant. It is electric, an anxious anticipation, counting every tree, snapping each detail in place like they unlock something magical to come.

We drive past signs for Bradley Airport and I glance over my shoulder to Thomas, fingers tapping against his jeans in anticipation.

"Almost there, champ." I grin at Evelyn, Thomas's excitement contagious.

As a father, it is strange to know so little about my son, especially because as a toddler Thomas was never far from our ankles. I can list the obvious things: he loves model airplanes and wants to join the air force. Anyone could walk into his room and ascertain as much. I also collect practical tidbits that come with occupying the same house: how he doesn't add milk to cereal because he hates for it to get soggy, or how he always wears a jacket even in the slightest chill. There is so much else I don't know, so many more important things...how he feels about school, if he has many friends, if he has started to notice girls. If he understands how much I love him. If he sees himself as different from the rest of the family, and if that makes him feel alone.

Truth to tell, his demeanor has always been a bit of a mystery. Jane is all Evelyn, brazen and adventurous, and Violet is much more like me, her heart on her sleeve, but Thomas...he is nothing like his namesake, although I do not fault him for it. He never knew his uncle and I wouldn't expect him to take on Tommy's personality because we gave him his name. His face does resemble my best friend's boyish features, sometimes there will be a certain tilt of his head, an ancient mannerism that jolts me. But he is built like I was at his age, a lanky height sure to turn broad as he grows, and his brown eyes are mine as well, steady and unchanging. Still, I wonder how this quiet and analytical boy was born from flesh and bone of his mother and me.

We veer off an exit and follow a side road hedged by a golden-brown meadow. The Buick bumps along as we sidle off the paved street onto a rough path, our tires kicking up dirt. We rumble to a stop halfway down the field and the dust settles around us. We step out of the car and Evelyn reaches into the back seat for the wicker basket and blanket, our three door slams resounding across the landscape. The sun is warm on my face despite the fall breeze, and Evelyn rolls up the sleeves on her wool sweater.

Thomas peers around at the wide, empty countryside, skeptical. "Dad, are you sure this is the place?"

I shrug, playing into his doubt. "I thought so…"

Then, we hear it. The low roar of an engine like distant thunder, then something more acute, a high-pitched whoosh, blasting through the clearest sky, as a galvanized fighter jet soars into view over the amber treetops. Its shadow sweeps the meadow and Thomas takes off in a sprint, whooping and cheering in its wake. Evelyn drops the basket and we chase him, our arms lifted to the air. The wings of the plane so low they eclipse the sun. The wind whips as we run, and it glides higher, the shadow slipping away until it is well past the trees. Thomas stands still ahead of us, mesmerized, watching the jet until it is smaller than a distant moon, until it disappears, leaving only a white stream like a brushstroke to show it had been there at all. He turns, awed, his face its own beam of light.

"Mom! Dad! Did you see that?"

Evelyn nods, her mouth agape. "Incredible."

A roar reverberates behind us again, another set of drills, this time three jets in a triangle. A sound that would have once caused me panic, but here we are untouchable, the peace we've settled into is a shield from even the horrors inside my own mind. Thomas gallops off, chasing the rumble as the planes soar the length of the field and vanish. I unfurl the flannel blanket on a gust of wind, and lie back, resting on my elbows. Evelyn settles next to me and unpacks the basket, unpeels the paper liner off a pumpkin cupcake and sneaks a bite, a smudge of icing above her lip. I sip apple cider, still steaming in the red plastic thermos, warmed by the scent of clove and cinnamon. We spend the afternoon like that, stretched side by side, watching our son run, his arms extended like wings, his eyes never leaving the sky.

We watch the footage in the living room, our inn full of guests visiting their families for Thanksgiving. JFK has been shot. A young woman next to me weeps. The roles of host and guest dismantled in the intimacy of our shared loss, as we were all stunned into silence, shook in our utter disbelief. When JFK was elected, he was only three years older than I am now. Forty-three years old and the president of the United States. I am forty and I run my parents' inn. An innkeeper. That's all I have ever been. Probably all I'll ever be. How can he be a few years older than I am and suddenly be dead?

The phone rings, jarring us all, and Evelyn excuses herself to answer it in another room, and I follow her, needing air.

"The Oyster Shell Inn, how can I help you?" she says, with false cheer. There is a pause, her voice shifts, concerned. "This is Evelyn."

She gives me a quick panicked glance, and lowers herself to sitting at the kitchen table. I sit beside her, and she moves the receiver between us, leaning together so we can both hear.

"Evelyn… I've heard so much about you… Maelynn loved you so much." There is a female voice on the other end of the line, a voice I don't recognize. "I wish this wasn't—" the voice breaks "—god, I'm sorry, I tried to pull myself together before calling."

She presses a hand to her chest, rubs her clavicle. "I'm sorry, who is this?"

"My name is Betty, I lived with… Maelynn was my…" Her voice catches. "I have terrible news." A pause. "There was an accident." There is a muffled sob on the other end. "Maelynn… she's gone."

A sharp intake from Evelyn. I falter, nothing I can do to protect her from this, the last thing we thought we would ever hear. Betty chokes out the details, and I grip Evelyn's hand. A head-on collision, the other car ran a red light. Maelynn died instantly. The other driver died later, at the hospital.

JFK murdered in a car; Aunt Maelynn killed in a car crash.

A motorcade. A gunshot. A red light. The squeal of tires. Different tragedies, different cars and cities, the same end.

Evelyn's chin crinkles, trying not to cry, and she leans into me. It doesn't seem possible someone as alive as Maelynn could be gone. I'm terrified this news could be enough for her to crumble again. I want to turn the volume down on the television, reverse the bullet, stop the cars, freeze anything that threatens our salvaged serenity.

"I'm so sorry." Betty coughs, her breath labored, trying to get the words out. "I wish we could've met under different circumstances...your aunt, this may be shocking, but she—she was the love of my life. And I think, well she told me, I was hers too."

Betty, the mystery man that turned out not to be.

The true love that Maelynn finally found.

Evelyn lets out a laugh, a relief, wiping at her cheeks. "Honestly, Betty, there is nothing about Maelynn that would shock me."

That night, we tell the children about what happened to Aunt Maelynn. We also talk about JFK and try to help them grasp the news. Jane cries, angrily wiping the tears as they fall. Thomas sets his jaw; his face somber but controlled. Violet, almost eight now, doesn't understand. She asks me so many questions when I tuck her in—about death and why it happens and where you go and what it means. Questions I don't have the answers for, outside of vague Christian teachings about heaven and hell, the loose structure Evelyn and I were raised in that we shed in adulthood like clothes we outgrew. Angels and a blissful eternity sounded more like stories than something we believed, ideas we wished were as real to us as death itself.

Her questions plague me as I try to sleep.

Evelyn asks, side by side in the darkness, "How has my mother, of all people, outlived everyone else? I wouldn't be surprised if she outlived us all."

I say nothing. I wouldn't wish that on anyone. To trudge along after those closest to you have died, to continue on without your love beside you. How lonely that would be, how horrible to keep saying goodbye, to exist in the spaces they no longer fill. I can't imagine my life without Evelyn, I have never known a world she didn't brighten; I wouldn't want to inhabit the darkness her absence would create. So, tonight, I grip her tighter. I hold her like holding her will make sure she never goes. But still I can't sleep. My heart thuds as I lie still, my stomach tight. I rest my head on her chest, grip her waist. She strokes my hair, kisses my forehead and tells me it will be alright. But no amount of soothing changes the truth haunting me.

Someday, I will lose her too.

Nights later, all the children are tucked in, the dining room is set for the morning, and from my spot under the quilt I watch Evelyn get ready for bed. The door to the bathroom is ajar and she is in her nightdress, running a comb through her hair.

I say, "You're doing better than I thought you would, with Maelynn." Evelyn is stronger. I can see it in her posture, the length in her neck, the square angle of her shoulders. She doesn't seem to carry Maelynn on her back, as she did Tommy when he died, faltering under her grief. "I was afraid it might be like last time."

"I don't really have a choice. We were younger then…the kids need us, the guests need us. I don't have time to fall apart."

"You can feel it, though."

"I feel it, trust me." She comes out to meet me, and sits on the edge of the bed. "I thought she was invincible." Her eyes well, remembering her aunt who was her dearest friend. "I wish she'd told us, about Betty. Like we would care? I don't understand why she felt she had to keep that secret from me… I can't believe she'll never visit again, that we'll never see her."

Betty told us Maelynn didn't prepare any will or final wishes.

Part of me believes she assumed she'd never die, or she wasn't worried about what would happen when she did.

We decided her body should be sent back to Boston for the funeral, she was beloved by many students who would want to say goodbye. Betty sent us the newspaper clippings and made the arrangements. In the letter that arrived along with the obituary she wrote, *I won't be at the funeral. I hope you can understand. I said my goodbye the day she died and I can't bear to do it again. Every day I wake up praying it is all a terrible dream.*

My stomach wrenches as I read her words. Someday, that will be me. Or someday, that will be Evelyn. No one in love gets out of this life unscathed.

There is a light knock on our door, and Violet, in one of Jane's old nightgowns, too long for her, peers inside. It has been years since Violet has entered our room after bedtime, complaining of monsters and ghosts in her closet. But recently, death seems to plague her in her dreams. I pat the quilt next to me and she pushes herself up to her knees, crawling toward me. She settles in my arms as Evelyn shuts off the bathroom light and slides under the covers alongside us both.

"Oh, sweetie, can't sleep again?" She strokes Violet's hair, damp from a bath.

"I'm afraid I'll have a bad dream."

"Well, then, let's think of happy things before bed," Evelyn says, and scoots closer to me. I feel her body relax and I am filled with a rush of affection. Violet rests her head on my chest and I'm struck with how little she still is. Maybe because she is the baby of the family, she has always seemed more fragile than her brother and sister. Or maybe it's because she has always seemed to carry more in her heart, as if she bears all the emotions in the house in her tiny frame.

"What kind of happy things?" She peers up at me, and her eyelids droop, even as she fights to appear awake.

"How about the story of when I fell in love with Mommy?"

"I love that one," she sings, and scoots closer. Evelyn adjusts her position against me on the other side and lets her eyes close. I catch her smile as I begin. Violet interrupts the story in all the usual parts, giggling when I mention the color of Evelyn's dress, asking questions about her uncle Tommy, which lead back to questions about Aunt Maelynn and what it means to die. I give simplified answers to pacify her, to quiet my wandering mind, until her eyes close and her fingers twitch against my chest.

I slide away from Evelyn, who shifts against the pillow in my absence, and carry a sleeping Violet to the room she shares with Jane. I peek at Thomas on the way, and through the darkness I can see the lump of his body under his covers, fast asleep. Jane is awake in bed with a flashlight, clutching a newspaper and scissors. She has spent the last few days glued to the television or buried in the news, cutting out and keeping articles in a shoebox. Smoke rises on her nightstand, the room thick with the stench of incense. We've been fighting her about burning it in her room, but tonight, it doesn't seem worth the battle.

I nod to her as I tuck Violet in. When I sit on the edge of Jane's bed, she doesn't acknowledge me, her flashlight gliding over the words. John F. Kennedy's face gleans from the front page with the headline "A President Remembered." Aunt Maelynn's obituary is taped to the wall by her pillow.

She is getting tall, going on thirteen and all limbs and attitude. I'm not sure when things between her and Evelyn began to change, both willful to a fault. They used to spend hours together on the piano; like Evelyn at that age, it was the only time Jane stayed in place, tackling more advanced material, delighting our regulars who remarked at how grown-up she was becoming. She used to love helping around the inn, keys jingling in her grip as she led guests to their room, or pointing out the way to Bernard Beach. But lately she prefers solitude, talks back to her mother and slinks off into her room, absorbed in researching the Cuban Missile Crisis and the Bay of Pigs and construction of the Berlin Wall, and devouring every current event as it unfolds around her.

"Hey there, Janey, you going to sleep soon?" I pat her leg, until she reluctantly meets my gaze.

"How could I possibly sleep? In case you didn't know, the world is falling apart." She scowls, places the flashlight between her knees to secure it and cuts out the front page.

"Well, then we definitely need some rest so we can face it in the morning."

"That's not funny."

"I'm not trying to be funny. But I don't want you to stay up worrying about things we can't change tonight."

"That's the problem. No one thinks they can change anything. We're all following along like a herd of cattle. And we're all going to slaughter."

It always surprises me how adult she has become, how cynical and dark her outlook has become at twelve and a half. "I know the world seems scary now. And I miss Aunt Maelynn, too, and so does your mom. But worrying all the time does not help—it will only make you feel more helpless."

"But we're all helpless. Aunt Maelynn was helpless. JFK was helpless. Both of them are dead and neither saw it coming."

"Sometimes things happen, and there isn't anything we can do but live the best life we can, and hope that we're ready for them."

She puts the scissors and the newspaper down, glaring at me. "But she did live a good life, and she finally found someone, and she was killed anyway. And JFK's son—to have to bury his dad on his third birthday? The way he saluted the casket...it's not fair, Dad." Tears form in her eyes, and she turns away, her cheeks red.

My throat constricts, the boy with his hand pressed to his forehead, the bare dimpled legs and buttoned wool coat, a heartwrenching salute from a toddler too young to understand. A final goodbye to a father he would never remember, whose face he would memorize from photographs, the way our children never knew my parents, their stories like folktales, never would they feel the heat from their bodies in an embrace.

"I know it's not. It's not fair. But like we don't have control over what happens in the world, we don't have control over when we leave it. All we can do is love the people around us while we can. That is all we can do." I reach for the scissors and the newspaper clippings and lay them on her nightstand. "Why don't you put these away for tonight? Try to get some sleep. Things always feel better in the morning."

She nods and grudgingly slides flat on her back, her flashlight casts our shadows against the wall. She clicks the light off and my eyes work to adjust in the darkness. I lean forward and kiss her forehead, partly surprised when she lets me.

"Sweet dreams, Jane."

"Good night, Dad."

I turn to leave and before I reach the door she calls out.

"Dad?" I pause in the threshold, and she continues, "I don't mean to be so rude to Mom all the time. Sometimes I can't help it, but I feel bad. Please tell her I'm sorry."

"You should tell her yourself. She'd appreciate it."

"Maybe. I wanted you to know, so you're not disappointed in me."

"I could never be disappointed in you. And I'll tell you a secret."

"What?"

"You are just like your mom was as a girl. And your uncle Tommy too. And they were the people I loved most in the world." She is silent, the covers up to her chin. "But I still think she'd like to hear what you said. It would mean a lot to her."

I shut the door behind me and walk down the hall to our bedroom, noting that the carpet we installed when we moved in over a decade ago is thinned and fraying around the edges. We will have to replace it soon. I open the door to our room, the ache of a full day's work weighing on my body. Evelyn is asleep, turned to face her nightstand. At night we lie together, the curve of her waist pressed into me. Even sleeping alone she has positioned herself to be held.

Her words linger, *I thought she was invincible.* I switch off the lamp glaring above her and slide under the covers. I move closer and she shifts her hips backward to meet me. I kiss the smooth skin on her shoulders. "Good night, Evelyn. I love you so much."

She murmurs, muffled words I can only assume mean the same. The thought enters my mind, my fear morphs into a silent vow. *I'll never live without her. Not even for a day.*

With that, and her body against mine, a sense of calm washes over me, and for the first night in a while, I sleep. I sleep and dream of a life without death, and an eternity to lie with the woman I love in my arms.

Fifteen

Evelyn

December 2001

Some days are good days, but today is not one of them. I spend most of it in and out of sleep on the couch, my shoulders and neck stiff with pain. When I wake in the late afternoon, Joseph is reading in the armchair. "Joseph?" I peer up at him, wipe my chin and lips, wet with drool.

He flips the corner of the newspaper down to see me, his face creases with worry that he attempts to hide with a sad smile. "How are you feeling?"

"Okay. Tired."

"I know."

"Violet asked if we want her to host Christmas."

"That's nice of her."

I whisper, fear creeping into my chest, although we are alone, "I don't want anyone else hosting Christmas."

I knew everything would be different once they knew. Even as I try to freeze myself in time this final year, their image of me will shift, morph like my brain scans. But this is our last

Christmas, and I don't want it marred any more than it already is with worry, with well-meaning advice or offers of help, a steady arm extended every time I stand, pitying glances around the room. I am their mother, their grandmother, not a patient under their care, someone to monitor or grant sympathy. So for now, I want one last Christmas with my family, even if it's my illusion. One more memory that includes me as I am, not as they will come to see me.

My eyelids heavy, sleep bidding me once more as Joseph says, "You don't have to carry everything on your own, you know."

I have no strength to argue, I can't see him anymore, my chest an anchor dragging me below the depths, where space and time cease to exist, where the pain I inflict disappears.

The next day is a good day. The windows are frosted around the edges, a gray afternoon that begs for indoor lighting even at midday, on this frigid Christmas Eve that promises more snow. Jane's back is straight, cozy lamplight glints off the glossy surface of the Steinway where she sits on its polished ebony bench. She doesn't look at me, but I sense her awaiting my cue.

We have practiced for months, the concert in January, which at first seemed both too long to wait and not enough time to rehearse, now is only a month away. I rehearsed on my own to feign faster progress when we met, my hands often not cooperating, striking the wrong chords, notes jumbled in my mind, the keys seemed closer together, or my fingers larger. The tremors set me off course, clumsy. Joseph refused to let me give it up, despite my protests. I relented, even with the nagging humiliation at my selfish desires, because I need the time alone with Jane. The afternoons disguised as piano practice that I can use to guide her toward a truth about her own life that she knows but is afraid to admit. A concert designed for me, encasing my ploy to gather us all together, Marcus forever imprinted in this gift we share, a path that leads her to him.

My fingers are at ease on the Baldwin as I begin to play, and Jane joins in on the Steinway, but still, I can't get it right. The first sheet of music, which we have practiced most often, is manageable from muscle memory, but after, I scramble, my fingers can't find the notes in time. Jane stops and waits patiently for me between each mistake while I reset and try again.

Again, we start from the top, again I'm too slow. I am scarring the music as I struggle. We stop, reset. Begin. The notes fly off the page, but my fingers don't respond fast enough, as though my brain signals are trudging through mud. What was I thinking, taking this on? Stop, reset. Begin again. I'm behind. I can't keep up. I can't do this. She is getting ahead, and I am falling apart. What becomes of a pianist who loses her hands? I slam my fists on the keys, and the ugly discord of my frustration reverberates through the house.

"It's alright, Mom. We still have time to practice. It's okay."

She is exceedingly patient, so understanding it verges on condescension, the same encouraging look I recognize because it was the one I used on her, when she was a child aggravated that the piano didn't make the music she wanted.

We still have time. But what if we don't?

"Let's hope you're right." I trace the keys; they are smooth and cold and familiar and strange under my fingertips. I feel her gaze, the air pulses with the question she is about to ask, *how are you feeling*, a conversation I'm tired of having, so I add, "Why don't we take a break, see how Violet and Rain are coming along in the kitchen?"

"Sure. I told Marcus I would save him some Christmas cookies."

I lean against her, happy for the opening. "I think he'd rather you were his Christmas cookie, dear."

"Oh my gosh, Mom..." Jane covers her face with her hands. "And you wonder why I don't bring him around?"

I shrug my shoulders, and say, before covering the keys, "I may have Parkinson's, but I'm not blind...and neither is he."

"Is it not *enough* that I'm a strong, independent woman?"

She says it tongue in cheek, but I couldn't be more serious. "Being independent, being strong, doesn't mean you have to be alone. It's important you understand." I pause. "Why are you so afraid to give Marcus a real chance?"

Jane's tone shifts defensively, caught off guard. "You know why."

"You're not the girl that ran off to California, and Marcus is nothing like that man either. And it was so long ago...don't you think it's time you let yourself love again?"

"Look what happens when you let yourself love! Look at you two, giving up everything for each other. Look at Maelynn. She finally settled down, and then she died, out of nowhere. You think that's a coincidence?"

"Oh, honey, you can't believe that." It feels absurd to counter, but I had no idea she was carrying this superstition, holding back from something good, sure the other shoe would drop. "Maelynn was happier than she had ever been with Betty. She loved Maelynn very much, I heard it in her voice every time we spoke. Loving Betty isn't what killed Maelynn. I am so thankful that the last years of her life were not spent alone. And it's *because* of the love that your father and I shared that I am okay with death. Because I really lived. It's time you let yourself have something real. It's worth it. It's the only thing that's worth anything."

In the kitchen, Violet and Rain have begun an angel food cake and I wonder if I added that to the recipe book. I must have. I can't remember. I wrote down all the children's favorite family recipes and put them in a bound book for Christmas this year. I have been working on it for months. Some days my writing is so tiny, impossible to make out, but I'm unable to write larger, no matter how hard I try. Sometimes I have trouble remembering—steps are jumbled and ingredients forgotten. Some days my mind is sharp and clear, and I write as much as I can until I need to rest. More often, the tremble makes my penmanship illegible, scratches and scribbles deface the pristine lines. I rip out entire pages, the torn edges left behind in the binding.

I perch at the table, watch Violet and Rain execute the familiar recipe, Rain's belly beginning to round beneath her wool sweater. It is like a ballet, the way they pivot between ingredients, without hesitation in this known landscape they could navigate blindfolded. Exhaustion creeps in, blurring the edges, but for now I am content to sit nearby, bathing in their company. The flour-dusted countertops, the festive aprons, the clatter of our movements as the sink fills with mixing bowls and measuring cups. I'm not sure when it happened, when I found the beauty in domesticity and embraced all the comfort it brings. One of my favorite things is to press my spoon through thickening batter and await the moment my family comes bursting through the door, rosy-cheeked with frozen toes to warm before the fire. The heaps of layers stripped in the foyer, hats and gloves propped against the radiator to dry. Sometimes I wonder where that little girl from the beach went. The girl who was afraid of heights yet desperate to fly. If she would recognize herself in me at all.

Joseph comes down the stairs, poking around for something tasty to steal. "Looks good, girls. When can we dig in?"

"Not until tonight. Everyone will be here at six. Thomas and Ann are even staying overnight. Imagine that!" I wink at Joseph.

"He's come a long way, our son."

"But he's still useless in the kitchen, so we told him six o'clock is fine," Violet says, and Jane nods, laughing. Rain dips her finger into the batter bowl and giggles when she catches Joseph's eye.

"Grandpa, you didn't see a thing." She smiles a wide, guilty smile.

I reach for Joseph, and he sidles beside me. I like the feel of his rough palms, toughened from working in the garden. I love to watch him there, finally in his element, the musk of earth and sweat clinging to him when he retreats inside. I wish I could smell it one more time on his skin. The doctors said it's common with Parkinson's, an early indicator of what was overtaking me. How I wish I could smell the cake baking in the oven, the buttery sweetness filling the house. But for now, it is enough to know it is there, while I am still here, beside my daughters and my oldest granddaughter, watching their subconscious choreography, gliding and shuffling and spinning around each other as they work.

"Mom, you sure you want us to leave you to finish up? We can skip it this year." Jane studies me, concern on her face. They are going to take Joseph to do some last-minute Christmas shopping, a tradition begun years ago when the Oyster Shell, packed with families visiting for the holidays, was too busy to allow him to shop in advance. He has the time now that we've closed the inn, our agreement after he turned sixty so we could enjoy retirement, but they look forward to seeing the stores together on Christmas Eve, decked in garlands and lights.

I shake my head. "No problem, a bit more mixing and I'll pop this last one in the oven. You go ahead." Jane opens her mouth to rebut, but I insist. "Go, I'm fine." Hesitant, they gather their things and are out the door in a flurry of scarves and mittens and puffy jackets with a promise to be back soon.

Once they are gone, I scrape the batter into the cake pan. About an hour to cook will be right. I write down what time they left in case I can't remember. Things like that have helped me lately. Joseph's idea. He is full of ideas to make this all easier on me. Some, like writing notes, or labeling photographs, making lists, help. Still, I am losing words.

The mixing has tired me. I need to rest up for this evening. Thomas and Ann will arrive soon, Tony will be here after he and Rain visit with his family, and Connor and the kids too. Since my talk with Violet, I've noticed glimpses of the tenderness that once existed between them, in the passing of a butter dish at dinner without being asked, or the casual plucking of lint off a sweater. It's not a loveless marriage, but I know love is not all it takes. I hope what I shared was enough, that how lost I once felt can provide a foothold for her, a way back to him. I'm thankful Violet and I differ in this crucial way; she can be guided, advised, her perspective reshaped through conversations, she can learn by watching others. Jane is more like me. No one could have told us, saved us from our mistakes. We had to see how it felt to run.

Jane, who still won't listen. Who won't invite Marcus over, who won't admit they're dating, who will forge the longest, hardest road so she can say she got there on her own. We met him at the news station years ago, but even in that brief exchange, she looked for excuses for us to linger, to watch him record his segment, and he stretched his neck to search for her as soon as the cameras cut, when their eyes met, both faces crinkled with affection. He was earnest in his hello, asked after our lunch plans with genuine interest, while their bodies hummed the same melody, drawn together in the space between them.

She talks about him enough that I've pieced together the rough outline of his life: how he grew up with a bunch of siblings in Roxbury, the years he spent as a war reporter, how he never married, always chasing his career and traveling. But I need to *know* him, and for him to know us. It will be important to Jane...after. I don't want her to wait as long as I did, as Maelynn did, to realize that loving someone doesn't mean losing yourself, that it can add more than it takes. I hope I have enough time.

Forty-six minutes left on the timer. The seconds drag. I keep dozing off. They will understand. But I can't forget about the cake. I can't ruin their favorite dessert. They would understand that too. There is little I can do wrong now that wouldn't be explained away, coddled, a toddler who can't help but make a mess. But I can't, not on this last Christmas. I need to stay awake. I try to focus on my most concrete thoughts, on Joseph. His silver hair, his thumbnail split down the center from a wayward hammer, his frame solid as an oak tree. I am flooded with guilt, thinking about my near-flight to Boston, all the years I almost threw away, when now all I wish is for more of our life together, the way it was back then. Thinking about our plan, all we will leave behind, and the arguments we've had over it. Me, insisting he can't do this; him, adamant he can't bear a life alone, and that my decision defines his. My decision, an impossible one, unthinkable. But the alternative is a different kind of demise, slow, debilitating, certain. Death isn't the only way to die. But on an evening like this, fresh snowfall and a cake in the oven, it feels like it should never have been my call to make.

My thoughts send me into a dreamless sleep. I am startled and frightened by beeping and the opening of a door, the house bursts with the buzz of voices and clicking of footsteps. Then I remember. My family is home. Is that the oven beeping? Did I cook? I am drunk with fatigue, but I resist the urge to drift back to sleep. It's a celebration, for someone, or something, I remember now. It's my family in the foyer, in the living room, swinging the wooden door into the kitchen. I need to be here.

Connor pushes open the door to the kitchen, trailed by four mops of red hair. Lanky Patrick on the verge of becoming a teenager, Ryan sporting a scraggly beard that is either an attempt at growing one or sheer college laziness. Confident and effervescent Shannon who shares Violet's petite figure, and...who is this, this oldest daughter with pale freckles faded by winter, this rounded face and cheerful disposition? I scan my mind for details...a clue. Is she in college, or has she graduated? Where does she live? My mind is blank, panicked, searching desperately for a name I can't find. I force a smile as they enter. It's a celebration for something. Christmas Eve. That's right. Christmas Eve.

"Mom, is something burning in here?" Violet rushes to the

oven, still beeping, yanks open the door, smoke billowing out. "Oh no."

The cake, the cake, I forgot about the cake. Violet carries it to the counter, the top singed. Connor throws open the nearest window, cold air rushing in.

The tickle in my throat, eyes welling. "I'm sorry, I thought..." But I can't finish.

Violet turns to me, catches my eye, my embarrassed tears. "Oh, Mom, no, no it's okay. We can scrape off the top. It's fine."

Heat spreads to my cheeks. "Throw it out. It's ruined."

"Molly, grab a knife." *Molly.* Molly, who works in Providence. She took the train in last night. Of course. Violet gives me another pitying look. "Mom, really, it's okay."

Molly puts her arm around me. "Hey, it's an excuse for more whipped cream."

Later, there is the tearing of presents and stories by the fireplace. Eggnog and cookies shaped like Santa and snowmen and jingle bells. Jane plays "Have Yourself a Merry Little Christmas" on the piano and I'm transported to years ago, when Joseph and the kids surprised me with a performance of that very song.

"I do have one more gift," I say, once the celebrations have settled, everyone strewn across couches and stretched out on the floor. Out of a large gift bag I retrieve a stack of wrapped packages, and motion for Ryan to pass out one to each of his cousins, and one each for Jane, Violet and Thomas too. "These took some time, and they aren't perfect," I hedge, as they begin to unwrap, hoping it's enough, that giving them something to hold, to keep, to remember me by, will make up for all I'm taking away. "I had to rip out some pages, but, well, you'll see."

There is only the sound of tearing paper, and then a hush follows. Rain, Molly and Shannon, together on the couch, bend over the covers of the bound recipe books, their hands clasped tight. Rain begins, "Grandma, this is... I can't believe you did this for us." Ann and Thomas sit together, flip through the pages with care.

"Mom, this is incredible," Violet says, sniffling. "How did you...when did you?"

"Oh no, Vi, don't look inside the front cover," Jane says, teasing, as she wipes tears from her eyes. Inside each, the inscription: *May these recipes always bring you home, bring you joy, and remind you of all the days we spent cooking and sharing meals, together by the sea.*

Lying wide-awake in bed that night, Joseph is asleep beside me. The clock on my nightstand reads 3 a.m. It is officially Christmas. Flashes of earlier years crisscross my mind, little bare feet pattering down the hall, little bodies crawling into all the spaces between Joseph and me, the joy of Christmas magic in their eyes. The air around us is chilled, my nose cold and exposed, but the heat beneath the quilt is cozy enough to invoke the deepest slumber. But I can't; I am haunted by my failing mind. The cake, Molly's name. What else will I forget? What if it doesn't click into place after a few moments? And yet—the joy in something as simple as baking with my daughters, of all the hugs as they came into the house—how many years of this will I miss? How many years will I take away from Joseph? He could outlive me. I could outlive him. That's the way it goes. If you don't plan it. If you don't run.

I memorize the way his lips part, his slow, loud exhales. When we first married, he slept on his stomach and I nuzzled against him. I took for granted the way we wrapped effortlessly around each other, sinking into one form. Now he lies on his back, wisps of hair stuck to the top of his head. His shoulders are still broad, but slimmer, frailer. I long to curl around him but tonight, like most nights, my body aches too much to be contorted to fit his. I want our young agile bodies one last time. The mornings where we woke entwined, letting the morning slide into the afternoon. It has gotten more difficult these last few years, but we still make love when we can. I'm afraid for the time that will be our last, because there will be no way to know it, not in the moment. No way to hold on to it in the ways I wish I could.

But for now, it is only Joseph and me, and this early morning, this final Christmas. With the snow falling lightly outside, the heat of his body pressing against me, this moment is all the magic I need. I reach for Joseph's hand. Even in sleep he closes his fingers around mine.

I know I am running, but to what, I'm not sure. My only hope is wherever I run, someday, somehow, we will meet again.

I edge myself toward my nightstand, flick on the light and pull a notepad from my drawer, penning a safety net, a way out of this vow he has bound himself in.

Because the only thing I'm sure of is this—I can't let him follow me.

I can't do this with him by my side.

Sixteen

Joseph

May 1969

Evelyn stands by the counter, beating eggs and directing Violet to sift flour as I tinker with the gas range, the pilot light out. Violet chatters as she rolls out dough for a piecrust for our Memorial Day party. "I still need a new dress. I'm not wearing anything from Jane's old bin."

At thirteen, she has started to resist the position as Jane's little sister, her hand-me-downs, their shared bedroom kindling for contention on both sides.

Knowing her mother stews inside her house alone all day when she isn't with us, Evelyn invited her over to help with preparations. Mrs. Saunders perches at the counter, squints at Violet's technique. "Oh, not so thin, you're going to rip it."

Thomas, fifteen, sits at the table cramming for finals. He's always studying, relentless about a good night's sleep so he can go on early morning runs, homed in on enlisting in the air force and becoming a fighter pilot. We encourage him to meet up with friends, to ask girls on dates, but he insists he needs to focus. I'm torn. I've seen war. I know what it can do, what it really means. But it's the one thing he speaks about with any enthusiasm, the only thing we can get him to talk about at all these days, and I can't bring myself to steer him away.

Jane pokes through the refrigerator, covering the counter in an odd assortment of sandwich ingredients. Things have been especially rocky between her and Evelyn these last few months. Jane hates her curfew and keeping her music down, she holes up in her room most of the time listening to the news on the radio. She comes home smelling of beer, babbling and incoherent, and sneaks out after we forbid her from leaving the house. Most of it is normal teenage behavior, I rationalize, and truthfully, things between Jane and me have always been smooth; she's smart and gets good grades, she's independent like her mother, and I've always trusted her to make the right decisions in the end.

But recently, Jane announced she wants to take a year off before college, to move to Boston this fall, after she turns eighteen. She'll rent an apartment with a friend and try to get a job at a newspaper or radio station. To get life experience, she says, before applying anywhere. We aren't exactly pleased; we were sure Jane would be thrilled to go off to college, and had saved for it. But we know better than to force her. Still, Evelyn is struggling to let her go, knowing in a few months she'll make mistakes without our safety net beneath her. Last night, they fought about Jane's graduation. I walked in on them, corralled in their doorways.

Jane braced against the door trim, cocked toward her mother. "It's stupid, and a waste of time. I get my diploma, whether I go or not."

Evelyn's voice was low, threatening, her arms crossed. "That's not the point. You worked hard to get here, what's the alternative? Drinking with your friends?"

Jane screeched, "I'm not going! Have you seen what's going

on in this world? You and everyone else, you're focused on all the wrong things."

"What's going on in the world has nothing to do with you, or this conversation. You have so much potential—"

"This is the shit I'm talking about! You don't care about anything that actually matters, you never have."

"Jane, enough!" I yelled, late on the scene, as she slammed her door and Evelyn stormed into our room. When we went to lock up for the night, there was money missing from Evelyn's purse, and Jane's bedroom windows left open, her bed empty. I want to address it, but reprimanding Jane in front of everyone, especially her grandmother, would only make it worse.

"We actually have something to tell you all. Thomas, Jane, are you listening?"

Thomas glances up from his homework, silently agreeing to pay attention.

"Kind of," Jane mumbles, her head stuck in the refrigerator.

"We hired someone to work here, to help out for the busy season. So you can enjoy being teenagers, so we can all enjoy this last summer before Jane leaves." Evelyn says this, a peace offering we had planned weeks ago, but there is an edge to her voice now, the missing ten-dollar bill not forgotten.

"What? Who?" Jane asks, her mouth full of sandwich.

"A law student from Yale, his name is Sam. He applied through Professor Chen, you remember him?" Her question is met by blank looks from the kids. "You should, he's stayed with us for years...well anyway, he set up some referral program all over the state for course credit, and asked if we wanted to participate. One student works here in exchange for room and board, and writes a paper or something about it at the end? I'm not sure exactly how it works. All I know is it's an extra set of hands. I know it'll be a bit different around here, but we're hoping it frees us up, gives us more time as a family since it's our last summer all together," Evelyn says, her excitement peeking through. "He'll start Memorial Day."

Jane chews her final bite slowly before answering. "You hired some strange guy to live here without even telling us? Great. Really nice." She drops her plate into the sink with a clatter. "I'll be in my room."

"Jane—" I call out, but she is already up the stairs, her only response the slam of her bedroom door.

Sam begins with us that Monday. He takes the train from New Haven and I pick him up. He is from Madison, Wisconsin, he tells me on our drive, and he is looking forward to a summer spent on the coast. He is lean, in the way that suggests he hasn't done much hard labor, his arm muscles undefined beneath his white T-shirt, but there's a certain confidence to him, and something else, like he could hold his own in a fight. On the drive we share brief histories, how my family had run our inn for generations, how he spent the last few summers in different parts of the country, seeking new experiences as a way to gain perspective, live a little between his demanding academic years.

"I spent last summer working along the Missouri River, trying to see what Mark Twain saw, when he was there working on steamboats. He's a Hartford man, too, you know. Raised his family right here in Connecticut. I read all his work while I was down there."

He says it casually, without hubris, and his easy smile reminds me of someone I can't place, Tommy, maybe, but not quite, and it makes me feel like I know him, somehow. His face is good-looking in an obvious way, magnetic, something part of me wishes I had known before bringing him home to my teenage daughters. He lounges in the car beside me like it belongs to him, like it's the most natural thing in the world to be here, arm out the open window, and as we round the bend to Ber-

nard Beach he says, "I can see why you've never left this place."
I like him immediately.

Evelyn and Violet are draping red, white and blue streamers
onto the porch when they hear us arrive, linen-covered tables
scatter the lawn, set with pitchers of lemonade and iced tea, croquet wickets and mallets in the grass. Sam lifts his single suitcase
from the trunk, and waves a hand in greeting, and they meet
us on the driveway.

"All this for me?" He winks at Violet, before shaking Evelyn's
hand, holding it a second too long. Violet giggles and thumbs
her curls, adjusts the hem of her sundress, looking suddenly a
bit older than I would like her to, giddy with his brief attention.

"Is this not how everyone welcomes new employees?" Evelyn says, gesturing around at the party. "Forgive us, we've never
done it."

Sam gives a hearty laugh. "Trust me—" his gaze lingers on
Evelyn "—this is already better than any place I've worked."

And it can't be my wife, blushing over this comment, pink
splotches rising on her chest. I consider saying something, telling him to watch his mouth, but no, it's in my head. Surely,
it's not what he meant, who would be so bold their first day of
work? A harmless compliment, a reference to the beach, to the
party, to this beautiful summer day. This stranger thrust into
our sanctuary setting us off-kilter. A kid. Too handsome for his
own good, maybe, used to a world where doors open, where
women can be made to feel beautiful with a glance.

We usher him inside, where we find Thomas at the table,
bent over his textbooks. Sam cocks his head to read the spines.

"Geometry proofs...man, I used to hate those. Until I realized
it's like winning an argument, a lot like what I do now, actually. Saying something and backing it up, line by line, until no
one can disagree." Thomas looks up at him, the faintest smile
on his lips. "I'm Sam, by the way. Sorry to interrupt."

"No, it's fine, it's, yeah, I think about it that way too. That's funny." Thomas puts his pencil down. "Thomas."

"Let me know if you need a study partner, I'm happy to help. Although from the looks of it," he adds, drumming the covers of the books with his knuckles, "you have it under control."

"Thanks, I appreciate that," Thomas says, concluding the longest conversation any of us have had with him in weeks.

We give Sam a brief tour, Violet leading the way, and give him some time to unpack and get settled in his room. Violet leaves to finish crafting centerpieces of driftwood and seashells, and we are back in the kitchen slicing tomatoes and chopping lettuce, burger toppings for later, when he rejoins us.

"How can I help?" he asks, as Jane plods down the stairs in a top that shows too much of her midriff. She stops at the landing when she sees him.

"Actually, Sam, meet our oldest daughter, Jane. Why don't you two head outside and set up the chairs?" Evelyn says, surprising me. I brace for Jane's resistance, hoping a fight doesn't break out in front of Sam, at least not on the first day.

"Sure," Jane says, agreeable in a way that is disconcerting, and he follows her out back.

"You really think that's a good idea?" I ask, eyeing the two of them as Jane guides Sam to the storage shed.

"Sam's in college. Maybe he can convince her in a way we can't." A benefit to this temporary hire that hadn't occurred to me, but had been clearly tallied by Evelyn. I watch them together as we chop, Jane's head tipped back in laughter, a sound I barely remember, setting up the party to usher in the summer season, her last with us. Sam gestures animatedly as they unclench folding chairs, closed tight like all the years of Jane's resentment, one by one, open to the sun.

We get into a flow quicker than I expect. Sam and Evelyn tag team most of the front desk operations, check-ins and checkouts, and I handle back of house, turning rooms and tackling projects I've been putting off. Regulars stop me in the halls to comment on how wonderful Sam is, how helpful, how welcoming. Hiring him does what we intended, cuts our work significantly, but now it is not only our new employee's help that we have. Jane slices cantaloupe beside Evelyn in the kitchen, lingers by the desk, answering phones and taking messages and chatting with Sam. Violet, enamored, pops up everywhere, seemingly anticipating his needs, showing how to jiggle the knob on the linen closet when it sticks, and where to find the 1970 calendar for guests who want to return next summer, and how to properly fold a fitted sheet. Thomas even chops wood outside when he sees Sam forming a pile, and I overhear him asking questions about Yale, about his classes and professors, life on campus. Not going to college had never bothered me before. I know enough to navigate my way through our ledgers, but Sam makes it sound like an awakening, learning about yourself more than the texts, the deepest knowledge that I always envied in Evelyn and Tommy. Regret creeps up for the first time, an opportunity missed.

One set of hands hired for the summer becomes four with the unexpected participation from our children, and there is more help than we need, not enough to do in this inn usually run by two. We throw barbecues for guests and neighbors, the whole yard thick with the tantalizing smell of meat and smoke. Sam shows Evelyn how to marinate chicken thighs in Cajun spices, something he picked up in New Orleans, our tongues sharp with the heat. We carry beach chairs overhead at low tide, claiming spots on the sandbars, staying until the water rises past our knees. Dinner parties of clams baked on the half shell and buttery lobsters devolve into dancing, couples slinking off to darkened corners of the beach. Mornings nursing headaches, foggy recollections tinged with embarrassment. Bonfires in the sand late into the night, our voices carrying out to Captain's Rock, laughter and liquor shared by flickering flames, faces lit by the moon and fire, foamy waves rolling in the dark.

One afternoon, Evelyn and I recline under a cloud-strewn sky. Jane pushes Sam beneath the water at high tide, surfacing on his shoulders, challenging Thomas and Violet to a chicken fight. Violet, no match for Jane, is tackled quickly, and roughly, and after the second round, she comes up sputtering and gasping, declaring the game over. She mopes back to the beach, wrapping herself in a towel.

Sam drags Evelyn out in her place, grabbing her hands to pull her to standing. Jane grumbles about having to be on Thomas's shoulders, but Sam assures her it is only fair to switch up teams. Evelyn looks back at me, shakes her head as though she has no choice, but she is laughing, and goes easily.

Together in the waves, Sam submerges to lift her, Evelyn's legs wrapped around his neck for only a moment, but I'm taken aback by the intimacy of it, the places of Evelyn only I know, pressed against the back of his hair, her swimsuit dripping, wet and friction and bare skin, before Jane topples her over. My chest tight with something I can't quite name, as I watch from shore.

Evelyn

Sam walks into the kitchen shirtless, his hair damp from a morning swim. I am brewing coffee to set out for guests. Violet, Jane and Thomas are still asleep upstairs, Joseph is in town to pick up paint to fix the peeling porch.

"Coffee." He sidles up beside me, holds out a mug with gratitude, a savior with a fresh pot. He smells of salt, of sweat, close enough the hair on his arms brushes mine.

I take a half step away, too aware of his body. "You were the one making whiskey sours."

This summer with Sam is unlike any other. The freedom hired help can apparently bring, the valve we had wrenched so tight all these years, loosened. An instrument finally in tune. The ease of it, handing over tasks I had wrongly assumed only the two of us could manage. Our busiest season passing swiftly, smoothly, neither of us stretched to the breaking point. The renewed novelty of Bernard Beach in July, without having to rush back, without feeling guilty about what isn't getting done. Parsing out moments of joy between tasks, watermelon eaten off the rind on the back porch, a sunrise stroll alone on the sandbar as the sky turns pink, the way I had always imagined it could be, but never quite was. Even Jane is changed, no longer scarce, her defenses down. The burden of the work awaiting us each morning, released. Giving us the ability to be irresponsible, spontaneous, for once, knowing it's not all on us to steer the ship. Lets me stop resisting, holding on to everything outside of my control with a white-knuckle grip. To exist in the night instead of turning in early to bed, to be reckless, to feel young, to *be* young, to welcome that teenage feeling of endless summer, to give in to revelry.

"A man on the moon." He flashes me a grin, closes the space between us once more. "We had to drink to that."

Walter Cronkite on the television, a broadcast lasting twenty-seven hours. The grainy images we watched in our living room, the windows open to our cheers and our yells and the sticky summer air, drinks poured and records spun and we could barely hear the updates over the din, every now and then someone shushing the crowd, only to be drowned out again by the laughter and clinking glasses. Neil Armstrong in his space suit, the American flag lifted as though by a breeze, an astronaut achieving the unbelievable. A man, like us. Walking on the moon. The future, limitless, no longer capped by the sky. The world a place of magic, of mystique, once more.

"It's still hard to believe," I say, turning to rest my back against the counter, facing him.

"Oh come on." He sips from his mug, eyes on mine, teasing me, reading me, seeing me in ways that are unsettling. "We knew this was only a matter of time."

"Well, sure." I feign competence, indifference. "NASA has been working on it for a while." I search for specifics, something to show I'm not so easily impressed, a moon landing a footnote on a long list of incredible things I've seen. "It was bound to happen sooner than later."

"Of course," he agrees, laughing. "But geez, Evelyn. You're a tough one to impress." Turning the tables on me once more, conversations with Sam a tennis match, a volley I try to keep up with at every serve. "A guy may as well not even try." He winks, and my stomach flutters. "Shower time. I'll be there if you need me."

The warmth between my legs startles me, the image of him naked between the stream of water, waiting for me. I immediately banish the thought. I could be his mother. This is how Sam speaks to everyone. I've seen him make old ladies blush, regular guests who stop by the front desk asking the way to the beach, requesting extra towels they never use. At bonfires, the tales of the women he's slept with, shared past midnight across embers, told not as conquests but as invitations to imagine him doing so. To imagine myself, what it would feel like to experience a different body, sweaty and pressing, against my own.

Sam's twenty-three, I tell myself, and that's how people are these days, freer with sex than we ever were, promiscuous now because of the pill, and open about it, an adjustment of our expectations, nothing more.

Then what is it that makes me eager to get downstairs, to hope he's awake, to catch him alone, to bask in the heat of his attention? The conversations that keep me guessing, have me lying awake, rethinking my answers, what I could have said, the different ways I could have preened, shown my feathers. The performances he begs for since he discovered I play piano, an interest we share. "I could listen to you play all day," he murmured once as he passed through the study, as though this hobby of mine is something sexy, smoke passed between parted lips. Something worth chasing once more because Sam says so, because he makes me feel like it's not too late, because he understands the one thing I've always had to explain, without me saying a word.

Joseph

Jane's eighteenth birthday falls on a sunny Saturday in late August, the final stretch of summer that feels both infinite and fleeting. Mrs. Saunders is beside me at the counter, threading cloth napkins into rings adorned with starfish. Sam and Evelyn are setting up outside, Violet and Thomas tasked with hanging linens and folding towels and sweeping the porch, Jane still fast asleep in her room.

"I don't know what we're going to do without Sam after Labor Day," I say, watching as he and Evelyn recover a tablecloth carried on a breeze, hold either end and secure it with clamps.

"Really? I'll be glad to see him gone. Inserts himself where he doesn't belong, if you ask me," Mrs. Saunders says, her gaze held a second too long on my wife outside, the exact moment Evelyn playfully shoves Sam, before going back to rolling napkins.

Usually I ignore her criticisms, often off base and steeped in envy, but as she says it, instances lift in my mind. Sam rubbing sunscreen on Evelyn's back that morning I was occupied on the roof ladder. Showing her how to mix vodka and ginger beer and lime juice, topping her off each time. Cramped together on one piano bench, trading performances. How he strips his bathing suit off under his towel, hanging it to dry while he waits his turn for the outdoor shower, naked except for the towel at his waist.

I find myself peeking through the kitchen window too often, until I feel Mrs. Saunders watching me, too, my attention a confirmation I never meant to give.

Jane stops halfway down the stairs, already dressed in her bikini, her disappointment evident that her entrance was wasted on her father and grandmother.

"He's out back," I say, jutting my thumb in Sam's direction, eager to break up the twosome outside. "Happy birthday, Janey."

She grins, and says, "Eighteen, finally!" and nearly dances down to meet us, planting a kiss on my cheek, to my astonishment, before rushing out the screen door into the glaring late morning sun.

"I wonder why she's so excited to turn eighteen," Mrs. Saunders says dryly, as Jane leaps onto Sam's back, exposing the little modesty her bathing suit bottom covered.

I dry wineglasses from last night in silence, unsure how to respond without her reading into all the things I don't intend to say.

We work with haste all morning, eager to get to the beach, and soon the sand is scattered with bodies stretched on towels slathered in baby oil, Jane's friends making wide circles in the water, smoke from their cigarettes going out to sea. Sam pulls his chair up alongside the other side of Evelyn's, Jane on his left. I overhear them all talking, impassioned snippets about a commune out in California, a trip he was planning to Morocco, some pilgrimage for spiritual enlightenment, the anti-war movement, but I am two chairs away, too far to engage in a conversation not meant for me. I try to think of something interesting to add, something Maelynn said once about her travels, maybe, but come up empty.

The day sinks into night, the party spilling out onto our lawn, guests as always interspersed and welcome to join in the festivities, to fill plates to the brim with potato salad and chicken wings, to spike their lemonade with gin. The drinks are poured and passed, passed and poured, and someone I don't recognize lights a fire out back as dusk falls. We send Violet to bed, despite her protests, and, a bit later, Thomas, who is furious to be looped in with his younger sister instead of the adults. Evelyn begins to collect dishes, though she dances while she does it, big stacks piled in the kitchen, cleaning left for another day.

The darkness gives the alcohol a feeling of wildness, or perhaps the alcohol gives the darkness a feeling of wildness, of the possibility that anything, and everything, could happen tonight. I lose track of Jane, and immediately look for Sam, who I have lost, too, in the throng. Evelyn is perched by the fire in clear view, in deep conversation with our neighbor Linda, and I am ashamed of the relief I feel when I spot her. When I sidle up beside them, Linda wanders off and never reappears. My head begins to get fuzzy, aware of bodies in motion all around us, but Evelyn is clear before me, asking if I need another beer, if I could refill her cup on my way. I don't need one, but our oldest daughter is eighteen, and we made it all the way here, across space and time and heartache and children, to raise one to adulthood, together, and I will certainly drink to that.

I wander through the diminishing crowd, and get caught in conversations I try to extricate myself from, to reach the table littered with mostly empty liquor bottles and grab a beer, mix a vodka soda with lime for Evelyn.

Behind the bushes, Jane and Sam stand a foot apart, in my view, but blind to me.

"Now that summer's almost over..." Jane starts, sounding nervous, muffled. "You know, I'm eighteen now." My stomach drops, not wanting to overhear this, split between an urge to intervene and to disappear, remembering how it feels to be a teen, the intoxication of first love, and a father's need to shelter his daughter, now grown.

"I know." Sam pats her arm. "Happy birthday, kid." Relief washes over me, layered with surprise, that he wouldn't take advantage of a girl so obviously infatuated, who pined after him all summer, who could easily be his before he leaves, and never be seen again.

"I'm not a kid," she says, her voice syrup, pulling him close.

"Sure," Sam says, peeling her arms off him.

"I could go with you, you know. To Paris. Like you said." She's dripping with desperation, her speech slurring, and now it's nearly too late, I need to leave, to have walked away already. She can't catch me here, would never forgive what I've heard.

"Listen, you're great. I've enjoyed hanging with you all summer. But, we're just not…" I can't see her face, but can hear her sniffle, her breathing quick, a wilted version of Jane I've never seen. "You're still so young. You know?"

She sniffles hard, leaning into him. "I'm not that young."

"How much did you drink?" He sounds annoyed, her affection a gnat to swat away.

"Enough to know I'm not too young for you." She tilts her chin up to his, and kisses him.

He pulls back, hard. "Jane, please, don't. Okay? You're embarrassing yourself." He looks behind him, and says, "If I wanted you, you'd know."

I feel his words like a punch, ready to hit back, but before I can say anything, do anything, Jane runs off, audibly crying, and Sam slinks off into the dark. I debate chasing after Jane, but what would I say? Her dad is probably the last person she wants to see.

Shaken and sobered, I busy myself clearing stray cups and empty bottles before heading back. Berating myself for not jumping in, for not protecting her from humiliation, heartache. I tie up overflowing garbage bags and haul them to the bin, anything to calm myself, steady my trembling hands before facing Evelyn, sure she will read me, and unsure what good it would do to confess what I overheard.

I force it out of my mind, and navigate the best I can through the shadows, the sky above a black swath reflecting nothing, stars swallowed in clouds. As I approach the fire once more, the lawn is mostly deserted. Sam has reappeared beside Evelyn, the two of them alone by the fire, and I'm jolted by the sight of him. A flare of anger at how he treated Jane replaced by something worse, because somehow when I approach it feels that I am the one interrupting, unwanted. A sudden flush of heat, a twinge in my gut, this feeling I can't explain, but know is true. My wife, who loves me, who wants me gone.

I hand Evelyn her drink, but stay standing by her side.

"Aren't you going to sit?" she asks, motioning to the open chair across from Sam. Their knees too close, nearly brushing. The laughter that stopped as I approached. Her smile waning as she asked, the courtesy tucked into the question, the invite sterile. The way he doesn't look at me at all, waiting for the answer, my presence an imposition to their fun.

"The beer is warm." I lift my bottle in response, my throat tight. "I think I may call it a night."

She gives me an uncertain look. "Want me to come in?" Asked out of obligation, a consideration expected in a marriage. She holds my gaze, and I can see it, the hope that I say no.

"No, stay. There's still a little fire left," I say, hating myself and hating him, and wanting to toss her over my shoulder and lay her in our bed, to see her skin flush with pleasure, to feel the charged air between them between us instead, but I don't. Because the worst part of me fears she would close her eyes, and imagine him.

"Alright, well, good night," she says, too easily, already shifting her body so I'm out of her line of view.

I turn away, wondering if, even though I trust her completely, I am making a mistake. Presenting a route she may follow, a chance to leave me gutted. But a choice that's hers to make, a way to know for sure if loving me was more than merely the circumstances of our lives, growing up together, forever entwined.

As I leave, Sam adds logs to the firepit, stoking the flames.

Evelyn

I can smell the smoke on my clothes, in my hair, as I stand, my head spinning. I shouldn't have stayed out, should've gone to bed with Joseph. Should never have put myself in this position, the drinks and the fire and moon poking through the clouded sky, a reminder that things are dangerous when everything is possible, when there's no limit to where a man may land.

I stumble away from the glowing embers, alone in the dark. Had I fallen asleep here, curled up in the cinders of my own shame? Who had left first? What time was it? No signs of pink on the horizon, the lights clicked off in the house. I push my hair out of my face and wipe my lips, my mouth cotton. Knock my knees against a reclined lawn chair as I pass by the table of liquor, all but drained, and nearly trip over Jane crouched by the bushes, clutching a bottle of gin.

"Jane?" I whisper, "What are you still doing out here?"

She laughs, a cruel, hollow sound. "You didn't think anyone was here, did you?"

"How much have you had to drink?" I peer at the bottle, hoping she's not the reason it's nearly empty. Not like I am in any position to talk.

"Why do people keep asking me that?" She clutches it close, like it will absolve her, the bandit declaring innocence while gripping the money bag.

"Come on, let's get you to bed." I attempt to lift her by the arm, but she wrenches away from me.

"Don't touch me!" she shrieks, backing away, farther into the bushes, her curls getting snarled in the branches.

"Jane, you're being ridiculous. Come inside." My head pounds, my vision swimming.

"I'm ridiculous? Look at you. At least I'm acting my age." She looks at me with hate, with disgust, with fury, and this fight is the last thing I need tonight.

"Fine, sleep out here. Christ." I can't keep protecting her, talking her out of her bad choices. It won't hurt her to sleep in the grass, maybe it's the wake-up she needs.

"Yeah, go ahead. Leave. It'll be good practice." Drunken

mutterings I can't begin to dissect, have no energy to understand, my bed calling to me, my husband beneath the sheets, waiting, my shame spinning circles, making me nauseous, even as I close my eyes.

Joseph

Normally we host a Labor Day party, a final send-off to summer before the inn slows for the season, but it feels flagrant, opulent, after a summer when celebration was our steady state. Without much discussion, we decide to ease out of the summer with a quiet weekend. School starts tomorrow for Violet and Thomas, and they are spending the day with Evelyn, picking out supplies and clothes. Sam is packing in his room, while I sip coffee alone in the kitchen. I offered to drop him at the train station, but a friend is driving him to the airport. Apparently, he got approval to miss the first couple weeks of classes for some European trip, details I tuned out as he began to talk. I've been avoiding him as much as possible since Jane's birthday, leaving the room as he enters it. Sam, who can skip weeks of classes at an elite university, travel without having worked for pay all summer. Who stayed with us as an experiment, a research project, our quaint town another box to check on his list of escapades. A taste of a life kept small, a tale to tell another man's wife across a roaring fire.

I was sure I would be shooing Jane out of Sam's room all morning, but she hasn't come downstairs. She's become impossible, surly and hostile, picking fights with Evelyn over issues I had been fooled into believing our summer together had smoothed. Nasty comments as she passes through a room, antagonizing everyone in her path, ignoring her mother when she asks her to help. I don't know if it's the imminence of Sam leaving that has brought on her bad mood, or the fact that he rebuffed her advances, or both, but the last week, she has been as scarce around him as I have tried to be. He appears through the swinging kitchen door, lifts his suitcase in hand in explanation.

"Ah. Ready, then?" I ask. He nods. I lean on the banister, and call upstairs to Jane. "Jane, Sam's leaving!" There is no reply, not even the pad of her footsteps toward her door. "Maybe she's still asleep. I'll tell her you say bye."

"Please do," he says. "Thanks, Joseph, for everything."

"Yep. Sure thing." I can't bring myself to meet his eye. "I'll walk you out."

A red Camaro idles in the driveway, he slips into it as though out of our waking dream, and I stand there until the car vanishes from view, the only sign he had been there the faint crunch of tires, the engine fading into the distance.

Seventeen

Joseph

January 2002

The children and grandchildren spend the morning scouring for samples and souvenirs at Faneuil Hall and Quincy Market, while Evelyn and I slip away before her rehearsal with the Boston Symphony Orchestra to visit our first apartment, the little one-bedroom in the South End. We take the orange line from State Street, Evelyn tucked in a plastic seat by the train doors while I grip the metal bar above her, and exit the crowded T at Mass Ave., a few blocks away from where we once lived. We meander along the sidewalk that is the strangest type of familiar, like a dream confused with a memory, or a memory confused with a dream, past things we recognized, like Wally's Café, a brand-new jazz club when this was our neighborhood—now half a century old—and things we don't, like a Shell gas station and a Dunkin' Donuts.

We turn off Tremont and our brownstone building is still there, as I remember it. The stone steps led to a heavy oak door, which opened to a dingy hallway, our apartment the first on the left. The iron fire escape that climbed up the side of the brick, the curved windows and little arched entryways that signaled below-grade apartments for rent. A thin mattress and table flush against the wall, the lodging house overflowing with families and young couples with little to their name. The years Evelyn and I spent mostly alone, newlyweds wrapped up in each other, cocooning from the grief we never could outrun.

Everything else has changed, though. The market across the street where we used to buy our milk is now a liquor store, bars on the windows. The sidewalk is cracked and crumbled in spots. There is a bike rack out front, a rusted frame with missing tires chained against it. The building is the same, but it is as though it has been picked up and transported to a new time. Which, I guess, it has. The street as I remember it doesn't exist anymore, although it's hard to believe something so alive in my memory can really be gone.

We sit together outside the apartment, our thighs and shoulders huddled close on a bench I don't recall. It is too cold to stay long, the wind whipping through Evelyn's hair. How intoxicating her chestnut curls had been then, how I buried myself in them as the morning sun crept through the blinds and I'd breathe her in, weakened by the softness of her naked form. She held me on top of her, ran her fingertips over my back and told me she felt safe under the weight of my body. Hours spent beneath the covers, nothing between our skin and the sheets but air warmed by our electricity. I recall Evelyn hauling groceries up the steep entryway, her foot stuck in the threshold to prop it open and her key tucked between her lips as she wriggled through. She insisted she was fine when I offered help but did not fight me, sweeping her hair out of her face, as I laughed, grabbed the overflowing paper bags and followed her inside.

I remember all these things as we huddle outside the apartment. We don't speak at first, but despite the cold it is the warmest of silences, each of us suspended in the past, offering thanks to a place that was once our refuge. She smiles for the briefest moment, and I wonder which day she has stumbled upon, wish I could turn back the clock, start there once more, relive this whole life with her.

She shifts uncomfortably on the bench, her brow furrowed, her contented smile replaced by a melancholy stillness. "What's wrong?" I ask.

She shrugs. "Today, the symphony... I should be so excited but... I don't know."

"What?"

"Once it's over, then what?" Her voice is small and fearful, like a child's.

"Then..." I pause, knowing what she means, that there comes a point when the days behind us far exceed what lies ahead, when all there is left to chase is memories. "It's about enjoying every day we have left."

She grows quiet.

"Are you nervous?"

"Now or never, right?" she jokes, and it feels forced. She spreads her gloved fingers in front of her and regards them like suspicious strangers. The doctors said the idea she could play at such a high level as her symptoms progressed was unlikely, verging on impossible. She practiced alone all week, and Jane came over last night to squeeze in one last private rehearsal. I lingered in the living room pretending to read, and my heart sank at each stretch of silence, signaling a mistake, confusion, momentary defeat. Then the music picked up, and I held my breath like watching a flickering heart monitor, listening for an outburst. They will rehearse with the BSO later this afternoon, and I pray that for today, her hands are her own.

Evelyn leans her head against my shoulder, watching people flow around us and each other, the city pulled by a tide all its own. I wonder what our life would have looked like if we had stayed here, if in another world this would be a farewell performance honoring a lifetime of achievement, instead of a consolation prize squeaked out before her final lap. A shadow of the real dream. If we never had children, if she saw the world, I wonder if she would've stopped missing home, if that life could ever have been enough.

I ask, "Do you remember when you moved here, after Tommy died?"

She murmurs her agreement.

"I was so afraid. I thought I'd never see you again." Even now if I close my eyes I can feel the flutter in my stomach, suitcase in hand, as she crossed the street to where I stood, waiting for her to notice me.

"Why are you bringing that up?" She faces me, hesitant. "I thought you wanted to remember happy times…relive our best memories."

I thread her fingers with mine, stroke her knuckle with my thumb. "I want to remember everything we shared, this entire life." I pause, trying to articulate my thoughts, the feelings surfacing on this pilgrimage, wistful for those two young kids, their life just beginning. "The best way I can think to say goodbye is to revisit it all…falling in love, having our children, the grandchildren, all of it…even the days we were lost. It's not only the happiest days, though they're a part of it." Her lower lip begins to tremble. "But it was also the hardest days. The days I was lost, the days I thought I'd lose you. When everything fell apart but you were all I needed." A tear falls down her cheek, her hand clasped in mine, a hold so tender I never want to let go. "Those are the days I loved you most."

Evelyn

Symphony Hall is brightly lit and cozy with the chatter of smartly dressed patrons. I peek out from backstage as they file in, the only evidence of the bitter January night settling in outside is the half-moon windows above the marble statues, black-ened by the evening sky. Glistening chandeliers flatter the ornate ceiling, shaped like upside-down Christmas trees, their bulbs like glowing stars. My body thrums with anticipation, every-thing crisp and clear. The hum of the filling seats, the scores propped up on music stands onstage, waiting. The risk of this high-wire act surging through me, the sheer undertaking, so easy to slip, so far to fall.

We've been here for hours, watching the other pianists and awaiting directions, but only had one chance to rehearse. The conductor showed us our marks, where we enter, where to stand for our bows. I was too anxious to take any of it in. Even the run-through of our performance was a blur. It went okay, not perfect, a few missteps that glared red in my mind. Jane assured me no one noticed, and I'm grateful not only to not be alone, but to have her beside me. My eldest, my first baby, who of-fered her arm as we entered stage left, who painted my lips and sprayed my hair backstage. Who would be talented enough to perform alone, if she chose. I am the one who needs to share the notes with her, a score designed for two. I need Jane to carry the performance if I stumble. Without her, the risk of failure, of humiliation, the overwhelming regret, is too high. Without her, this dream is out of reach.

"Looks like a full house," she says, peering out behind me. "You ready?"

"We're about to find out." I inhale, and breathe out slowly.

"Listen." Jane grabs my hands, pulls them to her chest. "I know you're nervous. I'm nervous. But this is it, the real thing, your dream finally coming true. Don't waste tonight being nervous. Enjoy it. It's amazing, and I'm so proud of you, and so proud to call you my mom—" her eyes well as she says it "—and I'm here with you, okay?"

I throw my arms around her, indebted to this incredible daughter of mine, this grown woman who stands beside me now, reminding me how far we've come. "Whew, okay." I dab at my eyes. "Let's have some fun."

I had heard our concerto for the first time when Joseph took me to the symphony, and I was struck by Mozart's dual arrangement. There was something joyful about it, soothing but playful, like someone bouncing through a lifetime of memories. A feeling of having truly lived: the grand opening, the drama and the hints of melancholy, the reflective, graceful finale.

A perfect farewell.

Joseph

As we take our seats, front and center in the audience, I notice the solitary golden plaque honoring Beethoven, the only artist deemed worthy of a carving. I had forgotten all about it until Evelyn repeated the story this morning to the grandchildren, a fun fact they could pocket and take with them as they entered the hall for the first time. The organ pipes are the only thing I remember, seeing them again I am still in awe of their magnitude, a mere mortal before the throne of the gods.

Onstage, two Steinway grand pianos gleam—stretched versions of the baby grand we have at home. There are two empty stools at the keys, and my stomach tightens with pride and nerves knowing Jane and Evelyn will soon be seated there. Evelyn has only gotten through a full practice once at home without pausing, without mistake. Her tremor has worsened, her joints tight and swollen, her patience and wrists so thin. Will she be able to see me here, right in front of her, sending her all of my strength, or will she be blinded by the spotlights?

The chatter has grown to a lively buzz as empty seats fill around us. Because of Marcus's connections to the *Boston Globe*, we are seated in the very first rows. I crane my neck at the growing crowd and check my watch—eight minutes until showtime. Jane and Evelyn have been backstage since the afternoon rehearsal. Violet and Connor, Rain and Tony, sit on either side of me, alongside the rest of the grandkids and Thomas and Ann.

I spot Marcus in the aisle, dapper in a knit suit jacket and tie, and wave him over. As he reaches our row, I stand and extend my hand. "So glad you could make it."

"I wouldn't miss it," he says with a grin, taking his seat. Evelyn had to convince Jane it was wrong not to include him after all he had done. Although the way she hid her smile as she acquiesced, the way Marcus's neck swivels as he searches the stage for her to appear, tells more of the story.

"I hope you'll join us for dinner after. It's the least we can do to thank you for everything you did, for making this happen. It means the world to us, truly, we can't thank you enough."

"I would love that," he agrees, as a hush falls over the audience and the orchestra files onstage, instruments in hand.

The conductor waves his baton and the delicate music whispers to us. A man in a tuxedo strides onstage and bellows, "Welcome everyone, to a very special night here at the BSO, a one-of-a-kind celebration of local talent, incredible musicians with roots right in our own backyard. I would be remiss not to begin with a big thank-you to the *Boston Globe* for their sponsorship of tonight's performance." He stops for applause, highlighting upcoming shows and ways to give back for more events such as this, then continues, "Please give a warm welcome to our first guests of the night. A mother-daughter pair from Connecticut. Both women moved to Boston in their late teens and fell in love with our city, so please help them feel right back at home here tonight." The crowd erupts into cheers. "Without further ado, here to play a rare piano duet, Mozart's Piano Concerto number ten, Evelyn and Jane Myers!"

I sit forward in my seat, barely breathing. Evelyn and Jane emerge in black dresses, mirroring the rest of the musicians. Evelyn holds on to Jane's arm, although whether out of necessity or nerves it is hard to say. She is so small, frail, next to Jane, who towers over her. My stomach clenches. They take their seats on the piano benches, smooth their skirts and wait for their cue. The music starts gently then picks up pace, the violinists in rhythm as one. My heart leaps, anxious for them to begin, barely hearing the music that preludes their accompaniment.

Then, Jane lifts her fingers to the keys and Evelyn follows, both in perfect sync with the instruments, with each other, their pianos distinct yet part of something bigger. The orchestra fades away and their solos ring clear through the rafters, filling the air with the sweetest vibrations. I've listened in on their practices at home as I washed dishes or skimmed the newspaper, but seeing them here, it is as if I am hearing it for the very first time. Evelyn is swept up in the music as the symphony swells around her and I am in awe of something I never fully understood until this moment. My eyes fill with tears, my fear falls away. Violet squeezes my hand, her cheeks wet. If there are other instruments or people onstage, I can't see them, Jane and Evelyn float above the scene, their fingers dancing with precision to the music below. It is hard to believe after all these years, Evelyn is playing with the Boston Symphony Orchestra. My wife, my love, her dreams scribbled in ink, her eyes always on the clouds. She is my symphony.

They finish the song in a rush of grandeur and my vision swims. Jane and Evelyn embrace, and they walk to the edge of the stage, right above us, to take their bows. My throat is thick with pride; years ago it was hard to imagine them ever sharing a room again, never mind a stage. A relationship we once thought irreparable, mended. Evelyn is vibrant, awash in the spotlight, and Jane beams beside her. Evelyn looks to the audience, and when she searches and meets my gaze, my chest is a bursting flame. She lifts her chin to the glow of the spotlights as though warming it in the sun, her smile luminous, and the crowd roars in applause. I take care to absorb every detail, to never lose the feeling radiating from her, and to hold on to the feeling of standing before her, of being the man she chose.

Evelyn

The symphony aglow in stage lights, the orchestra swelling around me and Jane in the center, its beating heart. I soar outside my body, leave behind my trembling hands and foggy mind, each note and chord ringing perfectly in my ears, the entire hall fills with music I weave myself into. This is more than I could imagine, more than all the lists and all the dreams and the biplane and the sunrises and the trips and everything I thought would make me whole. I am both the loom and the shuttle, the string and the weaver and the tapestry itself, an ethereal, glimmering celestial tapestry of stars, its beautiful song tuning out the fear and the pain, until I could burst into a spectrum of light—and this, *this* is how it truly feels to fly.

And there, waiting for me on the ground when it is over, when Jane and I take our bows, is our entire family in the first rows, shiny and clapping and cheering, and my eyes fall on Joseph and suddenly I know it had been real, and he had been witness to it all, to the life we shared together, and to this very night when I finally touched the sky.

Eighteen

Evelyn

May 1970

I don't know how it all got so far with Jane, so tense. There wasn't one incident I can point to, an argument that crossed the line, no cruel lash of a tongue I could apologize for. There was a fight about her graduation back in the spring, but that wasn't what unraveled us. It wasn't because she blasted the Rolling Stones or grew her hair to her waist or came home after curfew with red eyes or hung with a questionable crowd, although that's probably what she thought. I trusted her to grow out of it, to experiment and make mistakes on the way to finding her own path. I had a mother who didn't agree with my choices. I know what it's like to be misunderstood, cast off, because I didn't fit the mold of the daughter she wanted. It wasn't because she was desperate to leave home as soon as she turned eighteen; I've also been young, trapped, bursting to be free. It was more subtle, more insidious, harder to name.

I don't even think Joseph understands. I've never been able to articulate it; he recognized the tension but tread lightly on the surface, chose to see the best of us both, to tiptoe between our camps negotiating peace. She didn't treat him like she treated me; he wasn't the target of her scorn. He didn't rise to her judgment and overact, as I did, further cementing our fissures. He was safe, impossible to provoke, and he never pretended to be what he was not.

It was our constant clashes that uncovered my deepest insecurities. It was the way she began to see the world, focused on its darkness, on war, on corruption and scandal. Her curiosity edged toward obsession, her discontentment spiraled into outrage and, somehow, I was at the center of it all, a suburban mother who sold out, who gave up on my aspirations, who ran a bed-and-breakfast in a seaside town, completely removed from the tragedies she saw plastered on the front-page news. I was the embodiment of the problem, the one who could turn it all off by switching the channel, who buried myself in domestic pursuits so as not to feel anything.

I grew flustered beneath the weight of her judgment, wounded when she looked at me with disapproval, when she told me I didn't understand, I didn't care, that I was just like everyone else. She peeled me open and I was left raw and pulsing and ashamed, so I dug my claws into the only power I had. The ability to make rules, to punish, to forbid, and each time she slammed the door and I caught myself in the mirror I looked ugly and haggard and on the brink of madness. But to agree with her, to admit I was exactly as she saw me, was to disappear completely. So I flexed my talons and she tore at the walls until she could escape. And when she was gone, so was a part of me.

Jane moved to Boston nearly a year ago, right after her eighteenth birthday, and has had little contact with us since. We try to visit, but she always makes up excuses about why we can't. She skipped Thanksgiving entirely, claiming she had to work. We haven't seen her since Christmas. When she came home, she was skinnier than when she had left, her hair nearly to her waist. She was distant and strange, barely eating, ignoring me, and she disappeared as soon as dinner was over to catch an early train.

Since she moved out, Joseph and I have been two gears out of line, jamming and stalling, getting nowhere. All that's unsaid is palpable in our deliberate movements, two ships giving each other wide berths as we pass—he rushes to brush his teeth so he can leave the bathroom before I enter it, I stumble through making coffee before he wakes and leave him to sip it alone in the kitchen—and I don't know how to fix something not quite broken.

Since last summer, since Sam, even as I hate myself for it, my unrest keeps surfacing, tap-tapping against the glass encasing our model marriage, a diorama of a good life. I can't explain why, and now, with Jane not speaking to us, the raps are louder still, stirring old longings for something new. Baiting me to hound Joseph, baring their teeth. We lie in bed, another night when we barely touch, our bodies exhausted and our conversations strained. I turn away after we click off our lamps, and can't help but mutter, "We keep saying we're going to plan something, and then the inn gets booked up, and we never do."

He rolls onto his back, eyes on the ceiling, his patience worn thin. "If you want to travel, go for it. I can't have this conversation anymore."

"I hate when you do this. Pretend like I can just get up and go anytime, like that's a real option."

"I've never stopped you."

"I'm just saying, our lives could be over in an instant…and how have we spent them?" A conversation he never understands, the ticking clock only I hear. In two months I'll be forty-five, and it seems impossible to be halfway through this entire life, when I feel like I've barely begun. I imagine fifty years, then sixty and seventy, and the overwhelming feeling that anything worth doing should already have been done creeps thick into my throat.

Joseph clicks his lamp back on, sitting up. "What do you want from me? You say you want to see the world. I tell you to book a trip somewhere, and it's not enough."

I toy with the edge of the quilt. "I don't want to just take a vacation. That's not it."

"What is it, then?"

"I want to have lived."

Joseph laughs cruelly, slamming himself back down on the pillow. "Well, I must be a fool because I think we have a pretty great life here."

I whisper, "It is a good life."

He raises his voice. "Oh, god damn it, Evelyn. Maybe it's me you don't want then, huh? Maybe it's me that's not enough for you?"

An opening, my chance now, to assure him. To say, last summer we were all in a fog, we weren't ourselves, I certainly wasn't. To tell him I'm relieved it's over, relieved Sam is gone, but I can't seem to shake the guilt from that night, the things I should tell him but don't. The explanation would create a bigger chasm, leaving a rippling of unrest and uncertainty in its wake.

I burrow into my pillow, cowering from this, the sliver he is prying out, a truth that isn't quite one. "Don't say that."

He takes a deep breath, clearly trying to calm himself. "We have responsibilities. We have the inn, the kids."

"I know." I soften.

"I'm trying to give you what you want." A nice sentiment, the delivery barbed.

"I know. What do *you* want?" I inch toward him, imploring him to confess something new, desperate not to be the only one with my eyes on the horizon, sending up flares for rescue.

"You know what I want." He stiffens at the question. My wishes a personal affront to him, an insult to the life we've built.

His predictability incenses me, flint striking steel. "You always say that. But deep down, you *must* want more?"

"Our little life here with you, raising our family, *that's* my dream. It's boring to you, I know. I'm boring, loving you." He fumes. "You're so obsessed with wanting more, you can't see what's right in front of you."

I tuck my arms tight beneath me, away from the cold space between us, no way to make him understand. This stalemate between us, the parts of me I wish he found charming, sexy, admirable, instead of my biggest flaw, the barrier to my contentment. The first time I can't see a way through. The coast we built our lives along has become our battleground. It's never been Joseph I wanted to leave, but I can't stand being his second wife, the mistress to his inn, shackled by his inheritance, the ghosts of his parents, his duty disguised as a promised land.

I'm forty-five today, and all I can do is stare at the empty chair where Jane should be, my lips in a tight line. With no explanation, no call, she doesn't show, and it feels like a fire-tipped arrow shot into our castle, intended to hurt me, to prove how little she cares, standing back in the distance, eyeing the flames. After the dishes are cleared, my mother makes a few comments about how she is "not surprised" Jane did not come and how we should have "nipped her behavior in the bud." I take the deepest breath and exhale purposefully, eyes sharpened on my mother. She sees herself out, and Violet and Thomas make themselves busy in their rooms. I'm silent the rest of the night, scrubbing pots and swatting Joseph away when he tries to help.

"Please, Joseph." I rub a soapy wrist over my forehead, brushing the hair out of my eyes. "Leave me alone."

"I'm sorry, I—"

"I know. But I can't control how I lash out right now, so I am asking you to go away and when I come to bed, I swear I'll be fine."

He leaves me at the sink to take my frustrations out on a casserole dish with stubborn cheese residue. From the window I watch him hose down the pile of beach chairs left outside by the family from Jersey before retiring for the night. I come to bed a while later, calmer but bleary, my steps weighted. I can't focus, my toothpaste falls off my brush and into the sink twice before I give up, throw it in the drawer and crawl into bed beside Joseph, sheets kicked to his feet in the thick summer air.

My thoughts race as I stare at the ceiling fan, surprising myself with the question that emerges, the insecurity that sifts to the surface as a riddle, a test. "Joseph, why do you love me?"

"You know why I love you." His answer is quick, dismissive.

"No, I don't." I exhale, slow and controlled, concentrating on keeping still, composed. A tear escapes down my cheek. "I really don't understand." I turn toward him, miserable and selfish and unlovable. A mother on the verge of losing her own daughter, as though a daughter is a thing that can be lost, like a set of keys, when all I wanted, all I tried, was to be the kind of mother I had always craved.

He stumbles through an answer, caught off guard. "I love you because you're the only woman I've ever loved, the only woman I'll ever love."

"That doesn't answer the question. It doesn't tell me why." I'm pathetic now, a dog begging to be petted, to be told I am a good girl, worthy of all of the chances he's given me. But I need to hear it, need to know I didn't trick him somehow into chasing after me, for waiting me out, for his endless patience and confidence in this selfish person that's proven herself unworthy of his love. As though my life in Stonybrook was an opening act to all that still lay ahead, merely biding time until my true potential would be discovered, an excavated jewel. A story folks would tell one day, the tale of the woman who once ran that inn, right there, who went on to do so much more.

Not the story that projects itself in my mind, a sad old wretch, rocking alone on this very porch, who chased away the only good and true things she had ever known.

"There are so many reasons I love you, I could probably list them, but the truth is I can't help it. I never could. I love you because you have this light in you…" I begin to cry, and he strokes my hair. "People are drawn to you, I have always been, you're a magnetic force. You're a dreamer and a fighter with more heart than anyone I have ever met."

I can't take it in, even though I pleaded for it, this gushing affection I need to plug with something thorned. "Then why do I have a daughter who hates me?"

He slides closer, putting an arm around me. "She doesn't hate you, she's a teenager, trying to find her way."

"But I am an adult. I shouldn't have let her leave without saying goodbye, like my mother… I hate myself for that. I shouldn't have let our stupid arguments turn into something bigger. I want to visit, but she won't talk to me, she just hangs up. What am I supposed to do?"

"Why don't I go see her this weekend? Maybe she'll talk to me. I'll tell her you need to work things out, that she can't ignore you. She may be an adult now, but that doesn't mean she isn't our daughter."

I nod, my cheek wet on his chest. "And tell her I love her, okay? Tell her I want her in my life. She's my first baby for god's sake. How can she not know how much I love her?"

How much I love you too. I want to say. *I'm sorry, to you too.* But I don't, Jane the only territory I can breach while balancing this tightrope between us.

"I'll tell her. I'll tell her," he says and pulls me close like hushing an upset child, muttering words of comfort and assurances, prayers to false gods to keep her safe.

Joseph

I drive up to Boston, Jane's address in my pocket. I haven't been to the place before, but Jane wrote it down and left it on our dresser in lieu of a goodbye. Part of me is afraid of what I'll find, my stomach a knot when I arrive at her apartment in Brighton, on the outskirts of Boston. The thick stench of pot seeps out to the creaky front steps, unnerving me.

I knock on the door, and a muffled voice calls out, "Come in."

I turn the knob and feel dizzy, the room hazy with smoke. A girl I don't recognize sits on the sagging couch, braless in a tank top and underwear.

"Oh my god, I'm sorry," I mutter, averting my gaze. "I think I have the wrong place. I'm looking for my daughter Jane."

The girl squints at me, disturbed by the daylight streaming through the open door. "No, you're not wrong, man. Jane lives here. She's working. I think. She should be back anytime now. Sit. You can hang and wait for her." She slides over on the couch, making no move to cover herself up.

"No. It's okay," I protest, turning to go. "Tell her that her dad stopped by." I shut the door behind me, short of breath. Defeated, I make my way down the steps to head back to my car and nearly bump into Jane, startling us both. I reach for her elbow, paranoid by what I found, filled with an irrational fear she will run from the sight of me.

"What the hell, Dad?" She wrenches away.

"I saw your roommate in there. I saw the drugs. You're coming home."

She laughs, and it sounds strange. "Relax. That's Sheri. She's not my roommate. She's a friend, crashing with us for a little. But don't worry. I'm working, see?" She points to her outfit, tiny shorts and a low-cut top. I give a blank stare. "Bartending."

I drop my voice, trying to calm down. "I am not comfortable with this, Jane."

"Oh *okay*, you can live with Mom," she mocks. "But *this* you're not comfortable with."

"This thing, between you and you mother—"

"She never told you, did she?" She cocks her head, daring me. "Go home, go ahead, ask her what happened on my birthday."

I never knew what happened after I went to bed that night. Evelyn never brought it up, Sam left. In my mind, that strange summer had been exorcized with the changing leaves. The conscious decision I made, no matter how it hurt, to trust her. To let her go. To let her choose me. To prove our life together was what she really wanted. Her presence in our bed later that night was my answer, her thighs cool against mine as she slipped beneath the sheets, smelling of smoke from the fire, careful not to wake me as I feigned sleep.

"What are you talking about?"

"I saw them together, okay?" Her eyes are shiny with tears, but her jaw is set, furious.

I keep my voice even. Evelyn would have told me if anything happened. I am sure of it. "What did you think you saw?"

"*Think* I saw? I was standing right there." She's crying now, angry tears she bats away. "Sam asked her to run away to Paris with him. He had his hand on her knee, and they were leaning in close, and he said they could go, and they could drink wine, and play music and *make love*." She spits the last part out, a bitter poison.

Her words a sheet of ice. I can't speak, can't respond. It couldn't be. Evelyn would have told me. She didn't leave, she came to bed, there must be something Jane didn't understand, didn't see, but I can't grasp any of this, can't believe Evelyn would have kept this from me, unless, unless...a part of her wanted to go.

"You knew, didn't you? You knew, and you stayed..." She backs away, horrified.

I can't explain, can't find the words to tell her I did know, in a way. Not about Sam's proposition, or any of the details, but the energy I felt between them when I was near. She steps into her apartment, her eyes dark. "Then you're just as bad as she is." And closes the door.

Evelyn

July 1973

Food has always been my favorite part of any celebration, the only piece that isn't ruined by loss. When the room is quiet because everyone is eating, it's harder to tell there are voices missing. Joseph tries desperately to get the conversation started, my birthday dinner soundtrack currently the scrape of forks. "Thomas, how are your classes?"

Thomas has opted to stay in New York and take summer classes to graduate on time, juggling a double major in business and finance. He replies, "Challenging." A nonanswer.

I gaze at him, my only son. How unlike his namesake he seems, although it strikes me that Thomas is about the age Tommy was when we said goodbye at the train station the last time. Thomas sits at the table like a breath of air, necessary, steady, but nothing that draws attention. He cuts his steak with precision into bite-size pieces, places it smoothly into his mouth. His etiquette was not taught. It is discipline, masked by politeness. Tommy used to hold his steak knife like a saw, he'd tear through the meat and toss it into his mouth between boisterous laughs, wiping his chin with the back of his wrist. Then, he'd smile or wink, food tucked into the side of his cheek, and any faux pas was forgiven.

Tommy didn't grow older with us in my mind, but the image I have of him still seems older than me, somehow. Even as I've lived far past any age he had ever been. Frozen in our last moments together, at nineteen, he seems older than I feel, tonight, at forty-eight. Missing my brother became a low hum vibrating below the surface. I could hear it if I listened close, but mostly the throbs were masked by my heartbeat. I began to lose the image of his face first, the exactness of it, the sharpness of the details. Was his freckle on the left side of his chin, or the right? Were his eyes more gray or blue?

Then, it was the things I remembered him saying. Had he ever said them at all? One evening when the kids were little and catching fireflies as the sun faded low in the sky, *Male fireflies each have their own light pattern, you know,* echoed in my mind. But who had said it so many years ago? Was it Joseph? Tommy? The three of us were kids ourselves then, sitting on the dock, the air cooling around us, when fireflies began to flicker across the dunes. Something about the way the males attract the females, I couldn't remember. *Male fireflies each have their own light pattern, you know.* So silly, so insignificant, but I wanted to remember. I wanted to put a voice to the words in my head. I heard it in Tommy's first, then Joseph's, but neither sounded right. Had I been the one to say it? Was it something I had known on my own?

"Are you enjoying them?" Joseph tries again.

Thomas shrugs. "I'm paying for them to be challenging."

Poor Joseph—no amount of prodding is going to open Thomas up these days. Becoming a pilot was the only thing we could get him to talk about before; he was obsessed with learning what kept jets in flight, how they were put together, who tested new designs. We can't get him to talk about much of anything anymore. Not since the doctors found the murmur in his heart. The air force denied his application; he would never be able to serve.

After his physical I found the posters from his room, plastered with jets and helicopters, as I tossed out the trash. They were viciously ripped and torn; it was so unlike Thomas, destroyed so violently it unnerved me. All I wanted was to collect them in my arms, unfurl them and flatten them under the heaviest books, tape the pieces back in place and press them onto his walls.

Put his dreams back together, make them real once more. But I couldn't. And he wouldn't talk about it, no matter how we tried. Instead he retreated into his room, pushed himself to a breaking point. Get into college. Study harder. Outwork everyone. Outwork himself. He slipped farther away, applied to NYU and left a few months later.

Joseph sighs. "Well, then, I guess you're getting your money's worth."

I miss baby Thomas waving his pudgy fists so I could wipe them, those round cheeks and big eyes. He needed me for everything when he was a toddler. Now he needs me for nothing. He is only here tonight because he knows it would hurt me if he missed it; he has seen what Jane not coming home has done to us all. He is not cruel, although it is hard to know how he feels most of the time. I understand what the heart murmur meant for him, for his future, for his life, but he found his own way, a new path in New York. Still, I can't get him to talk without asking a question; I can't get him to laugh with anything more than politeness.

Joseph tries Violet, her yellow dress a glaring contrast to her mood tonight, uncharacteristically subdued, verging on somber. "And who are we going on a date with this weekend?"

"Funny, Dad." Violet wrinkles her nose at him. She's seventeen now, and completely unaware of how stunning she's become. Joseph says she takes after me, and physically, maybe, we have similar frames and hair. But she is comfortable in her skin in ways I never was, and her personality is all Joseph; both kinder and more giving than I have ever been.

"I didn't mean for it to be funny. I want to get to know these young men. The only one I ever really met was...what was his name? David?"

"Ugh, David?" She stabs at her potatoes, agitated. "Just because we went on a few dates doesn't mean he was The One."

Violet is never shy about her affection for the boys she likes, although they try to steal their kisses under cover of the front porch. Giddiness pours out of her with each, she'll lean her head against their shoulders, trace her fingertips along their arms. Then she finds some fatal flaw and won't see them again. Soon, a new boy knocks on our door. Joseph worries about how often they come and go. I tell him we should be glad she isn't too serious with anyone at her age. Maybe we can protect her longer, from mourning her first love, from feeling taken advantage of. But I worry too. What is she searching for?

Thomas sneers as he glances up from his plate. "Vi, you need to realize the world is not waiting around to hand you a fairy tale."

"Oh yeah, and how many girlfriends have you had?"

Thomas glares at her and takes a bite of steak.

I raise my eyebrows. "Your brother has a point. It's great to have high standards, honey, and you have all the time in the world to figure it out, but we want to be sure what you're looking for is...real."

Violet pouts. "Dad gave you the fairy tale."

I nearly laugh. Joseph, who works late on projects around the Oyster Shell to avoid me, his dinner plate wrapped in plastic wrap and left in the refrigerator, reheated after Violet and I eat. Coming upstairs after dark, exhausted and falling asleep without saying much more than good night. My body more used to the space between us than the warmth of his touch, our conversations limited to updates and logistics, guests checking in early, towels that need bleaching, items to add to the grocery list. He wakes before dawn and fumbles in the dark to get dressed, and I'm left under the covers, pretending to sleep, wondering how we got so off track.

I point my fork at her to get her attention. "There was a *lot* more to it than the fairy-tale parts, and we were lucky to find each other so young and last through all we did." The false assurances in my voice, wanting to show her the way, but not worry her, our hopeless romantic daughter not privy to the ways we've come undone. "It's not always easy."

Thomas, who has clearly had enough of this conversation, changes the subject. "Has anyone heard from Jane?"

We haven't seen Jane in three years. The last we heard was a letter with a return address in San Francisco, letting us know she moved from Boston to California. It feels so strange; her absence from the table is as striking as her presence. Celebrations feel pretend without her, performances of a happy family. I shake my head.

"Sorry, Mom," Violet murmurs.

"It's alright, sweetheart."

But it's not. I can't stop staring at Jane's empty chair. I miss my daughter. I know she is trying to find her way in this world, but I don't know why that means pushing us out of it. Pushing *me* out of it. I don't know if the path she has taken will be clear enough for her to trace home, but I don't want to talk about it, don't think I could speak without wondering aloud about her. What is she doing? Is she safe? Has she eaten? Is she working? Does she have enough money? When will I see her again? A primal panic, like when I placed my wrist near her newborn mouth, compulsively checking her breath.

Joseph went to visit her once, when she still lived in Boston. He was short with me when he got home, relayed only the barest information: she lived with roommates, worked in a bar, she seemed fine. But his shoulders hunched with worry, he shrugged me off when I pressed for details. It stung, how I couldn't scratch below the surface, sure he blamed me for Jane leaving on such bad terms. And ever since, he's been strange. Both of us avoiding conversations to avoid fights, burrs that dig in, carried through our day.

Thomas heads out tomorrow morning by train, back to New York. Violet has only this last summer home before she leaves for college, a summer of dates and stolen front-porch kisses.

Soon they will both be out of the house. I don't know if Jane's absence will sting less or more when it is only Joseph and me again. The inn, full of strangers and still so empty.

After dinner, Thomas will stay in his childhood room once more. Violet hugs Joseph and me before retreating for the night. I wonder if Thomas will consider his blank walls and remember what used to cover them. I wonder if tonight he will dream of fighter jets and parachutes, or if the siren's song of the train to Manhattan will be the lullaby that rocks him to sleep.

Nineteen

Joseph

February 2002

Today is my birthday, my seventy-ninth, and my last, and all I want is to surround myself with family, to embed myself in one more happy memory for them to hold. A storm blew in the night before, routine for February, blanketing everything in snow. Rain suggests sledding, and even though she can't participate with her growing belly, she offers to pour hot cocoa at the top of the hill. Evelyn decides to hang back at the house, nervous to be out in the cold, although years ago she would have been the one carving a snowy path for the rest of us to follow.

"You sure this is a good idea?" Evelyn asks. "I'm afraid you'll get hurt."

"Sledding on my seventy-ninth birthday seems as logical as anything this year."

She doesn't argue. We didn't expect Thomas and Ann to join, but they surprised me at the house with newly purchased snow tubes, folded flat in their packaging, that we pumped up before heading out together to Breyer's Hill.

"You first, Pop. It's your birthday," Thomas urges, and the rest agree.

I swing my legs onto our old Flexible Flyer, and am filled with nerves. It has been years, decades, since I have gone sledding with our kids, but Tony gives me a hearty push before I can overthink it, and the icy air on my face, flying over the white expanse of snow, wakes something in me. I feel invincible, the way I used to feel as I leaped from Captain's Rock, young again and free. I whoop as I soar through the powder.

It is climbing back up that reminds me of my age. I take two turns before I concede to the aches and stay at the top, assisting Rain in pouring steaming hot cocoa from the red plastic thermos that has seen many winter days like this one, sledding, or skating across Gooseneck Pond as soon as it froze solid. She leans against me as we watch them together, her curly hair wrangled beneath a knit cap, a mirror image of her mother, but with a steadiness and inner harmony all her own.

We clink our Styrofoam cups, and she sprinkles a few extra mini-marshmallows on their frothy surfaces. Connor and Violet squeeze onto our old wooden toboggan with Patrick, nearly too old to be caught sledding with his parents. Tony, always a big kid at heart, even married to Rain and a dad-to-be, pushes them off before hopping onto the back to ride along. Thomas and Ann glide alongside in their tubes, Ann giggle-screeching as they bumper-car and get knocked off at the bottom. Thomas falls onto his back into the pillowy snow with a chuckle that starts deep in his belly.

It is the perfect day. Except, I feel Evelyn missing in every laugh. I want to share every single moment with her.

The next morning, the rich smell of coffee greets me as I walk downstairs to the kitchen. Evelyn doesn't drink it, although sometimes she will get it started for me when she is up early, wandering the halls before dawn, but this is not one of those mornings. She is tucked in bed, covers to her chin, trying to force sleep.

The last few nights she perched on the toilet seat, mouth agape, as I stroked her toothbrush across the backs of her molars. She grips my arm when we walk through the house, her steps slow and unsteady. I've caught her twice before falling, once as she crossed the living room and once coming out of the shower, and my heart quickened with the flicker of fear of what would happen if I hadn't been nearby, dread rippled through my chest as I steadied her. Sometimes her face smooths to a masklike expression, her mannerisms and features cloaked in disarming stillness. Her tremor has spread, both hands quiver; the concerto the last music she played. Conversations repeated as though they are new. Her anxiety pulses as she shuffles across our wood floors, palpable as she anticipates lifting herself from a seated position.

I think, but don't say, *It's alright, it's not too much longer, my love.*

Instead I say, *I'm here with you, we have four months yet to share.*

Most days she doesn't want to see anyone. She can't bear the scrutiny, weighing her progression, her symptoms, her mood. The glances and furrowed brows, the worry the children express to me when she is barely out of earshot.

Thomas must be up. Or perhaps Jane, Violet or Rain, who are coming over for breakfast this morning, beat me to the coffeemaker. Thomas and Ann slept in his room last night, squeezed together in his old bed. I can't remember a time in years past that they stayed overnight. But since the Twin Towers fell, it's been different. Thomas puts his arm around Ann's waist when they sit on the couch; I've spied him stealing kisses as the door swings shut to the kitchen. Ann appears lighter under his affection, showing up to the dinner table with damp hair that dries with a natural wave I've never seen. They spend more time here on weekends, and took extra days off around the holidays to be with us, when usually they are out the door before dessert.

Thomas has been especially helpful with the logistics of it all, the details to carry out once we are gone. We named him executor of our will because he can best separate his emotions from the reality of all that comes with death. The paperwork and the phone calls and the scheduling, the distribution of things. The surreal nature of something so intimate as loss combined with the formal and legal and public ways you must share it with others. We told him we don't want to be buried. Instead, we want our ashes scattered beyond the sandbar, floating through schools of minnows, carried on the backs of crabs, drifting in and out with the tides, in the place we've always been and will always be. Like my parents are with us in the worn banisters of the inn, in the flour-dusted countertops and faded curtains open to the summertime breeze. Like Tommy is in the first brisk swim of the season, or our grandchildren leaping off Captain's Rock, he is the wind when it howls and the endless starry sky above. A cemetery is not where we feel them, it is merely the place they laid to rest.

Thomas pressed to know more about *how*, and we covered the grisly details the best we could, despite his misgivings. The stockpile of pills, the locations of our important documents and final wishes, the plan devised over a year ago that seemed such a hypothetical then, but now as it approaches I find myself researching alternate methods, all the ways pills can go wrong, desperate for something foolproof yet peaceful. An answer eludes me, so I shove it down, a bridge to cross only when there is no more road. Choosing to have faith in a good death with Evelyn, the same faith that propelled me from Connecticut to Boston and back again, certain that the only answer to a good life was one spent with her.

Violet makes extra portions of meals, stocks our freezer, picks up groceries, prescriptions. Jane calls each morning to ask how her mother is doing, and comes by a few times a week. She plays the piano for Evelyn, the music between them soothing what words cannot. Our children encircle us, buoying us from one day to another. The ways each can be useful are their offerings of peace, my gratitude deepening in lockstep with my shame.

Thomas wears a faded NYU T-shirt and sweatpants as he drinks coffee at the kitchen table; for years Evelyn and I were convinced he only owned suits and ties. Violet mixes batter for pancakes, Rain sprinkles diced potatoes with rosemary and paprika and coarse salt—Evelyn's recipe for home fries—and Jane peels apart bacon strips and lays them on a baking sheet.

"Good morning, girls. Morning, Thomas." I pat him on the back as I walk by. "Ann still asleep?"

He folds the newspaper and puts it aside. "Yeah. Mom?"

I pour myself some coffee, glance through the frosted windows to the garden, deadwood and twisted branches poking through the fresh snow. "Yeah, she's tired from all of the activity last night."

Thomas pauses, studying me like he wants to ask something, but he follows up instead, with, "It was fun yesterday, sledding. I can't remember the last time I did that."

"I'm glad you made it. Though I'll pay for it today, that's for sure." I rub my leg, work the tension in my calf.

Thomas sets aside his newspaper. "Dad, I wanted to talk to you and Mom. Ann and I have thought a lot about what we can do, how we can help."

I take a sip of coffee, relish the mug heating my palms. "You've already been more helpful than you know. Being here to spend time with us is all we want. We know you're busy, and it's a long way for you to come all the time."

"Well, that's what we've been thinking about." He toys with his near-empty cup. "We don't want to be so far anymore." I raise my eyebrows in surprise, and he continues, "Mom's getting worse fast, isn't she?"

Rain, Violet and Jane stop what they're doing, listening.

I open my mouth to assure him, but I can see it on his face.

The grimace, the certainty. It's on all their faces. They finally see what Evelyn has been trying to tell them all along.

"Ann and I have been looking at some houses in Stamford, so we can be closer to you and Mom, and Jane and Vi, and everyone. It's important to me, to Ann too. We want to help."

"Thomas, that's very thoughtful of you, but you don't need to uproot your lives because of us—"

"We want to. We don't want to be so far from the family. We don't want to miss anything anymore. It's not only to help... it's for us. Really."

My throat thickens, and I do my best to clear it, knowing Thomas is uncomfortable with emotion. "That makes me so happy, son. Your mother will be so happy."

"Why will I be so happy?" Evelyn shuffles down the stairs with small, weighted steps and a weak smile. Her wool sweater swallows her bony, hunched shoulders. It appears sleep was a battle she lost. Thomas looks to me but I wave my hand, gesturing for him to tell her.

"Ann and I want to move to Stamford, get out of the city. We want to be closer to family."

Evelyn's mouth falls open in disbelief. "But you love New York!"

"We'll both still work there. We'll commute in. Honestly, it's amazing we stayed as long as we did. Most people we know moved to the burbs ages ago."

Evelyn shakes her head, her smile wide. "I can't believe it. Really, Thomas?"

"It's time. We'll be able to visit so much more without worrying about train schedules and getting back to the city late at night. Especially with a little one around here soon." He tilts his head at Rain, who instinctively touches her bump and brightens. "We're tired of missing everything. We just need to find the house."

"That makes two of us, or should I say three of us." Rain

looks down at her bulging belly, covered in a striped apron. "Tony and I need to get out of our crummy apartment when the baby comes."

"Rain, you're welcome to stay here, it'll be…empty soon," Evelyn says. "Your grandpa and I discussed it before, hoping someday you could raise your family here like we did. We know how much you love it and, well, you two know this place better than anyone. But we never thought Tony would agree."

"Ahh yes, his famous Sicilian pride."

"It wouldn't be a handout, tell him that. We know he likes to make his own way, but we've been trying to decide what to do with it, honestly. It's too far for Thomas and Ann to commute, and Jane and Violet are settled with homes of their own. It's filled with so many memories, and to think of the garden going to a stranger…" She pauses, trying to rein in her excitement. "You'd be doing us a favor, Rain, please. At least talk it over with him."

"Really?" Rain's eyes are misted over. "God…it would mean everything to us. I love the garden…you know how much we both love this place. I'll talk to him."

"And, Thomas?" Evelyn turns toward him. "You have no idea how happy I am that you and Ann will be closer, that you'll be around more. I never thought I'd see…" She trails off, clears her throat and collects herself. "And you know you can stay as often as you'd like while you sort it all out."

Our children, all together again. Something twists in my chest. We should be here. We should be with them, spending every last second we have. What if it's too late?

What if it's not?

He casts his gaze to the floor. "Thank you… I wish we had done this sooner." Tears fall, and he hurries to wipe them away.

"Wish you had done what sooner, dear?" Evelyn's face is cheerful, curious, her thread to the last few minutes snipped.

The color drains from Thomas's face.

"What time is your train?" Evelyn chatters. "Your father can drop you after breakfast."

Thomas's voice is scratchy, eyes rimmed red. "I'm too late, aren't I?"

Evelyn shuffles to the table and sits beside him, patting his hand as he crumples, shoulders shaking. "There will be other trains, I'm sure."

I meet Jane's eye and she swats at a tear falling down her cheek. Rain grabs her hand. Only Violet has seen Evelyn this way; she gives me a sad smile of recognition, the moments like this we've already swallowed, a shared knowledge between us, the inevitable creeping in.

Evelyn gestures at the abandoned preparations for breakfast. "That looks like quite the spread, but if you all don't mind, I think I'll try to get a bit more sleep. I'm not feeling up to eating. Save me some, okay?"

She stands slowly and Thomas rises to help her, but she shakes her head. We watch her ascend the stairs on her own. Uncertainty and remorse pool around me as I'm left alone with the children, quiet in their own sorrow. Will we really be able to go through with it? Can we face them one last time and say goodbye?

"How often is this happening?" Jane asks, her voice hollow.

"More often than I'd like."

"Jesus."

"It's what we were expecting." I try to keep my voice even but it wavers.

"But this, seeing it…four months? We have four months with her? Is that real, Dad?" Her voice quivers. "That's all she'll give us?"

Four months. My heart lurches. *Take it back.* We can take it back.

"How do I even begin to tell her everything I want to tell

her? How do any of us…god, I wasted so many years mad at her, and now…"

"That's ancient history, Jane. You've had so much good time together, you can't—"

"I'll be here more. Whatever she needs, okay?" Her voice catches in her throat. "But you, Dad? I'll never understand it."

"Can you lay off?" Violet says. "This isn't easy on him either, you know."

"Explain it to me, then." Her eyes are wild, her fear and reality crashing in. "What if something had happened to Mom when we were little? Would you have ended it all then, when we were kids?"

"Of course not," I stammer, trying to explain. "I would've been devastated to lose your mother, and I'm not sure how I would have managed. But of course I would've been there for you kids."

Jane throws up her hands. "So why is this any different? You're still giving up so much."

Rain looks down at the tile, silent.

I continue with our practiced reasons, guilt ringing in every word. "You kids aren't kids anymore. You don't need me like you would have then. You have your own lives, your own families. The inn is closed. Your mom is my best friend, all I have—" I fumble with my words, trying to make Jane understand, to make them all understand what even I struggle to swallow "—besides you kids. Honestly, I don't know what I would've done, and I'm lucky I never had to know. But, Jane, we've had our life together. All that's left is the certainty one of us will go, and the uncertainty of when. So, it's our time to be together, with whatever time we can guarantee."

"Jane, let up," Thomas cuts in. "You don't understand because you've never been in love."

"Oh, *screw* you." She narrows her eyes at him, all venom. "No one else was going to say it!"

"Thomas—" I warn.

"Can we not fight right now?" Violet rubs her forehead.

"Dad, you can't let her do this. Listen to her, she's not capable of making this kind of decision," Jane says.

"Her body and memory may be faltering, but she knows exactly what she's doing," I say, clearing my throat. "We both do."

I hear Evelyn's movements upstairs, the pad of her feet against the carpet, the soft click of our bedroom door as it closes. Try to banish all the imagined years without her, but one thought remains. I can't save her. I never could.

Twenty

Joseph

August 1973

Evelyn and I plan a trip to fly to California together to check on Jane, to end the silence between us, to convince her to come home, despite Evelyn's fear she would refuse to see her. But the morning of the flight, Violet wakes up clutching her abdomen, writhing in pain, and one of us has to take her to the hospital. The tickets are booked, and we have already dipped into our savings, there is no chance to reschedule. We have to make a quick decision.

"I'll go, you stay with Violet," Evelyn says. "Jane's upset with me. I need to make it right."

"She may be more willing to talk to me," I say.

"But it's my battle, not yours."

"Trust me, okay? She doesn't want to see you."

Evelyn stops, wounded. I don't invite further discussion, and that's what hurts her most. But what she doesn't know would hurt more. I don't tell her about Jane's confession in Boston, the real reason she wasn't speaking to her mother, why she left so angry. Doubt seeped in after Jane told me what she heard. Was there more I didn't know? It stung that Evelyn never shared what happened, even if she chose to stay. Sam's clandestine proposal kept secret, why? To protect me, or because a part of her considered leaving? Evelyn could not go to California, could not be the one to bring Jane back, when Jane was still so angry with her, when there was so much she misunderstood. And I couldn't tell Evelyn, because now her secret was mine, because it created a nesting doll of things we didn't say.

Evelyn lifts her hands in surrender, turns her attention to Violet and lets me go.

Jane's old address leads to dead end after dead end, days spent talking to hippies on the street, showing her photo and tracing her steps, until I finally track her down. Unlike in Boston, the door is ajar, and I press it open. My eyes flicker across the shabby apartment. The mattress is on the floor, covered with a single frayed blanket and no sheets. Cartons of half-eaten food litter the counters. A cat with a ripped ear and patchy fur stalks through the debris with the authority of a wild animal that doesn't belong to them, but lived here first. The haze of smoke in the air gives me déjà vu. Jane in another apartment, angry, defiant, three years earlier. My head spins.

Jane, in the corner, is nodding off beside some drugged out hippie.

My breath is ragged, my heart races, my voice low. "Get away from her."

"Dad? What the fuck!" Jane snaps awake, hugging herself.

"Listen, man. We're cool." He raises his hands, offers a smile, his teeth yellow.

Blood pounds in my ears. I feel like I'm underwater, tumbling in a rip current, panicked for breath. "We're going home."

"What are you talking about? I'm not leaving."

"You don't have a choice. Let's go." My eyes stumble on the tracks on Jane's arm, her shoulders bony and legs like straws.

"You can't tell me what to do anymore." She shakes her head, her hair wild.

I want to grab her, and my body quavers with fury. "I don't give a damn. You are my daughter, and you're doing drugs now, Jane?" My voice catches in my throat, saying it, seeing her and knowing, for the very first time, how far from us she has truly been.

"We're just messing around."

"You can't believe that." I take one step forward, try to steady my anger, try to appear calm, in control. "Come home. Come on, let's go."

She laughs. "Why would I?" She turns toward the man and wraps her arm around him, the insides of her elbows red and pockmarked. He resembles the feral cat, mangy, all bones and scraggly hair. He squints at me, resting his head on hers.

I turn to him, my fists clenched by my sides. My leg throbs, my voice a growl, and I'm filled with rage. Rage at the bloodied child's foot jutting out of the rubble in Sicily, at Tommy's stomach ripped open, at my mother's tumor, at shrapnel tearing through my calf, at Jane's arms scarred and cratered, her eyes hollow. I step toward him with raised fists. "You're lucky I don't rip your throat out, you son of a bitch. I don't know what you've done to her—"

Jane screams, "Dad, stop!"

I turn to her, desperate. "I have two plane tickets, Jane. Come home. We miss you. Your mother can't sleep…she is so worried about you."

She clambers to her feet, propelled by her fury. "I haven't talked to her in years. She isn't even here. How worried could she be?"

I falter. "Violet got appendicitis…she couldn't leave her."

Jane cackles. "How convenient. Her precious Violet needs tending."

"This has to stop, between you and your mother. Don't you know how much she loves you? How much we both love you?"

"How could you stay with her? How can you trust her after what happened?"

"*Nothing* happened, Jane."

"Did she tell you that?"

I don't admit I never confronted Evelyn. Don't admit that in my worst moments, I imagine her kissing him, leaving me, the pain of it nearly driving me mad, bracing myself for the day she might. "There are things in a marriage that are hard to explain...you have to trust the other person. You heard what Sam asked her, but you never heard her answer. Obviously, she didn't run off with him."

"He wouldn't have asked if he didn't think he had a shot. It's so fucking embarrassing and gross. I can't believe you don't see it!"

"The choices we make are what matters. What happened with your mother...it's not a reason to cut her out, to pretend like she doesn't exist."

Jane doesn't appear to listen, as if she couldn't care less. Behind her, the junkie draws a pen across his forearm, a crude tattoo. I'm nauseous, the whole scene rushes away from me, my vision closes in. "Come home. Jane, please. Come home." I'm losing her, clawing at the edge of a cliff.

She smiles, and she looks like a skeleton, her face sunken. "This is my home. People here finally understand me."

"You're doing heroin..." The word chokes what air I have left; I try to reach for her. "You can't even see what's right in front of you."

"Don't touch me." Jane's face is unreadable, and she backs away. "You need to leave."

"I'm not leaving without you."

"You heard her, man, time to go." His words don't register. All I see is Jane. I want to hug her, hold her, pull her out of this place. I want her head heavy on my shoulder as I carry her home and tuck her in, safe and warm.

"I'll drag you out of here if I have to." I grab her wrist.

She rips it away from me, screeching, "*I said* don't fucking touch me." I reach for her again, and she screams like she's being attacked.

I lift my hands. "Don't do this…"

"You try to take me anywhere, I'll bolt. I swear to god. You'll never find me again."

"Jane…" Her name, my final plea, out of leverage, out of hope, no way to force her to leave, no way to trap her, to keep her safe from herself. She stares at me, cold. My offering feels meager, pitiful, but it's the only move I have left. This reminder, an escape hatch, a truth she must have forgotten. "You can always come home. Always."

Twenty-One

Evelyn

March 2002

Outside the wind rustles the evergreen trees, the ground soft and sodden with the last few days of melted snow. As spring approaches, there are only small icy patches left over in the shadiest corners of the yard, the greenery withered, the grass brown and littered with sticks and leaf debris that had been frozen over since fall. Joseph works in the garden, though it is only March, arguably too early in the season with the threat of more snow to come. But this morning we woke to the tips of green shoots poking through the mulch and he raced through breakfast, not even finishing his coffee, to clear their path, snipping and raking the decay left by winter. I wonder if he imagines Rain and Tony kneeling together in turned soil each spring hereafter, as it blooms again with color and life.

I haven't left this spot, attempting once more to write my letters, discouraged that Joseph had already finished his. Envelopes tucked inside the hinged seat of the piano bench for safekeeping, for *after*. It was my idea, something for the children to read when we are gone, in hopes of bringing them some semblance of peace. But it is hard to know what to say. Given the chance, how do we begin a goodbye, to include everything they will need to hear after we are gone? Especially when we are choosing to leave them behind. Leaving, when there are so many more important reasons for us to stay. I am filled with guilt and uncertainty once more. I wonder why we ever made this choice... one we can still take back. I want to reconsider everything, make Joseph see, before it's too late.

It's not only the message giving me trouble. I lose words, names; ideas dissolve before my pen hits the page. A new kind of loneliness I never imagined, trapped in the maze of my mind, but the threat is real and hangs around like an eerie fog, imminent, cloaked and haunting me. The seasons change and time moves too fast and I am behind, struggling to catch up, to hit Stop on the clock, to rewind and begin again, to have a choice that will allow me to stay as I was, not as I am. What can I say in the letters to comfort them when I am so scared myself?

The grandfather clock strikes nine in the morning, although this time tomorrow the clocks will read ten. A strange trick of daylight savings that reminds me how flimsy our sense of the world is, and rumbles a bitter anger coming in waves lately, so strong and sudden, like physical contractions of pain. How time is false and constructed, that it can change because we say so, and we can frivolously lose an hour while we sleep. No matter how I try to stay right here, in this moment, it will slip through my fingers like sifted flour, like the finest sand.

I try to focus on a memory to keep myself alert, a trick of Joseph's to help keep me in my own mind. After the symphony, we celebrated over dinner in that crowded Italian restaurant on Hanover Street. I work to re-create in my mind's eye how beautiful and imperfectly perfect they all were. Their smiles aglow in the candlelight, the hum of the other patrons surrounding us, tucked in our own cocoon of laughter and conversation. Jane beside Marcus, at last, where they belong. Everything a haze of dishes clinking and servers in black ties and aprons weaving between tables, but Joseph clear as day as he rubbed his thumb across my knuckles, fingers interlaced with mine.

This life, together. It was enough. It was everything.

"You know how much I love you, right? How thankful I am to have had you as my mom?" Violet's eyes fill, as we sit together on the couch, a fire in the hearth, tucked beneath a knit blanket, sharing stories, remember when's. These conversations coming often, assurances of love, of gratitude, and I echo them back to my children like a lullaby, *I love you, I love you, I will always love you. How lucky I was to call you mine.*

"It's only March, sweetheart," I tease. "You're a few months early for goodbyes."

She laughs, wiping at her eyes. "I'll bank some extras." She takes a deep breath, contemplative. "Do you think you'll be together, after? You and Dad?"

I twist my wedding ring between swollen joints. "I don't know what to believe. It's nice to hope, I suppose. If it were up to me, we would be together here instead." I meet Violet's eyes. "But that's not an option for me, not the way that I want it to be. I've lived a full and beautiful life. I couldn't have asked for more out of it."

"You know, I've been talking to Thomas and Jane, and, we have an idea." Violet smiles, a sly, sneaky grin.

"Alright…" I say, uncertain.

"Let's throw a party," she announces, eyes glittering.

I laugh, not expecting this. "A party."

"A party. Just family, just the ones who know. You and Dad said, at the very beginning of this whole thing, you wanted this year to be a celebration, right? And we can't keep sitting around here crying." She laughs, wiping her eyes. "So yes, a party. A celebration of life."

"You're going to throw us a funeral before we're even gone?" More laughter, surprising myself with how much I like the idea, how nice it would be to be there, to not miss anything, especially this.

"A *party*. Nothing sad. No crying allowed," Violet says, and crosses her heart.

"You said it," I tease, and hug her. "A party sounds perfect."

"Soon, you think?" Violet asks, studying me, concern etched in her face once more.

"How about May, the garden in bloom?" I say, hoping to emit confidence, to stave off my symptoms by sheer force of will. "Something to look forward to."

"May," Violet agrees.

"A party." I lean against her, thankful for my daughter, for this gift, a beacon to swim to as I tire, carrying me through. For something, even now, to celebrate.

Twenty-Two

Evelyn

August 1973

The night Joseph and Jane's plane is scheduled to land, I pace the foyer, sweltering in the August heat, checking the windows obsessively in search of a taxicab as guests pass through, oblivious to my agony. I keep vigil at the door, so resolute in my focus that the sudden crunch of the tires along the driveway startles me.

The cab stops at the edge of the walk, and the back door swings open. Joseph steps out with his leather suitcase. I wait for Jane to sidle out and join him in the thick and humid summer night, in the darkness made alive by buzzing cicadas, but nothing happens. The car hums, the waves crash in the distance, the air and trees stand still. Joseph shuts his door behind him and the cab backs up, disappears into the shadows, the steady crunch fading as it maneuvers down the driveway, and is gone.

My stomach lurches. I have seen him look that way once before, coming out of a car alone. Last time, I rushed to meet him, under the bluest summer sky. Last time, I threw my arms around him. Last time, it broke me.

Joseph remains a statue in the driveway, his grip on his suitcase limp. He doesn't search the windows for me, or glance back at the retreating taxi, doesn't seem to register he has arrived at all. He stands, shoulders stooped, staring at the shattered oyster shells beneath his feet. I press my palms against the cool metal screen, wanting to open it, to run to him, but I'm not sure he would see me if I did, not sure he would recognize my arms around his neck. So, I wait, frozen.

When he raises his gaze and meets mine, his face gives away nothing. He begins a labored march up the walkway, the rusted springs creak as I move to let him in. He enters the house the way a breeze sweeps through an open door, aimless and empty, a chill in its wake.

He disappears upstairs, and I find him perched on the edge of our bed, his suitcase untouched by his feet. I linger in the doorway, afraid to make my presence known. He leans down to untie his shoes, slips them off. Each movement arduous and painful. He looks older, worn and battered.

The silence pounds in my chest. He seems to be unaware of it entirely, as if he moves underwater. "Joseph," I whisper, afraid to make noise, to startle him. "What happened?"

He looks at me as if noticing my presence for the first time. He drops his gaze and lines his shoes together, toe to toe and heel to heel, before he speaks.

"She's doing drugs. Hard drugs. Heroin."

A punch that levels me. My breath quickens.

My body weakens as he tells me what he saw. The shabby apartment. The mattress on the floor, drugs and debris littered the counters, the yells of the neighbors and the smell of rot and filth. How Jane was nearly unrecognizable. The man who brought her to California, his eyes bloodshot and his sickly smile. The raw and red needle pricks in the hollows of her elbows.

"And I couldn't do anything." He tears at his hair. "I couldn't get her to come home."

My limbs feel like they are made of bricks as I cross the room
to sit beside him. I stroke his back, faking a sense of calm even
as my stomach wrings. "This is not your fault. She isn't a child...
we can't make her do anything she doesn't want to...even if we
wish we could."

He wrenches away from me, his voice ice. "You didn't see this
place. You didn't see her. This isn't about her being an adult. We
fucked up, we lost her, she's never coming back."

It feels like I have been slapped. "You don't blame me, do
you?"

He doesn't look at me, doesn't answer.

I stammer, losing control. "Please tell me you don't think this
is my fault, because I already feel responsible and I couldn't live
with myself if you thought that. I couldn't."

He concedes, slamming his knuckles together between his
knees. "It's not your fault."

I jolt to my feet, buoyed by my shame. "Yes, it is. I could have
done more, I should've tried to fix things before she moved out,
or while she was still in Boston. Should I go? I'll go by myself.
I'll go right now."

He shakes his head. "It won't do any good... I'm her father.
I'm supposed to protect her. And I couldn't. I couldn't do anything."

"It's not your fault."

"Well, it's someone's fault. Jane's gone, okay? She's never coming home, and she lives with some bastard who can't support
anything but a drug habit." His voice is hoarse, like he had cried
on the plane. I feel it rise again, acid in my throat. He coughs,
wrung out. "The way she looked at me... You wouldn't recognize her."

I don't know what to say, my mind a minefield of blame and
imagined scenes of Jane, twiggy and strung out with a needle in
her arm. I can't make sense of it. Her face is a blur, a combina-
tion of people I have known, my daughter but not my daugh-

ter, the way in dreams faces never match the person they are supposed to be.

"She thinks you cheated on me."

"What?" A jolt in my sternum, a knife pressed to my throat in the dark.

"With Sam, that summer."

"What?"

"She heard you two together, after her birthday."

I almost laugh, it's so absurd. "What does she think she heard?"

"She heard him ask you to run away together to Paris, to travel, drink wine and *make love.*" His voice is twisted and bitter when he says it. My gut churns at the memory. Sam's hand on my knee, the summer air thick with alcohol and smoke from the fire.

"Did she happen to hear what I said back?" I am haughty with the truth, the claims an impeachment I never saw coming.

"No. But I told her nothing happened."

"Do *you* think I cheated on you?" The simmering tension between us since Jane left hits me with force. A wall of heat I step into, barely able to breathe, questions answered with a cock of this gun, my racing heart. *"Oh my god.* You've been thinking this for years, haven't you?"

"No. I haven't." His voice is quiet, firm.

"I didn't. I would never."

"Why didn't you tell me about it?"

My voice raises an octave, incredulous. "Because it was so ridiculous! I told him he was completely off base, that it was incredibly inappropriate, that I was happily married, that he was a kid. It was a non-event."

"But why did he think he could ask?" I can hear his hurt now, the question he held back.

A rock in my throat. "I don't know."

"He must have thought there was a chance."

"There was *no* chance."

"But there must have been something he picked up on." His face is creased, pained. "I felt it, you know."

"Felt what?" My face is hot with this, the real accusation.

"Something between you."

I feel sick, something buried clawing to the surface. "This is why I never said anything. I didn't want you to read into something that wasn't there. I was so afraid it would create doubt... that it would make you question everything."

"You should have told me."

"I see that now." I touch his elbow, and he doesn't react, as though I am making a peace offering to the bed frame.

"What was it, then, between you?"

"Nothing—" I insist.

"Don't insult me, please."

"It wasn't anything romantic, Joseph. I swear." I fumble, trying to make sense of the escapist summer I suppressed so effectively it was nearly forgotten. "It was...god, this is so humiliating."

He says nothing, eyes on his shoes.

"He thought I was *somebody*. Interesting. He talked to me about travel, and music, and it was... I don't know, nice, to pretend I was something other than a mother. More than an innkeeper. He made me feel like it wasn't too late."

"I think you're interesting. I could talk to you about that stuff." His voice is gruff.

"I can't explain it." I don't know how to make him see, without insulting him, without digging a deeper trench between us that will bury me alive. "I was different, around him. I liked who I was, or I was pretending to be someone I wished I was. I don't know. But it was *never* more than that." I inhale, gathering steam. "Sam completely misread the situation. Leaving you was so far from the realm of possibility that I never told you, because telling you made it probable, somehow. Something I invited in." I backpedal, wanting to get it right. "Which, maybe I did, but I didn't mean to. I was so horrified and embarrassed that he thought he could come on to me. I kept going over every interaction and analyzing what I did, how I should've acted differently. I'm so, so sorry. I should've told you. I didn't want to make something out of nothing. But you're right. You deserved to know." The humiliation rises again, a metronome of shame, ticking away the years since I last spoke to my daughter. "God, Jane really thinks I cheated on you? All this time. *Jesus.*"

"I think it's only a part of the bigger issue we're dealing with here."

"What can I do?" My nose prickles, tears threatening.

"I don't know."

I feel so drained, the silence stretching between us like the miles he has traveled to land home in defeat, the years we have shared while he carried this secret. "I'm so sorry, Joseph. I hope you can find a way to forgive me."

"Nothing happened," he says, without warmth. "There's nothing to forgive."

"But I should've told you, you shouldn't have had to question something like that."

"I'm sorry I don't make you feel interesting..." An apology that feels like an end of a rope, a wounded man with nothing left to lose.

"No, no, no. Don't twist this around." I shake my head, stammering, "Yell at me, slam the door, tell me to sleep on the couch tonight. Do something."

"I'm not angry with you, Evelyn." His words a sigh, no fight left.

"You should be. *I'm* angry with me."

"It was so many years ago."

Hot tears fall down my cheeks. "I'm so ashamed...you actually thought I could be with someone else? That I'd ever consider it?"

"I wanted you to have a choice, an out, if you wanted it."

My chin quivers, trying to stifle everything. "I'm so sorry."

"I wish I could've fulfilled that need in you, I don't know, maybe we could've—"

"What? Sold the inn?"

His silence is an answer. "I'm sorry too."

There is nothing left to say. We sit in the half dark, not touching. Eventually we force ourselves into bed, exhausted with regret and shame, but neither of us sleep.

November 1975

I fold bleached towels, making a mental checklist of everything we need for Thanksgiving. Most guests are in town to visit family so we don't offer a full dinner, but I bake pumpkin bread for breakfast, butter spread across its crumbly surface, and set out hot spiced cider with orange slices in the foyer each evening. We have a small celebration, with my mother and Violet and Thomas, Thomas home only for the day, and Violet on holiday break from Tufts University.

I am desperate for their visit. Since Thomas started his job in Manhattan we barely see him, and although Violet is a junior in college I still expect to see her in her room, ankles crossed as she lies on her stomach on her bed, flipping through a magazine. It was easier to begin thinking of it as Violet's room, instead of *their* room, and sometimes in my mind's eye I can convince myself there is only one bed, instead of the pair of twins that sit empty and perfectly made, like tombs before me. The letters we've sent, money, phone messages, all unanswered. The nights we've sobbed until we're spent, clawing at this new reality, this nightmare we want to rescue Jane from, but can't. Sometimes it's the only way I can pass by their room at all. It is too hard to grieve her every day, to know that at any moment we could get a call that would bring us to our knees.

Joseph sits at the kitchen table going over the books and double-checking reservations when the phone rings. He glances at my lap full of linens and reluctantly reaches for the phone beside him. "Thanks for calling the Oyster Shell Inn, how may I help you?"

There is a pause.

"Jane?"

Joseph sits upright, the reservation calendar falls into his lap.

I drop the towel and gape at him in disbelief. After two years of silence since Joseph traveled to California—could it really be?

His voice cracks. "Of course you can, sweetheart. Of course you can..." Another pause. "No, no, don't worry, we'll book it, we'll take care of everything." Jane's muffled voice on the other end. "Okay. Talk to you soon. We love you."

He places the phone back on the receiver, and stares at it, as if he heard from a ghost. His eyes brim with tears when they meet mine, his lips parted in shock.

"Jane's coming home." He leaps to his feet, tips his chair over in his haste, and I jump up, scattering the laundry to the floor. He grabs me, wraps me in a hug as the strength goes out of my legs.

"Are you sure?" I grip him back, unable to believe it can be true.

"Yes. She's coming home." His embrace fills me. For two years, since he returned from California, since we talked about Sam, he has been a gust of wind. Silent except for the sounds he made by rustling through the leaves of the house. Coffee brewing. Shower running. Newspaper crinkling. Keys jingling. Staircase creaking. Car starting. Nothing I could say or do, no attempts at comforting conversation, gentle touch, giving him space, brought him back. But now he lifts me off the ground, spins me in dizzying circles. "Jane's coming home!"

"She said seven fifteen, right?" I pick at the skin around my nails, an ugly stress habit that's manifested since Jane left. I glance at the clock. It's not even six and we are nearly there.

"Seven fifteen." Joseph releases his grip on the steering wheel to clutch my hand, not as much to comfort me as to prevent me from tearing my cuticles. "Stop. It will be fine."

I nod but my throat is dry. Nothing about this is fine.

Outside it's so dark it could be midnight. The November sun sets earlier each day, signaling the slow creep of winter's chill that will linger long into spring. I button my wool coat—the heater on the passenger side is broken, the vent blows cool air until I slide it closed. Joseph said he would fix it but he has been so distracted; he must have forgotten. I don't bring it up. "Desperado" by the Eagles plays on the radio, and the lyrics are so apt a lump forms in my throat. Joseph doesn't pay attention to lyrics, music wafts through his eardrums to his passive enjoyment, so the irony is mine alone to weather until the song is over.

We pass a sign for Bradley Airport and Joseph gets into the right lane, anticipating the exit. I tuck my fingers under my thighs as much to stop my nervous tic as for warmth. It's been so long since he has held my hand in a moment of affection. Been so long since he drew me in for a long, spontaneous kiss or wrapped his arms around me, nuzzling my neck from behind as I washed up from dinner. It's as though he never came back from California, and only his shadow, an empty body with his likeness, returned.

We circle the parking lot until we find a spot, an hour early. We left the house long before we needed to, the afternoon spent puttering and pacing. Balls of nervous energy, anxious to get there, to see Jane. Now that we're here, planes gliding onto the tarmac, I'm terrified. What if she hasn't forgiven me for all those years we spent in silence? What if she blames me for how her life has turned out? Then a thought shames me as it flits across my mind, her skin, pockmarked and raw—*what if she isn't clean?* As we walk toward the terminal, I pick at my cuticles again. Joseph reaches for my hand, interlocks his fingers with mine. This time, he rubs my knuckles with his thumbs, and my breathing slows.

We stand under a sign labeled Arrivals and wait, as the minutes creep by. Joseph puts his arm around me and I lean against him, grateful. With every crowd that appears and dissipates my heart races, but each time it is a sea of strangers. I glance at Joseph's watch. *Seven twenty-five*. Another throng presses through the gates. Businessmen. A family in matching T-shirts, *California* glittering loudly over the Golden Gate Bridge. Flight attendants dressed in blue uniforms. And then in the distance, behind swathes of jostling limbs, there she is.

Jane has a tattered bag slung over her shoulder. The Vietnam War is over, but she looks like she walked straight out of a protest. Her hair is long and wild, T-shirt and jeans worn, and Joseph was right. She is skinnier than I've ever seen, her arms and legs toothpicks. I prepare myself for Jane to greet Joseph first, for her to be reserved or even cold to me. She scans the crowd but doesn't see us yet, her head swivels anxiously. We rush toward her and Joseph calls her name. She turns at the sound and spots us, elbowing our way toward her. As we approach, my breath catches. There, holding her hand, hidden from view behind her knees, emerges a little girl.

When Jane sees us, she heaves the girl onto her hip and barrels toward me, gripping me tight, this child—*Jane's child?*—wedged helplessly between us.

"Mom... I'm sorry. I am so, so sorry," she sobs, her shoulders heave.

I stroke her hair, my heart bursting and throat thick with tears, and say, "I'm sorry too. I'm sorry." She doesn't smell like cigarettes or alcohol or pot or grime, just faintly of sweat and unfamiliar scents I can't name, wisps of her old life I'll never know. The little girl unmistakably Jane's, the spitting image of the toddler I carried on my own hip a lifetime ago, an impossibility I know to be true. I embrace them both, too stunned to speak.

Jane pulls back, composing herself. "Mom, Dad, meet Rain. Your granddaughter."

The little girl peeks at us from behind a curtain of curls, her face pressed into Jane's shoulder. Granddaughter. Rain. How big she is, my *granddaughter*... I have a granddaughter.

"Jane, oh my god, Jane." Joseph, tears in his eyes, reaches a gentle hand out for a high five. Rain tentatively swats at his hand, smiles.

"Jane, I..." Every conversation I had rehearsed null and void in the light of her, Jane's baby girl. Except this. "We are...so glad you're home."

We usher them to the car, and on the drive my fear resurfaces. We got what we prayed for, our daughter returned to us, alive, safe. And more than we ever imagined, a granddaughter, all of fourteen months old, a miracle, a gift, perhaps even a reason for all of it.

But I have no idea where we go from here.

Twenty-Three

Evelyn

April 2002

I teeter outside, hold on to the walls until I reach the porch and make my way to my bench to sit beside Joseph. He kneels with his back to me, clearing yellowed stalks and withered stems to make way for fresh green shoots. The air has a chill to it, the breeze dragging tannins of winter despite the brightness of the spring sun.

He turns as I crunch through the debris. "How was your rest?"

I wonder how long I slept; I don't even recall lying down. "I dreamed about my mother again."

"Want to talk about it?"

I finger the buttons on my sweater as the breeze picks up, not wanting to ask for Joseph's help. "The way she was in the end, how scary it must have been for her... I can't imagine going through this without you. She didn't have anyone."

"She had you."

"She barely knew who I was by then." All those visits to

the nursing home, unsure what year in her mind I entered as I opened the door, or if she would recognize me at all. She had gotten lost in our neighborhood six times; when she was found wandering after midnight in the dead of winter, claiming to have a birthday card to deliver, we had no choice. The last four years of her life were spent there, the sharp smell of cleaning solution over the musky stench of decay was enough to make me want to turn around each time I stepped through the automatic double doors. Each day her reality shifting into a different point in time, where lost loved ones were alive, where ancient wounds were fresh and gnawing, and sometimes two people who never coexisted found themselves together in her mind. The stark rooms, silent except for the drone of a television or occasional incoherent moans, the blank stares on the residents' faces, the way time never seemed to pass from one minute to the next, from one day or week or month. The lives each one of them had lived, stories within their bones. The forgetting. The waiting. Waiting for loved ones. Waiting for a meal to be brought to their laps, fed to them from a spoon.

"I still think you were a comfort to her." He notices me fumble with the buttons. "Are you cold?"

I shake my head as a cloud slips away, wrapping me in sunlight. The dream nags at me again. "I feel sorry for her...she was so alone, her whole life." I had never seen my parents be affectionate, not like Joseph's parents. Mrs. Myers planted kisses on Mr. Myers's scruffy cheeks, he twirled her around the living room to a spinning record. I rarely saw my mother and father in the same room except for meals, saw them touch only to pass matches for their cigarettes. And the way I fought with her, the way I left her when Tommy died...was it she who wouldn't come out of her room, or me who didn't consider her unimaginable sorrow, a mother forced to bury a child, me who never pushed open her door, even to say goodbye?

"In my dream, she called for help and I didn't save her, all because she was angry with me and yelled at me." Another tear falls, and I let it.

Joseph is quiet, listening as he yanks the wilted brush, creating a pile beside him.

"I was angry at her for so long…she was so critical. But maybe that was the only way she knew how to get people's attention? I don't know…" I shrug, shame rises pink in my cheeks. All along I thought she cast me aside, but maybe it was me who never needed her. I was the one safely on land. I had Tommy, and Joseph, then Maelynn, and the children. She was trapped in the house like a restless spirit, mourning her son, abandoned by her daughter, ignored by her husband, drifting, waiting for someone to notice her. "I hate that it took losing her to finally understand her…" Our last conversation rings in my ears. "I couldn't be there for her before it was too late."

Joseph nods. "There's no use punishing yourself. Sometimes, it takes time to see things the way they really were."

I try to remember the dream even as it begins to fragment and slip from me. The details blur, but I can hear her call my name, crying for help. I feel the waves roll over my feet as she floats away.

Joseph continues to work as I sit with wandering thoughts. My mother's nursing home, how few men I ever saw there. Room after room of women who had lost their husbands, friends, family and often their minds. Which is worse to lose, the one you love, or your ability to recognize their face? Gratitude washes over me that I will never have to know years without Joseph, or years without the memories we spun together like the warmest wool.

I ask, "Are you afraid?"

The surge of love I feel for him is nearly unbearable, his crooked knuckles, the dull ache he kneads out of his leg after a long day, his affinity for night swims, every intimate detail that I carry, the affection I feel even for the dirt beneath his fingernails. If we were younger, I'd crawl through the grass and rest my head into his lap, my eyes on the clouds, or wrap my legs around his waist and nuzzle my nose into his neck, whispering, *Are you afraid?* but today it's an exertion to have come outside, to merely ask him from where I sit.

He sets down his spade and brushes his palms against each other, standing with effort to join me on the bench. Another stab of longing, yearning to fold myself into his lap once more. The women in the nursing home. Years living without their loved one beside them—but living. To make the plan is one thing, but to go through with it...

"Having second thoughts?" he asks gently.

"All the time. Aren't you?"

He doesn't have to answer for me to know we share the same trepidations; the repercussions of our decision heavy between us. Across the garden, a bedroom window is thrust open at Violet's house, rooting me back to reality. To have a conversation like this, with our family so near, to discuss the unthinkable.

"Do you think it will feel like anything?" I ask.

"I hope it will be like falling asleep, the way we're doing it."

The pills in the cabinet, stocked up prescriptions to help me sleep, to make me comfortable, from doctors who only heard me say the pain is too much to bear. Who didn't hear what was underneath, that there will be a day when what I lose is more than what I keep.

"What if there is nothing after?"

"Well, then we won't know the difference."

I consider this, and realize he's right. There is no way to know for sure. "Do you think it will be heaven?"

He shrugs. "I don't know what heaven could offer that could be better than the life we had."

I wiggle my eyebrows. "How about one where you don't scrub toilets?"

Joseph laughs, smiles sadly. "I hope there is an ocean. And a sun to warm us after swimming."

I lean against him. "I wouldn't mind if it was sort of like this, all over again."

Joseph brushes a strand of hair behind my ear, and I am young again, like two kids we once were, tangled in this very meadow. He meets my gaze, teary-eyed. "Like I said, this life with you, this has been heaven for me."

I swallow hard, the words that keep rising in me. *I don't want to die, not yet, not ever. I've loved my life, I've loved our life, I want to stay.*

Grateful we chose to wait until after the first few months of spring, to not miss the whimsical forsythia, the azaleas and tulips, the purple spouts of crocuses. "Have you thought about where you'll put a section for Rain's baby?" I ask. Rain, well into her third trimester. It won't be much longer. Another pang, a different kind of longing.

"There is some space by Jane's gladiolas, I thought it'd be nice for her flowers to be near her grandchild's."

"Jane is going to be a grandma. What does that make us?"

"*Very* old," he says, and I laugh.

"Look at it, Joseph." The garden is at the beginning of the beauty to come, as April turns to May and May to June, it will burst with color and life. It helps me remember their names, sometimes when I lose them, I imagine their flowers and the names find their way back to me. I want to see the blossoms that will represent Rain's baby, I want to see her baby grow and plant a garden of his or her own. I want to live here forever, to roll through the soft petals and press them to my nose. What a cruel side effect, to lose the scent of cookies in the oven, the sweet fragrance of a meadow. Had I known, I would have lain in the garden each morning, breathed in honeysuckle and rose. I would have filled the kitchen counters with fresh baked goods, cupcakes and muffins and sweet breads. I would have gone to Bernard Beach, inhaled the salt air and the musk of sandbars and seaweed. I would have lain against Joseph, breathed in his skin and soap and sweat and cologne. But you can't know. Sometimes, these things get taken without warning, and you can't get them back.

"Would you like some iced tea?" I ask. It is too late in the day for coffee, but it seems like the perfect moment for two glasses filled to the brim with ice, two lemon wedges, two straws and enough tea to sip away the afternoon.

"Sounds great. I can make it for us."

"No, Joseph, let me. I'll be right back." Before he can argue I press a shaking hand into his thigh, lifting myself off the bench. I make my way gingerly along the path, past Violet's daisies and the green stalks that will bloom into Thomas's lavender in later summer, to the porch.

I am there, almost to the steps, when I hit the ground. The blue sky fuzzy above as a rippling pain strikes white-hot across my back and my hip and my elbows. A warm stream of urine trickles down my leg.

Joseph above me, eclipsing the sun, asks if I am okay, if I can get up, if anything feels broken. I'm able to get up, but the pain sears like a burn. He lifts me carefully to my feet and guides me inside, inspects my elbows, scraped raw and bleeding from the cobblestone walk, miraculously the worst of it. He gapes at me, fear carved into his face. I have never fallen before. I've come close, stumbled from the shower or miscalculated a threshold, but I've always caught myself, or Joseph has steadied me. Never this.

"I peed myself, Joseph, I—" A sob rolls over me as he guides my soiled pants past my thighs. I weep as he holds me up, a doll in his arms.

Twenty-Four

Joseph

May 1977

Violet poses before a gilded mirror, her arms sleeved in lace, and tilts her head to put on a pair of pearl earrings. Bridesmaids, friends of hers from Tufts and Stonybrook, float around her in powder blue dresses, buttoning and adjusting and fluffing in a scene reminiscent of "Cinderella," a fairy tale I memorized from all the times she begged to hear it, those nights when she still fit tucked in the crook of my arm that seem both a lifetime ago and a recent memory.

Jane, the maid of honor, kneels by Rain, adorned in a similar blue dress. She has filled out to her normal lanky appearance, a far cry from the skin and bones that came home over a year ago. Her hair tamed and pulled back, her eyes clear and bright, her confidence growing as her shame dissipates, thriving under the distraction of a routine, changing sheets, scrubbing bathtubs, confirming reservations. My guilt from those lost years heavy and thick, for not being able to better protect our daughter, to prevent her deepest pain.

She thanked me once, months after she came home. We sat at the kitchen table while Rain ate diced strawberries. She avoided my eyes, wiping red juice from Rain's chin, as she said, "Thank you, for coming to California. For coming for us both." I told her I wish I had done it sooner. She broke down, telling us about her time there, the man she followed across country, the ache she mistook for love, all the ways it splintered and sucked her dry. Rain born so small and new, and the parts of Jane that woke up when she had her, wanting to be new again too. The shame that kept her away from us long after she was born; the craving, the need for family that eventually brought her home. I grabbed her hand and Evelyn grabbed her other and we held on because there were no more words, all the words that exist pulsing through our grasp, changing nothing, fixing nothing. All we could do is love her, this woman who crawled her way out of hell with her daughter, who holds on to us now. A lifeline to the girl she once was, to the woman she will one day become.

In the bridal room, Rain, now two and a half, practices scattering petals, dressed in a flower crown and frilled skirt, while Jane fusses with her hair. Violet's curls are pinned back in a low bun, and when I meet her green eyes in the reflection, I can't help but notice how much she resembles her mother on our wedding day. Evelyn was about her age, tender and iridescent, the brightest light radiating in any room.

"How do I look, Daddy?" She beams and twirls with grace, like the ballerinas in the music boxes she used to wind endlessly as a girl.

"Beautiful, sweetie. Beautiful." I blink furiously, hoping I can hold it together to get her down the aisle. I hug her close and kiss her cheek, then leave to visit Connor. The church buzzes with soft chatter and anticipation, rainbows of light stream through the stained-glass windows. Evelyn was checking all the guests are seated, and I pass her in the hallway. She is dressed in a glittering navy gown and her hair is curled and pinned in ways I haven't seen in years, her cheeks rose-dusted and lips painted a pale pink. Our fissure had ratcheted closed like it had been waiting, spring-loaded; any struggle or misunderstanding between us paltry next to this—our daughter, safely home. A grandchild, a whole new kind of tenderness. Her tiny hand, a salve.

Evelyn's beauty stops me, even in the pre-ceremony rush, and catches me breathless, sends me back to the moment she first stepped off the train. The highlights of our life together play on an infinite loop in my mind, stringing every moment that led us from there to here, from here back to there, and I am in awe all over again. Except, I love her so much more today than I did even then.

She reaches for my elbow. "How is she?"

"She's so beautiful. I can't believe she's getting married today."

"I know. Our baby is all grown-up."

"She looks so much like you, you know."

She smiles, coy. "You think so?"

"I do. I don't know if I can give her away."

"If anyone deserves her, it's Connor."

"He is a good man, isn't he?"

"He is." She straightens my bow tie and thumbs my chin playfully, and my whole body softens at her touch.

"I don't know where the time has gone. Where has it gone?"

Evelyn shakes her head and gives a light shrug, but she hasn't stopped smiling, a dreamy, giddy smile that reminds me of sun-soaked kisses on a deserted beach.

"Is Jane with her now?"

"Yes, and Rain too. She's practicing scattering the petals all over the room."

"Oh dear." She giggles. "Let's hope there are some left for the ceremony."

Her laughter fills me and makes me want to confess every single thing I love about her. The wrinkles around her mouth, the sharpening of her cheekbones, the softening of her thighs.

All the ways she has aged track every year we've shared, the proof on her body is the map that tells me I'm home, the scars and freckles I've traced with my tongue, that I could follow with eyes closed, the only place I've ever cared to know. I love her so much, and today I'm bursting to tell her over and over. But I don't, because *I love you* has become routine, the period at the end of a sentence rather than the explosion of affection that erupts the first time it's said. I need words stronger than *I love you*. I need a whole new emotion to describe the depths of which I care for the woman to whom I've given my life, and who in turn, has given her life to me.

"You better go check on the groom. I'm going to take my seat. It's almost time." She stands on her tiptoes to kiss me, and her fingers linger on my arm even as she turns away. It seems she is falling victim to the romance of the day like I am.

Connor is down the hall, on the opposite end of the church. I tap my knuckles against the door, and he shouts me in. His three brothers and his father circle him, redheaded with Boston accents, slightly stockier, taller, balding or mustached variations of the groom. I shake his hand and can sense a shift in him, from the young boy roughhousing with his brothers, to a man ready to devote himself fully to a woman. I direct him out of the door, his groomsmen and father follow closely behind. The ceremony is a blur of tears and applause. Violet radiates, and Connor trembles as he slips the ring on her finger. I study him during the vows, recognize the look of total powerlessness on his face. I know that expression well; it was the one I wore when I married Evelyn. It's the one I have every time she gazes into my eyes, undoing me effortlessly and completely.

At the crowded reception hall, Violet and Connor are announced to a ruckus of cheers and after they share their first dance, they invite everyone onto the floor. I gesture to Evelyn to join me, although in the past it would've been her dragging me out, with some resistance on my part. Since Jane has come home, nothing feels so serious that I can't dance with my wife. Evelyn presses her cheek to my chest. Violet and Connor sway near us, eyes locked in their own secret conversation, a love story all their own to discover.

I'm taken back once more to life as a newlywed. Of all the words we said without a sound, those days and weeks and months we hid beneath the covers. She made me so weak then. Even now I'm weak for her, heavy with the weight of my love and the ache of wanting endless years with her. To be able to start all over—young and new. To learn each other again. We met when we were kids, we were the only loves we ever had. It scares me to think if she had explored the world, if she had left Connecticut out of something other than grief, if she would have met someone else. If someone would have broken her heart, or worse, loved her as deeply as I do. If she would have settled for me if she had any other choice.

Evelyn shifts against me, raising her chin, her gaze on the glow around Connor and Violet.

"Remember that feeling?" she whispers, peering up at me.

"Remember it?" I stare into those ever-changing eyes. "I've never forgotten it."

She presses her lips to mine and I stroke her lower back, pull her closer. "I was hoping you'd say that."

The glimmer in her eyes as we dance, her contented smile, give me courage and I ask, "Would you have chosen me, again? If you had the chance to do the things you wanted to do? Would it still have been me?"

She is quiet, our bodies drift with the current of the other couples on the crowded floor, all lost in their own sweet undertow.

I'm not sure she heard me, but before I can ask again, she speaks.

"Are there things I wish I had done in this life? Things I have never done, and probably will never do? Things I wish I could change? Yes. I'd be lying if I said I didn't have regrets. But you, our children, everything about our life together…that's a choice I'd make again and again. It's always been you. Even when I was afraid. It's always been you."

She says the last part in a whisper, as if to herself. And we sway together on the dance floor until the songs and the people around us all fade into the most beautiful, soothing melody, like waves along the shore…until there is only Evelyn in my arms as the tide comes in and out, out and in, at once blurring and keeping time.

September 1983

We agreed to close the Oyster Shell for good after Labor Day, the mark of the end of the summer in Stonybrook, when the striped umbrellas are gone from the beaches and the seasonal cottages board up their windows for winter. We talked about it for years, built up our savings and imagined what retired life would be like, debated if we could really swing it, if we had the courage to shut the doors. We've lasted longer in the business than anyone else we know, over thirty years. There are a few other bed-and-breakfasts nearby, and we've seen the inevitable turnover of ownership, watched inns become private homes and private homes become inns. Most family-run places last about ten years before selling off or shutting down. The burnout rate is high because the demand on the innkeeper is constant—to share your lives with strangers, to be available and welcoming and invisible all at once. But selling the Oyster Shell, its cedar shingles as gray and weathered as I am, was never an option.

But now, our children are settled in their own lives. Thomas and Ann newly engaged, Violet pregnant with their third, and Jane once again the daughter we used to know, bold and adventurous, but not wild, not on a path of destruction. Just free. Eight years she and Rain lived with us, helping to check in guests, serve breakfast, change linens. I miss the patter of Rain's little feet in the hallway, Jane sipping coffee at the kitchen table, but I'm proud of how far she's come. Her own apartment, a steady job as a bank teller in town, taking journalism classes at the community college. It feels like as good of a time as any to turn the page. Unlike my parents, who were forced to close, to grieve it like a loved one, our dream wasn't swept away by gale-force winds. When we closed, it would be our choice, not because we were broken by the work, but because we wanted to spend our time however we like, to let our house become nothing more or less than a home.

The last guest checked out, the room turned, their car long gone from the driveway, Evelyn grabs my arm, threads it with hers, and we walk together to the end of the driveway. It is the perfect September day, the slightest breeze, clouds drifting lazily by.

"Will you do the honors?" Evelyn asks, handing me my pliers, and I work the faded Oyster Shell Inn sign off its chain.

We look at each other, the signpost bare, the sign in my hands. Evelyn asks, "Now what?" and we both laugh. She wraps her arms around me, and I rest my chin in her hair. Our world suddenly so quiet, just us two.

She begins carefully, "You should figure out *something*...this retirement is a gift, and I'd hate for you to waste it being bored."

I say nothing, deeply insecure. She squeezes me, demanding an answer.

"But what am I supposed to do?"

She wiggles her eyebrows. "Anything you want. That's the beauty of it."

Easy for her to say. She has other dreams, other wants, besides me. Lists of them. I wonder, not for the first time, if I love her more than she loves me, if I'm enough for her. Why do I love her so much? Because she is everything I am not, and everything I wish I could be. I envy her. Even in her darkest days she felt more than I have ever felt, gone deeper into herself so she could be born anew.

I wish I had more to offer, some interesting secret to confess. There are things I enjoy about our quiet beautiful life, like hot coffee after a shower in the morning, or the cold surge of water around my body in the first swims of summer. But I'm not a dreamer. And although she wishes that were different, I am not unhappy. People always seem to know what path they were supposed to take, but I've merely drifted in the current I found myself in.

I resuscitated my parents' dream, found my way without them all these years. Together Evelyn and I breathed air into dusty rooms, watched them bloom with chatter and life, raised our children and catered to guests as they did; we lived in the shadows of their memory, while they existed in the caverns of ours. There wasn't room, or need, for anything more. For me it had always been enough. We barely had time even for friends, although we did our best to be sociable, Evelyn always the life of the party while I struggled to make small talk. I never again found a bond like the one I shared with Tommy. Relationships came and went with the phases of our life. Outside of Maelynn, Evelyn's connections to other women were swept aside by bustling schedules and promises to get together that evaporated with the passing seasons. But like I said, I am not unhappy. And yet, I can't answer Evelyn's question.

"Are you listening?"

"Yes. I'm listening. I don't have anything to say. Is it so wrong to want to spend time with you?"

"You'll get tired of me if all we do is spend time together."

"We've been married thirty-eight years. If I am not tired of you yet I don't think I'll ever be." Her arms around me no longer a comfort, I slip out of her hold. "Let's head back. I want to find a place for this." I lift the sign in answer, something to do, for the moment.

She calls after me, "Think about it, okay?"

What do I want, Evelyn? God if I know. I want time with her, with the people I love. I want time with the people we lost. I want to go back to the beginning. I want to reach for her hand in the surf, my heart pounding. I want her to say yes to me all over again.

Twenty-Five

Joseph

May 2002

I hear the screen door creak open behind me. Evelyn appears
in a floral sleeved dress, her long silver curls swept back at the
nape of her neck, already dressed for the party. I've been out
here since breakfast spreading mulch, planting red zinnias and
combating an aphid infestation, trying to get as much done before I have to make myself presentable. The air is cool, but the
activity has my blood moving, and I am warm enough under
the sun.

She strolls down the path, something tucked discreetly beneath her arm. "How are Violet's flowers?"

"Alright." I point my spray bottle at the undersides of the
infested leaves, the shriveled daisies a feeding ground for pests.
"Let's hope this takes care of the problem."

She perches on her bench and in the morning light the dark
circles under her eyes are more visible, purple and translucent.
She shoves her hands into the pockets of her sweater, and says,
"I love this time of year."

Peak spring, the flower beds in full bloom, growing together into a kaleidoscope of color, the peonies like puffs of pink clouds, everything green and bright as it grows anew. A hummingbird flits around a honeysuckle blossom, black-eyed Susans quiver in the slightest breeze, the sun peeks out from behind a wisp of clouds. Many days spent like this, Evelyn keeping me company, reading or writing in notebooks while I worked. Sometimes I'd catch her gaze fixed on the violets instead of the pages in her lap, and I'd wonder where her drifting mind lands. Did she see me, desperate and waiting at the end of her walkway? Or was she in the very first moments, petals in her pockets, flowers in her hair?

She tilts her head back, warming to the sun. "Pretty morning."

"Beautiful," I agree, my eyes on her, the romance of the day, the excitement of the party, getting to me. Still, after all these years, so incredibly beautiful.

"I have a surprise for you." She reveals a carved wooden box hiding behind her and sets it in her lap.

I scramble, unprepared. "I didn't know we were doing gifts."

"We're not." Evelyn drums her fingers against its lid. "I've had this tucked away for you for a long time, searching for the right moment."

I tilt my head, intrigued, and brush the dirt off the best I can, wiping my hands against my worn jeans. She pats the spot beside her and I sit.

"I started writing you letters while you were away in the war and, well, I guess I never stopped." She lifts the lid off the box, and it is filled to the brim with envelopes, my name in cursive scrawled across the front of each. "There are letters for when I wanted to tell you how I felt, or when I needed to get something off my chest, and one for every big milestone we've had along the way."

"Evelyn..." Her name is all I can manage, overwhelmed.

"It's a celebration, right?" She beams, and I am without words. Sixty years of her innermost thoughts captured in these pages, waiting for me.

"I don't know how to thank you for this…" Again, as I often do, I wish for stronger words than *I love you.* She slides the box from her lap to mine, and I ask, "Do you want to be here when I read them?"

"I don't know… I honestly don't remember what they say. I never reread them. I just saved them for you, for someday." I wrap my arm around her shoulders, search fruitlessly for the response a gesture like this deserves. "At first, I wrote them because you were away and there was so much I wanted to tell you, but then Tommy…and we didn't speak. But I couldn't stop writing. It helped me to get my thoughts out. Then as the years passed, it was a way to capture our life together, little snapshots in time. I was never sure when to give them to you, nothing ever felt big enough, but tonight, the party, it feels like the perfect time."

She leans against me and reaches into the box for the letter on the very top. The envelope has yellowed, fragile to the touch, my name in faded ink across the front.

"Read them in whatever order you like, except start here. This is the first one I ever wrote."

"Is it alright if we read it together?"

She nods ever so slightly, and I weaken, realizing after all these years, even though I have parted her thighs with my tongue, have spread my palms across her bare stomach while our own children lay nestled in her womb, have plucked unsightly hairs from her chin with my fingertips, that this—sharing these intimate letters, makes her shy.

I flip the envelope over and tear gingerly through the seal. The paper inside has yellowed, too, and I slide it from its hiding place. In the top right corner is the date: *June 15, 1942.* The year catches in my throat, so long ago. It was around the time we enlisted, before I knew war, when Tommy was full of so much life, fearless and brash, eager to be a hero. I swallow hard, and silently read.

Dear Joseph,

You and Tommy just left, and I sit on Bernard Beach again, this time alone. I wanted to chase that train down the tracks. I wanted to beg you to stay. I wanted to do anything but stand there as you disappeared. I am scared, Joseph. I am scared of not seeing you again. I am scared of how the war may change you. I am scared you will come back and you won't love me anymore.

Love. I am uneasy using that word, like if I use it too much somehow you will take it back. You told me you loved me. You love me! Now I know, I can't bear the thought of you ever stopping. I am sorry I couldn't say it back. I'm furious with myself, regretting it since you left. I want you to know I do love you. I have loved you, desperately, for so many years, hoping someday you would feel the same way. And now that you love me back, you're gone. Please come home to me, so I can tell you in person. I love you. I have always loved you, and I will never stop loving you. I am yours.

Forever,
Evelyn

My vision swims as I reach the end of the page and I'm yanked back to the present, Evelyn leans against me in the garden, in a new decade, a new millennium. So many years since she wrote this, the innocent, unbroken girl waiting for me on Bernard Beach. All we've been through since then, war, and loss, and the life we created right back where we started.

How young and sure of the world I was then, how she was the answer to it all. *I have always loved you, and I will never stop loving you. I am yours.* How desperately I wanted to hear those words while I was away, how much I needed to hear them when I re-turned. How the thought of her feeling the same way, still, sixty years later, brings me to my knees. My affection for her is almost too much to bear, the tenderness of her love illuminates me from the inside, fills all of my empty spaces with the purest light.

Evelyn

The garden twinkles with string lights, winding paths traced with tea candles and lanterns. Tony and Rain have handled the cooking, pasta with meatballs rolled by hand, his grandmother's sauce, buttery garlic bread, and a salad tossed with olive oil and balsamic sent by family in Sicily. Red wine decanted on the table along with pitchers of ice water and strawberry lemonade, beside freshly snipped bouquets.

It feels like a wedding, a bar mitzvah, New Year's Eve, a buildup to something new, something awaiting that is an after-thought to the night itself, because tonight is why we're here, giddy with it, the merriment, the lights, and the flowers and the stars, with being together.

Violet approaches, hands me a flute of champagne. "You'll need this."

"There aren't speeches," I say, certain now there are.

Violet shrugs, grinning.

"Nothing sad, you said," I warn, accepting the drink, know-ing this night is already more than I could have asked for, that I can't promise not to fall to pieces if my children start saying sweet things.

"I didn't promise no speeches." She kisses my cheek, and car-ries another glass to her father.

Joseph finds me, putting his arm around my waist as Thomas clinks his glass with a butter knife, and we all turn toward him.

"First, I'd like to remind everyone that bets are open—" he

points to his nieces and nephews "—anyone want to guess the over, under, on how often your mom cries tonight?"

Violet swats him on the arm.

"Hey, you said keep it light," he teases.

"Yeah, not at my expense," Violet says, but she's grinning. Connor sidles up to her, hands her a glass, and she squeezes his arm in thanks.

"You two aren't like any parents I've ever met, or any two people I've ever known. It's hard to explain, what it's like, being raised by two people so in love. Truly made for each other. When I was Patrick's age—" he tips his glass to his youngest nephew "—it was mortifying, to be honest." Everyone laughs. "But now I see what a gift it always was. To be raised here, in this place. To have you guiding us. Not only helping us find our way when things didn't go as we hoped, but for supporting us in whatever we chose to pursue. Jane, with her journalism, and me, with moving to New York, helping Violet and Connor all the time with the kids, and never pushing your dreams on us. For closing the Oyster Shell when none of us wanted to keep it going. But still keeping this place for us all to come back to, this house that binds us together, where our memories live. A place we'll be able to return to, always, and feel close to both of you. I don't say it enough, I'm sure..." His voice breaks, and I wish I was near enough to put my arm around him, but he doesn't need me now, Ann is there, beside him, gripping his hand. "But I love you both, and anything good I have in my life," he says, turning to Ann, "I owe to you."

Violet dabs her eyes with a tissue, and she says, "Nice job keeping it light."

Thomas, teary, locks eyes with Ryan and says, "First speech in, and we're on the board." Violet laughs, hitting him again.

"I guess I'm up," Jane says, downing the rest of her glass. "Mom, Dad. How do I begin? Everyone knows we've had our moments, no need to go down memory lane. I kept things interesting, didn't I? We couldn't all be Violet, I suppose."

Violet lifts her palms. "Thanks for that." She shoots Thomas a look and he tilts his glass in cheers.

"You two are my favorite people on this planet." Her eyes are shiny as she says it, and she catches her daughter's gaze. "Sorry, Rain. You too. And that baby, while we're at it." She gestures to Rain's belly, her dress stretched tight. "But the two of you." She turns back to us. "God, you have saved me a million times, in a million ways, and I can't tell you how grateful I am. How lucky I feel to have made it this far, when it could have been so different. Those years that Rain and I lived here, I can't thank you enough. Can't explain what it meant to feel so safe, to share her childhood with you, to have you there for bedtime stories, and her first days of school, and every lost tooth. For helping me find solid footing again so I could build my own life, and make her proud. Becoming a mother taught me so much about us, Mom." She turns to me, and my eyes fill. "All the ways you were there for me that I was too stubborn to see. And, Dad, you were always my rock, the one place I could land, and you never let me forget I could always come home. And this will always be your home, too, *we* will always be your home..." She pauses and I think she will say, *with or without mom,* but she doesn't, and it hangs in the air as she continues, "Thomas was right about this place, we are lucky to have grown up here, but more than that, we were lucky to have you both, waiting here with open arms."

Joseph is crying now, too, and I can't take another, it's too much, I'll never be able to thank them for tonight, for feeling so loved, so lucky, so overwhelmed with gratitude, but before I can protest, Violet is standing, wiping her eyes. "And I'm supposed to follow that?" She blinks furiously, and smiles through her tears. "We had one rule," she says, shooting her siblings a look. "So instead of a long speech, because quite honestly, we all know I'd never be able to get through that. I'll just say this." She turns to us, eyes rimmed red. "We love you. We are so thankful that you are ours, that you raised us to love the beach, and each other, and because of that, because of everything you've given us, if we ever feel alone—" her voice catches "—when we hear the waves, we can close our eyes, and be right here again, with you."

We lift our glasses, tears streaming down our cheeks.

"Cheers," Joseph says, "we love you all."

The grandchildren clear the table and someone turns up the stereo, making way for a grassy dance floor. Marcus is here, and he leads Jane out with him, and I wonder how much context he has, under what guise she invited him tonight. But the way he holds her around the waist, the way she tips her head back in laughter, gives me my answer. There's nothing about her, about us, he doesn't know.

A song, "Brandy," by the band Looking Glass comes on, and Violet and Connor bob and sway to the beat, the grandkids joining in, singing. Thomas and Ann, and Rain and Tony join in, shouting the lyrics and dancing along, singing the story of a sailor, and the girl he left behind to chase the sea.

"Look at them, Joseph." My voice more breath than sound.

He squeezes my hand. "I know. Who would've thought we would be so lucky?"

Our three, and the ones they love, and the ones they made, all here tonight. Their lives now the only thread to follow; their choices and mistakes and triumphs and regrets, the people they will meet, the families they will create, their songs reverberating long after we're gone.

"They could not be more different." I laugh. "Are we sure they're all ours?" But in truth, they have never seemed as alike as they do in this moment. I can see Joseph in each of them, in Violet's easy smile, her affection with her siblings, Thomas's frame, his quiet confidence, Jane's devotion to her daughter. Violet threads her arms around Thomas, and around Jane, their youngest sister between them, and they dance, rooted together, three completely different people, branches of the same sturdy, steady tree. "They make me so happy, every one of them."

"I always hoped they would," Joseph says, kissing me.

"Let's join them, shall we?"

We make our way to the edge of the grass, and Thomas turns to us with a wide smile. Usually we are the ones to reach for a hug, to show our affection, but tonight he is unbridled, he is joy, and he is here, fully here, and he reaches toward us.

For the first time, he pulls us into his open arms.

Twenty-Six

Evelyn

November 1992

Sandstone Lane is veiled in the densest night when we turn into our neighborhood, our headlights cast an eerie glow. The tires crunch on the thin layer of snow iced over our driveway. Joseph is visible in the light emanating from the dashboard as he surveys the blackened landscape. "The storm must've knocked down a line somewhere."

"Looks like it." I can't even manage a nod, exhausted from the day spent greeting and hugging and accepting sympathy. My mother's funeral felt like a strange, bleak party, most of the guests were friends of ours, or our children, everyone in black as they spoke in hushed tones, but no one broken by grief, no raw emotion pulsed in tightly gripped hugs. The priest gave a generic reading, ashes to ashes, dust to dust, as I stood on aching feet, wondering how my mother had outlived so many others.

What a strange tradition, the way we say goodbye, kneeling over a casket, tiptoeing around small talk and muted circles, somber and bowed by decorum, how one's own mortality emerges naked and emboldened in the forest of faces, stalking through the room. It seems too late, detached from the real experience of loss, how it lingers, the sharp pangs that follow: a familiar scent, a song on the radio, a memory plucked out of thin air while washing dishes.

Joseph eases the car into the garage and I wait as he disappears in the darkness, fumbles for a flashlight on his workbench. The beam clicks on and I follow him inside, my body at once weighted and emptied. We dig through the cabinets for candles and matches and carry them upstairs, hollow in this big house for the two of us. We light the blackened wicks until the room is cast in a flickering yellow glow, and we undress and brush our teeth in the half-light. Joseph kindles fires in the hearths throughout the house, and I yank some extra blankets from the closet in case the heat dissipates through the night.

My last visit to see my mother in her nursing home morphs into a cloud of guilt and sadness, dragging me under. The hallway reeking of rubber, mothballs and bleach, a kind of place that will never quite be a home, the last conversation we ever had.

It started with her rant about Maelynn, how wild and selfish she always was, how she never visited her own sister. Clearly, in her mind that day, Maelynn was alive and well. Like Tommy was sometimes, and my father. I envied her naivety. I wish I could not remember, to believe everyone I ever loved was out of sight for the moment, in the other room perhaps, or too busy or selfish to visit. I should've let it go, should've left, but I couldn't. So tired of her screaming, so tired of her illness, so tired of being rational and calm and patient, never rising to her bait.

My voice deepened to a growl, the iron teeth of my buried resentment splayed open like a bear trap. "Why did you send me away to live with her, if you thought she was so terrible? Were you sick of me? Did you only want Tommy at home so you could pretend I never existed?"

She closed her eyes tight, as though in pain, but when she

opened them, there was something new, something raw and wounded, in her gaze. "Is that what you think?"

Her lucidity struck me silent, my chest heaving.

"If I was hard on you…it was because I was afraid for you. You reminded me so much of her…" She trailed off again, and I had trouble breathing evenly, her coherence as jarring as her screams when her mind slipped away. "Neither of you were ever satisfied with the life in front of you. I thought…I thought Maelynn was the only one who could make you see what I never could." She blinked, gave me an odd look, like she was trying to place me. "I didn't know what else to do, Tommy. Part of me hoped if Evelyn met her, she would see through her. The other part was afraid she'd fall for her, like everyone else. But at least if she did, she'd be with someone who understood her, who could be there for her in ways I never could."

Even in her confusion I heard her perfectly clear, aware of my salty tears only when they reached my lips. All this time I had been so angry. "I…"

"I thought I made a big mistake, that you got the worst of her. You left me, when Tommy died…but look, you're here now. At least you visit me." A tight smile passed over her lips.

I considered explaining why Maelynn didn't come, but there was no use, no need to tell her who had been dead for decades, when I would have to remind her again next time. Instead I stammered, "Thank you, for telling me."

"Telling you what?" She blinked, disoriented, her face shadowed with distrust. And like that, she was gone. I stood, taking my cue, my eyes stinging with tears.

She muttered something, turned away from me. Then she pivoted back, one knotted finger pointed at me. "You. What are *you* doing here?" Who I was to her then, I couldn't be sure. Her body trembled, her gaze darting back and forth, searching me. I apologized for disturbing her, assured her I must be in the wrong place as I backed out of the room. The last thing

I saw were her terrified eyes as I shut the door with a soft click, the image of her shaking under the covers, so small and alone, seared in my mind.

I get into bed with a sigh, and Joseph crawls under the quilt beside me and asks, "You alright?"

I rest my head on my elbow, curved to face him. My tears had found me the day I left her trembling in her room, once I was alone in my car. While washing my face in the sink, I see my lined eyes in the mirror resemble hers. And rolling dough for biscuits the way Mrs. Myers taught me, my hands are spotted with age. How little I understood...but today I was spent, wrung dry. "We knew this was only a matter of time."

"I know."

"I keep replaying the last time we found her wandering outside. She was so afraid, helpless..." I pause, remember her clutching me like a child as I slid a nightgown over her bare, bony shoulders. "What if I get like that? What if you do?"

"I don't know." His brow furrows and even in the shadows I make out the worry lining his temples.

My back is sore from standing all day; my legs tingle, restless, and I struggle to get comfortable. "I don't want to get forgetful, I don't want one of us to go to a nursing home. I want to stay here, like this, forever." Joseph veers on seventy, and I'm not far behind, our aches vocal but tolerable, our days still our own to spend how we choose, but for how long?

"Unfortunately, my love, I think that one is out of our hands."

I shift closer to him, our knees touch beneath the flannel sheets. The light flickers behind him, a candle burns out.

"It doesn't seem fair, does it?" he asks. I fall silent, my fingers toy with a hole in the blanket. "You can't be the first to go, Evelyn. I'd be so lost without you... I couldn't stand to be in this big house by myself."

"Well, you can't either. I'd be lost too..." I trail off, my chest fills with the visceral fear of something looming, one of us

crumpled over a casket, crawling into bed each night alone. I
shake the images from my mind. "You think any of them are
watching over us?"

"Who knows." Joseph shrugs. Then he asks, "Do you think
your father was happy to see your mother?"

Surprised by the question, I laugh. "He may have liked the
break these last couple of decades." The picture I have of my
father is vague after all these years, but I can still see the bushy
mustache, the cigar clenched between his teeth. I can't help
myself, imagining it fall from his mouth in shock at her sudden arrival after years of solitude.

Joseph joins and our laughter in the darkened room is a release, a knot coming loose. He asks, "And Tommy?"

"Tommy? He's too busy with all the girls to notice. I bet he
winks at all the angels and tells them they have the most beautiful wings."

"What about Maelynn?"

"I bet she and Betty are riding their chariot too fast and dis-
rupting all of the harpists." The thought of Maelynn and her
one true love, a woman whose image I concocted only from
her voice on the phone, bowling over an angel choir makes my
eyes tear up with laughter.

"And my parents?" Joseph barely gets the words out.

"They tried to start an inn up there, too, but no one in heaven
sleeps so they have the whole place to themselves, and they spend
all day cuddling in each room."

Joseph pulls me toward him, my head tucked below his chin.
"Sounds like heaven to me."

We sink into the peaceful silence that follows, the images we
created swirl in my mind. The candles burn lower and Joseph
strokes my hair with his fingertips.

"You know… Maelynn and Tommy, they wouldn't have
wanted to get old. They wouldn't have been able to take it."

I swallow hard. "Still doesn't make it easier, does it?"

"No, it doesn't." He is quiet, and then asks, "What will become of us?"

"If we're lucky, a little cloud home where we can cuddle and kiss and never be apart."

"I hope that's true."

"And if it's not?"

"Then I don't want to waste any more time wondering." He shifts his body over mine and kisses me. I run my fingers over his shoulders, press him against me. His hands explore the same paths they have traveled these many years, only the surface has shifted and changed with time. He makes love to me gently, and I give him the same love in return, tender and earnest. I try not to think of cloud homes, of chariots or harpists or all the things I have never been sure enough of to believe. Instead I think of his skin on my skin, his lips on my lips, the soothing repetition of our bodies' rhythm. I think of that rhythm as we lie together, breathing deeply, loosely entwined. I think of that rhythm as I fall asleep, tucked against him. I try not to think of chariots, of fire, of darkness, of dirt, of all that awaits us when the greater rhythm stops.

Twenty-Seven

Joseph

May 2002

She was having a good day.

She didn't stir much last night. When I woke, I was surprised to find her in a deep sleep. I cuddled close behind her until I felt her wake. She turned and burrowed into my chest, kissed me good morning. We made breakfast. Pancakes. Something usually reserved for the grandchildren. But she felt like having pancakes, and we don't deny ourselves any indulgences now. Not when we are so close. She spread strawberry jam on one of them, she said she wanted to try it. Do something she had never done, even though it was a small thing, a silly thing. She took a bite and laughed, shrugged her shoulders. I spread some on mine too.

She napped on the couch while I worked in the garden. After an hour I came inside and washed up, cleaned the dirt beneath my fingernails and dried them on a dish towel. I knelt before her on the couch. Slid my hand into hers, raised her knuckles to my lips.

Saliva dripped from her mouth. I wiped it with my thumb. She drooled often as she dozed, and once it happened while she was awake, in the middle of a conversation. She joked about it, something about being hungry, a joke to cover humiliation.

I whispered to her, still asleep, "I'm sorry you didn't get to do all you wanted." Her tremor, her bone-thin arms, the dual pianos rendered silent in the study. The tan-skinned memory of her so alive in my mind, swimming ahead of me as we raced toward Captain's Rock.

She stirred at my touch. She woke with a smile, as if departing a particularly pleasant dream. I asked, "What would make you happy today? We can do anything you'd like."

"Me?" She looked so content. Her green-gray eyes soft and dreamy. "I have everything I could want. I've done it all."

"I'm sorry..." I said, sheepish.

"What for?"

"I feel like I failed you."

"How can you say that?" She brushed her fingertips through my hair. "I played my concerto, didn't I?"

"There was so much on your lists you never got to do."

"The lists weren't what it was all about. They were a starting point, a way to feel alive." She smiled. "This year was more than I could've asked for. And it's not over."

"No, it's not over." I began to cry, knowing too soon, it would be.

She raised her eyebrows and said, "Being with you, that was my greatest dream of all." She kissed me and my salty tears slid between our lips.

We sat together in the garden, the flowers in full bloom. The morning air was warm, the sky a clear and endless blue, a perfect day for May. Her face turned pink as the temperature rose. Her skin so delicate, paper-thin. We decided to plant daffodils for Rain's baby. She was due in a couple of weeks.

Evelyn walked to the violets, her footing steady. She picked one and slid it behind her ear. It was something she would have done when she was young, spinning in the meadow of wild-flowers. She smiled and lifted her hands to the sky. They didn't even tremble as she said, "What a beautiful garden you have made for us, Joseph."

She was having a good day.

A brain attack, they sometimes call it.

A stroke.

Like a stroke of luck. A stroke of good fortune. A stroke of genius. All things I can't reconcile with the fall of her arms, her body, into the violets. The words crumbled beneath her tongue, her legs crumpled beneath her body. Her slack face.

Evelyn perched on the counter, pulling me toward her for a kiss. Evelyn with long wet hair, lying on her back on the dock. Evelyn with Violet on her hip, dancing in the kitchen. Evelyn at the piano, straight-backed and focused. Evelyn mixing cake batter with a wooden spoon. Evelyn swimming ahead of me in the waves. Evelyn wrapped in a towel after a shower. Evelyn in her violet dress emerging from the train. Evelyn laughing. Kissing me. Holding me. Her body nestled in the curve of mine in our bed. *Evelyn.*

The ambulance. The hospital. Curled against her in the adjustable bed, kissing her cheeks. Gripping her hand. The children were there right away...or it may have been a while. I can't be sure of when. The stroke of a clock. The stroke of midnight.

There wasn't enough time. We didn't have enough time. We were supposed to have more time. Another month together. Then we'd go together in each other's arms. Her arm was numb, she told me. She couldn't feel my touch. She couldn't feel me grab her, and she couldn't say what she was trying to say, she couldn't see me.

We were supposed to have more time.

She was having a good day.

We *made a beautiful garden together, Evelyn.*

That is what I wanted to say before she fell.

We made this garden. And it is beautiful.

Twenty-Eight

Joseph

December 2000

She is quiet in the car on the way back from the doctor. The radio clicked off, heat blasts through the vents. The drive home after each visit has been silent, racked with worry, questions, the desire for answers coupled by fear of what those answers will cost. We turn down Sandstone Lane; at Bernard Beach the waves stop short of a fresh blanket of snow, the strip of sand in between smooth and dark, a desolate bridge between crusted-over ice and steel-colored surf.

"It's good we caught it when we did. Now, well, at least we know." I rest my hand on hers, and it trembles beneath my touch. "We'll get through this. It will be okay."

Her mouth tightens the way it does when she tries not to cry, but a few tears leak out, slide down her cheeks.

I know she must be thinking about her mother, who had a different disease, but one that ripped her apart at the seams in the same way, stitch by stitch. Who screamed and threw things at the nursing staff. Who lost track of time and faces and conversations in the middle of speaking, who became like a child once more, alone and timid and afraid.

That won't be Evelyn...so many people live with this for years, for their entire lives, there are medications, the doctor said, things to help with the symptoms. An abnormal case, he said, but caught early enough...*stage one.*

It started with little things, things that were nothing really, considering our age. Soreness in her neck and back. Difficulty sleeping. Forgetfulness. Evelyn is seventy-five, I'm nearly seventy-eight, our bodies don't cooperate like they used to, they aren't supposed to. My leg seizes up at night. I can't read without glasses. Some mornings I spend on and off the toilet. We thought Evelyn's symptoms were natural. Our friends, too, complain of insomnia, losing their keys, aches and pains, it was nothing to worry about.

But she began to lose track of time, of names and places, of conversations she was present for. She fell asleep at midday and paced the halls at night. And then, the tremor in her left hand began.

The doctors refused to label it at first. They did not want to diagnose her until they ruled out some things that imitate it. Stroke, Alzheimer's, multiple system atrophy. Each scarier than the last. We saw a neurologist who specialized in movement disorders. There were so many doctors, brain scans. MRI. Blood work. Endless tests.

Evelyn has made me promise not to say anything to the children about the appointments. Not until we know more, she said, she didn't want to worry them. Not until we have answers. Then, not until everyone was together. Not before Christmas. Not at Christmas. Not until she is ready. Evelyn hides her tremor under blankets, sweaters, tables, tucks her hand beneath her thigh, anything to keep suspicion at bay. Here and there the children have shown concern to me privately, asking vague questions I bat away, grasping at clues to a riddle none of us wants solved.

Evelyn's expression when the doctor told her, when he put a name to what she would fight for the rest of her life, was one I had seen before, when I came home alone to find her at the front door of the inn. A mix of fear, anger, disbelief. It was a look I prayed to never see again.

Based on the test results, and the evaluations, we can say with confidence what we believe you are dealing with. There are medications we can try...

Evelyn sank further into herself the more he explained, her face hardened to an iron mask. He spoke out of one side of his mouth when he talked. He vaguely resembled an untalented puppeteer. In this way, I could almost convince myself this was a show, and we were the audience. He was speaking about someone else. The word *Parkinson's* did not have anything to do with my wife.

Parkinson's disease... But this was Evelyn. *My* Evelyn. The same Evelyn floating on her back in the ocean, painted toes poking through the surface. Evelyn, smooth and naked beneath our sheets. Evelyn's slender fingers commanding the ivory keys of the piano. I couldn't match the word *Parkinson's* to our life together. It did not fit.

The tires crunch along our driveway, leaving tracks in the snow, and I ease to a stop and turn off the ignition. The silence is louder without the hum of the engine, the whirr of the vents, the rolling tires. Neither of us makes a move to go into the house. As if staying in the car will keep what we now know trapped inside, as if we can suppress it as long as we don't open the doors.

Evelyn speaks for the first time, so faint I almost can't hear her. "I don't want to live as less than I am."

The doctor's droning voice, *There are five stages of Parkinson's, but based on your symptoms you're advancing quicker than normal...*

"I know. We have time before we need to worry."

"I *can't* live as less than I am."

I fake strength as she falters. "We'll face it as it comes."

It will continue to progress...

She shakes her head, irritation ripples beneath her calm. "You're not listening, I don't *want* to face what comes. Who knows how long I will be good to you, to anyone?"

"Don't talk like that."

"You saw how my mother was..." She breaks off. "I can't live that way, I can't."

"That was Alzheimer's."

Evelyn softens. "Semantics, Joseph. This will take me away the same. Maybe worse."

"But you're stronger than your mother. A lot of people live with this for a long time...maybe with treatment, medication you could fight it. We'll get through it together." My voice catches on *together*.

"There's no *getting through it*. I'll keep getting worse, and fast. You heard the doctor. I don't want to put you through what's to come."

"What are you saying?"

"I think maybe I'll live out this year—" she pauses, her voice a whisper "—and that's it."

"What are you talking about?"

"One final year."

"Don't joke."

"I'm not joking."

The heat begins to dissipate in the car, my breath visible when I exhale, unsure how to respond, my assurances weak and forced, edged out by looming dread. I think of my father, after my mother died, how he stared out the window, a phantom drifting through the deserted inn. How his grief took him once she was gone, a merciful death, his hell the lonely cavern shaped by her absence. "I don't want to live without you."

"It's better than watching me fall apart—either way you lose me. I don't see a better way."

I knock my knuckles together in my lap, wield my helplessness like a dull blade. "Well, then, I'll go with you."

"Don't be ridiculous. You aren't sick."

"I don't care. If you can talk crazy, so can I."

"It's not crazy. I don't want our children to know me like that, it's not how I want to be remembered. I don't want you to see me..." Evelyn drifts off and tears begin to trace the same tracks, slide off her chin down her neck. "I don't want it to end that way."

I stroke her hair, and my eyes swim. "And I don't want it to end."

She whimpers, "I'm scared."

"It'll be okay."

"Forget what I said. I'm sorry."

"I know. I'm scared too." I hold her then, my heart a pounding fist, the center console digs into my hip. *My mother's tumor. My father's empty eyes.* I hold her tight enough to fight the tremors, to shield us from the truth closing in, our fears the dark clouds before the storm surge.

One final year echoes through my mind.

Twenty-Nine

Joseph

May 2002

The sun pierces the drawn blinds and I grimace, roll toward her side of the bed. The sheets where she should be are cold, a stray silver hair glitters against her fluffed pillow, the quilt taut. Beside the rug, her slippers are left cockeyed, the door to her closet ajar. On her nightstand, a water glass, the edge faintly imprinted by her lips.

Three mornings I have woken without her. My eyes raw and bleary, the air is heavy and pins me beneath it. I watch the red digits on the clock blink ahead. Birds chirp outside the window, the waves roll at Bernard Beach. I stroke the corner of her pillowcase with my thumb. The complete emptiness reverberates through me, renders me motionless. Hollow.

Kissing her in the hospital bed, monitors beeping, unresponsive, but there, she must be there, she must be, her eyes closed and her body warm, I crawled right in beside her, held her and stroked her face. Telling her, *I love you, I love you, come back, don't leave me, I love you. Come back. My love, my life, I love you.*

Feeling her slip away, the children beside me then, all of us gripping her hands, her arms, holding and hushing her, soothing her, knowing there was nothing left to do except to assure her, to comfort her, to kiss her forehead and her cheeks, to say, *It's okay, if you have to go. Okay? It's okay, my love. It's okay. I'm here. We're here.*

The tiny squeeze of my hand, the only way I know she heard me, knew we were all there beside her.

Then, she was gone.

Last night in my restless, tortured sleep, I dreamed she was swept out into the ocean, and she yelled for me through roaring waves. I treaded water, desperate, her screams sharp, but I never reached her. She appeared again at the bottom of the ocean, floating peacefully, eyes closed, hair drifting in the current, and I grabbed for her hand, to drag her to the surface, but she sank deeper, and I dove but she slipped from my grasp. I woke crying out, but there was no one to answer me. Now I lie awake, sure it was all a cruel dream, and imagine the curve of her body tucked into mine, her heat radiating beneath the covers. I plead for another whole life together. This one wasn't long enough.

The children have been here and there in fragments and blurs but I can't understand when they speak. I am underwater, sounds muted, diving toward Evelyn. I drift alone in the waves. Plates are pushed my way, but I have forgotten how to swallow, and I refuse them. Three days have passed without my permission, with only my vague knowledge of the sun rising and darkness falling once more. Time ceases to exist, and so do I.

Can she really be gone?

We had planned the details nearly a year ago. We selected the funeral home across town, instructed that the bouquets should be trimmed fresh from the garden, requested Billie Holiday's "I'll Be Seeing You" on the piano. We were to be cremated, our ashes scattered by our family on Bernard Beach. It was all a surreal to-do list, hypothetical logistics of which I felt completely removed. I was never supposed to see her carried out to sea.

I haven't dressed or brushed my teeth or shaved. I am thick with the stench of my grief, my stale tongue and bristled cheeks. But today I stand in the scalding shower and let it burn, my vision spins from the heat. I press my forehead against the wall. Soapy rivulets sting my tear ducts until the stream runs cold, and I am gooseflesh and shivering. Her towel hangs on the rack next to mine and I resist the urge to wrap up in it, wanting to cocoon myself in her floral scent and also preserve it, to leave it there, folded and ready for her.

I dress in the suit I wore when we married. It had been tucked in the attic beside her wedding dress, and the purple one she wore as she stepped off the train. So many clothes came and went over the years, boxed to be donated or handed down in over-stuffed bins, but we could never bring ourselves to give those away. The jacket is musty and loose in the shoulders but it still mostly fits. If she's watching, I think she'd like to see me in it again. I will get to see her in her favorite dress one last time today. I don't know if I will be able to bear it. She has always been so beautiful in violet.

A button on my sleeve is loose, and without her, that is how it will stay. A tube of her lipstick lies on its side, tipped over on the vanity, and I stand it upright. Raise my gaze to the mirror and am startled to see an old man in my suit, weathered skin, body stooped and withered. I don't recognize him. I look away, search for an alternate truth, but the hand I find toying with the button is liver-spotted with protruding blue veins. I expected to find her small fingers interlaced with mine, but they are empty and ugly and clammy and I thrust them in my pockets. Her skin soft as petals, after today, will be ash. Ash to scatter across the beach where we hunted on our knees for razor clams, where we first kissed, where our children learned to swim, where we sat side by side in sand chairs as golden afternoons faded to twilight. The shoulders, the stomach, the inner thighs I kissed, the map that has always led me home.

How will I find my way, without her?

I pad down the hall, my hand glides over the worn banister, down the creaking steps to the kitchen. No one creaks behind me, no clink of dishes before me. Her aprons hang by the pantry, her half-finished mug of tea beside the sink. Step with leaden feet through the swinging doors to the living room, past the pianos with their silent, gaping mouths, through the foyer and out the screen door, to our last goodbye.

It isn't fair. It hasn't been enough. It could never be enough.

Thirty

Joseph

May 2002

The sun streaming through the window warms me, floods each detail of the hospital room in crisp light. The ringlets fall from Rain's tied-back hair, propped up with pillows in bed, Tony in a vinyl chair by her side. Jane sways, shifting her weight from one foot to the other, her face illuminated by the bundle in her arms. Her first grandchild—a whole new kind of endless love. Marcus lingers by the door holding a glinting balloon, and his crinkled eyes betray his bubbling affection as he admires her.

Last week we scattered Evelyn's ashes, standing together on the sandbar, watching them float away on the wind like wisps of a dandelion. Connor stroked Violet's hair as she sobbed into his chest, their marriage a teetering boulder that had to fall to find solid ground. Thomas whispered a choked goodbye as we turned back to shore, his red-rimmed gaze on the horizon and Ann clutching his arm. Rain picked a bouquet of violets, scattering them on receding waves. My feet were bare and my pants rolled to my knees as we stood together, in the moment

I was never supposed to witness, but there I was, my sunken prints proof as I turned away, footprints that would disappear with the incoming tide. Marcus put his arm around Jane and she leaned into him, rooted and steady. She let him hold her up.

Today, he shares the moment by giving it fully to her.

"She's perfect," Jane whispers. A milestone we never experienced with our oldest daughter, when it was her turn. Was she alone in the hospital? Was she afraid? We never welcomed our first wrinkled and pink granddaughter swaddled in newborn cloths, never saw the blissful exhaustion on Jane's face, now mirrored in Tony and Rain. What we missed, meeting Rain at fourteen months, we always tried to make up for. Now this newborn, our great-grandchild, enters the world as I plan to leave it. What will I miss, when this hello is followed so soon by a goodbye?

"Eve," Rain says. "We named her Eve."

Eve. With skin so pink and new and her eyes so wide and unblinking. I am torn in two; I am trapped inside a well barren with grief and Eve is fresh falling rainwater, pouring in and raising me up. Shattering and healing me. *Eve.* Evelyn's ashes carried away on the ocean breeze, glittering through schools of minnows and nestled in the shells of hermit crabs, she has made her way back to me once more.

"Dad, do you want to hold her?"

Jane places the baby in my arms, and the sweet smell of her overwhelms me. She is wrapped in the blanket Evelyn sewed, a pastel yellow, and my stomach lurches with the ache of missing her. Each day without her an empty eternity.

Look at the beautiful garden we have made, Evelyn. Together.

At home I kneel by the edge of a flower bed and dig, sweat gathers at the base of my neck in the heat. The topsoil is dry from a streak of warm May afternoons but underneath it is cool and moist. The bulbs in my palm are hard and brown, conceal the buds of sunshine they hold within them, daffodils for Eve, the first flowers to bloom each year as winter fades away. I dig a patch of shallow holes, then press the bulbs into the soil. Smooth the top layer of dirt and water them, the cool liquid washes over the earth, gives them life.

Next year and each year after, Rain and Tony will sit on this bench, the Oyster Shell Inn their home, hold Eve in their arms or watch her walk and run and dance among the flowers when these daffodils usher in spring, their blossoms golden and radiant.

There is so much beauty here to be seen.

Inside, the ivory keys are cool to my touch, but smooth, comforting. I sit at the Baldwin where Evelyn spent so much of her time, filling our home with her music, soothing melodies finding me as I worked in the garden. I press one key and it lets out a low echo. It is so quiet here.

I stand and lift the cover off the bench, where her sheet music is kept, and where our letters lay hidden. We planned to leave them on the counter on our last day, for our children to find. I'm not sure if Evelyn ever finished hers. Her writing got so small, difficult to read, toward the end. Though my envelopes were sealed months ago, I worry what I had to say wasn't enough, was never sure how to begin to say goodbye.

I shuffle through the sheet music for the letters tucked beneath, sift past mine to find hers. Four white envelopes where there should only be three. I flip through, *Jane, Thomas, Violet* all in a tight, pained scrawl. Beneath them, the fourth letter is labeled *Joseph*, in the looping cursive I remember.

My hands tremble as I tear it open. I sink back onto the bench and read.

December 24, 2001

Dear Joseph,
If you're reading this, it means I've left you before I said I would.
I am so sorry, sweetheart. Please know wherever I am, I miss you

terribly. I've never known a world without you in it, and I don't want to imagine the next one without you either.

You are asleep beside me, as I write this. You should see yourself when you sleep, it is one of my favorite things, even with your hair all mussed and your mouth hanging open. If I wasn't afraid to wake you, I'd steal a kiss right now. Open-mouthed and everything. It's Christmas Eve, well, Christmas morning now, I guess. It's the middle of the night, and as usual lately, I'm wide-awake. I can feel myself going where you can't follow. I notice my lapses, and it scares me. But in a strange way, it assures me, too, tells me I'm making the right decision, even though leaving you all behind is the last thing I want. This isn't something I can will myself through, not something I can outrun.

Which brings me to this. If I'm already gone, don't go through with it, please. You still have so much time, and the children didn't expect to lose me yet. I hope they can see now it was never really my choice. But it is yours. Don't do anything because you promised me. I know you carry guilt for things outside of your control, and my fear is you will somehow add losing me to the list. Please, Joseph, don't. Let me put you at ease. There is nothing to feel sorry for. You are the reason for all my joy. You are my life, my biggest dream come true. You saved this family, and in every way, you saved me. How can I thank you for never letting me go?

It has been an incredible, beautiful life together. I couldn't have asked for more. And still, I don't know how to say goodbye to you. It wasn't part of the plan, you know. And maybe that's the point. There couldn't be a plan, not really.

I love you, Joseph. I love you for waiting for me so many years ago. And wherever I am now, there is no rush to join me, because I will wait forever there for you.

Love,
Evelyn

I read it over and over, the lines blur with my tears, weak and lost in her words until I can't hold myself up. I lean against the piano keys and the house echoes with the low notes pressed beneath my arms. The hum that follows trembles through me, at once emptying and filling me with its sweet sadness.

Thirty-One

Joseph

June 2002

Waves seep away from my bare feet as I sink and wiggle my toes in the wet sand. Last weekend Bernard Beach buzzed as it always does at the start of each season, wave runners circled Captain's Rock, music blared from speakers, swarms of beachgoers toted coolers and called out to friends they hadn't seen since Labor Day. Today the beach was quieter, filled with local families settling into their summer rhythms, carrying sand chairs and waving hello as they claim their usual spots, giving each other wide berths along the crescent shoreline.

The Long Island Sound stretches before me, the tide rises as the sun begins to fade. This morning I woke to gentle rolling waves and birds chirping through the open window. I traded my coffee for a brisk swim to Captain's Rock, my body jolted by the cold as I dove off the dock, my skin red and tingling as I toweled dry. The family trickled in over the next few hours, widening our claim on our section of Bernard Beach. The tide was going out when we arrived, revealing glistening sandbars we dragged our chairs onto, passing cellophane-wrapped sand-wiches and cherries and crinkled bags of chips. The water slid away from our ankles as the morning slid to afternoon, expos-ing the smooth hard mud beneath, dotted with spiral shells of hermit crabs, clusters of mossy-brown snails and, to the trained eye, the occasional squirt of a burrowing razor clam, a telltale dimple in the sand left in its wake. An unseasonably hot day for the first of June, more like July or August, signaling an ex-tended beach season to come, summer days stretching before us like an open hand.

I stand at the edge of the icy water until my calves are numb. A lone seagull cries as it swoops overhead. I see a glint of glass, and hope, as I always do, it is the messages sent adrift last sum-mer, somehow, someway, finding their way back to us. The words I never got to read, her final letter, still floating out there, somewhere. But as always, it is the break of a wave, a trick of the light. The sun is getting lower, but my skin holds the heat from the rays even as the temperature drops. We are the last ones left on the beach, as the sky ripples into clouds streaked purple and pink, reflecting across the sea. Light and sound hushed, calm. This was always her favorite time of the day.

I turn back toward our semicircle of blankets and chairs. Rain and Tony are tucked under a striped umbrella, Eve cradled in Rain's arms. Jane lounges nearby on a blanket with Marcus, propped up on his elbows nursing a watery iced tea. Violet and Connor sit together on beach chairs, tunnels of sand dug by their heels before them. Violet laughs at something Connor says and he rests his hand on her knee, light moments that add up to something more, the way globs of watery mud stack and so-lidify to form a drip castle, tiny grains of sand creating a foun-dation on which to build. Thomas and Ann meander toward us, stopping to peer at a horseshoe crab washed ashore on their walk back from the jetty.

The sun sinks lower, a half circle settling on the horizon.

Time to go.

And yet, my skin is still tinged with its heat. The clouds sweep watercolor strokes of magenta and orange over a fair blue sky. The faintest breeze dances on my skin. I breathe in the salt air, the musky and healing scent of the ocean that will always be hers.

I pat Thomas on the shoulder, pull him toward me.

"You don't have to go yet, do you, Dad?"

"It's time. It's been a perfect day."

He holds me tight. Ann wraps her arms around me and buries her face in my neck. The rare show of affection takes me aback, plunges me deeper into the reality I have been chasing away since I woke. Violet bites her lip and forces a smile, her curls lift in the wind; Connor is stone-faced and resigned, but both stand to embrace me. I kiss Rain's forehead, and Eve's cherub cheek, then hug Tony and Marcus. Jane weaves her arm through mine, insists on walking me to the edge of the beach.

When we reach the road she whispers, "Tell her hi for us, will you?"

I nod, a sob caught in my throat, and hold her tight.

As I turn away my legs are weak, unsteady. I don't risk looking over my shoulder, although I feel all of their eyes on me, dragging me back with force, like the gravitational pull of the moon on the tides.

I press on, memorize each detail of my path one last time even though I could navigate it blind. Knowing my way like I knew every blemish and curve of Evelyn, worn maps imprinted in the deepest corners of my mind.

These are the dunes covered in swaying switchgrass, a long-ago hiding place where Evelyn nibbled my ear under the glittering stars. This is where the path becomes Sandstone Lane, blistering asphalt that burned the bottoms of the grandkids' feet each time they raced barefoot to the beach after it was paved. Here are the towering oaks where Thomas once lodged a toy plane. Here are the cedar shingled cottages, their scratchy crab-grass and rickety front porches and clotheslines draped with fluttering linens. Here is the row of swamp rose that curves along our driveway, where there was once a wooden sign that I carved and Evelyn painted to declare the Oyster Shell Inn open once more. Here is the crunch of the path leading me home, the front stoop where my mother shook out towels, where Tommy barreled into the kitchen, the front door where I'll always see Evelyn waiting for me to return.

Inside, I make my way to the study and to her dueling pianos. I can almost hear her music rise up to meet me, a familiar song of which I've lost the name. My fingertips graze the ivory keys. I play a solitary note, and it sings.

I open the hinged bench and find the letters and the prescription bottle hidden inside. Swing past the door to the kitchen. I place the letters on the counter, two stacks, one for each of us. I trace my fingers over her handwriting, deteriorating with each envelope. The symmetry of mine penned with steady hands.

I pour myself a glass of water from the sink. It is so cold, so refreshing in my throat and I down it in two eager gulps. I finger the pills on the counter. I pour another glass of water. The sun sinks fast.

There isn't enough time.

There isn't enough time.

There will never be enough time.

I press a palm against the cap, apply pressure and twist it open.

But there is still time enough.

I turn on the faucet, and tip the bottle, the pills cascade and disappear down the drain.

I open the screen door with a creak and step onto the porch and into the garden. The flowers glow in the evening light, a tapestry of our family, woven into the earth. The daffodils have not yet begun to bloom, although I imagine them each year hereafter, bursting golden through thawed ground, reaching toward the sky.

I thought I loved Evelyn when she was beside me, but I was wrong. On these days without her, when I can mistake the breeze for the softness of the undersides of her arms intertwined with mine in sleep, when I can hear the musical notes of her laugh and look up to see Jane, when I can hold Eve, and know our great-granddaughter may have her ever-changing eyes, when I am asked for the story about the train and I am still here to tell of her floral perfume that lured me like a spell, when I can open a window and inhale the brine of the sea that always belonged to us, listen to the music of the waves we made our own, lulling me from my grief into the deepest peace, *these* are the days I love her most.

I lie down on the earth among the violets, breaking the last promise I ever made to her, a promise she never wanted me to keep. Whisper a new promise, a tomorrow without her.

What a beautiful garden we have made, Evelyn.

I tilt my face to the setting sun and smile, soaking up the last of its warmth.

Acknowledgments

I began writing *The Days I Loved You Most* over ten years ago, at twenty-two years old, in the summer of 2013. My road to publication was long and winding, and for that, in hindsight, I am incredibly grateful because it prepared me not only for the release of this novel, but for what it takes to build a writing life. The first five years this book was a secret project I turned to for the joy of it, to see where the story took me. The last five years were spent chasing the dream to see my novel in the world. Revising and querying agents, and revising again and again, ten drafts to the final, much of which was done while pregnant, caring for a newborn, pregnant again and raising two boys under two. This book was shaped in the pre-dawn or late in the night, in the moments stolen during naps, or with a baby strapped to my chest. Audio snippets captured while pushing a stroller, lines scribbled furiously while preparing lunches before they flitted away. In rare marathon writing sessions, thanks to sitters and grandparents, which provided gloriously uninterrupted windows so I could sit with the tougher scenes for the time they deserved. Evelyn and Joseph were with me for a third of my entire life, through new beginnings and losses, marriage and babies, rejection and validation and years of doing the work, all the while riding on faith and hope and rooted in a deep belief that this book would one day find its home. None of this would be possible without all the love and support surrounding me, and although it is impossible to thank everyone who guided and championed me along the way, I will do my best to try here.

To my incredible super warrior of an agent, Wendy Sherman. There is no one else I would want to be on this journey with. Wendy, I don't know how you do it all, how you make every client feel like both your number one priority and your dearest friend. You are the reason this book is in the world, the reason the doors opened after all this time, that all my wildest dreams have come true. You work tirelessly, my fiercest advocate at every turn, and somehow make it all seem effortless. I couldn't be luckier to have you in my corner. To the rest of the team at WSA, but especially Callie Deitrick, for being so incredibly supportive and warm along the way.

To my brilliant and thoughtful editor, Erika Imranyi. Thank you for your passion for my story, and for seeing *The Days I Loved You Most* the way I had always hoped it would be seen. I could not trust your editorial eye more, and am in awe of your ability to hone in on exactly what needs to be tweaked, while giving me total freedom to make the changes that felt right and true to me. *The Days I Loved You Most* would still be a Word document without your vision for breaking it out, without your faith in this debut author, and it is far better for the revisions we embarked on together.

To the entire team at Park Row Books and Harlequin/Harper Collins, I am so lucky to call you home. I will never be able to thank you enough for everything you've done. You have changed my life, you are the reason I can call myself an author. To each and every one of you who touched my book along the way, but especially, Loriana Sacilotto, Margaret Marbury, Amy

Jones and Heather Connor for seeing and believing in the potential in Evelyn and Joseph, to Rachel Haller, Lindsey Reeder, Brianna Wodabek and the entire marketing team for working so hard to bring my book to readers, and to Emer Flounders and Justine Sha for being the publicity team of a debut author's dreams, to my copy editor, Gina Macedo, for catching every little thing, to Nicole Luongo for making the process seamless, and to everyone in the Sales, Art and Production team who have had a hand in making my novel shine. And special thanks to Carol Fitzgerald at The Book Reporter for the beautiful website and spreading the word.

To Jenny Meyer and Heidi Gall who have brought *TDILYM* to a global audience. Talk about wildest dreams. Jenny, having you on our team is an absolute joy, and your name in my inbox means only wonderful things. Thank you for working so hard for me and this story, for expanding my reach beyond what I ever thought possible. The wonderful relationships I have with my international publishers, and the many translations of this novel, are thanks to you.

To all of the editors and teams abroad who have made me cry with their love letters to Joseph and Evelyn, who have welcomed my book into their publishing houses with such enthusiasm and have shepherded my career overseas, I will never be able to express what it has meant to me. To Darcy Nicholson and Lisa Krämer for being incredible advocates for this story, for your passion and all of your hard work in making me feel at home from thousands of miles away. It's been a joy to work with each and every publishing team around the world, and my life will never be the same because of all of you.

To Lauren Parvizi, Hadley Leggett and Erin Quinn-Kong, my unicorn of a writing group, the rare kind I always hoped to find but never knew existed, three women I can't imagine this wild ride without. May magic find us all, as long as we are still writing.

To Alice Peck, who saw a glimmer in this story before anyone else, who drew out what made it most special and taught me to bring it to light. Thank you for being a dear and kind friend, for being a haven for my story to blossom into what I had always hoped it could be, and for seeing it that way, somehow, before it ever was. For encouraging and guiding me through the early and most vulnerable years of edits and queries, for always believing in what we would become.

To Lidija Hilje, your edits were a gift when I didn't know where to turn. You seemed to know my book better than I did, and still, somehow years later, hold it so completely in your mind in a way that astonishes me. I cherish our friendship, your vocal support of my work, our brainstorming sessions and the safe space you created to share each update along the way.

To Sarah Branham, for ratcheting my novel to the next level at a crucial juncture. You unknotted my puzzle of a structure and I am in awe of your brilliance. This book finally leapt over the biggest hurdles because of our time spent together, and I am forever grateful for how much you championed me.

To my early readers and dear friends. Megan Price and Caitlin Lash, Maelynn is named for you, a joke that surely went on too long, and yet, here we are, because I promised you I would. Thank you for all the storyboarding sessions and for taking me and my notecards seriously. Dominika Sillery, my most trusted reader from our early workshop days. Thank you for always believing in me, and in how far this could go, from the start. Michelle Merklin, for the drafts you read so quickly, despite babies and work. There isn't a thing I've written you haven't read since we were kids, and I don't envy you for slogging through the early work. Carolyn Kaleko, for the challenge we embarked on together that gave me the courage to write a novel in the first place. Who has lived with these characters nearly as long as I have, who talked me through countless scenes and drafts, the overflowing bathtub was your brainchild, and Joseph should really blame you for the mess. Thank you for mentally preparing me for how hard publishing would be so I could face it head on, and then for walking through every moment of it with me, for making me feel never once, alone, in chasing my dream.

Much research went into this book along the way. Thank you to Kathleen Pendleton at the Boston Symphony Orchestra, to George Mellman for the detailed tour, for providing the Beethoven anecdote, and the orchestra librarian for helping me choose Evelyn and Jane's concerto. Special thanks to Mary Incontro for making sure Evelyn and Joseph's perspective in their seventies rang true. To Jim and Mary Brewster of The Captain Stannard House, for allowing me to shadow you and pick up sensory details about running a bed and breakfast in a seaside Connecticut town. Joseph's keys jingle because you let me follow you around.

To you, the reader. I am a writer because I have always been a reader, because of the wonder and comfort and joy I've always found in the pages of a book. There are so many ways to spend your time, and I'm thankful you chose to spend some of it in Stonybrook, with me.

To my teachers, especially my earliest English teachers who encouraged me with notes and library passes and books handed down. To all my teachers at The Greater Hartford Academy of The Arts, but especially Benjamin Zura who lovingly and famously wrote "meh" on the top of most of our poems and taught me to take critiques in stride at a young age. To the other students in our workshop, I've never felt safer to create and to share, and I hope you are all writing wherever you are.

To all of my close family and friends who have supported me in myriad ways. Even my brother, who prefers to "wait for the movie," promised to read this book (this is a test, Brian...call me if you see this). Thank you for lifting me up, sharing in the setbacks, celebrating the wins and cheering me on every step of the way. You know who you are, and life is sweeter and more fun for having you in it. Joseph and Evelyn were an island, but because of you, I never had to be.

The Days I Loved You Most is set in a fictional town inspired by a very real place that is deeply rooted in my soul. A seaside Connecticut town where, like Joseph and Evelyn, my family has left footprints for six generations, a place of love and legacy and belonging and childhood. To my Grandma and Papa, for giving me the beach, for teaching me to love it, for teaching me what love is. You met when you were fifteen and eighteen, and that love lives on, long after you are gone. Even your middle names, Bernard and Bernadette, my favorite coincidence, a matching set from the start. Bernard Beach is for you.

To my dad, for being so fun to share good news with, for being one of my loudest supporters and biggest fans. To my mom, for my love of reading, for all the library trips, the hours spent on the couch together as I read aloud, the books on tape in the minivan. Thank you both for letting me go to arts school at fourteen to study creative writing, for coming to my readings, for never once thinking it wasn't worth my while. For giving me a childhood by the shore, and for unscheduled summer days where I was left to read in a hammock and chase my whims and hobbies, to play in the woods and the streams, to write in my little notebooks, for the freedom to imagine, to explore, to figure out who I wanted to be, for letting me believe no matter what I tried, I could fly.

To my boys, Teddy and Jordan, the best things I've made by far. I hope you know a love like Joseph and Evelyn's, and I hope you know that you can always come home. You are the sixth generation on our beach, and there has been no greater joy than sharing my most special place with you, except of course, in being your mom.

To Jonathan, I began writing this novel when we had been dating for six months, and now we have been married eight years, and together over a decade. Our relationship has always known this book, and I am awed by your continuous and un-wavering support of my dream. Every love story I write, I write because of you. We are the lucky ones. We always were.